His gaze dropped to her mouth.
What would she do if he kissed her right now?

She opened her mouth, then snapped it shut. "You know, I actually came down here to thank you, not bicker. But for some reason, you bring out the worst in me."

He flicked her nose. "It's called foreplay, sweetheart."

She swatted his hand way, then jabbed him in the chest. "See, right there. Why do you have to do that?"

"Do what?"

"Say things that make me want to smack you."

He leaned forward so their faces were inches apart. The breeze picked up a wayward strand of her hair and blew it into his face. "That's not what you want to do to me."

ALSO BY ERIN KERN

BACK IN THE GAME

Champion Valley #2

ERIN KERN

FOREVER

NEW YORK BOSTON

Copyright © 2017 by Erin Kern
Excerpt from *Changing the Rules* copyright © 2018 by Erin Kern

Cover photography by Claudio Marinesco. Cover design by Elizabeth Turner. Cover copyright © 2017 by Hachette Book Group, Inc.

Forever
Hachette Book Group
1290 Avenue of the Americas, New York, NY 10104
forever-romance.com
twitter.com/foreverromance

First Edition: October 2017

Forever is an imprint of Grand Central Publishing. The Forever name and logo are trademarks of Hachette Book Group, Inc.

The publisher is not responsible for websites (or their content) that are not owned by the publisher.

The Hachette Speakers Bureau provides a wide range of authors for speaking events. To find out more, go to www.hachettespeakersbureau.com or call (866) 376-6591.

ISBNs: 978-1-4555-3600-9 (mass market), 978-1-4555-3599-6 (ebook)

Printed in the United States of America

OPM

10 9 8 7 6 5 4 3 2 1

BACK IN THE GAME

ONE

I want to sign up for ballet lessons."

Stella paused in the act of locking the doors to her dance studio and eyed the tall, broad-shouldered kid who'd caught her at the end of a long day.

"You want ballet lessons?" she repeated.

Matt West nodded. "Yeah." He cleared his throat as though nervous. "I know some of the other guys on the team are taking lessons from you. They said it helped with, like, their balance and stuff."

Stella turned to face him. She always had extra time for a student in need, but technically Matt wasn't a student. And the other football players she was helping had come in with their parents.

"Matt..." She crossed her arms over her chest. "Does your dad know you're here?" Not that Stella was *looking* to see Brandon West, but she needed to make sure she had his permission to get Matt enrolled.

"Uh...not exactly," he answered.

She turned the key in the lock again and pushed the door open. "Why don't we go inside and talk?"

As Matt followed her inside, Stella wrestled with the uncomfortable and conflicting feeling about what to do. It wasn't the kid's fault his father was sex on a stick who'd given her more fantasies than anything she'd had as a teenager. It also wasn't Matt's fault her one and only date with his dad had ended in disaster.

She should come up with an excuse. Tell Matt she didn't have space in her schedule. But when she glanced at him and spotted the hopefulness in his brown gaze, she knew turning him away wasn't an option.

"Why don't you tell me what made you decide to come see me?" she said.

Matt rocked back on his heels. "Some of the guys said your classes were cool. And you were helping them and stuff."

"Do you have an idea of what specific things you'd like to work on?" she asked. "I'm assuming your coach gave you areas that need improvement."

"Yeah, you know"—he shrugged—"I have issues with my balance and flexibility. Coach says I might have a shot at a scholarship if I work on those things."

She could totally help him with that. Except...

"I would love to get you signed up today, but I need your dad here."

Matt winced and shook his head. "I can't just, like, sign his name on whatever release form you have?"

If only. Because that would work better for the two of them, but she couldn't go against her own rules. "It's not really a release form, just more like signing over permission. And since you're under-age, your dad has to come in here and sign you up." Unfortunately.

Matt was silent a moment, as though searching for a way to get around having his dad involved.

She offered him a sympathetic smile, because she remembered what it was like to be seventeen. "You can't go behind your dad's back, Matt. You need his permission."

His shoulders slumped. "But I know he won't go for it. He'll say ballet is for girls and I need to find another solution."

Sounded like how Brandon would react. "Maybe you're not giving your dad enough credit. Maybe he's more progressive than you realize."

Matt laughed and shook his head. "Trust me, he's not."

"Why don't you try first?" she suggested. "Go home, broach the subject with him and just see what he says."

"I don't know," he admitted. "When I was six, I asked for a Ken doll for my birthday and he bought me a set of army guys instead."

In that case... "Maybe..." *Dear God, don't say it.* "Maybe I could talk to him for you first," she blurted out, because apparently, her mouth didn't get the memo. "Give him an explanation of ballet training and its benefits."

Matt's face brightened so fast that it almost overshadowed her insane plan to put herself in Brandon's path. "You'd do that?"

She shrugged as though it was no big deal. No big deal to come face-to-face with the man who sent her into more cold showers than a shirtless Ryan Gosling. "Sure. But you still need to talk to him. Don't let your dad think you were deliberately trying to go behind his back."

One side of Matt's mouth curled up, and holy kick-in-the-stomach if he didn't look just like Brandon when he did that. "But I kind of already did."

"Yeah, but you don't want him thinking that you did," she corrected.

He scratched the side of his face. "But won't he know I did after you talk to him?"

Hmmm, good argument and one she wasn't prepared to answer. "I'll handle that when I talk to him. I'll let him think it was my idea and I came to you instead of you coming to me."

Matt blinked, then slowly shook his head. "Yeah, I don't think that'll work."

She placed a reassuring hand on his arm, even though her own doubt made her fingers tremble. "Trust me on this. I can handle your dad."

Yeah, piece of cake. Because the last time she'd tried to "handle" Brandon West, she'd thrown up rotten sushi all over him.

Brandon West had just picked up his double bacon cheeseburger with extra tomato when a shadow fell over his table, piercing the solitude he'd been enjoying with his solo lunch. For a second he waited for the person to realize they had the wrong table, when his gaze touched on the outline of long hair, narrow shoulders, and hands firmly planted on hips curved to such perfection that Brandon almost whimpered.

Until he remembered who those hips belonged to and the crystal-clear blue eyes that came with them. Eyes that were filled with trouble almost as often as they held promises of steamy kisses and twisted bedsheets.

He chewed slowly as she plopped herself down in the wrought-iron chair across from him and gave him a smile so wide that he almost made the mistake of thinking she was dropping in to say hi.

"I need to talk to you about something."

"All right, fine."

Brandon watched in horror as she reached across the table and snagged an onion straw off his plate.

Before he could tell her to keep her hands to herself or, better yet, move the hell along, his server appeared. As though he were waiting for an opportunity to give Stella a reason to stay.

"Can I get you anything?" the guy asked.

Stella tilted her face up to the waiter. "I'll just have whatever he's having—"

"No, she's not staying," Brandon interrupted.

"Maybe just put mine in a to-go box," she suggested. "Mr. Grumpy Pants is a bit socially inept," she whispered to the server.

"Christ," he muttered to himself.

The waiter left without another word, probably because he still wanted his twenty percent tip. Smart man.

"Start talking, Stella," he said.

"I think you should put Matt in ballet training," she said in a rush.

Brandon paused with his glass of Coke halfway to his mouth.

"Ballet isn't just for girls," she continued. "Some of the best dancers in the world are men. Ever heard of Mikhail Baryshnikov?"

He just stared at her. What the hell was she talking about?

"Okay, dumb question," she pointed out. "But never mind that. It's not about turning Matt into a ballerina. It's about helping him with balance and flexibility." She forged on when he didn't say anything. "I've helped a lot of kids on the team. They've—"

"Stop," he said with a raised hand. "Explain."

She nibbled on her thumbnail, which was way more endearing than it should have been. "Okay, this isn't really going the way I planned it."

"The way you planned what?"

"See, here's the thing—"

"Stella," he interrupted when he sensed another load of bullshit about Mikhail what's-his-face or whatever else she planned to say to him. "Why are you talking to me about Matt? If he wanted to take a class with you, he would have told me."

"But he thinks you won't let him," she admitted.

"Hold up a sec. Are you telling me Matt came to you and asked for ballet training? For football?"

Stella sat there, then slowly nodded.

"Why didn't he come to me first?"

Stella huffed out a breath as though she'd already lost. "Okay, here's the thing," she started. "And this isn't how this whole thing was supposed to go—"

"Yeah, got that," he stated.

She blinked at his interruption. "Is the issue that you don't want Matt taking ballet? Or that he didn't ask you first?"

He paused, then bit into his burger. "Both."

Stella blew out a breath. "That's lame. Can we set aside for one minute the circumstance in which Matt came to see me?" Stella said with exasperation. "Let's get back to the ballet thing. Matt wants to take lessons with me and since he's a minor, you need to sign him up."

That was it? In that case . . .

"I don't think so," he finally said.

The server delivered the food. Stella blew out a breath, then took an enormous bite, leaving a smudge of mayonnaise on her lower lip. "Mmmm," she said. "Now that's a damn good burger." She kept talking, but Brandon could only stare and ball his hands into fists to keep from swiping the mayonnaise away with his thumb. "I'll have you know that not one of them has had their masculinity questioned, or whatever it is you're worried about." She paused as though waiting for his response. "And now you've tuned me out."

God, she was cute when she was annoyed. Brandon sighed as he picked up his napkin. "Hold still a minute."

But she jerked away when he reached toward her. "What're you doing?"

Jesus, what did she think he was going to do?

He resisted rolling his eyes at her. Barely. "Lean forward a little and sit still for a sec."

Finally she complied, leaning forward just enough for him to reach her with his napkin.

Sweat built up between his shoulder blades when her blue eyes darkened and her breath hitched. Despite the heat arcing between them, Brandon managed not to touch her more than necessary, even though he wanted to ditch the dirty napkin and skim his fingers along her jaw.

He dropped the napkin to his plate and cleared his throat. "You had a spot of mayo on your mouth."

Stella automatically reached up and touched her lower lip, even though Brandon had taken care it. "You could have just told me," she muttered.

He offered her a crooked grin. "What fun would that have been?"

She narrowed her eyes at him. "You're sick."

She had no idea.

"You were saying something about masculinity?" he prompted, desperate to get the conversation away from Stella's mouth. Even if it was to talk about ballet.

Stella gazed at him for a moment, then dug back in to

her burger. "I just think your hang-up with ballet is possibly threatening Matt's masculinity."

He rested his elbows on the table and enjoyed the red coloring her cheeks. Yeah, she was good and worked up. "You think that's what's worrying me?"

"Well, then what's your problem?"

His problem was her. Seeing more of her than he already was. Bad enough he saw her at all the football games and bumped into her around town. He was trying to keep a friendly distance because she bothered him. Like, fantasizing about what she looked like under her clothes bothered him. How was he supposed to keep himself in check if she kept putting herself in his way?

"Just bring him to one class. If he hates it, you don't have to bring him back."

"I already told you, it's not happening."

Stella pushed her half-empty plate away. She stared at him for a moment, then leaned her elbows on the table. "Okay, how about this," she said, completely undeterred. "I waive my enrollment fee and if after one month you don't see a difference on the field, you can pull him."

Brandon chomped on his burger some more.

She dropped her head back and heaved a sigh. "Why won't you let me help him?"

"Because I don't think it'll help."

"But you haven't even tried. Talk to some of the other kids on the team. Ask them how it's helped them."

Brandon wiped his hands on a napkin, then tossed the napkin down. "Why are you so hell-bent on this? Why does Matt's football performance matter to you?"

Stella lifted one elegant shoulder, which had been bared when the neckline of her loose top had slipped. "Because when a kid comes to me and asks for help, I like to try and find a way to make it work. And he really wants a scholarship."

Brandon watched her for a moment, moving his gaze over her features, touching on her narrow chin, the smattering of freckles across her nose, and her clear eyes, which were as blue as the sky above them. Her hair was a hot mess today, thrown into a messy ponytail, darker on top then fading to blond at the ends. As much as she confused him, she also amazed him. She was all spitfire and sass in a lithe body. Her legs were long and lean, a testament to years of dancing that had shaped her body to resemble a man's wet dream.

Bottom line, he liked Stella. She pushed his buttons and turned him on. And that was also why he needed to stay away from her. He'd been burned too badly in the past to let himself fall for a pair of big blue eyes and kick-ass legs. The last woman he'd been serious about strung him along and left him high and dry with a toddler after years of empty promises.

"What else?" he prodded.

She blinked at him. "What else?" she repeated.

"You're not doing this just because you like Matt. You don't know him that well, so there has to be something more."

She opened her mouth, then shut it as though rethinking whatever she'd been about to say. He wasn't sure she even knew why pursuing this was so important to her. Maybe she didn't like to be told no. Maybe she didn't back down from a challenge.

Or maybe she had an ulterior motive that he didn't even want to think about. Stella didn't strike him as deceptive. Using Matt to get close to Brandon. No, she was better than that.

Stella leaned her elbows on the table. "Okay, you want to know the truth?"

He steepled his fingers together. "Please."

"I think you've realized by now that I'm a doer." When he arched a brow at her, she forged on. "I'm also a fixer. And I like to help people. It's one of the reasons I became an instructor. When I see someone I can help, or where I can step in in some way, I go for it. I don't like to sit back and not *do* something."

Brandon nodded. "That's admirable."

She beamed a smile at him that punched him in the gut. "Thank you."

"But my son isn't a charity case."

Stella rolled her eyes at him. "I didn't say that, Brandon."

"And he's not someone you need to fix."

"I didn't say that either."

"So where do we go from here?" he pressed.

"You let me help," she answered with a shrug, as though it were that simple.

As much as he wanted to, Brandon couldn't bring himself to disappoint her. "I'm not sure yet."

Her mouth slowly curled into a grin, as she knew she had him. "Doesn't sound like a no to me."

He stood and tossed some bills on the table for a tip. "No promises."

TWO

Brandon spent the entire drive to the high school kicking himself for allowing Stella to get under his skin. Again. He'd made a rule to keep his distance from her since their one date a year and a half ago. She thought it was because she'd thrown up on him. If he were smart, he'd let her keep thinking that. No, the problem was he'd liked her too much. It hadn't taken him long to realize he could fall too easily for her. He couldn't afford to jump into anything with Stella, then be left high and dry when she decided to leave. Because people always left. He'd learned that the hard way with his ex, Trisha. And the Blanco Valley rumor mill was in full swing with whispers of Stella going back to Chicago to choreograph for her former company.

Brandon pulled into the high school parking lot and exited his truck. Practice had long since ended, but the head coach was on the field with Matt, giving him extra attention and instruction.

With Blake Carpenter in control of the team, everyone was pretty confident the Bobcats could have a repeat of last year's winning season. Matt desperately wanted more playtime, and Blake wanted to give it to him. Brandon's cousin was a fair coach who loved his players, but he was also practical.

Brandon couldn't think of a better man to coach the kids. Not only was Blake one of the best people Brandon knew, but he'd also been a legendary quarterback who'd dominated the game for almost fifteen years before he'd retired a few years ago.

Brandon spotted the assistant coach, his friend Cameron, on the sidelines.

"How's it going?" Brandon asked him.

Cameron had removed his baseball cap, revealing matted, shaggy dark hair. "It's going," he answered. "He did good at practice. He just needs to work on his coordination."

Stella's face instantly flashed across his mind. Hadn't she said something about coordination? Damn, he didn't want her to be right.

But Matt's the one who wants the lessons.

And it still rankled that his own son felt like he couldn't come to him about that. Was Brandon that much of an ogre? Maybe he needed to work on being more approachable.

On the field, Blake demonstrated a blocking move, which Matt attempted to replicate. Blake did his demonstration again, then gave the ball to Matt.

The scene reminded Brandon of his own football-playing days. When he'd been young and optimistic and the only thing he'd cared about, besides Trisha, had been the glare of those stadium lights. The sounds of the band. The crowd. Hearing his name through the speakers as he'd thrown himself across the end zone to score those precious points. That had all been during a time when he'd thought he was set. He'd go off to college with Blake, play some ball, and hopefully get drafted.

Every guy's dream, right?

Well, he'd been no different. Only, God had had other plans for him in the form of a seven-pound screaming infant and—*poof*—he'd gone from being a football god to an eighteen-year-old construction worker trying to make ends meet for his new wife and son.

"I noticed the recruiters on the sidelines," Brandon commented. "Isn't it a little early for that?"

Cameron lifted one shoulder. "Not necessarily. Some of them like to get an early start. See which kids show the most promise."

Brandon knew Matt wanted to play ball in college. The only thing the two disagreed on was where the kid should go. Brandon wanted him to go to University of Colorado Boulder because it was in state, thus cheaper, and they had an excellent business program. But Matt wanted to attend the University of Texas...aka the Longhorns...aka football central...aka way beyond Brandon's financial capabilities. He certainly didn't want to burden his kid with financial issues. However, he wasn't sure how he could keep Matt from applying to UT without cluing him in.

"But, Dad, that's where Adrienne's going," Matt would say, referring to his girlfriend of five months.

That was all fine and good. Adrienne's parents could afford to send their only daughter to any school she wanted. It just so happened to have an incredible football team, which was just about all Matt cared about, and it was double the cost.

It was one of those subjects he kept putting off. But it

was only a matter of time before the two went head-to-head about it.

"Did you notice the recruiter for CU?" Cameron asked.

"Yeah." Brandon kept his gaze on the action on the field. "I also noticed the guy with the Longhorns shirt."

Cameron waved a hand in the air. "I told you not to worry about that. Do you know how many times I changed my mind about college?"

"Yeah, but you didn't have a girl tugging you around by the pecker," Brandon reminded his friend.

Cameron dipped his head. "You have a point. But the school year just started. Anything could happen. Do you know how many high school relationships come and go?"

Yeah, Brandon knew that. His own relationship with Trisha was excellent proof.

Cameron held up a hand, because he knew full well the relationship Brandon had had with Trisha. "Hey, I didn't mean anything by that."

Brandon shook his head and waved his friend's concerns away. "Don't worry about it. I was young and stupid."

"Weren't we all?" Cameron countered with a tilt of his mouth.

"I wanted to get your opinion on Boulder," Brandon told him. "What do you think about their football team?"

Cameron puffed out a breath and watched Matt. "They're not bad. I mean, I wouldn't call them a powerhouse, certainly not compared to the Longhorns." He stared back at Brandon. "But Boulder isn't where Matt wants to go."

Brandon lifted his eyes to the darkening sky. "Don't remind me. I can't even say the word *college* without him getting all pissy."

"What's wrong with UT?" Cam asked.

"Nothing, except I can't afford it. Not to mention I don't

want him following a girl he thinks he loves only to have the relationship end."

Cameron's brow pinched. "I thought Matt had a college fund."

"He does." Which was tied up in Brandon's business. "But it's not enough for a school like that. He'd have to get a scholarship, and we both know my son won't be getting any football scholarships to the University of Texas."

"Stranger things have happened," Cameron pointed out. "Then again, playing football for the Buffs wouldn't be so bad either."

Brandon scrubbed a hand over his rough jaw. "Try telling Matt that."

"He's a kid. We didn't listen at that age either."

And wasn't that the truth? He hadn't listened when his aunt, Blake's mother, had warned him about Trisha. "She's flighty," Blake's mom would say. "The girl's got her head in the clouds and you need to put her behind you." Unfortunately, Brandon hadn't listened because he'd been so enamored with her too-big-for-her-face green eyes, long legs, and infectious sense of humor. Five months later she'd called him to meet her behind the bleachers at the school. Through a stream of tears she'd informed him she was pregnant and that her daddy was going to kill her if they didn't get married. So he'd married her, telling himself everyone was wrong about her. That Trisha loved him and Matt and would never leave for greener pastures.

He'd never been so wrong or so heartbroken.

"Give the kid some time," Cam urged. "Applications aren't due for a few months anyway. And right now I need him focusing on the team and making state. If you have a kid who plays for a state championship team, he'll have a better chance of getting offers."

Brandon and Matt drove home after practice. The second they were in Brandon's truck, Matt dug his earbuds out of his backpack and stuck them in his ears.

Because heaven forbid the kid have a conversation with his father. At least one that didn't begin and end with him grunting some non-answer. Music blared from Matt's phone, which Brandon could hear through the earbuds, effectively cutting off any hope Brandon had of talking to his own kid.

Brandon pressed the accelerator and went through a green light, taking them through town and toward home. Haystack Mountain loomed in the distance, jutting above the valley, soaring past even the clouds with the sort of majesty that only God could give. The legendary Champion's Valley sign, built out of white boulders during the Bobcat's winning team run that lasted about fifteen years, had been strategically placed lower on the mountain so that anyone in the town could see it. A constant reminder that their team used to be great and could be great again.

Brandon drummed his fingers on the steering wheel and shot Matt a glance.

His hair, as dark and unruly as Brandon's, was matted with dried sweat and plastered to his head. Matt's legs, long and lanky, also like Brandon's, were stretched along the floorboard in front of him. Bottom line, Matt was a mini version of himself in both looks and personality.

He slugged the kid on the shoulder, motioning for him to remove his earbuds.

"Yeah?" Matt asked after he'd yanked the things from his ears.

"I talked to Cameron while you were on the field with Coach," Brandon told him.

Matt shifted in his seat, trying to stretch his long legs out even more. "And?"

"He says you're doing better."

Matt nodded, then lifted his arms to plug his ears again. Brandon reached over and yanked the things out of Matt's hands.

"Hey," his son protested.

"I'm trying to have a conversation here," Brandon told him. "Coach worries the recruiters are distracting you."

Matt shrugged. "They're not," he answered.

Brandon tossed Matt a quick look, then placed his attention back on the road. "You're telling me the guy from UT wasn't throwing you off?" Matt stared down at his lap. "Matt," Brandon said when he didn't respond.

"Maybe a little. I mean, I wanted to impress the guy."

Brandon shoved down the irritation that always bubbled up when the subject of college came up. "First of all, your focus needs to be your team and not recruiters. Second of all, I've already told you that you can't go to UT."

Matt looked at him. "I can if I get a scholarship."

"And what if you don't?" Brandon countered. "What's wrong with UC? It's a good school," he said, not waiting for Matt to answer his question.

"Nothing," Matt said with a shrug. "But their football team's for shit."

Brandon knew he didn't need to correct his son for the language. He simply slid him a raised brow look that most parents perfected when disciplining their children.

Matt got the message loud and clear, because he cleared his throat and fiddled with his earbuds. "Sorry. They're not very good."

"The football team may not be that good," Brandon agreed. "But they have one of the best business schools in the state."

Matt heaved a sigh and shifted in his seat. Brandon already knew what the kid was going to say before he said it.

"But that's not where Adrienne's going," Brandon concluded, because he'd heard it a dozen times already. "Look, I like Adrienne. She's a sweet girl. But you don't have to go to school where she's going."

"You and Mom stayed together after high school," Matt pointed out.

True. But Brandon wasn't about to give the kid a point for it. "The circumstances were a little different, Matt. And you know darn well that we didn't stay together," Brandon said as he turned into their neighborhood.

"So my relationship with Adrienne is expendable because I haven't knocked her up?"

Brandon shot Matt a look. "Boy, you'd better check that tone."

Matt cleared his throat and glanced out the window. "Yes, sir."

Brandon tightened his hand on the steering wheel and resisted the urge to run his hand over Matt's hair, like he'd done when he was a kid. "What I mean is, don't put all your eggs in one basket," he told his son. "Keep your options open. You never know where your relationship will be in a year. Do yourself a favor and focus on the Bobcats' season for now. Don't worry about the recruiters." He glanced at Matt as he maneuvered his truck onto the driveway of their house. "Otherwise Coach will make you do extra sprints."

Matt rolled his eyes. "Don't remind me. I don't ever want to do that again."

"I have some meetings and then I'll be back to make dinner," he told Matt.

Matt nodded and opened the passenger door. He slid out, tugged on the back door, and reached for his football bag, then hesitated as though he wanted to say something else. Brandon expected another argument for his case. But Matt surprised him.

"Love you, Dad," Matt said after a minute.

"Back at ya, kid," Brandon responded just before Matt slammed the door shut. "Don't forget to put that stuff in the wash. And feed the dog!" Brandon yelled as Matt walked away from the car and toward the front door.

Matt's response was a backward wave just before he let himself through the front door.

THREE

The Screamin' Bean—Stella had no clue who had come up with that name, but it was funny as hell—was packed wall to wall with people for the Meet the Bobcats event. Blake, the team's rockin' and super-hot head coach, had organized the event for the first time, to give the people a chance to meet the players off the field.

"People will be more excited to come to games if they see the players as students and kids, and not just players," Blake had told her one day.

The Screamin' Bean had agreed to hold the meet and greet because, well, it boosted sales for them too. So score for them.

Stella let herself in the door and spotted her best friend, Annabelle, and Annabelle's sister, Naomi, standing underneath a poster that read "We love our Cats!" Someone had used a paw print as the *o* in *love* and then glued orange and black glitter all over the poster.

Clever.

She waved at the two women and was about to head their way when Lois Jenkins, a member of the Beehive Mafia, aptly named for their attempt at reviving the hairstyle, broadsided her.

"How're you doing this morning, Stella?" Lois asked.

The question had Stella grinning. Lois, even with her periwinkle polyester pants—try saying *that* three times—was a nice woman. When Stella had first moved back to Blanco Valley to care for her granny Rose, Lois had been a regular visitor. And after Granny succumbed to cancer, Lois had attended the funeral and stayed after the luncheon to help Stella clean up.

"I'm good today," she answered the woman.

"I'm so glad you're here." Lois placed a sun-spotted hand on Stella's arm. "I was worried you wouldn't come."

Stella glanced around the packed coffeehouse. "Are you kidding me? I wouldn't miss this. And my best friend is engaged to the coach."

Lois's face lit up. "Oh, I'm so glad those two got together. You know, the girls and I were rooting for them."

Stella stepped in line for the counter, just wanting her cup of coffee and a scone.

"We were wondering how long we would have to put pictures of him on our Tumblr before some woman snatched him up," Lois stated.

Stella glanced around and caught Brandon's eye. Because there he was. Not that she'd been looking for him, but how had it taken this long for her to notice him?

Because he's tucked away in a corner talking to some woman.

Why would it matter that the woman he was sharing a table with looked like a contestant from the Miss America pageant?

Her gaze had just bounced on him when he shifted his attention and his eyes caught hers. For just a moment, even though it felt like an eternity. He looked at her just long enough to take a sip of his coffee, his eyes boring into hers over the rim of the paper cup. Then it was gone. Over. Done with because he placed his attention back on his companion.

And Stella felt an ache all the way down to her bum knee.

"I'm sorry? You said something about taking Blake's picture?"

They moved closer to the counter. "Oh yes, the ladies and I put their pictures on Tumblr so the women of this town can see what they're missing out on."

Stella studied the woman, who was about four inches shorter than her. "Mrs. Jenkins, are you saying your Tumblr page is a dating site in disguise?"

Lois held her hands up in the air and shook her head. "I hear nothing, say nothing. If those men want to flaunt themselves around town looking the way they do, then they'd better be prepared for a little attention." Lois leaned closer and whispered, "Just the other day, Patty got a shot of Cameron Shaw mowing his lawn. But don't tell him that because I don't think he realizes he's currently front and center at the Queen Bees. Do you know how hard that man is to spot? He doesn't showcase himself the way those other two do jogging with their shirts off all the time."

Stella didn't think Brandon and Blake would say they were showcasing themselves, but whatever.

"But anyway," Lois went on, staying by Stella's side in the line. "The Tumblr page was Patty's idea. Virginia wanted no part of it at first. Said it was indecent and inappropriate." Lois shook her head. "I swear that woman walks around with a bug up her rear end."

"Uh-huh," Stella muttered as she kept one eye on the

counter and the other on Lois. Funny how that particular eye kept wandering to Brandon, kicked back at the table, long legs stretched out and brushing against Miss America's bare legs. Brandon said something to her and the woman laughed.

Not that she cared.

"...and that reminded me of the man across the street who puts his yard gnomes in pornographic positions," Lois went on without pause in her story.

"How dare he!" Stella said automatically. Because she was only two people away from the counter. Then she could have her coffee and think clearly. Which meant *not* thinking about *that* guy.

Lois continued with her story. "I threatened to complain about him to the HOA, but do you know what he said to me?"

Stella blinked and shifted her weight off her bad leg. Was Lois waiting for her to answer that? "I can't imagine," she told the woman.

Lois thumped one of her soft-soled shoes on the tiled floor. "He said it was his yard and he could do whatever he wanted with it. But the next day the yard gnomes were gone." She snapped her fingers in the air. "Just like that. But between you and me, I think Virginia snuck down there and did something with them. She doesn't like things like that."

One person left at the counter, then Stella could excuse herself. Not only were there way too many people in here and her claustrophobia was being a bitch, but also her knee was throbbing like hell. She'd had to wear her brace this morning, because she'd been bad and hadn't been using her ice machine.

Evan Christiansen, the Bobcats' safety, bumped her

shoulder, then took another step back and stepped on her foot. The kid had no idea he'd invaded her personal space because he was cracking up some of the other players, saying something like, "How sweet is that?"

Sweet would be for everyone to take a giant step back and give her some space. Why did everybody have to crowd her? Didn't they understand that when the walls started closing in, she couldn't breathe?

Normally her claustrophobia wasn't much of an issue. The breathing techniques she'd learned during physical therapy usually worked. Ten to twenty seconds of deep and even breaths were enough to calm her pounding heart and prevent more sweat from dripping down her back. She'd gone almost three years since her last attack. Three years since her pas de deux partner had dropped her during a lift because Stella had freaked out and thrown them off balance.

"Honey, are you all right?" Lois asked, obviously noticing Stella's quick breathing. Or maybe it was the perspiration coating her chest.

Either way Stella needed to rein it in, and *fast*.

"I'm fine." She turned toward the counter and caught Annabelle's gaze.

Her friend tilted her head and mouthed, "Okay?"

Stella could only nod because, *great*, if Annabelle could tell from across the room, then the whole coffee shop probably could see she was on the verge of a panic attack.

Lois stepped closer and Stella almost came out of her skin. Stella backed away from the counter and shook her head, because her throat had dried up and, seriously, she felt like she was going to hurl. She was about to tell the barista never mind, which really pissed her off because she'd waited this long for her damn coffee, when she bumped into a hard chest.

Strong and steady hands braced on her shoulders and Brandon's deep voice came from behind her. "Black coffee and a cranberry scone."

She didn't want him ordering for her. She didn't want anyone doing anything for her, because, damn it, she should be capable of handling a simple coffee order by herself.

Except she wasn't because her throat had closed up to nothing and people were standing way too close. Touching her. Rubbing up against her and it sent prickles along her skin. Even Brandon, with his hard chest, pressing close enough to her back that she could feel the definition of his pecs, made her skin hot and itchy.

Didn't he know not to stand too close? Hadn't she told him she didn't like people invading her personal space? She was pretty sure she'd mentioned that on their one date, without telling him everything about her claustrophobia/panic attacks.

The only one who knew the full extent of it was Annabelle, and she'd never tell anyone.

The coffee and scone were handed to Brandon, who threw some cash on the counter. He nudged her backside with his hips.

"Outside," he told her. Demanded was more like it.

Stella was vaguely aware of Lois's inquiry. "Is she all right?" the woman asked. "She looks a little green."

"She's fine," Brandon answered. He gave Stella another nudge. "Get moving, woman, before you puke."

"How'd you know what kind of scones I like?" she asked as she weaved on unsteady feet toward the front door, hobbling with the one leg she couldn't bend because of the brace.

"Lucky guess," he claimed. "Just go."

And not a moment too soon they were outside, in the warmth and sunshine, where she could breathe and not have people crowd her and step on her toes. There was one free table, where Brandon set down her coffee and scone on. He added napkins and sugar packets before taking a seat in the plastic chair across from her. Stella took her own seat and stretched her bad leg in front of her. She wrapped her hands around the hot paper cup while the scrumptious man across from her lifted one hip off the chair, then tossed his wallet, cell phone, and car keys on the table.

Stella picked up the scone. "This wasn't a lucky guess."

"Just eat it," he ordered as he settled deeper in his chair. His wide shoulders, barely contained by a black West Custom Homes polo, were twice as big as the chair. "You need the sugar."

Stella blinked at him, wondering how he'd known. How he'd been able to tell just by looking at her that she'd been about to come out of her skin. Was it because he had great intuition? Or because he knew her that well? Which was silly, because they'd only gone out once. All their other encounters had been brief run-ins around town.

"Trisha started having panic attacks after Matt was born. I recognized the look on your face," Brandon said as though he'd known what she was thinking.

Stella bit into the scone, allowing the thick, sugary pastry to slide down her throat. Her heartbeat was almost back to normal. "I wasn't having a panic attack."

Lies.

Brandon snorted and tipped his chair back on two legs. "Says you."

"I wasn't," she insisted. She didn't want anyone's pity, nor did she want to rely on anyone.

"Sure," he said in a low voice. He pointed to the scone. "Eat."

She narrowed her eyes at him and lifted the pastry to her mouth. "So bossy." She took another bite of the scone, then washed it down with coffee. It was too strong, so she added a packet of sugar to it. Or maybe four.

Brandon watched her movements with a slight tilt of his mouth. "Addict much?"

"I'm not an addict," she argued as she swirled the sugar around in the cup. "I just like my things sweet."

"You know, they say the first step to getting better is admitting you have a problem," he told her as his grin widened.

Stella managed an elegant shrug while trying to get her leg comfortable, which was pretty incredible considering she felt like a lumbering oaf with her brace on.

Brandon glanced down at her leg as though he wanted to do something about it. But he just sank deeper in his chair and stared at her with those whiskey-colored eyes.

"Won't your coffee date be missing you right about now?"

Dear mouth: shut up!

Stella watched in horror not only as her brain ran away with her, but also as Brandon's mouth turned up in a grin so delicious that she almost whimpered. Honest to God whimpered while her toes curled in her Toms.

"You're not talking about Emma, are you?" he asked.

Oh, so the Barbie doll has a name.

Stella stole a sip of her coffee to hide the hammering pulse at the base of her throat. "She's probably wondering where you've gone."

Will you please stop talking? Just keep your mouth shut and drink the damn coffee!

But Brandon, the underhanded but so-freakin'-hot bastard he was, smiled even bigger. A smile that created lines at the corners of his eyes. "Emma's a big girl. I'm sure she's fine."

I'll just bet you think she's fine.

"But if you're that worried about her, I can ask her to join us," he added.

Stella only stared at him.

"Didn't think so," he chuckled. "Just drink your coffee, Tinkerbell."

She did as instructed, only because it was so good. *Not* because he told her to. "Tinkerbell was a blonde," Stella pointed out. "So your comparison is grossly inaccurate." A mob of high schoolers walked past their table, and Stella attempted to move her pest of a leg out of the way. But there was nowhere for it to go, seeing as she couldn't bend it, and there was no room under the table because Brandon's legs were the size of freakin' tree trunks.

"She also had an attitude the size of Texas," he argued while reaching under the table, picking up her leg, carefully and slowly, then resting it on his thigh. "I see what you were doing there. Trying to throw me off with all those big words."

And, yeah, that felt better since it alleviated the pressure of all the blood rushing to her knee. On the other hand, having half her leg just chillin' on Brandon's thigh—and there was nothing soft about that baby—pretty much confirmed what she'd instinctively known about him.

He really was hard, and cut and steely everywhere.

His hand rested firmly on her ankle. "Leave it," he instructed when she tried to shift her leg back to the ground. "Now, isn't that better?" he asked with a devilish gleam in his eyes.

"I wouldn't go that far," she countered, refusing to give him the satisfaction.

"Is it contact with people you don't like, or contact with me?"

Both.

"We should go back inside," she blurted, trying to shift her leg off his thigh. "Maybe the crowd's cleared out."

Brandon's hand only tightened on her ankle. Firm yet gentle because he knew how fragile she was.

I'm not fragile.

Another lie. The tough girl, I-don't-need-anyone attitude she presented was smoke and mirrors. People didn't see it because she was that good of an actress.

Brandon sees it.

She forced the thought from her mind. Nothing like a little denial.

"It hasn't," he responded. "Just sit and eat."

So she stayed only because he was holding her leg. Not because he told her to.

"How often do you get them?" he asked.

Stella lifted the paper cup to her lips and took a shallow sip. "Get what?" she replied with a coy lift of her shoulder. Over the years, she'd gotten good at pretending. At playing that she was so much stronger than she really was. The jokes and independence were just a shield for the shy little girl who'd craved stability.

Brandon shook his head. "You're good, I'll give you that. All right, if you don't want to talk about it..." He leveled her with a look. "But don't think I'll forget."

Why would she ever think that? Brandon West was the type of man who remembered everything. And that made him dangerous.

Her phone vibrated in her back pocket. Brandon watched

her as she dug the thing out, his eyes strong and steady and making her hands sweat so damn bad that she almost dropped her phone.

She touched the screen and saw a text from her mom.

The YMCA is offering a kickboxing class and the instructor is a total Channing. Want to take it with me? We could, like, box each other and stuff.

God love her mother. She referred to anyone good-looking as a Channing after Channing Tatum and swore she was going to incorporate the phrase into modern vernacular. Stella refused to use it because...well, she wasn't anything like her mother. Stella was more of a Chris Hemsworth kind of girl, and she had no desire to "box and stuff" with her mother.

Did you forget I have a leg I can barely walk on, much less box? Why are you at the Y?

"Something important?" Brandon queried from across the table.

"Just my mom," Stella answered. "She's supposed to be looking for a place to live but somehow ended up at the Y."

"Where's she living now?"

Aaaand cue rehearsed speech. "She came back after Granny died and she's been living with me."

Brandon's lips twitched. "Is that fake enthusiasm I hear?"

See? The man sees everything.

Not many people knew Stella's history. They didn't know she was a product of a one-night stand and that she'd never met her father. They didn't know her mother had the emotional maturity of a sixteen-year-old. Nor had she told many people she'd moved at least twice a year when her mom found yet another man who promised to take care of them.

Promises that had never been fulfilled.

"My mom and I..." Stella's words trailed off as she searched for the appropriate way to describe Gloria Davenport. "Have a special relationship."

"And by special you mean she drives you to commit homicide," he guessed.

Bingo.

Her phone buzzed.

I got bored so I stopped by the Y. Shall I sign us up?

Stella's teeth sank into her lower lip as she replied. *So you got bored after you found a place to live? And, again, busted knee, Mother.*

"My mom is different," Stella explained after replacing her phone. "She likes to have fun and I'm..."

"The straight-laced one," he finished for her.

Was he laughing at her? Because the half grin turning up the corners of his mouth was really doing funny things to her insides. The parts of her that were asleep most of the time because there hadn't been anything, or anyone worthy, of waking them up.

Not true.

"I just don't fly by the seat of my pants like she does. She goes where the wind takes her and I like order."

Brandon studied her from his kicked-back position in the chair, his thumb moving in slow, even circles over her ankle. The contrast of his worker's hands to her dancer's legs shouldn't have affected her. It shouldn't feel...erotic. Who knew skin could be erotic? Who knew a simple touch by a man's thumb could make heat bloom across her midsection?

But it wasn't a simple touch. No, Stella knew that. Nothing about Brandon was simple.

He only infuriates you because he gets you.

"Is that something you get from your dad?" he asked,

sliding the question in so effortlessly that Stella almost missed his attempt at prodding her.

Well played, Mr. West.

"I never knew my dad," she found herself saying.

He tilted his head and studied her, his chestnut-brown eyes demanding to know all her secrets. "And that's not something you like to talk about, is it?"

She spun her forgotten coffee in circles. "How could you tell?" As though she really had to ask.

He lifted a thick shoulder in a casual shrug. "We all have closets we try to keep closed."

"Including you?"

"I'm no different than anyone else."

Oh, yes, you are.

"And what're yours?" she prodded, the same way he'd prodded her. Only she'd had to come out and ask. Brandon had a way of sliding casual questions in so easily that Stella had no idea she was answering them until she'd revealed something she didn't want to reveal.

The thumb on her ankle continued to work in circles. "You really think I open up that easily?"

"Why not? I did."

He shook his head. "See, that's where you're wrong. All you did was deny."

She lifted her chin and leveled his look with one of her own. "I haven't denied anything."

Only denying about denying. No big deal.

Both his thick, dark brows slid up his forehead. "So you admit to having panic attacks?"

Seriously, he just did his sneaky thing again.

"There are ways of overcoming those, you know," he told her.

His thumb stopped moving, but his hand remained on

her ankle, keeping a firm hold as though he suspected she wanted to bolt. And he would be right. Not because she was being touched, though it was odd that being touched by Brandon didn't set off the same panic that being touched by others did, which was something she wasn't going to explore. Just yet.

"I'm perfectly fine," she told him.

He nodded. "All right. Another thing you don't want to talk about. I get it."

Did he?

Before she could ask, a shadow fell over their table, blocking the midmorning sun.

And there stood Matt, tall and dark-haired and looking so much like Brandon that it knocked the air from Stella's lungs.

"Dad, Adrienne and I are going to walk to the diner and get some lunch. She's going to give me a ride home when we're done."

Brandon looked up at his son, but his expression didn't change. Except maybe the muscle in his jaw tightening.

"Don't you need to stay with the team?" Brandon asked.

Matt lifted his shoulders, which were broad like his father's. "It's starting to break up, so Coach said we could leave if we wanted to."

Stella watched the interaction between the two, noticing how Brandon remained silent for a moment, as though battling some sort of internal conflict. Did he not like Matt's girlfriend? Or was there something else going on? Brandon seemed better at hiding his issues than she was.

Then, after several seconds of silence, Brandon nodded. "All right. But you're still on yard duty. I want the grass cut and edged before you go to bed."

"Got it," Matt responded. Just then, Adrienne came out

the door and the two linked hands. Brandon's dark gaze followed them down the street.

On impulse, Stella turned in her chair to catch Adrienne press a kiss to Matt's jaw. The kid's reaction was to drop a kiss of his own on the girl's head. Stella felt a pang at the young love, knowing that's what her own mother wanted and had spent her entire adult life chasing, dragging her young daughter with her. Perhaps there were people who simply weren't built for relationships. People who weren't destined to experience that kind of euphoria.

"They're cute together," Stella commented.

Something dark passed over Brandon's face, but then it was gone. "Yeah," was all he said.

She studied him and noted the stiffness to his shoulders. "You don't like Adrienne?"

"I like her fine," he stated.

Except Stella suspected there was more. "You just don't like her with Matt."

Brandon shook his head. "I didn't say that."

"You didn't have to."

He wagged a finger at her. "You don't get to sit there and be all secretive and then try to figure me out."

"Why not? Seems only fair." Also, she wanted to turn the line of questioning off her. And maybe watch him squirm for a while.

Brandon West doesn't squirm.

No, he wouldn't. The man was too solid. Too big and firm. And the man across from her, who'd been eating her up with his eyes and making her skin itch, heaved a sigh. "I just don't want them to get too serious."

"They're teenagers," she reminded him. "Nothing is serious at that age."

His eyes darkened. "You'd be surprised."

With his gravelly words came the understanding of the shadowy look behind his eyes. Stella leaned back in her chair and gazed at him. "Oh, I get it. You don't want him to be like you."

"Every parent wants better for their kid," he agreed.

"No." She shook her head. "It's more than that for you. You don't want him to make the same choices you did."

Brandon's strong chest puffed out when he took in a deep breath. Yeah, she'd nailed it. He didn't want Matt to be as irresponsible as he'd been.

"I just want him to use his head," Brandon admitted without really agreeing with Stella's assessment. "To be honest, I never expected their relationship to last that long. I thought it was more of an infatuation."

"Maybe it still is."

He shook his head. "No, it's more than that."

"How can you tell?"

His gaze zeroed in on her, warming her from the inside out. "I can tell when a woman is interested in a man."

FOUR

Honey, you need to get laid. You're too rigid."

Stella lay on her back on her living room floor, moving through her stretches, and ignored her mother's observation. Gloria always had observations, most of which were what Stella needed to do more of, improve on, or stop doing.

"I know you heard me," Gloria pressed from her spot on the couch.

Stella pulled in a deep breath and closed her eyes. Maybe if she left them closed long enough, she could pretend her mother wasn't there. Lord knew Stella loved her mom. But having her back in Blanco Valley, living with her of all things, could try the patience of the Pope.

"Honey . . . ," Gloria said.

"Mom," Stella replied with her eyes still closed. She pressed a finger to her lips. "Shhhh."

"I'm just saying," her mother went on. The leather couch squeaked when Gloria shifted positions. "There's just something about a nice, long orgasm that does wonders for a woman's stress."

Good Lord. Stella exhaled and sat up. She jabbed a finger at her mother. "That right there is why people go to therapy." She stood from the floor and abandoned her stretches. Her knee was about as loose as she could do for herself.

Gloria picked at the chipped paint on her thumb. "Sweetie, people go to therapy because they're uptight and don't know how to release their stress." She lifted one shoulder. "Just have yourself a couple orgasms and save yourself the money."

Stella stretched her back. "You say that like they just spontaneously happen."

"Well, they do," Gloria said with sly tilt of her mouth. "When you're underneath a man who knows how to strum a woman's body."

Stella held up her hand, then bent to roll her yoga mat off the floor. "There is some serious shit wrong with you." Not to mention Stella didn't even want to think about how her own mother knew that. No doubt from all the years she'd spent chasing one man to the next all over the country. Most of them younger with quick smiles and even quicker promises. Gloria Davenport practically defined the word *cougar*.

"The only thing wrong with me is that I'm not getting any," Gloria went on. "Where are all the good men in this town?"

Stella stored her yoga mat in the hall closet. "There are plenty of good men in this town, but you refuse to consider anyone less than ten years younger than you."

"Honey, old men are boring and stuffy."

Stella considered her mother. "Not true."

Gloria lifted a brow. "Because you have so much experience with old men?"

"Neither do you," she pointed out. "Have you ever tried giving a man your age a chance? You might be surprised."

Gloria stood from the couch. "Tell you what. I'll give a man my age a chance when you give any man a chance."

At her mother's words, Brandon's face flashed across her mind, sending her stomach somersaulting. No doubt he could give her one of those nice, long orgasms her mom kept bringing up. Multiple times. And, if judging by the way he'd stroked her ankle the other day, he'd do it with little effort.

The problem was, Stella had been ruled by her libido before. She'd allowed herself to divulge in the fantasy every woman dreamed of. She'd met a handsome man who'd swept her off her feet. Promised her all kinds of happy endings and rocked her world in bed. The spell Rick had had over her had pulled Stella's focus away from her dancing, and she'd turned down an opportunity to choreograph for the Chicago Ballet Company. She had just retired from her injury when the artistic director had approached her with the invitation. Only Rick had already spun a tale of leaving Chicago for a job opportunity where he'd take care of her and they could be together forever.

Stella had been torn between accepting the job she'd always dreamed of and moving forward with a man who had promised her the world. In the end, she'd chosen love, and it had bitten her in the ass. Big-time. Two months after leaving Chicago for Indianapolis, Rick had ended their relationship, leaving Stella with no choice but to return to Chicago and beg her former artistic director for a position.

"I'm sorry, Stella," he'd told her. "When you left, I gave the job to someone else. We started rehearsals a month ago."

She'd gone from being a principal dancer with one of the biggest companies in the country to an unemployed single woman with a bum knee. Shortly after that, Granny Rose had gotten sick and she'd left Chicago for Blanco Valley.

After that ordeal, Stella had sworn to herself that she'd never give anything up for a man again. No matter how enamored with him she was.

And now she had a chance to fix the mistakes of her past. Her former artistic director had called her back in the spring and offered her a chance to choreograph for *Rapunzel*. Stella had jumped at the opportunity to return to Chicago and do what she loved best.

At twenty-nine, she finally felt like she had her act together. She owned a successful dance studio and in six months she'd be back in the professional world, just like she'd wanted.

She left the living room, and her mother, and headed for the kitchen for a bottle of water.

When Granny Rose had passed away, Gloria had shown up on Stella's doorstep with two suitcases and a world of guilt riding on her shoulders. Guilt for not being there when her own mother had died. And guilt that Stella had stepped up to take care of the woman.

"I should have been there with you," Gloria had sobbed the day of Granny's funeral. "You were so good for her and I was nowhere to be found." She'd gazed at Stella with eyes so full of regret and sorrow that Stella's heart had cracked all over again. "I'm so sorry, baby."

Of course, she'd forgiven her mother. Gloria could be trying, but she was still Stella's mom, and they were all each other had left. A few days after Granny's funeral, Stella had asked her mother how much longer she planned on staying.

"This is it, honey," Gloria had told her as they'd worked together to put fresh water in all the vases of flowers they'd received. "I'm back for good."

As soon as the words had been spoken, Stella had a moment's panic. Not that she didn't love spending time with her mom, because she did. *Some* time. Not *all* the time as it had been since Granny had died. And her mother was still around, filling her pantry with junk food, telling Stella to have orgasms and flirting with the FedEx guy.

Gloria was back on the couch with the laptop perched on her legs. "The cute personal trainer at the gym is single."

Stella slipped her flip-flops on and walked toward the sliding glass door. "How do you know that?"

"He changed his relationship status on Facebook," Gloria told her.

"You're Facebook friends with him?" Stella asked.

Gloria shrugged. "Not exactly. I kind of stumbled across his profile."

"Stumbled across his profile?" Stella asked her mom in disbelief. "Or you did a search of the guy and went right to his page?"

"Or that," Gloria agreed.

Stella lifted her eyes to the ceiling and opened the door. "Mom, you're not going to find anybody by trolling through people's relationship statuses."

"Why not?" Gloria closed the computer and stood. "Now that I know he's single, I can go down there and...I don't know"—Gloria waved a hand in the air—"get trained and stuff."

Trained and stuff. Good heavens.

Stella walked to the back deck and picked up the hose so she could water her flowers. Gloria followed.

She shot her mom a glance as water filled the first pot. "Mom, when have you ever set foot inside a gym?"

"What does that matter? I'm not getting any younger, so

it's about time I start taking care of myself. Why not have the help of a young, handsome man?"

Uh... because none of your other relationships have worked?

Stella kept the thought to herself and moved on to her next plant.

"Besides," Gloria went on. "I'm going to need someone to keep me company when you leave."

Good grief, not this again.

"Mom, I told you I'll only be gone for about six weeks." *Your relationships never last that long anyway.* Another thought she held back.

"I finally come back to this place, and you're leaving. Why do you have to leave me here?"

Sometimes Stella felt like she was the mother, always having to reassure Gloria that everything was going to be okay. Always looking out for her and making sure she had her act together. Gloria was a leap-first, think-later type of person. Usually Stella had to do the thinking for both of them.

"First of all," Stella said, filling the second pot of flowers with water and moving to another. "I'm not leaving you. You say it like I'm abandoning you, and that's hardly the case." She glanced at her mother over her shoulder. "You know why I have to do this, Mom."

Gloria lowered herself to the edge of the deck. "Yes, I know. You already passed it up once, and all that."

Don't make light of it or anything...

Not that she expected her mom to understand. Gloria had never followed through with anything in her life. At least not anything that didn't have a penis.

"It's just that..." Her mom's words trailed off and Stella waited for her to continue.

When she didn't, Stella prompted her. "It's just that what, Mom?"

"Well"—Gloria folded her arms around her knees—"we're finally back together again, and you're leaving."

The water from the hose flowed over the rim of the flowerpot as Stella considered her mom. She shut off the hose and set the thing down.

Gloria's shoulders were hunched over, her long hair tied back in a low bun at the base of her neck. At forty-nine, her mother should have gray streaks running through her chestnut strands, which were several shades lighter than Stella's own hair. The brilliant color was just as shiny and bright as it had been when Stella was little. She had no idea what her mother did to keep her hair the envy of all women, but damn, she was a little bit jealous.

She sat next to her mom and nudged the woman's shoulder.

"Think of it this way," Stella began. "You won't have me here giving you a hard time for chasing around younger men."

Gloria snorted, which Stella guessed was supposed to be a laugh. "I hardly chase," she argued. "But sometimes these men don't know a good thing when they see it. They simply need a nudge."

Or maybe younger men don't want to settle down.

A reality Gloria refused to face.

The two of them stared down at the lawn in silence for a few moments.

"Just promise me you'll come back," Gloria said in a low voice.

"You know I will." Stella didn't want to think about how much she and her mom were alike. More alike than she wanted to admit, because Stella didn't like to do the mushy stuff. She didn't do sentiment. It made her itchy and uncomfortable and tongue-tied.

Gloria leaned forward and picked at a blade of grass. "I just figured you'd eventually get tired of me."

"Oh, well that's still true."

Her mom turned her focus to Stella and the two of them stared at each other for a moment. Then Gloria burst out laughing and Stella eventually followed. Because laughing was easier than admitting that she might actually miss her mom while she was gone.

Brandon was considering slapping Matt's phone out of his hand. The kid had been texting his girlfriend since they'd left the produce section, all the way through dairy and halfway down the junk food aisle. He'd been attempting a conversation with Matt, but so far he'd yet to progress past a two-syllable "uh-huh." Really chapped his ass. They were supposed to be shopping for dinner and so far Brandon had done all the shopping while Matt dragged his feet with his nose buried in his Samsung.

"Grab some oatmeal cookies, would you?" Brandon asked as he gave his list a cursory glance. Without looking up from the phone, Matt made a swipe for Fig Newtons and tossed them in the cart.

Brandon glared at Matt's phone and counted to ten. "Get some chocolate syrup, too, so I can pour some over my head before I run around outside naked." They weren't even on the right aisle for the chocolate syrup, but Matt made a blind grab anyway. His hand made contact with a bag of Milano cookies, before they landed in the cart. Brandon yanked the phone out of his son's hand, then smacked him upside the head.

"Ow! What gives?" Matt rubbed the spot where Brandon had hit him.

"You weren't even paying attention," Brandon pointed out.

"Yeah I was."

Brandon jerked his head toward the half-full cart. "What'd you just put in there?"

Matt leaned over and gazed at the contents. "Uh...cookies?"

"And what did I ask for?

Matt blinked. "Cookies?"

Brandon rolled his eyes and replaced the Milanos back on the shelf. "Put the phone away," he instructed.

They moved down the junk food aisle and turned down the next one. Matt shoved his hands in his pant pockets and hunched his shoulders. "Are we almost done? I have homework to do."

Brandon snatched a box of Cinnamon Toast Crunch off the shelf. "Is homework code for girlfriend?"

Matt's look turned more solemn. "No, I really have homework."

Brandon lifted a brow, then did a double take at the dark-haired woman at the end of the aisle studying a box of Pop-Tarts in one hand and holding her cell with the other. Brandon pushed his cart toward Stella.

Why? Because he was sick in the head and needed help. Like serious help. Because Stella Davenport drove him crazy. When she wasn't setting his neglected hormones on fire, she was lecturing him about sticking his seventeen-year-old in ballet lessons.

Woman had lost her damn mind.

Or maybe he was the one who'd lost his mind, because he was actually walking toward her instead of hightailing it in the other direction.

"The cherry Pop-Tarts have two hundred calories and sixteen grams of sugar," Stella was saying as he and Matt approached. She put the cherry flavor back and chose another box. "The chocolate fudge also have two hundred calories, but seventeen grams of sugar." She glanced at Brandon, then pointed to her cell and mouthed the word *mother*. "I say go for the chocolate fudge. You only live once." Stella paused as she listened. "This store doesn't have vegan Pop-Tarts, Mom." She blew out a breath and dropped her head back. Then she put the chocolate Pop-Tarts back and reached for the wildberry. "Those have one hundred and ninety calories and sixteen grams of sugar. They don't have unfrosted ones either and even if they did, who in the world eats unfrosted Pop-Tarts? That's like scraping the cream out of Oreos."

Beside him Matt chuckled. Stella tossed them a glare and Brandon bit back his own laughter. She was so damn cute when her cheeks were all red and flushed. Brandon imagined that's how she'd look after being thoroughly kissed.

Stella switched the cell to her other ear. "How about something besides Pop-Tarts?" She listened for a moment. "I'm not reading the nutrition facts for every Pop-Tart flavor there is. Well, how about I surprise you?" She replaced the wildberry and went for the birthday cake flavor and threw them in her cart. "Okay, then. Wait, what's that?" Stella shouted. "You're breaking up real bad, Mom. I gotta go, love you." She blew out a breath and terminated the phone call.

"I feel like I need an exorcism."

"Your mom sounds funny," Matt quipped.

"Yeah, well, it's all fun and games until she has you reading the fat content of all the Pop-Tarts."

Brandon lifted a brow at her cart. "So you went with birthday cake?"

She shrugged both shoulders. "I have a sick sense of humor." She took her time perusing his and Matt's cart, taking in everything from the salmon to the cookies. "Interesting combination."

"This kid doesn't know the meaning of the word *healthy*." Brandon jerked his thumb at Matt, who gave Stella a huge grin. As in a shit-eating-I-just-won-the-lottery grin. Shit. His kid didn't have the hots for Stella, did he? Not that Brandon blamed him. Matt would have to be blind not to be enamored by Ms. Davenport.

Matt nudged Brandon's ribs. "You picked out the cereal."

"Because it's the one *you* like."

Stella folded her arms over the cart handle. "I wouldn't have pegged you for a health nut," she said to Brandon.

"He just likes to tell people that," Matt piped in. "But he's a closet junk food junkie."

Brandon turned toward his son. "Who killed off the rest of the ice cream last night?"

"That was after you ate half the gallon."

Stella leaned forward, giving Brandon a whiff of her hair, which was dark and shiny and smelled like summer and fresh air. Though it wasn't summer, Stella had always reminded him of long summer days and warm breezes.

And look at him with all the poetry.

"You're not an emotional eater, are you?" she questioned.

"He totally is," Matt answered.

Brandon just glared.

But Matt ignored him. "Last year when the Broncos lost in the playoffs, he finished an entire bag of barbecue chips."

Brandon glared at his son. "That was because you ate the last hamburger."

Matt's grin grew. "Actually Cameron ate the last hamburger. I ate the last hot dog."

"Either way," Brandon cut in. "The two of you hogged the food like a couple of toddlers."

"Sounds like the both of you have issues," Stella joked.

Matt chuckled; then his face sobered. "Hey, my buddy Evan said he's taking classes with you."

Stella's brow lifted, which accompanied an evil curl of her lips. "Really?" she asked with a pointed look at Brandon.

"Don't start," he warned.

"I didn't say anything."

"Because it's not happening," Brandon reminded her.

"You keep saying that."

Matt bounced a look between his dad and Stella, brows pulled in confusion. "What's not happening? What're you talking about?"

"Nothing," Brandon immediately answered.

Stella turned her attention, and her sweet smile, on Matt. "I told your dad he should bring you to my studio for ballet training. To help with your balance and coordination with football."

Matt's attention continued to volley between Brandon and Stella. "Oh. Really? You guys talked about it?" Matt glanced at his dad. "What did you say?"

Stella shot a warning glare at Brandon. "Several of your teammates are doing it. And"—she held up a finger to cut Brandon off—"it is helping them. Just ask."

"It's not happening," Brandon stated.

"I believe I was asking Matt," Stella argued.

"But he's a minor, so I'm answering for him." Brandon settled his arm on his son's shoulder and pushed their cart down the aisle.

"You can't do that," she called after him.

"Just did," he called back.

She was silent a moment, and Brandon thought, for just a second, he'd won another round. Then she spoke and Brandon reminded himself there was no winning with Stella Davenport.

"I'm going to break you, West," she warned just as he and Matt reached the end of the aisle. "You can't keep ignoring me."

Brandon shot one last glance at her before disappearing down the next aisle. Hands on hips. Lips set in a firm line. Feet braced apart. Yeah, she was a force to be reckoned with. He also knew she was right. He wouldn't be able to ignore her forever, because a woman like that was impossible to ignore.

Beside him, Matt was grinning like someone had stuck a hanger in his mouth. "What?" Brandon practically growled.

"I like her," Matt answered with a noticeable bounce to his step.

FIVE

Stella placed her hands on her student's hips and held them still. She moved behind the girl so the two of them were facing the floor-to-ceiling mirrors.

"When you *tondu*, your hips need to stay level." Stella pointed to the girl's skirt. "Watch the line of your skirt right here. This needs to stay straight and not lift when you move your leg. Try again."

The girl, eleven-year-old Elizabeth Dale, was in Stella's intermediate beginner class. She'd started ballet at eight, which was typically older than most girls. Stella had started dancing at three and by Elizabeth's age she'd been in advanced classes and on pointe for two years. But Elizabeth was a sweet girl and had determination, a factor that was just as important as experience. Stella had held the girl after class to work on a few techniques.

She stepped back from her student, and when she did, she caught a quick glimpse of two men. One was Elizabeth's father, who was a single parent after his divorce three years ago.

And the other man was Brandon, leaning against the jamb of the open doorway that led from the dance room to the observation room.

And damn if her heart didn't skip up to her throat at the sight of him. All tall and casual with the way he was just leaning there, as though waiting for the bus. Arms crossed over his thick chest. A black polo with *West Custom Homes* stitched across his left pec stretched tightly over his wide shoulders, as though the shirt was borderline too small. Tight at the shoulder, yet loose at the waist, because he was all trim and in crazy good shape.

His gaze followed her across the room, his expression unreadable.

She cleared her throat and broke eye contact with him, but she could still feel his gaze on her.

How did he do that?

Stella led Elizabeth to a photo on the wall. It was a black-and-white snapshot of Stella onstage, lights illuminating her from behind, casting a soft halo of white around her body. Her hair slicked back in a tight bun, she wore a light blue dress with spaghetti straps and a skirt with multiple layers of gauzy material that had floated around her like silk.

The familiar lump rose in her throat as she remembered that performance like it had happened last week.

"Is that really you?" Elizabeth asked.

"Yes," Stella said, gazing at the photo of her in the middle of an arabesque. Her left foot was up on pointe, her right leg extended behind her, stretched above her waistline, much higher than a human leg should be able to go. Her left arm was in front of her, pointed toward the audience and her right was extended to the side.

As though remembering, the pain in her knee turned up a notch, reminding her that she could no longer do things like that. Her body had been too abused, pushed too hard to achieve things the human body wasn't designed to do.

"How long did it take you to be able to do that?" Elizabeth asked.

That performance had been two years before her initial knee surgery. "A long time," Stella said in a thick voice, already feeling the emotion of what she'd lost weigh her down. What she wouldn't give to have all that back. The freedom and exhilaration of moving across the stage, being one with the music, feeling the lights warm her skin and the fluidity and flow of the movements. As natural as breathing.

She swallowed, hard, trying to push it down. One would think she'd have become a master at keeping the feelings back. At quelling the disappointment she'd had in herself, that she hadn't been able to push through her physical therapy and come back.

Stella had known when to throw up her white flag even though her artistic director had told her to give it more time. She'd been able to feel her body giving, protesting and slowly breaking down from years of abuse and always pushing to be better, more flexible, and never stop.

"I've gotta go. My dad's waiting," Elizabeth stated, pulling Stella from her thoughts.

"Of course." She smiled at the girl. "Just practice what we went over in class today and I'll see you next week."

The girl glided across the floor, light on her toes, the way dancers moved with effortless grace. Stella absently rubbed her knee when Elizabeth's father muttered an "Excuse me" from behind Brandon, obviously trying to get through the narrow doorway. Brandon, who was taller and wider, and probably five to six years younger than the girl's dad, glanced down at the man. He didn't move right away, instead casting a glance in Stella's direction as though he didn't want to give the man access to her.

And why would he have a problem with that? He couldn't possibly be jealous, could he? No, that was ridiculous. Brandon did not strike her as a jealous guy, and he had no reason to be envious of the other man.

As much as the thought of Brandon displaying even the tiniest bit of jealousy on her behalf gave her shivers, she knew it wasn't possible.

After a second of pause, Brandon moved aside and Elizabeth's father entered the room. He patted his daughter on the shoulder, then reached Stella's side.

"Thanks for taking the extra time with her," Wayne said.

"It's my pleasure," she told him while removing her ballet shoes and rolling her toes on the floor. "She's got a lot of promise. It's just a matter of muscle memory."

Wayne glanced back at Elizabeth, who was packing her dance things away in a duffel bag. "She loves coming here. Ever since her mother and I divorced, she's struggled to find something to hold on to."

If there was anything Stella understood, it was the need for something firm to grab ahold of. In a world where things came and went, foundations crumbled, and promises were broken, finding the one thing that could offer comfort like nothing else could be a real challenge.

Stella nodded. "Any time she needs extra help, I'm here."

Wayne jingled the change in his pocket. "Listen, she and I are going to grab some dinner at the new pizza place by the lake. They serve out of an Airstream trailer, but it's supposed to be really good."

Just like every week, the man tried to ask her out. He was perfectly nice and his invitations were always so innocent, and Stella always felt like she was kicking a puppy when she turned him down. Even though she was in no position to be picky, because men weren't exactly beating down her door, Wayne just didn't float her boat. Didn't make her hot. Didn't make her sweat.

No, that honor was held for the man whose gaze was burning a hole in the back of Wayne's head.

A part of her, a very small and sadistic part, was tempted to take Wayne up on his offer, just to make Brandon see what he was missing out on.

But then the human side of her knew that wouldn't be fair to Elizabeth's father. He really was a nice man and deserved to have a woman who reciprocated his feelings.

Stella plastered the same polite smile on her face that she gave him every week. "That's a really nice offer, but I have some choreography for an older class that I have to work on." Not true, but she'd already gone through every other excuse with him, so she had to resort to making things up.

Against her inner voice trying to ensue some common sense, Stella snuck another peek at Brandon.

Yep. Still there.

Wayne chuckled, making her remember she was in the middle of a conversation with a perfectly nice man. "You know, you keep turning me down enough, I'm going to think you're not interested."

Good God, did he have to make it so awkward? How was she supposed to respond to that?

She swallowed, trying to channel every ounce of charm she possessed. The last thing she needed was for him to pull Elizabeth from her class. "It's not that. I just have a strict rule of not dating parents of my students," she explained. "It can complicate the situation."

Wayne nodded and offered a smile, one that didn't quite

reach his eyes. "Understandable. But if you ever change your policy, give me a call." He fished a business card out of his wallet and handed it to her.

She accepted the card and glanced at it.

Wayne Dale, Attorney at Law.

Her black leotard and black bike shorts, which were pulled over her pink ballet tights, didn't have pockets, so she held on to the card with one hand while still grasping her ballet shoes in the other. "Thanks," she told him. "I'll keep that in mind."

With one last smile, he turned and strolled out of the room, taking Elizabeth with him.

Then she was alone, standing in the middle of the room, Brandon still leaning in the doorway. They stared at each other and something zinged through Stella's system, the same thrill she experienced when plummeting down that first drop of a roller coaster and her stomach took a nose-dive. The room, normally filled with classical music and moving bodies, was now too quiet and too large, swallowing her up. Then Brandon moved, pushing away from the door-jamb with an effortless grace he shouldn't possess, and strolled toward her. Her heart thumped harder with each step he took, reminding her of how small she was.

"I hope you let the bastard down easy," Brandon commented in a voice that was deep. Deeper and grittier than normal.

"What do you mean?" she queried instead of clueing him in.

Brandon glanced back at the now empty observation room. "The guy had rejection written all over his face."

The pang of guilt she felt when turning Wayne down pinched her stomach. "Would you rather I had accepted his invitation?"

Brandon slid his hands into his pockets and gazed at her with hooded eyes. "Depends on what the invitation was for."

She held up the business card. "He just offered his services."

"I'll just bet he did," Brandon commented, then took the card from her. Without breaking eye contact with her, he crumpled the card up and tossed it toward the trashcan in the corner of the room. And landed the shot like he was an NBA star.

Seriously, did the man suck at anything?

"Hey," she protested. "Maybe I wanted to keep that."

"You're not going to go out with that guy."

Damn, the man was good. She crossed her arms over her chest, allowing the ballet shoes to dangle from her fingertips. "How do you know that's what he wanted? Maybe I'm in need of a good lawyer."

One of his dark brows lifted. "You planning on suing someone?"

She narrowed her eyes. "Only people who stick their nose where it doesn't belong."

He chuckled, a sound that danced over her skin like a cool breeze on a hot day. "Touché." His gaze, as hot as the rest of him, skittered over her body, touching on her thighs before assessing the rest of her that was covered in spandex and tight-as-shit cotton. "But you can't dress like that and not expect a guy to notice."

Was he saying that he noticed? She glanced down at herself, and the bike shorts that were barely longer than a bathing suit bottom. Okay, yeah, most men would look at a woman dressed like she was. But she was a ballet instructor. She couldn't very well instruct and lead by example in a pair of sweats.

"What's wrong with how I'm dressed?" she wanted to know. "It's standard dance attire."

Brandon rocked back on his heels. "I'm just saying. Doesn't leave a whole lot to the imagination."

Since when did he care?

"I didn't realize you have a problem with how I dress," she said.

His pupils filled his coffee-colored eyes. "Didn't say I had a problem with it. But you slap a pair of spandex on legs like that, and men will take notice."

The heat in her midsection spread, then warred with irritation over his suggestion. Was he jealous? Teasing? Or was he just used to telling people what to do? Having his way?

She tilted her head to one side and decided to give him a dose of his own medicine. Make him squirm for a while. "Are you saying you notice?"

Something flashed across his eyes, but it was gone so fast that Stella wasn't sure if she'd imagined it or not. "Well, I'm not blind."

She waved her hand in a circular motion. "Meaning..." *Yeah, squirm away, big guy.*

"Meaning you have a kick-ass body, Stella, and you know it." The smirk playing havoc with his mouth turned into a full-blown grin. "You weren't expecting me to say that, were you?"

The ballet shoes dropped from her fingertips as she jammed her hands on her hips. "Do you torture me for some sick pleasure, or are you just naturally like that?"

He reached out and tugged on a strand of hair that had slipped from her ponytail. "So suspicious. Maybe I just like to put some color in those cheeks of yours."

She swatted his hand away. "There are other ways of

putting color in a woman's cheeks," she said, because, holy hell, her mouth had a mind of its own.

His brow knitted. "Is that an invitation? Because I thought you didn't date parents of students."

If she were a smart woman, and sometimes she seriously doubted the amount of brains in her head, she'd not issue an invitation to Brandon West. Because he'd take it without a backward glance. She held up a finger. "First of all, I don't teach your child. And second of all, how did you know I have that rule?"

Brandon took a step closer to her. "I could hear every word of your conversation with that guy."

"Or you were just eavesdropping."

"I don't eavesdrop."

Stella couldn't help the laugh that popped out of her. "So you don't listen to other people's conversations or do anything else you're not supposed to? Because I find that hard to believe."

"What're you implying, Stella?" he asked as he took another step closer. "That I'm a rule breaker? A bad boy? I thought women liked bad boys."

Yeah, but he was hardly a boy. No, Brandon West was all man. All hard, lean muscle that boys only dreamed of having. And why did he have to stand so close? Did he mean to invade her personal space? And why did she let him?

The familiar building of panic and sweat that always followed a claustrophobic moment started with a slow simmer in the pit of her stomach. The man towered over her, staring down at her out of eyes so dark that all she could see was her own reflection. Which meant he was too close. So close the heat from his skin brushed over hers like a puff of breath.

She took an instinctive step back, needing her space,

needing room to breathe because Brandon sucked all the air from the room. But the inch of space she put between the two of them wasn't enough because he was larger than life.

He grabbed her wrist, wrapping his thick fingers around her arm. "What's wrong?"

A sweat broke out along her forehead when he touched her. She pulled her hand from his hold.

He held his hands up. "Sorry."

She shook her head and tried to explain, but the words were caught in her throat. "It's not you. It's…"

Damn it! Her entire adult life, she'd worked so hard to overcome her anxiety. Had pushed through and told herself she was stronger than her panic attacks, that they wouldn't define her. But something about Brandon brought all of that to the surface. Because when she saw him, she saw every beautiful man who'd charmed the pants off her mom, literally. Then Gloria had snatched Stella from whatever friends she'd managed to make and uproot her world over and over. Only, the thing was, Stella knew, in her heart, that Brandon wasn't anything like that. He was a good man, but Stella's fears wouldn't allow her to see that far.

She turned from him, not wanting the man who'd starred in all her fantasies to see the anxiety on her face. The horror in her eyes for losing it so easily. He hadn't even put his hands on her, and her body had threatened to explode. Her eyes dropped closed to hold back the tears that had pooled.

"Stella," he said in a low voice.

She shook her head and pulled in a deep breath, willing her hammering heart to slow the eff down. "It's not you," she said again, because, apparently, she was incapable of saying anything else. Because, if nothing more, she needed Brandon to know he hadn't done anything wrong.

"You said that already," he told her.

"I don't like people getting too close to me," she explained.

He came around so he was facing her. "I can see that." His brow knitted with concern. "But you weren't like that with your student," he pointed out. "So is it just men? Or me?"

"You asked me that once before," she reminded him.

He nodded his agreement. "Yeah, I did. But you didn't really answer me." He paused and let the statement hang between them. "Did you?"

So what if she hadn't? Why was he so curious?

Um.... maybe he was just wants to help?

"You never did tell me why you came by," she mentioned, instead of letting him in. Better to keep him away so she didn't make the same mistake her mother always made.

He stared at her as though he wanted to argue, which he probably did. He wasn't the type of guy to let a subject just drop. No, it would come up again. But he wouldn't pressure her; she knew that.

"I thought about your offer to help Matt," he told her.

"Oh?" she asked now that her heart had slowed down. "I thought ballet was for girls."

"Are you still interested?"

"Are you going to tell me I was right all along?"

One corner of his mouth kicked up, sending her heart into her throat. The man had a melt-your-bones smile and knew just when and how to use it.

"If I do that, will you agree to work with him?"

She lifted a shoulder in a casual shrug. "I'd work with him anyway. I just wanted you to admit defeat."

His half-smile grew. "Anyone ever tell you that you have a sick mind?"

"You just remember my no-dating-of-the-parents rule." She waved a finger at him. "Don't be trying anything funny."

"If I try anything, Stella, it won't be funny and you definitely wouldn't laugh."

She didn't doubt that for a second. And that's what scared her.

SIX

Brandon drove away from the studio gripping the steering wheel and adjusting himself in his Dockers because *damn* that woman. Stella Davenport had no idea what an inferno of sexiness she really was. And the worst part? She didn't try to be sexy. She just...was.

Women like her, and Brandon had known a few, just exuded the stuff like heat from a flame. Or a bonfire, in her case. The way she walked. The way she tilted her head and exposed the creamy column of her neck. The way she was constantly sucking her full bottom lip between her teeth.

Yeah, Stella was a powerhouse. Perhaps he'd always known that about her since she'd shown up in town about two years ago. Since first bumping into her, literally, he'd known there was something different about those see-through-you blue eyes. She'd accused him of cutting in front of her in line at a hot dog stand at the Fourth of July fair. He may or may not have spotted her standing there, looking out of place and gorgeous in her red spaghetti strap tank and white skirt. He may or may not have casually inserted himself into the line right in front of her just to get her attention. And Stella wasn't the type of person to let something like that slide. No, she'd certainly voiced her disdain for "line jumpers," as she'd called him.

He'd turned to apologize, barely hiding the grin on his face, when Beverly Rowley of the Beehive Mafia had beat him to the punch. "Brandon West, you get that gorgeous tushy of yours to the back of the line like everybody else," she'd called from three people back. "Lois has her camera and she's not afraid to use it."

Stella had coughed into her hand, he suspected to hide a chuckle. So he'd dipped his head toward her in apology and excused himself. Not that he'd been sorry. He'd stepped in front of her just in time to get an impression of soft, plump breasts when she'd bumped into him.

Yeah, Brandon thought as he turned onto his street, Stella Davenport really was something else.

Beautiful.

Smart.

Funny.

And closely guarding some very private secrets. If anyone recognized inner turmoil, it was Brandon because he'd gone through his own for a very long time. His parents' deaths when he was six years old, followed by Trish's departure, then divorce.

He also recognized the anxiety all over her face when he got too close to her. Only her issue was more than just anxiety. She didn't want him to know, of that much he was sure. Because Stella was a proud woman and wouldn't want anyone to know she had weaknesses. His house came into view and he stuffed back a groan at the sight of the familiar bright yellow Jeep Wrangler.

He hadn't been lying the other day when he'd told Stella he liked Adrienne. She was a cute girl who had high goals in life and had good, upstanding parents. His son could do a lot worse when it came to his choice of girlfriend.

No, the problem wasn't how Brandon felt about Adrienne. The problem was how Matt felt about her. He recognized the dreamy look in the kid's eyes whenever she was around. Matt had the same worship and borderline obsession that Brandon had had with Trish. And look where that had landed him. Elbow deep in baby shit at the age of eighteen.

Too young to have a clue what to do with a kid. Too young to be married and playing house. He'd thought they could really make a go of it. Become a family and have more kids.

Only Trisha had other plans.

But that wasn't to say Brandon would change anything. Having Matt was the best thing that had ever happened to him. He'd loved that boy from the second he'd laid eyes on the screaming, red-faced, seven-pound newborn at two-fifteen in the morning. From the second Brandon had gazed down into his son's beautiful eyes, Matt had been his. Always would be, and it was Brandon's job to guide Matt, teach him and prepare him for the real world.

Even if that meant protecting him from the same mistakes he'd made at that age.

He parked his truck in the driveway next to Adrienne's Jeep, hauled his work bag off the passenger seat, and exited the vehicle.

As he made his way up the walk, his cell rang.

Blake's name flashed across the caller ID.

"What's up?" he greeted his cousin.

"Hey, can you bring Matt to school thirty minutes early tomorrow? I have some new drills I want to try with him."

Duke lumbered down the hallway and let out a gruff bark. "Hush," Brandon told the dog. Duke's response was to stick his wet nose into Brandon's Dockers. He moved past the dog and set his bag down. "For just Matt or the whole team?"

"Just Matt," Blake answered. "I want to work on these with him before practice."

Duke trotted down the hallway after Brandon, his too-long toenails clicking on the hardwood floor. Damn, he needed to cut those things. "Have you mentioned this to Matt?"

"He actually asked me," Blake answered.

"He did? He didn't say anything to me."

"I told him I'd call you. It would be three days a week for the next month."

Brandon leaned against the kitchen counter. "Listen..." Shit, he'd never been good with words. "I appreciate the extra time you've been giving him."

"Now don't get all mushy on me," Blake answered. "It's just football."

Brandon shook his head even though Blake couldn't see him. "No, it's more than that for you. Not many coaches would dedicate so many after hours for just one kid."

"Matt's not the only one I'm doing it for. But if he were the only one who needed the time, I'd still do it."

Brandon blew out a breath. "Yeah, you would." They were both silent for a second. "I'll bring him earlier in the morning."

"So," Blake said after a second. "I heard Stella finally got to you."

Shit, not him too. Did the three of them have a conspiracy going?

"So I'll have Matt at the school at six-thirty."

"Yeah, that's what I thought," Blake answered with a snicker.

They disconnected the call and Brandon opened a cupboard, pulled out a bag of doggie treats, and tossed one to Duke. The dog caught the thing in the air and swallowed it in one bite.

Matt's bedroom door was closed, as he suspected it would be, even though Matt knew damn good and well to leave the thing open. He gave Matt's door a quick knock before cracking the door open.

The kids were on the bed, sprawled across Matt's rumpled Denver Broncos comforter. One pillow had been kicked to the floor and the other was underneath Matt's head. The boy was on his back, one arm wound tightly around Adrienne's shoulders as she snuggled against his side.

A signature postcoital position.

When the two kids spotted him standing there, they jumped apart, scrambling to opposite sides of the bed. Brandon lifted a brow at Matt as Adrienne smoothed her hair down and cleared her throat.

"Hi, Mr. West," she greeted with a half-smile.

"Hi, Adrienne." She really was a sweet girl. But, shit, calling him Mr. West made him feel old.

"Hey, Dad," Matt finally said.

Guilty much?

"Homework done?" he asked the kid.

"Uh, yeah. We did that already."

And what else did you do?

The question was almost out of his mouth, but he kept

himself in check. After all, there was no reason to embarrass the kids. They were embarrassed enough, if the pink glow in Adrienne's cheeks was anything to go by.

You don't know they were doing anything. Nothing wrong with a little snuggling.

The argument popped in his head, reminding him that not all kids were how he and Trisha had been.

"Did you do the trash?" he asked his son.

"Uh..." He glanced at Adrienne, who was busy fiddling with her hair. "Not yet."

He almost told the kid to get up and do it right away but changed his mind. No need to be an ogre about it. "Just make sure you get it done before you go to bed."

Adrienne jumped up from the bed and grabbed her backpack. "It's okay, I have to get home anyway. My parents wanted me back by eight."

Now you've scared her off, asshole.

Matt scrambled off the bed as though he was afraid she'd disappear into thin air. "I'll walk you to your car."

Brandon left the room and walked to the kitchen. Behind him he heard Matt and Adrienne's voices just before they disappeared out the front door.

Had he been too hasty in assuming they'd been doing something they shouldn't have? Matt had always been a good kid and didn't have a history of getting into trouble.

Brandon had done the best he could on his own, and considering he'd been mother, father, chauffeur, counselor, disciplinarian, personal chef, and accountant all in one, he thought he'd done a pretty good job. So why was he so paranoid?

Because all teenage boys think about one thing. No matter how good they are.

The front door opened, then closed. Duke lifted his head

and perked his ears when Matt's footsteps sounded down the hall.

"Are you using protection?" Brandon blurted out when Matt came into the kitchen.

Matt stopped short and his eyes widened. "Am I what?"

Brandon crossed his arms over his chest and leaned against the kitchen counter. "You heard me, Matt. I want to make sure you're being smart."

Matt shoved his hand through his dark shaggy hair. "Dad," he said with a laugh that sounded shaky. Too shaky.

"I'm serious, son. I probably should have had this talk with you a long time ago. But I need to know. If there's anything you need to tell me—"

"Dad, relax, okay?" Matt interrupted. "We're not..." He shook his head and ran his fingers through his hair again. "I mean, Adrienne and I aren't doing anything." He swallowed hard, making his Adam's apple bob up and down like a buoy in a storm. "We don't do that."

A breath Brandon hadn't realized he'd been holding blew out, deflating the tension that had been building up inside him.

"Good," he responded with a single nod of his head. "Good." Awkward much? "Because you should wait. It's not something you should go around doing with just anybody."

"Adrienne's not just anybody, Dad," Matt argued.

Brandon nodded. "I know she may not seem like that now. But you're seventeen, Matt. You don't have enough life experience to know whether she's somebody special yet."

"Is it because you don't like her?"

Why did everyone keep asking him that? "Liking her has

nothing to do with it. And I do like her," he found himself saying for the second time in as many days. "I just want to make sure you're being smart." When Matt only blinked, Brandon explained. "Sex, Matt. We're talking about sex."

"Yeah, I got that." Matt nodded, then let out a strange laugh/cough thing. "Geez, Dad."

Yeah, you're not the only one who's uncomfortable, kid.

Brandon held his hands up. "Just want to make sure we're on the same page."

Matt turned, but not in time for Brandon to catch the roll of his eye. "Don't worry. I won't make the same mistake you did."

Brandon was across the kitchen so fast that Duke jerked his head off the floor. "Hey. Listen to me." He grabbed Matt's elbow. "You're not a mistake. Don't ever think that."

Something flashed across Matt's eyes. "I know," he said on a low voice.

"Do you?" Brandon pushed. Since the day Matt had been born, Brandon's biggest fear was his son thinking he was a mistake. That he or Trisha wished they could take it all back. "I'm not saying I wouldn't go back and do some things differently. But don't ever think that I regret having you." Matt was his entire world, and he'd be damned if his own child thought he was a mistake.

Matt's throat worked again. "I don't think that, Dad."

Brandon nodded and dropped his hands. "Good."

"Uh…" Brandon rubbed the back of his neck. "Look. I like Adrienne, okay? I think she's a sweet girl. Just…" Geez, why did he have to be such a blubbering idiot? Talking to his own kid shouldn't be this hard. "Just make sure you're using common sense. If I could go back and do it all over again, I would have waited until I was older."

Matt cleared his throat. "You don't need to worry. Adrienne's not that kind of girl anyway."

Brandon gazed back at his son, recognizing the dreams and innocence he'd once possessed. "Do you love her?"

Matt's attention darted around the room, landing on Duke, then shifting back to Brandon. "I'm not sure. I think I might."

"Because it's okay if you don't know. You're still young."

"Did you love Mom?"

The question threw Brandon for a loop because Matt hardly ever asked about his mother. He wasn't sure how to answer, since he wasn't even sure of the answer himself.

He sucked in a deep breath. "Yeah. When we were together, I did." It was bad enough Matt thought his own mother had abandoned him. But he also didn't want Matt to think Brandon didn't care about Trisha or didn't love her enough to try and make it work. He'd always been careful to make sure Matt understood that he'd once been a part of a loving family unit.

Matt only nodded. "I'm going to take the garbage out, then I'm going to hit the sack."

"All right," Brandon replied. Shit, had he completely botched that? Matt was his son, and they should be able to talk about stuff. Anything, because wasn't that what fathers and sons did? At least he and Matt always had, up until a few years ago when Matt had been overcome with the sullenness that plagued ninety percent of teenagers. He wasn't sure why he'd expected his kid to be any different. He strolled out of the kitchen as his cell phone buzzed. With an exhausted sigh, Brandon dug the thing out and tapped the screen without checking the caller ID.

"Yeah," he greeted.

There was a short pause; then a hesitant female voice said, "Brandon?"

He stopped short outside the kitchen as his heart rolled up into his throat, threatening to bring up the hasty dinner he'd shoved down. "Trisha."

SEVEN

I'm not calling at a bad time, am I?" his ex-wife asked.

Brandon cleared his throat and stretched out on the couch. "No," he answered, instead of asking her what the hell she wanted. It had taken a long time, several years, for him not to feel anything at the sound of her voice. When he'd realized she wasn't coming back, his longing had turned into resentment. And with each phone call, he'd wanted to demand why. Why they weren't important enough for her to stick around. Why her own dreams took precedence over the child she'd given birth to.

Now he wasn't sure what to feel. Longing? Anger? Brandon was confused except for the mild annoyance that she thought she still had the right to check in on them. As though she actually cared about their well-being.

"What do you want, Trish?"

Her soft sigh flowed through the phone line. "I left the circus," she told him.

A thousand responses flew through his mind, including one that had him asking why he should give a shit. Because he didn't. Only he sort of did. After all, it was the same gig that had taken her away from them in the first place.

It didn't take her away; she walked out on you.

Yeah, he could sit there and blame Ringling Brothers until the cows came home, and it wouldn't change reality. That she'd chosen to leave. Packed her bags and turned her back.

"Why?" he asked anyway, because, shit, he was only human and curious as hell.

"I..." Her words broke off and a sinking feeling settled in the pit of Brandon's stomach. "It just wasn't where I wanted to be anymore."

He gripped the phone tighter. "And why is that?" he asked, even though the voice in the back of his mind told him not to give her the time of day. They'd had conversations similar to this before.

She sighed. "I want to be back in Matt's life."

"What makes this time different from all the others?" He hadn't meant for his words to come out so harshly.

"I don't expect you to believe me," she said in a quiet voice. "But I've left for good and bought a house in Oklahoma City."

Which meant...what?

Brandon pinched the bridge of his nose as his thoughts automatically went to Matt, as they always did. Because the kid was always his first concern, his well-being and happiness meaning more to Brandon than his own did. Because that's what being a parent was about. Sacrificing your own happiness and stability to provide and look after this other human being that you were responsible for. Something Trisha had never understood.

He forced down the old resentment that always bubbled up when he talked to her.

"Why are you telling me this, Trisha?" he asked, needing her to cut to the chase.

There was a moment of silence before she answered. "I told you, I want to be back in Matt's life."

He chuckled without a trace of humor. "And you think it's that easy, huh? That fourteen years after you walked out on us, you can call, say you left the circus, bought a house, and I'll just go ahead and open the door for you?"

"Of course not," she admitted. "I understand it's been a long time. And I understand that I put you through a lot." She blew out a breath. "I...can't make up for what happened. For the hurt and disappointment that I caused you."

Brandon waited for her to continue, but silence fell. Damn, he shouldn't feel anything. Her words weren't supposed to create an ache in his chest. But they did because Matt's happiness was all that mattered to him.

"All right," he finally muttered, knowing he'd kick himself later for allowing her another chance. At least a chance to explain herself.

"How is he?" Trisha asked after a moment.

It was the same question she always asked, and Brandon always answered. "He's good. He has a girlfriend."

Brandon could practically hear Trisha smiling. "What's her name?"

He swallowed before answering. "Adrienne."

"How long have they been together?"

Brandon leaned his head back against the couch and closed his eyes. "About five months."

Trish paused before responding. "Is she a nice girl? Good enough for him?"

Like she had ever cared. "Yeah, she's a good girl. She's been accepted to UT."

"Smart and ambitious," Trish said with a smile in her voice. As if she was pleased, even though this was the most interest she'd ever shown in Matt's life.

"Trish, what're you doing?" he asked, putting a halt to her questions. "Why are you asking me all this?"

"Because I want to know how my son is doing," she replied.

"You've had fourteen years to know how your son is doing," he pointed out. "Why the sudden interest now?" Matt had only been three when Trish had left for good. Fourteen years was too long. Too long for her to be so disconnected, then try to waltz back in.

"Look, I don't expect you to throw me a welcome home party," she told him. "I thought maybe"—she cleared her throat—"that maybe I could just talk to him. I would really love to hear his voice."

The tremor in her voice was unmistakable, sort of how she got after Matt was born and she couldn't get the kid to stop crying. She'd look up at Brandon with tears in those big sad eyes, and he'd step in and fix everything. Just as he'd always done and eventually Trish had stopped trying with her own baby. Brandon had taken over because his wife had given up.

"I guess I just need to know that he's okay," she went on. "Maybe reconnect with him and—"

"And what, Trish?" he countered. "You'll come back into his life, then crush him again when you leave?"

The silence on the other end of the line was thick and filled with...regret. Brandon could feel it reaching out and gripping his throat. That's why Trish was calling. She had regrets and guilt and needed to make sure...well, he wasn't exactly sure what her end game was. But it was hard to erase fourteen years of her popping in and out, calling every few months as though she cared. And then disappearing for a year or two before he'd hear from her again.

"There's no need to be unkind," she responded in a soft voice. "I know I've made a lot of mistakes, ones that I would take back if I could. But I can't and that's something I've had to live with." She blew out a breath. "I just wanted to call and see if I could reach out one day next week and maybe you'd let me speak with him."

He'd known that request was coming, because she always asked, hoping it would be the one time he'd actually grant her wish. But he never did, for Matt's sake. He didn't want his son to get sucked in by Trish's temporary interest in his life, only to have her disappear. And then Brandon would be stuck with answering questions about why she hadn't called in six months. And anyway, the phone calls had been nothing more than her way of absolving her own guilt.

"How do I know you're serious this time?"

"I guess you don't," she admitted. "I'm just asking for a chance, Brandon. One last chance. And I know I'm a day late and a dollar short. And I'm not looking to take him away from you, or anything like that. You're a good dad, and he's always been lucky to have you. If you could just let me—"

"It's not a matter of me letting you," Brandon told her. "But whether or not Matt will even want to talk to you."

"I understand that," she amended. "But I have to try."

His hand tightened on the cell phone as the clock on the wall ticked an echo in the silent room. "Let me talk to him first," he found himself saying. "Try calling back next week."

* * *

The football field was dark and quiet when he and Matt arrived the next morning, but Brandon's mind was still running a hundred miles an hour after his conversation with Trish last night. She was scared. Scared that Brandon wouldn't let Matt talk to her. Scared that Matt wouldn't have any interest in her. Brandon thought he wouldn't care either. He shouldn't, however shitty that was. But he did. He cared what Matt would think.

"What's wrong with you this morning?" Matt questioned as they approached Blake.

He offered his son a half-smile to hide his turbulent thoughts. "Nothing."

The harsh wind lent an extra crispness to the already brisk morning air. The sky was slowly changing from dark to lavender as he and Matt walked across the freshly mowed field toward an already waiting Blake.

Blake checked his watch, like he thought Brandon and Matt were late, even though they both knew the two of them were right on time.

"I have a meeting at seven-fifteen, so I can't stay long," Brandon told his cousin.

Blake took a sip of his coffee and turned his attention to Matt. "You ready to lay it out?" Which was Blake code for "Prepare to have your ass kicked."

Matt dropped his gym bag on the ground. "I'm ready for anything you have to throw at me."

Blake's mouth quirked in what some would consider an almost grin. "Let's do it, then."

Brandon sat back and watched the two, his gaze tracking Matt and having flashbacks of his own football days.

Twenty minutes went by before the team started shuffling onto the field.

Cameron was close behind, a Bobcats sweatshirt warding him from the chill and a thermos of coffee in one hand. He stopped by Brandon and sipped his coffee.

"Lookin' good," Cameron commented. "Blake tell you he's starting on Friday?"

Brandon glanced at Cam. "No. Is Matt aware of this?"

"I don't think Blake's told him yet."

Of course he hadn't, otherwise Matt would have said something. Or would he have? Matt could be so mysterious sometimes.

Cameron elbowed Brandon. "What's eating you?"

Was he walking around with a "Piss Off" sign on his forehead? Brandon's gaze tracked Matt on the field, turning thoughts over in his mind before answering Cameron. "Trish called last night," he found himself saying.

Cameron's brow flew up his forehead. "No shit? What'd she want?"

"She left the circus and wants back in Matt's life."

Cameron was silent a moment as he sipped his coffee. "Are you going to let her?"

"I don't know," he answered.

Cameron studied him. "You still don't trust her."

Bingo.

"You know," Cam continued, "no one would blame you if you told her to piss off."

His friend's words cut deeper than they should. No, he didn't completely trust Trish. But something in her voice had reached out to him. Tugged at him.

"She's still Matt's mother," Brandon answered. He wasn't sure why, but he felt compelled to defend Trish. After all, without her he wouldn't have Matt and he couldn't bring himself to completely hate her.

"Yeah, but she put you guys through hell," Cameron

pointed out. "How many times has she waltzed in and out without any explanation?"

Yeah, Cam got it. He knew the hell Trish had put them through. And maybe Cam was just being a good friend, looking out for his and Matt's best interest.

"I think she means it this time," Brandon answered.

"How can you tell?"

Brandon watched Matt on the field, taking in Blake's instruction with the sort of determination Brandon had instilled in him. Finally, he just shrugged, because he wasn't sure how to answer Cameron.

Cameron took another sip from his thermos. "So what else has got your panties in a twist?"

Brandon slid his friend a look. "You have such an eloquent way of putting things."

Cam shrugged. "Just saying. You seem...off."

Because he was off. He'd been off since Stella had crashed his lunch.

How was he supposed to handle her? How was he supposed to wrap his mind around the contradicting vibes she was constantly throwing off?

The lady messed with his head something fierce.

"Just thinking about work," he told his friend.

"Really?" Cam questioned as though he didn't believe Brandon.

Hell, Brandon didn't believe himself. He heaved a sigh. "No," he admitted.

More of the football team lumbered onto the field. Blake glanced at them, then made a note of the time.

"Woman problems?" Cameron said while watching Matt. He glanced at Brandon. "You have that look about you."

"And you're so familiar with woman problems?"

Cameron's girlfriends rarely stuck. His friend's idea of a relationship was a roll in the sack a few times before he moved on to something else.

"I've had my share." Cameron turned from the field when Blake and Matt finished up. He laid a hand on Brandon's shoulder. "You want my advice? No woman is worth the headache."

How would Cam know? "I think you'll eat those words one day."

Cameron shook his head. "Never happening. Been there and bought the whole T-shirt factory. Trust me. If she's getting under your skin, cut her loose."

Good advice, if one didn't know Stella Davenport.

EIGHT

The Bobcat's band fired up, rolling into the traditional fight song, as Cody Richardson, the quarterback and practically a god around town, rushed for thirty yards and moved the game play closer to the end zone, giving the Bobcats a chance to put another six points on the board. They were down by three, having been knocked out of the lead when Cody had thrown an interception, sending the fans into a chorus of groans. The Beehive Mafia, who'd taken their seats behind Stella, kept shoving their polyester-covered legs into her back and arguing about which coach had the best ass.

Stella had wanted to slam her hands over her ears when the conversation turned from Cameron Shaw's backside, which seemed to be their new favorite, to which of them could con the assistant coach into "helping a little old lady cross the street."

"Maybe you could stumble and accidentally grab one of

his pecs," Lois had suggested to Beverly about ten minutes ago. "They look nice and tight too."

Stella had almost regurgitated her drink when she heard that.

"I'm still trying to get my hands on Brandon West," Beverly commented. "The kid got smart and started jogging with his shirt on."

The fact that they referred to Brandon as a kid was as bad as listening to them talk about him as though he weren't sitting right in front of them.

As in, next to her.

As in, pressed all over her side and rubbing up against her and throwing off heat like some... well, like someone who was hot all the damn time.

And she didn't mean his body temp either. Though his skin seemed to be warm all the time, urging her to wrap her fingers around his thick forearm because her hands were cold and he was wearing short sleeves. At eight o'clock at night. In October in Colorado.

Yeah, pretty much hot all the time.

She cast him a sly glance out of the corner of her eye to see his reaction to the conversation behind them. He gave none but kept his hard gaze on the game below as he watched Matt.

And how had she ended up pressed to his side in the first place?

She was supposed to be here with Annabelle. But Ruth, Annabelle's epileptic mother, had suffered a seizure and had to be rushed to the emergency room. Stella had received the text message from her friend just as she'd pulled into the parking lot. She'd sent a quick reply to call when she knew how her mother was doing and then entered the stadium alone. She'd made it halfway up the bleachers when she spotted Brandon talking to a woman next to him. Stella recognized her as a mom of one of the other players. If she remembered correctly, the woman had been divorced for several years.

Whatever.

Brandon could talk to whomever he wanted. Why should she care?

Brandon's gaze shifted and connected with hers the split second before she turned around.

And what was she supposed to have done then? So she'd continued her ascent, trying to avoid the obvious I-don't-want-to-sit-next-to-you-so-I'll-watch-the-game-from-the-Porta-Potty move. The woman next to Brandon had kept chatting away while he tracked Stella's movements up the bleachers. Then she'd been next to him, and instead of offering a hello, he'd simply lifted a dark brow at her.

As though to say, *Yeah, you were caught.*

An hour later, the stands had practically doubled in occupancy, forcing her and Brandon to be even closer to each other, allowing her to get intimately acquainted with his left side. Which included a corded bicep, covered in a thin black Bobcats T-shirt that was pulled tight over his bulky shoulders and loose at the waist.

Stella had always been a sucker for a man who knew how to hone his body. Brandon obviously knew how to work his. He knew how to wear a pair of jeans to make a woman weak in the knees with those lean hips.

"I'll catch him one of these days," Lois commented. "I'll just sic my granddaughter on him. She could snap a picture of him before he even realizes it."

"You'll just scar that child for life, Lois," Virginia warned. "I live right next door to the man. I'll get a picture of him."

Stella tried to tune the conversation out, but it was hard since the ladies were right behind her and making no attempt to be discreet. She cast another glance at Brandon and expected to see that hard jaw doing all kinds of clenching, making his face go hard and chiseled. Not that she noticed.

Instead, the corner of his mouth twitched as though he found the conversation amusing. Not horrifying like she did. Horrified at the idea of Lois tasking her pubescent granddaughter, pigtails with pink bows and all, to stalk a thirty-four-year-old shirtless man to take pictures for her horndog grandmother.

"Maybe they don't realize you're sitting right in front of them," Stella suggested to Brandon.

Brandon didn't take his eyes off the field as Matt took his position for the next play. "They know," he told her. "But they're going to get more than an eyeful if they're not careful," he said loud enough for the other women to hear.

Lois leaned forward and focused her laser-sharp hazel eyes on Brandon. "You wouldn't do that to a little girl, would you?"

Brandon cast the woman a glance. "Push me far enough and see."

The crowd surged to it's feet when the other team was penalized ten yards, giving the Bobcats the advantage. Lois tried pushing herself to her feet three times before Brandon hooked a large palm through her elbow and helped her up.

He helps little old ladies, Stella warned herself. *Even ones who stalk him with their camera phones and use their granddaughters.*

Stella stood with the rest of the crowd, trying to place even a millimeter of distance between herself and the man next to her. The one who always smelled like he'd just stepped out of a steamy shower and was *constantly* crowding her.

He cupped his hands around his mouth and shouted something to Matt. Of course Matt didn't hear as the play continued and the Bobcats intercepted the ball and gained fifteen yards. The band fired up once more and the crowd surrounding her and Brandon threw their hands in the air, waving their foam fingers and orange and black pom-poms.

The familiar and unwanted itch started at the back of her skull and worked its way forward as the woman next to her pressed too close. Stella's heart kicked into double time when the noise level of the crowd heightened. The breathing technique she'd learned helped slow her heart rate down but didn't stop the sweat that dotted her forehead.

Had there always been this many people at the football games? And after so many years of thinking she had her claustrophobia in check, why was it becoming a problem again? What had triggered it?

Was it because she'd been skipping her medication?

"You okay?" a deep voice said close to her ear.

Too close. Like whispering-against-her-skin close. Funny how it could feel that intimate with so many people crowding them.

They took their seats again and Stella put on her brave face. One she used to show her mom when they'd move to a new city and Gloria would fuss over Stella nonstop.

"Do you need Mommy to buy you a new toy?" her mom would ask after they'd settled into yet another apartment.

Or, "How's your room? Is it big enough?"

After a while Stella would just nod and say everything's fine. Just so Gloria would stop worrying that her daughter was so emotionally stunted that she couldn't handle another move.

Because you couldn't.

But what her mother didn't know, had never known, was that it hadn't been the moving around that had traumatized her. It hadn't been changing schools twice a year or not being able to make friends.

No, what had flipped the switch was far darker and life-altering than any city or school change. Traumatizing enough to produce panic attacks and a fear of intimacy so great that she'd failed to have a serious relationship in... well, since Rick.

"Stella?" Brandon said when she'd slipped into a trance, remembering all her past mistakes.

"Yeah, I'm fine." Funny how that always slipped out of her mouth so easily.

"Sure?" he questioned. "Need another scone?"

His concern had her smiling.

"The snack shack doesn't sell scones," she pointed out.

"How about a sip of my drink, then?"

And put her mouth where his had been?

He's looking at you, waiting for an answer. Say something.

"I'm allergic to soda."

Really?

His deep chuckle sent a shiver down her spine. "That's creative, I'll give you that. But also a lie." He handed her the cup. "Drink. You need the sugar."

She narrowed her eyes at him and accepted the soda. "You've said that before."

"Because it's true. Plus your pupils are dilated. Drink," he ordered again.

Her pupils weren't dilated from her claustrophobia. Nor

from her anxiety. No, it had nothing to do with her panic attacks or the crowd closing in on her.

But everything to do with the man closing in on her.

And why did he always have to notice things about her? How was he always picking up on her distress or the need for her to have some breathing room? How did he pick up on it when no one else did?

She pulled in a cleansing breath and offered him a smile. "Thanks," she muttered before taking a sip of the cola. It was still cold and bubbly and slid down her throat like silk. She'd always been a soda junkie, much to the dismay of Annabelle, who'd been trying to get her on more healthy alternatives. Like water.

Water was boring. Stella loved drinking a nice, big, sugary Coke. Maybe slip into a sugar coma because, *man*, what a way to go.

A better way to go would be with the guy who keeps brushing his thigh along yours. Maybe in bed, or a dark corner somewhere where people do dirty things.

Where had that come from?

From the same place all her other dirty thoughts originated. That box labeled *Brandon West: Keep the F Closed.*

Stella handed the drink back to Brandon. "Thanks," she said.

He took the Styrofoam cup, allowing his fingers to brush hers. Just the tips, and just enough to ignite a memory of their one and only date when he'd extended his palm to help her down out of his truck. Like the gentleman he was. A gentleman with a drool-worthy ass and biceps that could crush walnuts.

"Welcome," he muttered, staring down at her, daring her to move closer.

Just a little. Just enough to feel the heat of his lips.

Then again, it could have been the fact that they were surrounded by people and he had no choice but to lean close.

Yeah, that was it.

Okay, time to change the subject. "You know, if you get Matt signed up for some lessons this week, I'll wave the registration fee."

His mouth turned up in an almost-smile. "Persistent little thing, aren't you?"

"Little?" she repeated as the game moved into the fourth quarter with the Bobcats still holding the lead. "I'll have you know that I'm five-seven."

"I'm aware of how tall you are." He placed those whiskey-colored eyes on her. "But to someone who's six foot one, five-seven is little."

Okay, then. Whatever.

She narrowed her eyes at him. "Are you making fun of me? Wait, don't answer that," she said when he opened his mouth to answer. "Okay, how about this. You bring Matt in and not only will I waive the registration fee, but I also won't make him wear ballet shoes."

Brandon looked at her like she'd just started spewing pea soup everywhere. "He wouldn't wear ballet shoes anyway. What kind of kid do you think I'm raising?"

"The kind that wants to succeed," she told him.

Yeah. So there.

"Okay, no ballet shoes," she went on. "And he can wear whatever clothes he wants, even though my old ballet teacher would be rolling in her grave."

"You're really into this ballet training thing for the players, aren't you?" he asked.

Stella glanced at the game as the visiting team kicked a field goal and the Bobcats' fans sent out a groan in unison. "Or maybe I just want to help your son? Ever think of that?"

Brandon considered her for a moment, running his gaze over her features, touching on her eyes, then dropping down to her mouth. "Or maybe you're using it as a way to get into my pants."

The sharp pain that pierced her stomach almost sent her soda back up her throat. Was that how he thought of her? As some desperate pants-chasing woman who had to use people's kids to get laid?

Just like her mom.

"I'm sorry," Brandon said when Stella hadn't done a good enough job of hiding the hurt and disappointment he'd caused.

"You must have dated some pretty shady women if that's your first thought," she commented in a casual manner in order to hide how he'd wounded her.

"Let's just say some of the women I've dated haven't always been on the up and up," Brandon commented. With the same casual air as her? Or was that an act?

So he had wounds too. What a fine pair they made. Just a couple of lone wolves who were once bitten, twice shy.

"They obviously need to have their heads examined," Stella said.

The crowd around them roared when the Bobcats intercepted the ball and gained twenty yards. Out of the corner of her eye, she saw Blake running down the sidelines, motioning for number thirty-three to haul ass.

Beside her, Brandon nudged her shoulder with his, rubbing all that steely goodness against her sweatshirt. Even through the thick cotton, she could feel the definition of muscles.

"Are you going to go to bat for me, Stella?"

Why did he have to say her name like that? All gravelly and husky like he was turned on just as much as she was.

"Something tells me you have no problem fighting your own battles," she told him.

One side of his mouth kicked up. "No, but I'd love to see you tumble around with a couple of women. Maybe covered in some mud too."

She jerked her gaze to his. "What is it you think women do when we're together?"

"Pillow fights?" he guessed. "Slumber parties?" When she only gaped openmouthed, he chuckled. "Don't kill my fantasies, Stella. At least let me have the pillow fight thing."

"Sure." She gave his shoulder a gentle pat. Mistake, much? "I'll give you that if it makes you feel better. But here's a reality check. Women don't walk around like they're starring in a soft-core porn film."

"You're crushing me here," he told her with a grin.

"Someone has to set you straight. That way you're not disappointed when the next woman you go out with doesn't ask you to spank her."

There you go, Stella. Keep talking about sex with a man you've vowed to stay away from.

No man was supposed to have that kind of pull over her anymore. Because she was stronger than the vulnerable lovesick fool she used to be. The one who'd trip over herself if an attractive man gave her the slightest bit of attention. Yeah, that used to be her.

But not anymore. She'd steeled herself against that kind of temptation. Because she was strong and independent and didn't need anyone but herself to fulfill a dream.

In other words, the opposite of her mother.

In other words, stay the hell away from Brandon West.

But just as the Bobcats won game four, with the crowd

surging to their feet around her, Stella knew that would be impossible.

The crack of the shotgun echoed in the otherwise noiseless forest, at the same time glass from the empty Jim Beam bottle went flying all over creation. Brandon pumped Cameron's Winchester SXP, lined up the next shot, and shattered another bottle. The crack echoed in the forest, sending a flock of birds scattering from a nearby aspen.

He turned to his friend with a shit-eating grin. "Still think I can't shoot for shit?" he asked Cam.

Cam stood with his arms over his wide chest, his face stone cold except for the curl of his mouth. Yeah, game on. "It's the gun," Cameron responded. "My five-year-old neighbor could shoot with that thing."

"Let me have it," Matt demanded.

Brandon stood back while Matt moved to the next bottle that Cam had lined up on a downed log. So far they'd obliterated about half. Cameron had missed two bottles and Brandon had only missed one.

But Cam still insisted he was the better shot.

"The sun was in my eyes," his friend had griped.

Sun my ass, Brandon had thought. His competitive friend couldn't handle someone being better than him at anything. He'd been nagging Brandon for days, like a little old lady, to come shooting in the woods. Brandon had finally relented with Cam's last text, which had read:

I'm assuming you're forfeiting the trophy over to me if you bail on me again.

The "trophy" being a tattered one-dollar bill they'd been exchanging since college, that had dates scribbled all over it. Each one had tried to up the other with keeping the bill the longest. So far Cam had three weeks with the dollar bill tucked away in his wallet. Which he always "accidentally" let fall out so Brandon would be reminded that Cameron kept trumping him with his Winchester.

Well, not anymore.

Cameron had turned competitive but Brandon could dish out as good as his friend could.

Except he was about to be shown up by his seventeen-year-old.

Matt braced his feet apart, the butt of the gun tucked against his shoulder, and he lined the barrel up for his shot. With one eye closed, Matt squeezed the trigger and blew apart an old Pappy Van Winkle brand bourbon whiskey bottle.

"Damn, kid," Cam muttered.

"Yeah, but do that again," Brandon said.

Matt grinned as he pumped the barrel and moved on to the next bottle, a clear Old Tom Gin. He aimed for the shot and squeezed the trigger, sending more birds scattering all over the sky as the sound echoed throughout the mountains. Matt's shoulders slumped as he missed.

"What I thought," Brandon commented.

Matt handed the gun over. "Guy can't stand being out-shined by his own kid."

"Damn straight."

"Pathetic," Cam commented as he yanked the gun out of Matt's hands before Brandon could take the thing back. "Stand back, children, and watch how it's done." With laser-intensity focus, Cam shouldered the Winchester, closed one eye, and squeezed the trigger. He proceeded to shatter the next three bottles.

"Dude," Matt whispered when Cameron lowered the gun.

"Show-off," Brandon mumbled, but couldn't help the

grin that crept onto his face when Matt's mouth continued to hang open.

"You want to shoot like a pro, kid, you know where to find me," Cameron commented as he slung the gun over his shoulder.

Like the cocky bastard he was.

Brandon held his hand out. "Give me the thing."

"Uh-uh," Cam answered. "You know the rules." He wagged his finger, then shouldered the gun again. When one of them missed, they had to pass over the gun to the next person. The game stopped when all the bottles were broken, and whoever broke the most won the dollar bill and wrote the date of the win down.

Cameron had written the last three dates down.

Time to take the guy down a peg.

Except he needed to miss first, which he apparently wasn't planning on doing anytime soon. Brandon and Matt watched as Cameron blew apart two more bottles before aiming a fraction of an inch off and missing the third.

"Which one of you thinks they can beat me now?" Cam taunted. Similarly to how he used to egg people on in high school. Cam was the kid who used to throw the first punch for shits and giggles. His attitude had almost gotten him thrown off the football team multiple times. After being benched for several weeks their senior year, Cam had cleaned up his act and kept his nose out of trouble.

Didn't mean the guy didn't still love to talk shit, then grin his way into a good fight.

"Let me have it," Matt offered.

Without a word, Cam handed the gun over and stood back next to Brandon when Matt lined up the shot.

"Too high," Cameron coughed into his hand, but Matt didn't hear or didn't listen. Kid was stubborn like his old man.

Who are you calling old?

Matt broke one bottle and missed his second.

"I think it's safe to say I won't be getting that dollar bill," Matt grumbled.

"Yeah, women have a way of messing with a man's concentration," Cameron commented as Brandon took the gun from Matt.

And then he wanted to knock the shit out of his friend.

"Um...," Matt started, then swallowed so many times Brandon thought the kid would choke on his own saliva. "I wasn't thinking about anything."

"Save it, kid," Cameron argued. "Anyone with half a brain can see how lovestruck you are over this girl. Just be careful with her."

Then Matt rolled his eyes with the perfection he'd mastered by the age of ten. "Now you sound like Dad. I already told him Adrienne's not that kind of girl."

"That's how they all start out," Cameron pointed out.

Brandon shouldered the rifle and took aim.

You don't want him to be like you.

Stella's soft words intruded on his concentration just as he squeezed the trigger. And missed.

More birds took flight in the clear fall air, squawking at the intrusive noise, as though mocking him for being an idiot for allowing Stella to break his concentration.

And that conversation was weeks ago. Why was he thinking about it now?

Because you think about her way too much. More than you should.

More than what could be considered healthy, anyway.

"Like I said," Cameron taunted as he yanked the Winchester from Brandon's useless hands. "A woman has a way of breaking a man's concentration."

If Matt hadn't been within listening distance, Brandon would have told his friend to fuck off. But he didn't. Trying to set a good example and all that.

Matt's brows tugged over his eyes. "Dad doesn't have a girlfriend."

Cam snorted as he positioned the rifle, closed one eye, and squeezed the trigger. And shattered a vintage Bacardi. At the moment, Brandon wished the thing was filled with liquor so he could chug the stuff down.

Instead of taking the next shot, and essentially finishing the game off with the last two bottles, Cameron slung the gun over his shoulder and grinned. One of his shit-eating, I'm-about-to-get-into-trouble smiles.

Brandon knew that look and steeled himself for the onslaught of ribbing in the name of brotherly love and good humor.

"Of course he doesn't have a girlfriend," Cameron agreed. *And, yeah, we both know what I'm talking about.*

The taunt was all over Cameron's face and Brandon knew that if they'd been alone, it'd be no-holds-barred. The only reason Cameron held back was because of Matt. He knew Brandon wouldn't want the kid knowing that he'd been walking around with a hard-on ever since laying eyes on Stella Davenport.

Although, how Cameron knew this was anybody's guess. *It's because he knows you as well as you know yourself.*

Yeah, that was true.

Which was why he'd kept his thoughts about Stella to himself. As well as his fears. His abandonment issues. And, okay, he was man enough to admit he had those demons floating around. How could he not when everyone he'd ever loved had left? Except for Matt.

But he's leaving too.

Brandon shoved that thought away because he wasn't ready to come to terms with that yet.

"Dad, can I go to the batting cages with Tyler?" Matt asked, yanking Brandon from his thoughts.

He turned to his son, ignoring the knowledge in Cameron's eyes. "I'm taking you to Ms. Davenport's studio after this."

Cam leaned forward. "Are you trying to kill the kid?" he muttered near Brandon's ear.

"Just shut up and take your turn," Matt told him.

Cameron wisely kept his mouth shut and sent bullets into the last two bottles, earning him another win.

The sound of the rifle echoed off the snowy peaks of the mountains, bouncing from one direction to the next.

Sort of like his heart did when he was around Stella.

NINE

"Can Adrienne come over for dinner tomorrow night?" Matt asked.

As Brandon drove through town toward Stella's studio, his ESSP—Extra Sensory Stella Perception—surged through his system and woke his dick up like someone had Tased his ass.

Damn thing had a mind of its own.

And he supposed it would after being neglected for far longer than was healthy for a man his age.

"I told her you make really good steaks," Matt went on. "And she asked if she could bring something. I told her to bring potato salad."

And what would Stella be wearing this time?

No doubt that sorry excuse for a ballet outfit. Not that Brandon had known a lot of ballerinas, but weren't they supposed to wear like tutus and shit? Pink tights?

Not teensy little bike shorts that barely covered the bottom of those perfectly round ass cheeks. And certainly not a skintight tank top that revealed just how in shape the woman was. How high and round her breasts were. No ballerina he'd ever seen dressed like that.

"Dad, are you listening?" Matt asked after the kid had been carrying on a conversation with himself. While his father thought about Stella's breasts and tried to adjust his hard-on.

He cleared his throat and tightened his grip on the steering wheel. "Yeah, dinner," he stated. Like the caveman he was.

"What did I say about dinner?" Matt questioned.

Yeah, what had he said?

That Stella has a nice ass. One you want to run your tongue over.

Except no. That wasn't what Matt had said. That's what the devil on Brandon's shoulder said.

The devil that needed to shut the hell up.

Hadn't he said something about Adrienne? Yeah, that was it.

"Yeah, invite Adrienne over for dinner," Brandon answered. "I'll make some steaks."

Matt kept looking at him like he didn't believe a word of it. "Is Cameron right? Is there some woman you're interested in?"

Define interested.

Brandon shot Matt a glance. "Of course not." Yeah, because that was convincing.

Apparently Matt didn't accept Brandon's denial because dark suspicion clouded his brown eyes. "Really? Because it would be okay if you were. You don't have to, like, sneak around and stuff."

He pulled the truck alongside the curb in front of Stella's

studio. "I'm not sneaking," he told his son. "There's no one." At least one that existed outside of his fantasies.

And why wouldn't it be okay to jump into something with Stella?

That question had bounced around in his mind for the past few months. Even after she tossed her cookies all over his brand-new shoes, he was still intrigued by her. Turned on as hell. And maybe that was the problem. It was his hormones talking and not his head. Those babies had gotten him into too much trouble in the past, and he needed to keep a level head.

Pretty hard to do when the woman was always shaking that firm rear end at him.

And he'd tried not to notice. Really he had. But he was a red-blooded heterosexual male who'd gone way too long without a woman. Especially a woman like that. Between building his business and raising a son, his dating life had all but expired. Grown moldy. Evaporated.

Then along came Stella Davenport, with her mischievous blue eyes, sassy sense of humor, and too much sex appeal, and that dormant side had jolted awake like he'd been doused with smelling salts. And yeah, he liked what he saw.

"Dad?" Matt said as they still sat in the idling truck. "Are we going to get out?"

Brandon blinked himself out of his thoughts and unbuckled. "Yeah, sorry." He shut the vehicle off, just as his phone beeped. He picked the thing up and touched the screen just as Matt paused before exiting the truck. "You know you don't have to come in with me," Matt announced. "I can walk in by myself."

Brandon glanced at Matt. "I have to talk to Stella for a minute."

Yeah, that was a good excuse. Totally believable.

Matt shrugged his whatever the way all teenagers did in their odd universal language he'd yet to figure out. Even though it was the same language he'd used.

He shut the truck door just as his phone buzzed.

Booster meeting at four-thirty, Blake said.

Booster meeting? On a Saturday?

Thanks for the heads-up, he responded.

Sorry, Blake answered. *Forgot. Just be here.*

I'll be there, he responded to his cousin, then pocketed the phone.

He and Matt entered the studio with piano music echoing across the empty space. There wasn't a class, but the sight of the woman in the room stopped him short.

"How does she *do* that?" Matt whispered to himself.

Brandon wanted to know how Stella did a lot of things, mostly how she managed to turn him on by simply being. But yeah, he'd like to know how in the world she could contort her body in a way that would have left most people being air lifted to the nearest emergency room. She had one leg resting on a wooden bar, while she was bent over backward, head dipped back and right arm reaching over her head to brush the floor. Her neck, long and slender, was arched in a way that perfectly exposed places meant for kissing and teasing.

"I would, like, break my back or something if I did that," Matt commented, completely unaware of Brandon's tenting action in his jeans.

Honestly, was there anything worse than a hard-on in front of one's kid? Especially when he'd been preaching to Matt about taking things easy with his girlfriend.

Some example.

Matt cleared his throat to announce their arrival.

Stella straightened and removed her leg from the bar.

"Sorry," she told them. "I get caught up sometimes and lose awareness of my surroundings." She practically floated, because that was the only way Stella moved, toward a stereo system and shut the music off.

Brandon's blood pressure shot up another notch when Stella closed the distance between them. She had on her usual attire of short black bike shorts and bare legs. Only this time, instead of a skintight tank top, she had on a loose T-shirt, with a neckline so wide the thing hung over one shoulder. With no visible straps.

Damn, was she naked under that thing?

All he'd have to do was hook his index finger in the hemline and give it one good tug.

Yeah and she'd let him too.

Brandon glanced from Stella to Matt when he realized the two of them were staring at him.

"You said you wanted to talk to Ms. Davenport," Matt reminded him.

Uh, yeah. Talk to her.

Stella's perfectly shaped brows arched up her forehead. Then she held her hands up in surrender. "Don't worry, I don't have any shoes for him to wear."

Matt laughed like it was the funniest damn thing he'd ever heard.

Brandon scratched a hand along the back of his neck. Nervous much?

"I just wanted to know about how long it'll be," he finally said.

His too-observant son narrowed his eyes.

"I have to step out and make a few calls," he added. Because that was way less creepy than lingering in the doorway and watching her.

Stella moved those elegant shoulders and her T-shirt slid

farther down her arm. "Thirty or forty minutes, maybe. I don't have any classes today, so there's no time frame."

Matt gestured toward the bar where Stella had been stretching. "I don't have to do any of that, do I? Because I'd probably break my spine or something."

Stella's grin widened, then turned into a laugh. She placed a comforting hand on Matt's shoulder. "Don't worry, only the more experienced dancers can stretch like that. For now we'll just work on balancing on two feet. But if you'd like to sign up for more ballet classes, I could probably get you there."

"Uh..." Matt's mouth hung open, but Stella saved him from having to answer.

"I'm kidding," she told the kid.

"I'll be back in a half hour," Brandon told Matt. He turned to go, then faced Stella. "If he's in a pair of tights when I come back, we're going to have words."

The corners of her full mouth twitched. "Scout's honor," she answered.

Yeah, right.

She'd slap a pair of tights on Matt just to get a reaction out of him. Stella Davenport was trouble like that.

"Coach will kill me if I break my ankle," Matt said as a single drop of sweat ran down his forehead.

Stella couldn't help but laugh. The kid was so sweet, trying his hardest to hold the positions but looking more awkward and uncomfortable than anything else. "If you do it right, you won't break anything. That's sort of the point of all this. Don't lower yet," she instructed when Matt tried to lower off the balls of his feet. "Hold it for a few more seconds."

His grip on the bar tightened, his knuckles turning white

with exertion as he balanced on the balls of his feet. It was a standard stretch for any ballerina and one Stella could do in her sleep. But for Matt, who'd never even stepped foot inside a studio before, it was no doubt more challenging than tackling a running back to the ground.

"I don't know how you do this stuff," Matt commented.

Stella squatted behind him and pushed her index finger into his arches, urging him to tighten his hold. "The more you do it, the easier it gets. After a while it becomes more muscle memory than anything else." She straightened. "You can lower now."

They'd been working for about twenty minutes, starting with basic floor stretches, moving into plié squats, then balancing. The kid was a trouper, she'd give him that.

She turned and snatched some Kleenex off a shelf by her stereo and handed them to Matt. "Unless you're going to tell me real men don't wipe their sweat off."

Matt's mouth curled and, holy moly, the kid was the spitting image of his dad. "Sounds like something my dad would say."

Speaking of...

He accepted the tissue and swiped it across his brow and down his temples.

"What kind of deal did you have to strike to get him to agree?" she asked.

"What do you mean?" He was trying to be coy even though she saw right through his act.

Teenagers were notoriously transparent.

When she jabbed her hands on her hips and lifted a brow, he relented.

"I told him I would cook dinner for a month," he told her.

Stella tilted her head and realized what a strong bond the two must have. "That's actually not bad," she agreed.

Matt tossed the tissue in the trash. "He tried getting me to wash his truck too, but I told him not to push it."

"Sounds pretty fair."

Stella studied him for a moment, noting the similarities between the two and the differences, which were few. Matt's eyes were a shade darker than Brandon's, bordering on a rich chocolate. But they had the same thick dark hair, the same square jaw. Heck, even Matt's stubble, already grown thick for a kid his age, resembled his dad's. And Brandon was hardly ever without his edging-on-midnight shadow, which had proved to be both a curse and a blessing for Stella.

And, not for the first time, she wondered what Matt's mother looked like. Little was known about the woman, at least that's what Annabelle had always told her. And Stella wasn't about to ask, even though she was more than curious. That right wasn't hers because all she and Brandon shared were mild flirtations.

Yeah, but you want more.

Well, of course she wanted more. What woman wouldn't want more with a man like him?

But she couldn't. Jumping into something with Brandon West would impede the plans she'd already carefully laid out. Because planning was everything to her. Planning kept her sane. It gave her a sense of stability.

"Sounds like your dad's pretty fair," she commented to Matt. "Like you two have a good relationship."

Matt shrugged his bulky shoulders. "Yeah, he's cool I guess."

Which was teenage code for "I love the hell out of him."

"But you're more than just close with him," she guessed. "It's okay. I won't tell anyone that you actually like your dad."

Matt ran his hand along the top of the bar. "I mean, it's always been the two of us, so..."

"Even since you were born?"

Yeah, this is me subtly asking about your mom.

He shrugged again. "My mom left when I was three. I don't really remember her. Only what my dad used to tell me about her."

Which is?

Which is none of your beeswax.

Good grief, now she was talking like her mom.

"I was raised by a single mom," she explained. "It takes someone special to raise a kid by themselves." Okay, okay. So Gloria hadn't been a total f-up of a parent. She could have walked away. Could have dumped Stella Lord knew where after her biological father took off to drive trucks, or so her mom had always told her.

"Yeah, he's cool," Matt said again. "He takes me shooting and stuff."

Stella would guess that "shooting and stuff" was the male species way of bonding, which she didn't get.

"What kind of stuff do you shoot?"

"Just old bottles," Matt answered. "Cameron collects them for us to shoot."

Stella shook her head. "No offense, but blowing up bottles doesn't sound like fun."

Matt's serious expression turned playful. "Have you ever shot a gun?"

Hell no. "Sure," she lied. No reason to sound like a square. But Gloria had despised guns and everything they stood for.

No good ever comes from a gun, she always said.

Personally, Stella didn't see anything wrong with owning one as long as a person didn't have ill intent.

One of Matt's dark brows arched. "Really? Because you don't really seem the type."

Stella jabbed a hand on her hip. "Hey, don't let the ballet shoes fool you. I'm tougher than I look."

The kid held his hands up in surrender. "I'm not trying to say you can't handle your own. I just can't picture you holding a rifle."

She led Matt to the middle of the floor and placed him in front of the mirrors. "As long as you don't shoot Bambi, we're cool."

Matt looked at her in the reflection. "We occasionally go after opossums, but we've never actually hit anything."

Stella grinned. "Is that your way of saying you're all lousy shots?"

"We're actually pretty good. But the opossums are better."

"Spread your legs and turn your feet out," she instructed. "And why opossums?"

Matt assumed the position. "Dad hates them. They sneak into our backyard and terrorize Duke. Then they dig holes under our fence and Mrs. McAllister blames Duke for it and threatens to call animal control."

"Lower into a squat, straighten, then lift to your toes," she told him, watching to make sure he was executing the move correctly. "How does Mrs. McAllister not know it's the opossums?" Matt's balance wobbled when he lifted to his toes. "Tighten your core," she told him.

"My dad thinks she knows," he answered. "She just likes to stir trouble. He's been tempted to leave a dead one on her back patio, but he doesn't want to give her a heart attack."

Plus the fact that Brandon would never do anything like that, especially to an old woman. Even if that old woman was meddlesome and constantly snapping half-naked pictures of him. Not that she'd ever sneak a peek of one occasionally. On Annabelle's phone, of course.

Or your own phone. At night, when no one is around to catch your peeping ass.

Okay, whatever. So she'd seen the pictures. So she'd lingered longer over them than she should have. So she'd drooled a little. At least she wasn't looking at them at night anymore. Not after the first time when she'd gone on to have dreams about the guy all night.

Do not *start fantasizing about Brandon in front of his kid. Seriously, draw a line somewhere.*

Except her imagination had no line because she was sick and twisted and sexually deprived.

"Do two more of those, then we're done," she told him while he moved into the next rep.

He lowered after his last rep and wiggled his legs. "No wonder you're in wicked shape," he told her.

Stella smiled. "Most people don't realize how exhausting ballet can be. You'll develop muscles in places you didn't realize you had muscles." She patted him on the shoulder. "But congratulations. You survived your first ballet lesson."

His mouth quirked. "Yeah, just don't tell anyone. Better to have them believe it's my natural talent, and not from doing... What were those called again?"

"Plié and relevé," she answered. "Great for calves and thighs. Next week we'll work on pirouettes."

The suspicious look on his face almost had her laughing. "What's that?"

"It's where you spin around on one foot. Preferably your toes." When Matt's mouth fell open and red highlighted his cheeks, Stella giggled and placed a comforting hand on his arm. "I'm kidding," she soothed. "Don't worry, we'll wait until you've been doing this for at least three weeks."

"Um...thanks?" he replied.

"You need to loosen up, Matt," Stella laughed.

Matt swiped his phone off the floor, where he'd set it next to the mirror. After touching the screen a few times, he pocketed the thing and glanced at Stella. "I've got to go meet Adrienne now. Thanks again, Miss Davenport."

"Anytime, Matt. And tell your girlfriend hello for me."

And then he was gone, sauntering out the door with the same loose-limbed confidence Brandon always had. It probably came naturally to them. Good genes, or something. Either way, there was something about how the two of them moved that could melt concrete. One of the first things Stella had noticed about Brandon was how he carried himself.

Confidence.

One of her biggest weaknesses. And that man had it all over his six-foot-one—or however tall he was—leanly muscled, powerful body.

Yeah, there was all kinds of power in those lean hips. The kind that could pin a woman to a mattress as easily as it could lead her across the dance floor. Stella was a sucker for both, and if she wasn't careful, she'd allow herself to succumb to that temptation.

Been there, done that. She couldn't go there again.

Too bad you can't seem to stay away from him. Stella moved to the stereo and was just about to flick the music back on when a deep voice, one from her darkest dreams, cut her short.

"Where'd Matt go?"

She spun around and clapped gazes with Brandon, automatically moving her attention to his black Bobcats T-shirt and how the thing hung loose over his narrow waist. Maybe if he were to twist to the side, just a bit, she'd get a glimpse of some hard muscle.

Just a little movement.

Maybe she'd "accidentally" drop something and ask him to pick it up.

No, that's something Mom would do, and you're not that desperate.

Except sometimes she was.

Sometimes she forgot how it felt to be in a man's arms. To feel his steady heartbeat beneath her cheek. How comforting and safe a set of strong arms could feel wrapped around her much more petite frame.

When was the last time a man had held her like that?

Obviously too long if she couldn't even remember what it felt like.

"He went to meet his girlfriend for coffee," she told him after shutting her thoughts off.

He stepped farther into the room, car keys dangling loose from his fingers. "He went to meet Adrienne?"

"Yeah. He didn't tell you?"

Brandon shook his head as he stopped in front of her. "No, because he knew what I would say."

"Being sneaky, is he?"

"Like he thinks I was born yesterday," Brandon said. "Like I didn't pull the same shit when I was his age."

Stella arched a brow. "I find it hard to believe that you weren't a perfect angel."

His mouth curled into a grin so delicious that her stomach actually quivered. "Believe it. I was far from perfect."

She tilted her head. "So why are you surprised by Matt's actions?"

"Because it's different when it's your own kid."

"You're not going to give me the whole when-you-have-kids-of-your-own-one-day speech, are you?"

Brandon twirled his keys around. "Depends on whether or not you plan on having kids."

"Oh," was all she said.

His brown eyes stared down at her. "Do you?"

She blinked. "Do I what?"

The curling of the mouth came back. "Plan on having kids."

She puffed out a long breath. "That would require a man, which I don't have, so..."

"But you don't have to have a man to want kids," he pointed out.

She wagged a finger at him. "But you said 'plan.' That's different than want. Of course I want kids, but I don't plan on having them any time soon, because..." She waved her hand in a circular motion.

"Because you don't have a man in your life?"

She grinned at him. "I knew you were more than just a pretty face."

His eyes narrowed. "You think I'm pretty?"

"You don't like being called pretty?"

"There isn't a man on Earth who likes being called pretty. Pretty is for girls and men who wear skinny jeans and fedoras."

"And you wouldn't be caught dead in a fedora. Is that right?"

"Not really my style, no."

"And what is your style?"

Brandon paused before answering. "This is a strange conversation."

She offered him her own smile. "That's because normal is boring." Now she *really* sounded like her mom.

"Actually, normal is not boring," he argued. "Normal is

nice." He gestured toward her knee. "Having a better day to-day?"

Okay, change of conversation. She could take a hint. She glanced down at the bandage-free knee and managed to hold back a grimace at the ugly scars marring her skin. "Slightly. Still hurts though."

"What do you do to help with the pain?"

She lifted her shoulders, wishing the conversation had stayed on him. "I work with Annabelle sometimes, but other than that, there isn't much I can do."

"You're not one of those all-natural girls who doesn't believe in medicine, are you?"

The questions were all over his whiskey-colored eyes. And, yeah, there was a story behind her reluctance to take pain pills. But nothing that she was willing to share with him right now.

"I just try to go without them if I can," she told him.

"Trying to be independent?"

"Independent from what?"

He took a step closer, crowding her, and it took all of her breathing techniques and will power not to step back. "Things that make you dependent."

Stella steeled her features, trying with all her might not to allow the surprise to flash across her eyes. She didn't need him knowing how close to the truth he was. She didn't need him knowing how her mother had gone through a rough patch and had become addicted to Vicodin after a breakup with one of her many boyfriends. Stella had watched helplessly as her mother had become a slave to pills she hadn't even needed in order to get over the heartbreak from a man who wasn't worth the time of day.

But she hadn't known. Gloria had no clue the guy she'd mourned the loss of had violated her only daughter.

Not rape. It had never gone that far. But Stella's sense of trust and security, when the bastard would "accidentally" grab one of her boobs, had been breached. Over the five months he'd dated her mother, the asshole's "innocent" encounters had become not so innocent. Going from accidentally brushing up against her to cornering her in the kitchen one night and shoving his tongue down her throat. For a fifteen-year-old girl, it had been traumatizing. Especially since it had been her first experience with a kiss.

After that, the thought of any man putting his hands on her made her skin crawl. Just the very idea of any human being, especially one she didn't know, getting close enough to feel their breath or the brush of their skin sent her into a panic.

She blinked and focused on Brandon's statement. Yeah, she didn't like being involved with things that made her dependent, be it men or pills. Which is why she chose not to take anti-anxiety medication.

And that included Brandon West.

When she got a whiff of his aftershave, probably something named *Orgasm in a Bottle*, she stepped back.

The confusion must have shown on her face, because Brandon took another step toward her, until her back hit the shelves where her stereo was. "Are you okay?" he asked.

He's not trying to crowd you.

Yeah, she knew that. It was nothing more than his male instinct to protect. To find the problem and fix it, as all males were inclined to do. And Brandon wouldn't back down until he figured her out. But she didn't want him figuring her out. She didn't want him to know what had really happened to her, because then he'd take it upon himself to help her. To protect her from herself, and she was just fine the way she was, thank you very much.

"I'm fine," she said. A little too quickly.

He held his hands up, a gesture she recognized as his way of backing off. "Sorry. Sometimes I forget."

"It's okay," she blurted out. *Yeah, what?* "I mean, I'm fine. You don't have to be afraid to get too close to me."

Yeah, just keep on spitting out those lies.

He narrowed his eyes as though he didn't believe her. Smart man. "Why don't I believe you?"

"What do you mean?" she queried as though she were all cute and innocent. The truth was, she was neither.

"Just that I can't figure you out," he answered. "One minute you act as turned on as I am, and the next you're throwing out all these back-off signals." He shook his head. "You're like a Rubik's Cube."

She let the *turned on* comment slide. "Did you just compare me to a child's toy?"

He stared at her for a moment. "Actually, now that I think about it, a Rubik's Cube might be easier to solve. So what's his name?"

"Who?" Even though she knew damn good and well what he was talking about.

"The asshole who did this to you," he stated.

She swallowed, which sounded like the stereotypical, audible gulp in her ringing ears. "Why, are you going to go kick his ass for me?" The question was meant to come off as light. Joking. Because that's what she did best. But the quavering in her voice probably gave her away. How long had it been since she'd talked about it? To someone who'd listen? To someone who'd see through the concrete wall she'd built between herself and everyone else?

Brandon wasn't that person.

Yes, he is.

She thought he was; she just didn't want him to be. She

didn't want to open that box and expose the ugliness that had haunted her for so many years. Because what would he think of her? What would he think of the girl who'd been too scared to knee the shithead in the balls? What would he think of the girl who'd been too frightened to tell her own mother? No, it was better for him to think she was the fearless, independent woman who'd practically bullied him into ballet lessons.

Yeah, that was better.

"That was a hypothetical, by the way," she clarified. *Lie, lie, lie.*

"Sure it was," he commented, his voice sardonic, yet skipping along her nerve endings like fingers across a piano. "Is that why you don't date?"

Bingo. "I date," she fibbed.

"I'm not talking about our one dinner," he clarified. "Some cocky bastard took advantage of you and now you've sworn off men. Is that it?"

Her pulse did that fluttering thing again, the one that had perspiration gathering in between her breasts and heat rolling into her cheeks. Stella wasn't about to let him know how close to the truth he was. Her boyfriend from her dancing days, Rick, had swooped in with all his suave moves and charisma, making her heart pound. She hadn't tried to resist Rick because he'd seemed like the real thing, giving her all sorts of promises for the future. Telling her he'd take care of her, that she could follow him anywhere. So she had, ignoring the warning bells in the back of her mind that she was following in her mom's footsteps. Giving up everything for a guy who promised the world. And then Rick had abruptly ended their relationship, leaving her high and dry and picking up the pieces.

Brandon's gaze roamed her face, touching on the heat

flaming her cheeks and the heartbeat spinning out of control at the base of her throat. Her pupils were probably dilated too.

"What happened to you, Stella?" Brandon asked in a quiet voice. Throaty, making the moment feel intimate when she wanted to run in the other direction. Tell him to mind his own damn business, that he didn't have a clue what he was talking about.

When the truth was, she wanted to lean in to him. To unload the darkness she'd tried to bury but was still lugging around with her like an elephant on her back.

He could make it go away, that voice whispered. The one that sounded like her mother. The one that had pulled her to turn down her choreography job for a man.

"It's nothing," she whispered, because she couldn't force her voice past the lump in her throat.

"I don't think it's nothing," he argued. "I think something that makes you afraid of men is far from nothing."

Her chin notched up. "I'm not afraid of men."

"You're just afraid of being intimate with one," he corrected. "I'm not asking you to be intimate with me, Stella," he went on without giving her a chance to object. "I'm just asking you to open up to me."

But that was the thing. The two concepts were the same to her. It was an intimate matter that involved far more than just opening up to him. It meant exposing the real her, a person no one really knew. Who was nothing but a scared little girl, the antithesis of the person she'd forced herself to become in order to leave the ugliness behind.

His gaze dropped to her mouth, as though imagining what it would feel like to fuse them together. Her lips tingled just thinking about it.

"You're not going to tell me, are you?" he guessed.

She swallowed again, trying desperately to force that lump down. "No," she whispered with a shake of her head.

He nodded, but the disappointment was all over his face, darkening his gorgeous brown eyes. "All right. I won't force you to talk if you don't want to. But there's one thing you need to understand about me, Stella. I won't get into a relationship with someone who holds herself back."

She blinked and resisted the urge to run the tip of her finger across her lips, missing contact that wasn't even there to begin with. "Relationship?"

"Just putting that out there," he told her before taking a step back.

She shook her head. "Why—"

And then his hand was there. Gliding over her cheek, his big, rough palm cupping the side of her face with the gentleness of a lover's caress. But instead of feeling seduced or manipulated by her own hormones, Stella felt...comforted. At ease with a man who knew better than to touch her. And what did that say, that he was willing to take the chance of being kneed in the balls?

That he cared.

Oddly enough, the only reaction in her overly sensitive body was the butterflies in her stomach. Followed by heat blooming across her midsection that matched the warmth flaring over her cheeks.

God help her, but she was turned on.

The urge to push him away had been replaced with the impulse to grab a fistful of his shirt. To tug his head toward hers so their breath could mix.

"Stella," he finally said. "You might be able to hide from the rest of the world, but you can't hide from me."

"I'm not trying to hide from you," she hedged.

His soft chuckle brushed across her heated skin. "Sweetheart, we're playing the most erotic game of hide-and-seek I've ever seen."

Is that what they'd been doing? Even as she denied it to herself, Stella knew Brandon was right. Ever since they'd met, the two of them had danced and circled each other like a couple of MMA champions. With neither of them willing to admit defeat. So they'd continue to dance and tug and pull until one or both of them relented.

And which one would that be?

It couldn't be her. She was leaving in December.

Brandon's brow crinkled. "What?"

Had she said that out loud?

He had her tied up in so many knots that now she was just blurting stuff out without thinking.

"I'm... going back to Chicago for a little while." With nerves of steel, and ignoring all that inviting hardness his body was throwing around, Stella pulled away from him and ducked under his arm. She paced across the dance floor, the itch to dance away her stress pulling at her limbs. "I was offered a choreography job by my former artistic director."

"I know," he stated, his tone changing from the husky bedroom voice that had curled around her like a warm blanket to indifferent. Matter of fact. "Blake told me. And I can only assume Annabelle told him," he answered.

Had his eyes gone flat?

"I swear I need a new best friend," she muttered.

"So you're leaving, then," he said.

She folded her hands in front of her. Opened them, then refolded. "Only for a little while."

He nodded, but the darkness clouding his eyes indicated he didn't understand. "Until you decide not to come back," he concluded.

"Why wouldn't I come back?" Even as she asked the

question, she knew the thought had entered her mind. More than once. How easy it would be to stay in Chicago, especially since the reason she'd come to Blanco Valley in the first place—her grandmother—was no longer relevant. But something had always held her back. Maybe it was the sense of stability she'd finally created for herself. Perhaps it was her students she'd come to love. Possibly it was the community itself, the people, the students, the atmosphere that was like living in a storybook. The snowy peaks that sheltered their little town. The yellow-leaved aspens that danced in the crisp air. Hell, even the Beehive Mafia was endearing, in their own camera-obsessed way.

"Aren't you looking for a permanent position there?" he asked.

Why did he ask it in a way that made her feel guilty? She had nothing to feel guilty about. This was something she'd wanted for a long time. "Well, yeah, but there's no guarantee."

He took a step toward her. "So if they don't offer you something, you'll be back in Blanco Valley?"

Was he fishing for something? "Where else would I go?"

"Because people change their minds," Brandon answered matter-of-factly. "They get a taste of something better and they decide it's worth leaving everything for."

Were they still talking about her?

"Sounds like you're talking from experience," she guessed. She came closer to him, noting the ticking in his square jaw, highlighting the muscles that lent his face that chiseled look.

He didn't respond, just kept grinding away at those teeth as though holding back his own nightmares. "We weren't talking about me."

"I know, but I'm asking anyway," she pressed. Because

whatever had put the hidden layer of distrust in his eyes intrigued her.

"I don't want to talk about my past any more than you want to talk about yours," he informed her.

Oh, yeah. There was something there. Brandon understood her reluctance to open her heart to just anyone, just as she understood his.

"Maybe you should take your own advice," she said.

"What advice was that?"

"About not getting in a relationship with someone who won't open themselves up."

One of his dark brows quirked. "I guess it's a good thing we're not in a relationship, then."

She forced a nod because something about his words sounded so final. As though he were making the decision for the both of them. "Agreed." When he didn't say anything, just continued to stare at her with those soulful eyes of his, she added, "So we'll just keep doing what we're doing."

And wait a minute. Weren't they just standing, like, five feet apart? How had they maneuvered back to each other? So close that she could count each dark stubble shadowing his jaw? So close that the heat he always threw off warmed her chilled skin down to the pit of her stomach?

"And what are we doing, Stella?" he asked in a voice as smoky as summer mountain air.

His breath fanned her face, sending chills down her spine and creating images of him whispering in her ear as his big body pinned hers to a soft mattress.

"I . . . ," she breathed. "Don't know."

His mouth curled, transforming his face from shadowed to melt-your-bones gorgeous. "I think that's the first honest thing you've said to me since I got here."

Her brows tugged low over her eyes. "That's not true."

His hand gripped her chin, cradling it in a gentle way that allowed his thumb to explore her lower lip. Because *explore* was the only way to describe how he was touching her. As though discovering something he'd been seeking for a long time but hadn't been able to find.

"Sweetheart, you hedge better than a politician," he murmured, lowering to her mouth.

"I'm not really sure, but I think you might have just insulted me." Because how could it be an insult when his lips were hovering over hers like early morning mist over a lake?

"Or maybe you just think too much," he countered.

Yes, she was definitely guilty of that. Like thinking why didn't he just kiss her already? Or thinking she could just slide her hands over his shoulders the way his hand was currently sliding back into her hair. And how his palm was a perfect fit over the back of her skull. Firm and warm. That's how his fingers felt cradling and massaging and sifting through the strands of her hair.

"I'm thinking you have a funny way of interacting with someone whom you're not in a relationship with," she remarked.

He grinned against her mouth, the movement prompting the gentlest contact of skin against skin. His lips were soft, surprisingly soft for a man, and sent a tingle across her own lips. A tingle that would grow to a full-blown flame if he didn't kiss her already.

She gave in to her compulsion and curved her hands over his shoulders, familiarizing herself with the grooves and muscle and bone. He was hard, like granite under a layer of smooth, warm skin. Warmth that couldn't be contained by the soft T-shirt he wore. His heat burned into her, penetrating her cool skin and curling around into her stomach.

Was it just her, or had their almost-kiss a few months ago not been this hot? This intense? She didn't remember her panties almost going up in flames or her desire threatening to choke her.

"A kiss doesn't equal a relationship," he told her.

She nuzzled her nose against his. "But we're not kissing."

"Keep telling yourself that, Stella." Before she could respond, before she could even exhale the breath she'd been holding, his mouth was there. Fitting over hers, exerting a gentle pressure that had her fingers digging into the flesh on the back of his shoulder.

When her eyes dropped closed, her other senses took over and magnified the virile man who was so much bigger and harder than she was. His arm enclosed her waist, tugging her closer, inch by slow inch until she was flush against him. Chest to chest. Feet to feet. Leg inserting between hers so that his muscled thigh was nestled perfectly in between her softer flesh.

Best. Kiss. Ever.

Brandon West could use his mouth as a lethal weapon to bring women to their knees. Because if he hadn't been holding her to him with such firmness, she would have sank the second his mouth touched hers. And then she didn't have time to think about all the other things she wanted him to do to her, because his tongue smoothed over her lips in gentle, yet not-so-subtle invitation to open the hell up.

He didn't have to ask her twice. Without thinking about where they were, or the cars and people hovering around outside, even her looming anxiety, Stella obliged and parted her lips. With a hesitation that was sweet, yet longing, his tongue slowly pursued hers, touching just the tip before retreating again.

Since it wasn't enough, since the minimal contact had opened an emptiness she'd been living with for a long time, Stella did her own pursuing. Her tongue chased his, testing the warmth of his mouth. When he groaned against her and tightened his hand on the back of her head, the heat was kicked up a notch. The passion she'd once possessed but that had gone dormant from lack of use awakened with an explosive burst of fireworks. She returned his groan with one of her own when he tilted her head to change the angle of the kiss, allowing him to dive deeper.

And she let him, because Brandon West was an overpowering man who held her passion and trust in the palms of his hands. The question was, what would he do with it?

Their tongues continued to dance and weave around each other until someone opened the front door of her studio, and the outside sounds of cars and people intruded on their moment of intimacy.

"Oh!" the startled voice announced, ripping her and Brandon away from each other like two teenagers who'd been caught necking by the principal.

Her mother stood by the door, her eyes wide to match the smile on her face, as though to say, *Score one for the team, honey.*

Only Gloria Davenport.

She held her hands up and backed toward the door. "Don't mind me," she told them. Then offered Stella two thumbs up. For Pete's sake. "But good job, honey. Way to take my advice."

And then she was gone, blowing back out the door as quickly as she had interrupted them, taking Stella's dignity with her.

One of Brandon's dark brows lifted, showing nothing of

the passion he'd exhibited just a second ago. "Advice?" he repeated.

"Ah...," she began, not sure how to explain Gloria Davenport to someone who didn't know her. "Just ignore her. She obviously hasn't taken her medication today."

The slight curl of his mouth widened. "You look like her."

Please God, don't say that. "Okay."

His brown eyes narrowed, scrutinizing way too much. "Is this another thing you don't want to talk about?"

Right on. She lifted a shoulder and pretended her heart wasn't still pounding from their kiss. "I have no issues with my mom." At least none that she was willing to share.

Brandon nodded. "You know, one of these days all those walls you've thrown up are going to come crashing down."

As Stella watched Brandon saunter out of her studio as though he hadn't just knocked her socks off with his mouth, all she could think of was how right he was.

TEN

Y ou ready to spill yet?" Blake prodded for the umpteenth time since they'd ended their jog twenty minutes ago. The morning air was cool, dancing over Brandon's bare arms and cooling the sweat dotting his skin from their thirty-minute excursion through the park.

He and Blake, along with Duke, walked across the street to the Screamin' Bean for some coffee. Since the town was still buzzing from the Bobcats' win the night before, he and Blake had scored some free joe. They'd snagged an outside table and Brandon tied Duke's leash around a lamppost. The dog lowered to his stomach and watched the people as they passed by on the sidewalk.

In the meantime, Brandon ignored his cousin's inquiry and sipped his coffee. Casually, as though he didn't damn well know it was only a matter of time before Blake pried that shit from him. Because that's what the man did.

"Can't we just enjoy this beautiful morning?" Brandon

asked, knowing Blake would see right through Brandon's stall tactics. Because where could he possibly start?

Blake shrugged his shoulder. "Fine, then. Don't tell me what's eating your ass. No skin off my back."

Brandon's brow furrowed. "Did someone skip their Midol this morning?"

Blake lifted his cup and pointed a finger at Brandon. "You think I don't see past all your jokes, my friend. But I know you."

"And what do you think you know?"

"You're doing that thing you do," Blake said. "Where you clam up when something's bothering you."

Brandon wanted to call bullshit, but Blake would have seen through it. But he didn't know what the hell was going on with Stella, so...

"I'm worried Matt and Adrienne are having sex," he blurted out. Yeah, like ripping off a Band-Aid. A large-ass Band-Aid that left his skin red and raw.

Blake blinked and slowly lowered his coffee cup. "They're kids," he replied, casual as you please, as though they weren't talking about Brandon's own kid.

"What the hell does that have to do with it?" As though Brandon didn't know. As though he and Trish hadn't been doing the same thing at that age. And why was he such a chickenshit with his own kid?

Blake shook his head. "Again with the sarcasm. You're really looking for a foot up your ass, aren't you?"

Brandon set his cup down and scrubbed a hand over his face. Should have shaved that morning. "Sorry," he muttered. "Got a lot on my mind."

"Clearly." Blake sighed and glanced at the people around them. "Matt's a good kid."

Brandon blew out a breath. "Yeah."

The two of them were silent for a moment. Then Blake spoke. "He's got common sense, right?"

Brandon sipped his coffee, then lowered the cup. "Most of the time."

Blake nodded. "So he knows to use protection, right?"

"That's not the point," Brandon answered with a shake of his head.

Blake just blinked as though he didn't understand. "I'm not following you, bro."

Brandon wasn't following either. And now that he was talking about it, he felt like an ass for worrying about something he probably didn't need to worry about. That he ought to just talk to Matt instead of unloading on Blake. "I don't want them having sex at all."

Blake leaned back in his chair and rolled his eyes. "Seriously? They're kids, Brandon. Probably horny as shit. They're gonna do what they're gonna do."

Brandon narrowed his eyes. "Great advice."

Blake laughed, which only pissed Brandon off more. "Cam's right—you do have a bug up your ass. What gives?" When Brandon just stared, Blake pushed. "This isn't just about Matt."

Brandon leaned forward and rested his forearms on the table. "I don't know," was all he said. When had he turned into such a grumpy prick? Blake was usually the designated grumpy one in the bunch. Especially after Annabelle...

Shit.

Was that what was happening to him? Stella had made her presence known and now Brandon couldn't see straight, just as Annabelle had done to Blake.

"I know what your problem is," Blake commented.

Yeah, here it came. "If you tell me I need to get laid..."

Blake swiped his drink and took a sip. "The only way

that'll work is if you can get Stella Davenport to agree."
When Brandon's back teeth ground together, Blake's grin
widened. "Yeah, you think we all don't see it. Do you
suppose I wouldn't recognize the signs after what I went
through with Annabelle? You've got the same glazed-over
look that I had."

The same uncomfortable feeling coursed through Brandon's system as the one he always got when Stella was too
close to him. When he could see the gray flecks in her eyes
and smell the sugar on her skin. And when he got images of
sweaty limbs and tangled sheets.

Pissed now, as much with himself as with his cousin,
Brandon stood and swiped his keys off the table. "Eat shit,"
he growled.

Blake's devious chuckle followed Brandon as he stalked
away. "Yeah, have fun with that one," Blake called out.

"What do you think of these pants?"

Stella stared at her reflection in the bathroom mirror as
she tried, and had been trying for the past twenty minutes, to tame her thick wavy hair to do...well, anything
other than what it normally did. Which was float around
her head in thick waves that refused to conform to Stella's
demands for some control. She'd already smoothed some
serum in, but all that had done was make the strands stick
together.

"They look great, Mom," Stella told Gloria as she ran a
brush through her hair again. No change. "They really make
your eyes pop."

Gloria stopped her side-to-side turning and glared at her
daughter. "Blue jeans make my eyes pop?"

Stella didn't take her gaze off her hair. Screw it. The
stuff was going up in a bun. After all, it was just dinner

with Annabelle. Who the hell was she trying to impress? Stella opened a drawer and yanked out a hair tie. "I don't know, Mom. They're jeans. How would you like them to look?"

Gloria's hand jabbed on her hip. "Like I'm smaller than a size eight."

Stella shot her mother a glance as she wound her hair on top of her head. "Mission accomplished, then. Men will be tripping over themselves to get to you."

"Now you're just being facetious," Gloria accused.

The bun on Stella's head loosened and little hairs popped up, including some at her temples and the base of her neck. She expelled a sigh. "Seriously hate my hair."

"Honey, do you know how many women would kill for hair like yours? I mean, it has this natural gorgeous wave that you don't even need curlers for."

Stella shoved the hairbrush back in the drawer and slammed the thing shut. "Yes, I know. Grass is greener and all that."

"Okay, so, back to my jeans," Gloria urged.

Ugh. Stella spun around and eyed her mom. "First of all, where are you going?"

"Line dancing at the VFW."

Seriously? "Then they look good." Stella pushed around her mom and headed toward her bedroom. Gloria was supposed to be in her own place by now. As in, away from Stella. As in, on the other side of town where she wouldn't be bugging Stella about how she looked in her jeans.

Gloria hurried after her daughter. "Well, what if I told you I was going somewhere else?"

Stella riffled through her closet for a pair of boots. "Where else would you be going?"

"I don't know. A date?"

Stella turned with a pair of black boots in her hand. "Then you still look fine."

"I don't want to look fine. I want to look smokin'. I want to look—"

Stella paused in the act of pulling on her boots and held up a hand. "Please stop."

"What is wrong with looking smokin'?"

"Nothing if you're not my mother." Stella yanked on her other boot and zipped the thing up. "Rule number one about living with me. Don't ask me to compare you to a twenty-one-year-old college student. Rule number two." Stella stalked around her mom and went to her jewelry box. "Stop air-drying your underwear in my bathroom."

"Honey, they're too delicate for the dryer."

"Understood. But dry them in your own bathroom." Stella chose a pair of silver dangling earrings from the jewelry case. "I don't like looking at your thongs while I'm doing my business on the toilet."

Gloria lowered to the bed. "When will you be home?"

Stella finished fastening her earrings in and eyed them in the mirror. "It's Annabelle, so expect me home by eight."

"If you get done early enough, you could always meet up with us for some dancing."

Line dancing with her mom? Stella would rather run around town in a bikini made of Cool Whip. "Thanks, but you go on ahead. I'll probably just pick up a Redbox movie after dinner and come home."

"Honey, don't be such a dud. You're never going to meet a man by having dinner with a friend and watching movies by yourself."

"Maybe I don't want to meet a man," Stella retorted.

Gloria lifted her eyes to the ceiling. "It's not natural to be alone."

Stella turned from the mirror. "I was thinking tomorrow we could go out and see some apartments." *You know, since you aren't doing it by yourself.*

"Eager to get rid of me?" Gloria teased.

Absolutely. "It's not normal for a grown woman to live with her mother."

"Well, you're not living with me. I'm living with you."

Stella snagged her black clutch off the bed and pointed it at her mom. "Not normal either."

"It is in some cultures," Gloria muttered as Stella placed a kiss on her cheek and bid the woman good-bye.

Fifteen minutes later, Stella pulled into the parking lot of Maguire's, a sports bar/pool hall that was never short on action and big-screen televisions displaying every ESPN channel. Stella disapproved of the place, based on the fact that they had placed Steve Young ahead of Johnny Unitas on their quarterback wall of fame. Not that she had anything against Steve Young, but two places ahead of Johnny Unitas? But they had the best blue cheese burger in the county, which Annabelle was obsessed with, so here they were.

Stella parked on the side of the building and then made her way inside. The place was rowdy, as usual, with the majority of the televisions and the crowd devoting their time and attention to the Denver Broncos game. Stella glanced around for Annabelle and didn't see her at the bar or at one of the tables. Her gaze bounced from person to person, touching briefly on Steve Young's smiling face as he sat on top of Johnny Unitas's photo on the quarterback hall of fame wall.

Blasphemers. All of them.

Stella was bumped from behind by a woman who was too busy giggling at some man who'd spilled beer down the front of her John Elway jersey. If someone spilled beer on Stella's John Elway jersey, if she had owned one, she certainly wouldn't have been laughing. She moved out of the way and retrieved her cell phone from her purse.

"Hello?" Annabelle answered after a few rings.

"Hey, are you here?" Stella asked her friend.

"Yeah, I've got a table by the hall of fame wall," Annabelle answered.

"I'm over by the front door and I don't see you," Stella replied as she maneuvered through the crowd, not seeing her friend anywhere.

"I'm looking right at the front door and you're not there," Annabelle said.

"Well, now I'm next to the bar."

Annabelle paused before answering. "Still not seeing you."

Stella's gaze roamed the tables by the wall, but Annabelle wasn't seated at any of them. They were all full of people either watching the game or eating their dinner. She sat on an empty stool and closed her eyes. "Are you at the Maguire's in town?"

"No, I'm at the one in Pagosa Springs."

Because of course.

Stella pinched the bridge of her nose. "Why would we drive all the way to Pagosa Springs for dinner?"

"Because the Maguire's in town is obnoxious and full of drunk people. The one here is way better and quieter. Just hop in the car and come down here."

Stella glanced around the place. "I don't want to drive all the way down there."

"Well, I've already ordered drinks," Annabelle countered.

And wasn't this the greatest way to spend a Thursday night? "That's all right. I'll just grab some food to go and head home. I've got a headache anyway."

"You sure? I can ditch the drinks and meet you there."

Stella turned around on her stool and faced the bar. The guy next to her elbowed her in the ribs when he jumped from his seat to yell at the television. "No, stay and enjoy your drinks. I'm just going to head home."

"Sorry for the mix-up," Annabelle offered.

Stella blew out a breath. "No. biggie. I'll call you later."

They disconnected the call and Stella replaced her phone in her clutch. She spun around on her stool, looking for a table because the bar was packed with obnoxious fans who kept sloshing their beer and screaming at the game refs to remove their heads from their asses. Stella wanted no part of the game action, but her stomach let out a low rumble because she hadn't eaten anything in hours. Unfortunately, there weren't any tables available so she was stuck at the bar. Perhaps she'd just order something to go so she could get home to her quiet house and curl up on the couch.

Just as she was about to turn around, her gaze landed on a couple in the back. At first she didn't think much of them, but the woman with wavy blond hair who'd been busy fawning all over her companion shifted and revealed the man sitting next to her. Stella almost did a double take but knew her eyes hadn't deceived her. Brandon West could hardly be mistaken for any other man. At least in Stella's mind. He was too commanding. Too powerful and too mesmerizing.

He grinned at the woman next to him and then laughed

at something she said. The restaurant was too raucous for her to hear him, but she knew the sound. Deep and low and rumbling like the growl of a jungle cat. A shiver snaked down her spine at the memory of his laughter and how it had curled around her moments before their kiss. Stella blinked, realized she'd been staring, and averted her gaze seconds before Brandon's connected with hers.

But had he actually seen her?

The connection had been so quick, a mere moment and nothing more than a whisper of a glance. But Stella had been hooked, like she always was with him, and she looked again. Because she was masochistic like that.

Yeah, he definitely saw her. The woman next to him snagged a fry off his plate and tossed it in her mouth. Brandon kept his attention on Stella as he lifted his glass of beer, or whatever he was drinking, to his mouth and took a slow slip. Stella should have turned away. After all, blatantly staring at someone from across the room was rude. Especially when the person in question had been in the starring role in several of her fantasies. And said person was on a date with someone else.

Yeah. So rude.

Except she couldn't tear her gaze away when Brandon's throat muscles worked to swallow his drink. The Adam's apple in the thick column of his neck moved up and down in a way that shouldn't have been sexy. How many men's necks had caused a rash of sweat to build up in between her breasts? And why was she still staring?

Seriously, creepy.

But Brandon stared back as though he knew he had her right where he wanted her. Only when the woman next to him spoke did he break his gaze from Stella's and place it back on his date. He leaned forward and dipped his head down as the woman said something in his ear. Brandon's mouth curled up and Stella couldn't stomach any more.

Was she jealous?

Not just no but hell to the no.

What would she be jealous of? The amazon with the thick blond hair who kept placing her hand on Brandon's arm? Or the way Brandon kept laughing at whatever the woman kept saying?

Again, hell to the no.

Nope. No jealousy for her.

Stella spun back around on the stool and the guy next to her elbowed her in the ribs again. She was just about to tell the guy to gain some control of his extremities when the bartender approached her.

"If you're going to sit there, you have to order something," he told her.

Stella thought about her quiet house waiting for her and the soft couch begging to be sat on. However, thoughts of Brandon and his date were overpowering those desires.

"I'll have a Bloody Mary. And a basket of onion rings," she tossed in, just for the hell of it.

One of the bartender's thick brows lifted as though he saw right through her ploy to act all slick. Like she was the cool chick who frequented bars and knew her way around drinks.

Yeah, let him think whatever he wanted to think.

"You got it," he said instead of calling her out for the fraud she was.

Stella didn't drink. Like, ever.

Normally she couldn't stand the stuff. Hated the bitter taste and the way it burned down her throat and sat like acid in her stomach. But the scene behind her, the man who kept inserting himself in her life, and the whore who couldn't keep her hands to herself only reminded Stella of how alone she was. By herself. No one to cheer on a football team with. No one to grope in a public restaurant.

Sure she had friends. Annabelle was awesome, but she had Blake now. Ever since they'd gotten engaged, her friend had been spending less time with Stella. Not that Stella begrudged her friend her happiness. After everything Annabelle had been through with a cheating husband, she deserved a happy ending. And Blake Carpenter was the perfect man to give her that happy ending.

So, no. Stella didn't resent her best friend. Jealous a little? Sure, who wouldn't be? Jealous of the way Blake looked at Annabelle. Jealous of the way he only had eyes for her. But, yeah. She was lonely.

So why not take a night to herself? Why not throw her inhibitions out the door and let loose? Did the fact that she was by herself make her a tad pathetic?

Probably, yes.

Most likely.

But screw it.

Screw Brandon and screw his whore.

Her drink was placed in front of her on top of a white cocktail napkin. Stella immediately picked the thing up and took a sip. Yeah, that was nasty stuff. How in the world did people drink this shit?

And why did it seem like she was the only one on the planet who couldn't stand the taste of alcohol? Maybe there was something wrong with her.

Man, she really was a square.

A square who would rather be curled up on her couch or dancing in her studio. Just her and the music. Pretending that she didn't have a busted knee and no man to wrap his arms around her.

And that thought conjured another image of Brandon leaning forward so his date could whisper sweet nothings in his ear.

Ignoring the burn, Stella tossed back another swig. The bartender narrowed his eyes at her as he refilled a beer glass.

"You might want to slow down with that stuff. It's not meant to be chugged."

Stella wanted to tell the guy what he could do with his warning. Instead, she offered a sweet smile. "Is my food ready yet?"

The guy didn't take being dismissed kindly. His thin lips pursed from underneath his thick Fu Manchu. "Yeah, I'll get right on that."

See that you do.

In the meantime, she would just sit there and play with her drink. And by play, she meant drink. And then drink some more.

Before she knew it, her glass had emptied and her onion rings had been set in front of her. She slammed the glass on the bar and asked for another drink. Because that's what they did in bars, right? Slammed the glass down and demanded more drinks?

At least, that's what they did in movies.

And the movies were always right.

But why was that funny?

Had she giggled out loud?

"You sure you can handle some more?" the bartender asked.

Why couldn't the guy mind his own damn business? "Of course." She waved her finger above the glass. "More, please."

He lifted a brow and removed the glass from the bar. "You've got a designated driver, right?"

A designated driver? Shit, she hadn't thought about that. Maybe she could call Annabelle to pick her up on her way home. Yeah, she'd do that.

"Of course," she answered again. "What kind of person doesn't designate a driver?"

The guy shook his head and went to refill her glass. Nosy bastard.

The game on the television moved into the fourth quarter with the Broncos down by fourteen. Or was that twenty-four? Shit, she couldn't read the numbers on the screen.

Yeah, maybe she'd had too much to drink. Time to call it quits. Except the bartender set another full glass down in front of her. It would be rude not to drink it, wouldn't it? Clearly he'd gone to the trouble to make her another one.

So, yeah. She should drink it.

But maybe she ought to call Annabelle first to come pick her up. Might as well while Stella's brain was still functioning seminormally.

She twisted on her stool to retrieve her phone from her clutch, and the thing fell out and landed on the floor.

"Crap," she whispered to herself.

She was reaching down to grab the thing when the guy next to her hopped off his stool, actually fell was more like it, and his big-ass boot landed right on top of her phone.

"Hey," she chastised, but the guy with no neck—*we'll just call him No-Neck*—didn't hear her.

He stumbled around his stool, giving Stella the opportunity to swipe her phone off the nasty floor. And, damn, the screen was cracked. No-Neck, who'd elbowed her so many times that she practically had a mold of his elbow in her side, had broken her phone.

She swiped her hand over the cracked screen and pushed the power button.

Nothing.

"Hey." She grabbed the guy's shoulder.

No-Neck high-fived the other drunk asshole he was with, then turned around to face her.

Stella waved the broken phone in his face. "You broke my phone."

No-Neck squinted his bloodshot eyes as though he couldn't see the thing clearly. Probably because he couldn't. "Nah, that wasn't me." Then he turned around to walk away.

What the . . . ?

She grabbed his brawny shoulder again. "Yeah, it fell on the floor and when you stepped off your stool, your boot landed on it." She waved the phone in his face again. "See, the screen is cracked and now it won't turn on."

He swayed backward and laughed. Because the situation was so damn hilarious. "I think I would know if I had stepped on a cell phone."

Hardly. He hadn't even known he'd been elbowing her the entire time.

"Well, you did. And now my phone is broken," she accused.

"What do you expect me to do about that?"

Yeah, Stella. What's he supposed to do about it?

She glanced around the bar, which she shouldn't have done because she spotted Brandon again. He and his date had left their table and were deep in a game of pool. The woman was bent over the table like she was inviting Brandon to do her from behind. And Brandon was leaning on his pool cue, not watching his date but watching Stella. Eyebrow lifted as though he sensed trouble and would come to her rescue if she so much as lifted a finger.

She didn't need rescuing by anyone, let alone Brandon West. In fact, some days she felt like she needed rescuing from *him*.

No-Neck was still waiting for a response, so Stella crossed her arms over her chest. "Well, for starters you could loan me your phone so I can call my friend."

He narrowed his eyes at her and dug around in his back pocket. "What else?"

"What else?" she repeated.

He handed over his phone. "You said 'for starters,' indicating there's more."

She took the phone and dialed Annabelle's number. "You can pay for my drinks." Because that'll teach him to step on someone's phone.

The other end of the line rang while No-Neck dug a twenty out of his wallet and tossed it on the bar.

Stella ended the call when Annabelle's voice mail picked up. "She didn't pick up. Just let me— Hey!"

No-Neck had swiped the phone back and replaced it in his pocket. "You said one call. You made your call."

"I asked if I could call my friend, but she didn't answer—"

"Not my problem." And then he ambled away, taking his stupid no neck and working phone with him.

"Are you kidding me?" she called after him, even though she knew he wouldn't come back even if he heard her.

Wasn't that great? Here she was, semidrunk, no phone, and having to watch Brandon and his whore eye-bang each other from across a pool table.

"This sucks," she muttered to herself as she retook her stool at the bar. Her drink was still there, as were her half-eaten onion rings. But at least No-Neck wasn't there to elbow her anymore.

"Coulda told you not to mess with Big Frank," the bartender informed her.

Stella propped her elbows on the bar. "Really? That's his name?" How original.

The guy moved his shoulders. "It's what we've always called him. He's a loyal customer but ornery as shit." He pointed to her almost empty Bloody Mary. "You gonna want another?"

She stared at the thing for a moment. Then picked up the glass and downed the last bit. "Sure, why not."

"You get a hold of your friend?" the guy asked.

"Yeah, she's coming," Stella lied. No reason to sound more pathetic than she already looked.

"Because you're in no condition to drive home."

She pushed the glass toward him to urge the refill. "So you keep insinuating."

He snagged the glass with a muttered "whatever." A few minutes later he replaced it with a full one and left without comment. Smart man.

Sometime later, because Stella had no idea how long she'd been sitting there, she'd finished her third Bloody Mary. Did time go by faster when one was drunk? Because she was pretty sure she was there.

And the reason she knew this was because she kept laughing at the woman at the end of the bar who had barbeque sauce smeared on her cheek. The stain sort of looked like a deformed cat with a missing ear and Stella couldn't stop staring at the thing. She chuckled again, and some of her drink came up her nose.

Damn, that burned.

And now she had to pee.

Except where were the bathrooms?

"Where are the bathrooms?" she asked the bartender,

who kept having the gall to ask her what was wrong. Did it look like something was wrong? Couldn't a woman get shit-faced by herself without something being wrong with her?

"In the back," he told her. Then he yanked the glass off the counter. "And you're officially cut off."

Hey, just like they said in the movies. Was she cool or what?

Yeah, the coolest.

The bar stool read her mind and tilted to the side in order to help her down, not that she needed help. She almost thanked the thing for its thoughtfulness, then realized it was a freakin' bar stool.

And wasn't that funny as shit?

She laughed again and stumbled away from the bar.

Yeah, it was funny. Funny as hell. And she was cool. Cool and funny.

Where had that guy said the bathrooms were? In the back? But where was the back? She spun around, pretty sure she'd been heading for the front door. Except she spun too fast and the ground tilted.

"Whoa." She instinctively reached out to steady herself and came in contact with something soft and round. Plushy, yet firm.

A woman smacked Stella's hand away and glared at her. "As cute as you are, I don't swing that way, honey," the lady said.

Wait, had she grabbed the woman's boob? Shit, she had.

"I don't either," she reassured the lady. "But you have a nice rack. Hey, do you know where the bathrooms are?"

The woman pointed to the left. "In the back."

Yeah, so she'd been told.

She kept walking, placing one foot in front of the other because the floor was being an uncooperative douche. Why wouldn't the thing hold still?

Seriously rude.

Damn, this place was big. Stella swayed past the pool tables and managed to keep her gaze in front of her. Because she'd had just about enough of Brandon and his chick with the model-envy hair and do-me boots.

Whore.

And yeah, he was an ass too. Because...well, he just was.

"Ass," she muttered, then giggled when a guy she walked past gave her a funny look. He probably wouldn't understand her joke anyway.

Then there was a door with a picture of a toilet on it. Had the thing appeared out of nowhere? Whatever, she had to seriously piss and there were toilets inside. Enough for her.

She pushed through the wooden door and stumbled in. Damn, the place stank. Like...urine and men.

The guy who'd been washing his hands reached for the towels. "Dude, you're in the men's room."

"The hell you say," she shot back. Because this was totally the women's room. Wasn't it?

The guy smirked and strolled past her. "Okay, then."

Shit, the floor was spinning again. She placed a hand on the wall to steady her pounding head.

Now that she got a look at her surroundings, the place was filthy. Women's bathrooms didn't normally smell like sweat and piss. At least the ones she'd been in. Only men could nasty up a bathroom, especially a public one.

Shit.

And yeah, there were the urinals. With a guy standing at

them, doing his business. Feet braced apart, wide shoulders, dark, unruly hair.

Oh God.

Bile rose in Stella's throat as white-hot heat flooded her cheeks.

Brandon glanced over his shoulder at her as he zipped. "If you wanted to get a look at my junk, all you had to do was ask."

Normally she would tell him to shove his half-smile up his ass, but her dinner, along with the three freakin' Bloody Marys she'd consumed, churned in her stomach. And this was why she never drank. Not only was she a lousy, cheap drunk, but she also lost all inhibitions and acted like... well, like her mother.

And, man, this place *stank* something fierce.

Stella placed a hand over her mouth as a familiar watery taste formed. "Stop looking at me like that," she warned Brandon as he turned from the urinal and strolled toward the sink. Strolled, like the cocky badass he was. Totally enjoying her moment of drunken humiliation.

At least the Beehive Mafia wasn't there to snap one of their stupid pictures for their stupid blog or whatever the hell.

The room whirled again when she turned, and the door to the bathroom shot open, and who the hell kicked open a door like that? The thick wood clocked her right in the head, snapping her back and making the room spin even more than it already was.

She was vaguely aware of someone apologizing, probably whoever had blown through the door like he owned the damn place, as stars burst in front of her eyes and ice picks stabbed through her forehead.

"Shit," she whispered as she stumbled back until she

came in contact with the wall. She gripped her head with her hand and squeezed her eyes shut.

Yeah, that was probably going to leave a bruise. Then she could tell the hilarious story of how she cracked her head in two in the men's bathroom.

"Hold still," a deep voice said as two hands gripped her shoulders. She was moving somewhere. Where, she couldn't tell because her eyes were still closed. Partly because her head was splitting in two, honest-to-God-brains-spilling-out, and partly because she didn't want to look at anyone's "junk," as Brandon had so eloquently put it.

The bathroom sink turned on; then a wet cloth touched her head.

She jerked back at the contact and opened her eyes. "Do you have to touch so hard?" she demanded.

Brandon grinned. Such an ass. "You're bleeding. Now shut it and hold still."

Somehow, in the middle of her alcohol-fuzzy brain and lightning strikes in her head, Stella managed to scowl at him. "I really hope you washed your hands."

"Drunk off her ass and still cracking jokes." He ran a fresh towel under the water and touched it to her head again.

"I'm not that drunk."

He grinned again. "Honey, it's practically coming out of your pores."

"Hey, is she all right?" a guy behind her asked. "I didn't even see her standing there."

Brandon glanced at the guy. "Yeah, she'll be fine. She just can't be left alone because she confuses easily." He turned his whiskey eyes back to hers. "Now, I told you the women's restroom is the one with the picture of a girl on it," he said slowly.

The guy standing behind her moved to the sink to wash his hands. "You know her?" he asked Brandon.

"My sister," he answered as he dabbed the damp wash-cloth over her forehead. "She's special but likes to be treated like the rest of us."

Shithead. Her knee shot out, way too fast, because her head spun again. Didn't matter, though, because Brandon easily dodged her effort to knee his junk.

Seriously, she was going to kill him.

His grin grew and her insides tumbled. Or was that vomit? Shit, she couldn't tell.

"Easy, honey," Brandon placated. "You remember what the doctor said."

"Gonna murder you," she whispered.

He ignored her threat, probably because she'd slurred it, and tossed another paper towel in the trash. "You need some antiseptic and a Band-Aid," he told her.

"I can manage that on my own, thanks." She turned to leave the hell she'd slipped into and almost plowed into the wall again.

"Yeah, okay," her nemesis said, then took her elbow in his warm, large hand and steered her out of the men's room.

Did he have to walk so damn fast? Seriously, she was only so coordinated at the moment and his legs were eating up the floor like...someone with long legs.

Good one, Stella.

And now she was referring to herself in the third person.

They maneuvered through the throngs of people and eventually made it outside. The cool air was welcome on her heated face, which helped settle her stomach a little.

"What about your date?" she asked, because obviously her mouth didn't know when to shut the hell up.

He tossed her a confused look. "What?"

"The woman who kept rubbing herself all over you." *Seriously, shut up!*

His confusion turned into laughter. The kind that had his head thrown back and danced down her spine like the tips of his blunt fingers. Bastard.

"You're so cute," he told her, then flicked the end of her nose with his index finger.

She swatted him away but his hand had already retreated. So her reflexes were a little slow.

"My car's over there." She pointed toward the back of the building when they reached his truck.

Brandon snorted and pulled his keys from his jeans pockets. "Yeah, right."

She yanked out of his grasp. "I can drive."

"Nope."

A heavy sigh flowed out of her. "Brandon..."

He leaned against his truck and folded his arms over his chest. How was he only wearing a T-shirt when it was, like, fifty degrees outside? Didn't the man ever get cold? And why did all his shirts look like they were two sizes too small for him?

"Don't you own any shirts that fit you?"

He blinked. "What?"

"I mean, why do they have to be so tight?" she went on, because... yeah. "Not everyone wants to see all that muscle. Some women actually get turned off by it."

His brow pinched. "Seriously, what?"

She lifted her eyes to the night sky. "Never mind. I can find my own way to my car."

His hand shot out and grabbed her elbow. Why did he always grab her? And why did she always like it? "Stella, you get in that car, you'll end up wrapped around a telephone pole."

"Not your problem," she tossed over her shoulder.

He yanked her back and pinned her against his truck. "Yeah, it is. You get in that car and you're not giving Matt any more ballet lessons."

She narrowed her eyes at him and tried to ignore the solid muscle pinning her backside to her vehicle. "Low blow, West."

He opened the passenger door without breaking eye contact with her. "In," he ordered.

"Well, since you asked so nicely." She did as she was told, squinting against the bright interior light.

Without saying anything else, Brandon opened the glove compartment and withdrew a small first aid kit. Inside was a small packet of ointment and several Band-Aids.

"Such a Boy Scout," she teased. A new round of lightning passed through her skull, punishing her for trying to speak. How hard had that door hit her anyway?

Brandon was silent a moment as he tore into the ointment and squeezed a dab on his thumb. "You learn real fast to be prepared when you're a parent," he said in a low voice. "Try not to move."

His touch was gentle, but the contact still stung and sent sharp jabs of pain through her skull. "Ow."

One side of his mouth kicked up. And it really was a nice mouth. Full and soft and close enough that she could lean forward just enough to feel it. A simple touch was all she wanted.

"Focus, Stella," he told her.

How did he always know?

He finished with the ointment and tore open a bandage. "So, are you going to tell me what you were doing in the men's room?"

"Well, it certainly wasn't to look at your junk." Although she wouldn't have minded. Except, no.

Brandon applied the bandage with gentle ease, smoothing his fingers across her forehead. "Always with the joking."

His touch should have hurt. The soft pressure of his fingers should have exacerbated her already throbbing headache. Instead her eyes drifted shut when his hand smoothed down her temple and tucked a strand of hair behind her ear. Of all the men in the town, why him? Why did she have to be attracted to him?

Except it was more than a garden-variety attraction. She knew it. Hell, he probably knew it too. Her feelings for him toed the line of something deeper. Something that had settled into the forbidden part of her heart and refused to leave. She knew for a fact that it was more, because his touch didn't freak her out. Her anxiety had eased around him and Stella couldn't remember the last man who'd been able to get this close to her.

"Do you want me to back off?" he asked, as though sensing her thoughts. Because he knew she had a problem. He was so in tune with her, so perceptive and aware when no one else had been able to pick up on it.

She shook her head. "No, it's okay."

"You sure?" he pressed, resting one arm on the open door of the truck and the other on the roof. "Because by now you're usually hyperventilating."

Lovely of him to point out. "I'm fine."

"But you're still not ready to talk about it."

"Talk about what?" As if she didn't know.

"Why being around men makes you so skittish."

Skittish wasn't the word she'd use, but she didn't correct him. "No."

He nodded and glanced around. "All right. Then how about you spill about tonight?"

Definitely not going there. She shrugged like she was all casual. "What about it?"

He removed his hand from the roof of the cab and smoothed another strand of her hair down. "Let's start with why you were so drunk that you wandered into the wrong bathroom."

Um...I was jealous of the model you were with and drank too much? "Their bathrooms aren't labeled well."

"Yet, no one else had a problem," he pointed out.

Touché. "I guess I had more to drink than I realized." And that was all he would get out of her.

He narrowed his eyes. "Why?"

She threw her hands up. "Why do you care?"

"Because you don't seem like the type to drink yourself stupid."

She tilted her head at him, then closed her eyes when the movement caused a new wave of throbbing. "And what type am I?"

"Smarter than that."

"You think you know me so well."

He shifted closer, close enough for his knees to brush hers. "I know you better than you give me credit for." His grin was back. "That kills you, doesn't it?"

She shifted back in the seat so their legs no longer touched. "What's killing me is the line of questioning. Why can't you just let me go to my car?"

"Already told you, you're not driving."

She turned in the seat, staring out the windshield and crossing her arms over her chest. "Then just take me home."

He stared at her for a moment longer, then slammed the

truck door. A second later, he was in the driver's seat and turning the vehicle on. "I need your car keys."

"Why?" she asked without looking at him.

"So I can come by in the morning and get your car. I'll bring Matt and drop it off at your house."

She shot him a look. "You don't need—"

"Keys," he ground out.

Okay, he was mad. Fine, she could be mad too. They could just be mad together and *not* kiss, because that was the last thing she wanted.

Throwing one final glare at him, Stella looked around for her bag and...

"I think I left my purse inside."

With a heavy sigh, Brandon threw his seat belt off and opened his door. "Do not move," he ordered before exiting and slamming the door behind him.

Must he slam everything? Didn't he know how much her head hurt like a freakin' bitch? She dropped her head back against the headrest and closed her eyes. How had her night gone from having dinner with a friend to this? Sitting in Brandon West's truck, alcohol buzzing through her system and her head splitting open? She, Stella Davenport, civilized former professional ballet dancer, was acting like some drunk sorority girl who'd lost a bet and was now making an ass of herself in front of the hottest guy ever.

Score for her.

This was why she kept to herself. This was why she didn't date. Setting aside the whole can't-stand-to-be-touched-thing, Stella didn't have a clue how to kick it with the rest of the cool people. Perhaps she'd never really learned how. When she hadn't been dragged around from one home to the next by her mother, she'd been in a studio dancing. Or onstage. One could say she was socially awkward. Hell, she didn't even know what to do with a gorgeous guy who was obviously into her.

She knew Brandon was into her. That was no secret. Problem was, she didn't have the faintest clue what to do about it. Only, she acted like she did. Case in point, when Annabelle and Blake had been dancing around each other. More than once she'd told Annabelle to do the guy already. Giving her grief for not acting on her feelings.

Was she a fraud or what?

Hypocrite.

Terrified.

So she'd just stay away from him. Best solution all around. She could move forward with her choreography job and he could move on... with someone else?

Yeah that's what he should do.

The truck door opened, and Brandon climbed in. He pocketed her keys and tossed her clutch into her lap.

"You could have just handed it to me," she grumbled.

Brandon didn't say anything as he put the truck in reverse and backed out of the parking space.

Fine. She could do the silent treatment too.

The throbbing in her head increased, so Stella leaned back and placed the palm of her hand on her forehead. As though that was supposed to help.

Brandon leaned across the space, not even bothering to keep his arm from brushing across her legs, and opened the glove compartment. After digging around, he withdrew a bottle of pills and tossed them in her lap. Then he handed her a half-drunk bottle of water that had been chilling in the cup holder.

She shook out two pain pills and accepted the water with a mumbled "thanks." But then she hesitated before taking a sip of the water. Something about placing her lips where Brandon's obviously had been was too...intimate. Too close. One step away from sealing her lips to his, which she'd been thinking about way too much tonight. And even though they'd shared a drink before, Stella still wasn't comfortable with it.

"What's wrong?" Brandon asked, making Stella realize she'd been staring at the bottle without drinking. "You're not worried about cooties, are you?"

"Who even uses that word anymore?" she said before tossing the pills back and washing them down. She replaced the bottle in the cup holder and they sat in more silence. Fantastic.

"For your information," Brandon stated, breaking the thick tension in the small cab. "Melanie is a repeat client. She's an investor who flips houses and uses us for the renovations."

Stella snorted. "Melanie," she muttered to herself. Stupid name. Sounded like it belonged to a poodle, with those stupid pink bows in their ears.

"What's that?" Brandon asked with a glance in her direction.

"Nothing." She smiled. All fake and stuff.

His brow lifted, as though he was on to her shenanigans, then slowly placed his attention back on the road. One arm was draped casually over the steering wheel, his powerful legs relaxed and as stretched out as the seat would allow. He was a big guy who dwarfed the interior of the truck and sucked all the oxygen out of everything.

"You know, I don't care who you spend time with." Why? Why, why, why couldn't she shut up?

"Kind of seems like you do," he retorted without looking at her.

She crossed one leg over the other and bounced her foot. Nope. Not going to respond to that. Let him think what he wanted to think.

"Why would I care?" she shot back because she knew what he thought and, damn it, he was wrong.

Brandon grabbed his cell phone out of the middle console and thumbed the screen. "Because you want to get into my pants."

Her back teeth ground together and her head twitched. Her whole head actually twitched. "Whatever." Then she turned to look out the window, staring into the dark night so Brandon wouldn't see the pink staining her cheeks. Damn it, she could feel the heat flaming her entire face.

"Fine," he said in return.

Stella closed her eyes and blew out a breath. "Great."

"Perfect," he agreed while bringing the phone to his ear. Stella could hear the other end ringing from her seat. "Matt," Brandon greeted when his son picked up. "Just calling to check in and to let you know I'll be home soon." Brandon was silent while Matt responded. "Also, tomorrow's extra garbage day, so I need you to grab all those bags of leaves and mulch from the side yard and put them on the curb." He paused for a moment, then said, "Did you give Duke his heartworm medication? No, you know how he is. You have to shove the thing down the back of his throat." Another pause. "All right, I'll see you in a bit. Love ya." He disconnected the call and tossed the phone into the empty cup holder.

The wall she'd immediately erected around her heart cracked at the "love ya" thing. Because she was such a sucker for parents who were all into the parenting thing. Like those health insurance commercials that showed families playing a game of softball and high-fiving each other and stuff. Those always provoked the waterworks because that's how families were supposed to be. They were supposed to look out for each other and say I love you and put each other's needs first.

Like Brandon did with Matt. He was a good dad, which was such a turn-on. No idea why, and it pissed her off because it was just another reason why she couldn't resist the man.

She turned from the window and glared at him, throwing out the familiar defense mechanism that never failed her. "Why do you have to be so obnoxious?"

"Because you let me," he answered, immediately falling back into their conversation.

And look at them being all on the same page and stuff.

"What does that even mean?"

He shot her a quick glance. "That you refuse to shoot me down."

That...Okay, yeah, he was right. She had refused to outright shoot him down. Had she ever told him there could never be anything between them? Nope, pretty sure she hadn't. And how could he think otherwise when she all but panted like a dog in heat every time she was around him? Always mentally undressing him? Blushing?

But still, did that give him the right to annoy the shit out of her?

"Maybe," he went on, "I'm not the obnoxious one. Maybe you're rubbed the wrong way because, you know"— he wagged a finger between the two of them—"this."

"There is no 'this,'" she replied, mimicking his finger-wagging thing.

"There's something," he argued. "You can lie to yourself all you want, but it's there and it's not going away."

"You know, you're the one who's made it clear he doesn't want any kind of a relationship," she reminded him.

"Because you're leaving," he added.

"So it's my fault?"

He moved one thick shoulder. "Just stating a fact."

But what if she weren't leaving? *Don't say it . . .* "What if I weren't?"

He glanced at her. "But you are."

What was she supposed to say to that? "It's not like I'm leaving forever. I'm coming back after the job is done."

"So I've been told before."

Stella watched him for a moment, noting the ticking in his shadowed jaw. "Not every woman is like your ex."

"Thanks for stating the obvious." They were both silent a moment. "Sorry," he amended. "It's my default nature."

Boy did she understand that.

He heaved a sigh and scrubbed a hand over his face. "How are you expecting this conversation to go, Stella? One of us compromises something about ourselves and we run into your house for a quick bang?"

"You don't have to put it like that."

"How would you like me to put it?"

"Not like an ass," she shot back. Couldn't they get through one conversation without either fighting or shoving their tongues down each other's throats? How did Annabelle and Blake do it?

They love each other.

No, they were *in* love.

Huge difference and Stella often didn't understand how to make sense of the two.

"I'm sorry," he muttered.

Stella stared out the window while Brandon pulled into her driveway. "For?"

He threw the truck in park and sighed. "I don't know. Just seemed like the right thing to say."

"Why apologize if you don't know what you're apologizing for?"

"Damn, Stella." He leaned his head back and closed his eyes. "You're the most infuriating woman sometimes."

Now he knew how she felt. Wanting to strangle a person while kissing them at the same time. Quite the predicament.

Instead of saying anything, because she was sure she'd only make the situation worse, Stella unbuckled and opened the truck door. "Thanks for the ride."

Brandon undid his seat belt as well and got out of the vehicle.

"You don't need to walk me up," she said without looking at him.

Brandon didn't respond as he withdrew her car keys from his pocket to unlock the front door. How did he even know which one was the right key?

The porch light was on and Stella stood back while Brandon unlocked the bolt. The hand gripping the keys was big and tan. Such capable hands. Strong and confident. Stella probably would have fumbled and dropped them on the ground before getting the door open.

She brushed past him and flipped the hall light on. Brandon slapped a palm on the door before she could close the thing in his face.

"Brandon, don't," she told him. "You don't do casual and I'm not giving up my job for you."

He stepped closer to her, wedging himself in the opening of the door. "I would never ask you to do that."

Because he was a good guy. A good guy who wouldn't dream of standing in the way of something he knew meant that much to her. But had she ever told him just how much this opportunity meant to her? Or was this just another way he'd figured her out? Stella wasn't sure and the uncertainty made her squirm.

"I know, but..."

He stepped closer, and his chest brushed against hers. The cotton of his shirt did nothing to disguise the steel planes of his chest and the dips and grooves of muscle that would be perfect to drag her tongue over. He dipped his head like he was going to kiss her, glancing the tip of his nose along hers. But his mouth only hovered, frustrating her and turning her on at the same time.

A wave of heat bloomed across her chest and roamed its way down to the pit of her stomach. It flared over her face, pulling her skin tight across her skull and turning her even breaths into a struggle. When she tried to pull more air into her lungs, Brandon's hand grasped hers, lacing their fingers together and cutting off her deep breath. The contact turned her breath into a gasp.

He immediately let go and took a step back. "Sorry," he said in a gravelly voice. "Sometimes the urge to touch you is so strong that I forget you don't like it."

Yeah, except that wasn't why she'd gasped. She *had* liked it, to the point where she wanted to touch him back. His shoulders were begging for her hands to curl over them. Then maybe lean in for a kiss because it sure felt like where they were headed.

"You don't need to freak out every time you touch me," she informed him.

"I don't want to make you uncomfortable, Stella."

She gripped the door with one hand. "You don't."

He tilted his head at her. "I think I do."

Okay, he did. But not for the reasons he thought. He assumed her rapid heartbeat was because of her anxiety and fear of getting too close to someone. When actually her pulse kicked up because she wanted him. She wanted his touch. Craved it in a way that was so foreign to her, she didn't know how to handle it. Every time he was near, her body transformed into something she didn't recognize and it freaked her out. Instead he thought she was some nut case.

To prove him wrong, Stella closed the distance between them and curved her palm over his waist. Where she was soft and curvy, he was cut and solid. She skimmed her thumb over the ridge of his oblique and grinned when the muscle tensed.

"You don't have to prove anything to me, Stella."

She lifted her gaze to his and momentarily allowed herself to get lost in all the unspoken promises that could exist between them. "I'm not trying to prove anything to you."

He leaned into her and curled his arm around her, resting his palm in the comfortable curve of her lower back. His breath fanned across her face and for a moment, just a moment, the panic started. It unfurled without her permission, and she'd spent so many years allowing it to control her, robbing her of intimacy and shared moments. Her face heated and beads of sweat erupted across her chest. Her heart continued its uneven beating and moved into her throat, choking her and robbing her of breath. And for the first time, Stella cursed herself for not being stronger than her demons, for allowing her fears to overrun her sense of stability and comfort.

"Breathe with me," Brandon murmured. "Don't let it control you."

Her eyes dropped closed, pushing away the sounds of the surrounding night. The ticking of the hallway clock. The crickets. The leaves rustling on the breeze. A second ago they had closed in on her, gripping her like icy fingers and trying to pull her away from the man in front of her.

Stella leaned her head against Brandon's chest, focusing on his heartbeat and the steady in and out of his breathing. The solid wall of muscle. His hand moving in slow circles over her back. The other hand playing with her fingers, then holding them in a solid grip. Like a promise. That he would never violate her or force her to step outside her comfort zone. And she knew he would back away if she gave him the word.

Except she didn't want him to. Because this was...nice. To be held. Understood. Something she hadn't allowed herself to indulge in for longer than she could remember.

Her hand loosened its grip at his waist, releasing the soft cotton that had been bunched in her fingers. With her next slow exhale, she flattened her palm and slid it around and up his back. Inching along and allowing her fingers to explore the groove of his spine.

"That's it," he urged in a low voice next to her ear. "It's just you and me."

No one had ever taken the time to comfort her, or even be aware of the battle raging just below the false confidence. She'd time and again thrown all that out there to save face. But there was no saving face with Brandon. He kicked right past her defense mechanisms, where she was most vulnerable. The thing was, he didn't seem to care. He hadn't judged, hadn't asked what was wrong with her like most guys did when she had a panic attack.

He eased and soothed and understood. Hadn't once tried to push her past what she was comfortable with. As soon as he sensed her unease, he'd back away and give her the room she needed.

Man, she loved him for that.

Loved him.

Shit.

Then he did something totally unexpected. He started humming.

Stella couldn't tell what the tune was. And it didn't even matter because the deep rumbling of his chest, vibrating against hers did more than just calm her waning anxiety. In its place was awareness. An acute, sensitized awareness of every little inch of them pressed together. From her breasts nudging the curved perfection of his pecs, to their stomachs kissing each time one of them breathed, down to his feet bracketing hers.

Brandon didn't have any moves up his sleeve, of that much she was sure. There was no ulterior motive, no end game resulting in him getting laid. He was doing this for her because he was selfless and giving and way too good for her.

"What're you humming?" she asked against his chest.

The hand on her back tugged her closer. "Just something I used to hum to Matt when he was a baby."

She pulled back and looked at him the same time her uterus skipped a beat.

"And now you're crushing on me," he stated.

Crushing? Try falling.

He withdrew her hand from his back and lifted it to his mouth. Her breath caught in her throat when he pressed his lips to her knuckles, long enough to feel the firm heat of his lips. Then he released her.

Wait, that was it? He wasn't leaving, was he?

She opened her mouth to object, but he beat her to it.

"You're not ready for more, Stella."

Okay, yeah. He knew what she'd been about to say. She wanted more. She wanted to fist her hands in his shirt and drag him through the door. She wanted him to press her to the solid wood and show her something other than the gentleman who'd coaxed her through an oncoming anxiety attack.

Instead he left. Turned and strolled toward his truck, leaving her to gape after the solid perfection of his ass and wonder where they went from there.

ELEVEN

The Bobcats lost their sixth game in a crushing overtime defeat.

Four days later, Brandon stood back and watched practice, hands draped over the chain-link fence as Blake ran the team through drills and plays. Recruiters were all over the place, watching the kids, talking to the coaches and making notes on their clipboards. Both the schools that he and Matt had been considering were in attendance. Brandon snagged his kid's attention and motioned for him to focus on his coach.

"If you don't smile, your jaw's going to shatter," a soft voice said next to his ear. Only one woman he knew was almost tall enough to reach his ear.

Brandon turned his head and caught sight of Stella. But she didn't stay to chat. Just patted him on the shoulder and rushed past, swaying that sweet ass as she made her way to Annabelle. The two immediately started laughing it up. Stella tossed one last look at him, waved, then turned back to her friend, her long ponytail swishing over her shoulder.

What the hell?

Had something changed between them since he saw her a week and a half ago?

When he'd sensed a serious freak-out coming on, all he'd been able to think of was holding her. The panic had flared in her eyes and tore at his heart. How long had she been living with that? Had she been battling that alone? And what about the asshole who'd made her that way? Because Brandon was almost certain a man had triggered her intimacy fears. He sincerely hoped it wasn't what his mind had conjured up. That she hadn't been violated in the worst way imaginable. But there had been a violation. Something that had rocked her trust in other people, specifically men.

Another reason why they couldn't go beyond mild flirtations. Or maybe some kissing. As much as he would love to tangle in the sheets with her, Brandon knew Stella wasn't ready for that. Underneath the glib joking and scorching kisses was a woman not yet ready to surrender herself that way. So he'd wait.

He took out his phone and sent her a text. *What drug are you on?*

A second later came her reply. *I resent your implication.*

He grinned as he countered her. *Seriously. You're being nice to me, so what gives?*

I'm always nice.

Really? He glanced at her from the thirty or so feet away she was standing with Annabelle. He could practically see her eyes rolling from behind her sunglasses.

Okay fine. I thought about staying for a chat, but Rhonda

Powell is sitting at the top of the bleachers, plotting for a way to take a bite out of your sexy ass.

He lifted a brow in her direction and answered her.

You think my ass is sexy?

You know it is, so get over yourself.

He hooked his elbow over the chain-link fence and texted her back. *Why don't you come over here and talk to me instead of typing?*

Brandon watched her fine backside as she climbed the bleachers with Annabelle, her head bent over her phone as her thumbs flew across her keyboard.

You're the one who started texting me. Besides, Rhonda scares me.

He leaned against the fence and texted Stella back. *Nuhuh. You're not scared of Rhonda. Fess up.*

On the field, Blake blew his whistle. Brandon watched the action, keeping one eye on Matt and the other on his phone. After a moment, too long actually, she answered.

Yep, totally petrified. She's all yours if you want her.

She was so full of shit it was practically coming out of her ears, but he didn't call her on it. The conversation needed to happen face-to-face. Because something was up. When he'd backed away from her at her front door, he'd seen the invitation in her eyes. She would have let him in the house if he'd persisted. She would have let him take her to bed. She'd wanted it just as much as he had.

So why was she all of a sudden acting all buddy-buddy and endorsing a fling with Rhonda Powell? Especially when Stella knew good and well that Brandon couldn't stand the woman.

A ribbon of irritation snaked through his system. He'd never known anyone who played more games than Stella Davenport.

Without thinking, Brandon shot her a reply.

Why would I go out with Rhonda when I can give Melanie a call?

He pocketed the phone without a second thought, sent Stella a mock solute, and headed onto the field.

Yeah, he'd probably pay for that later. She'd no doubt turn back into the ice queen who ignored him half the time. But wasn't that what he wanted?

Shit, he wasn't sure anymore.

All he was sure of was that he'd reacted in the heat of the moment, said something he shouldn't have and probably hurt her.

Damn, he'd never had a more complicated relationship with a woman he wasn't even in a relationship with.

He could feel her eyes on the back of his head as he stalked across the grass, daring him to come back and finish it. Yeah, they'd finish all right.

He came to a stop next to Cameron.

"How's it going this morning?" he asked his friend.

Cam's eyes scanned the field from behind dark sunglasses. "It would go better if Drew Spalding would get his ass out of here. Man pisses me off."

Brandon glanced across the field where Drew was with Mac Armstrong. The two men were gesturing toward the scoreboard and talking it up. "You know he only does it to piss you off, right?"

"Yeah, well, it works," Cameron replied.

Brandon slid his hands into his back pockets. "Why can't the dude just let it go?"

"Let go of the fact that I banged his wife?"

Brandon held his hands up. "You said it, not me."

"Whatever," Cam answered with a lift of his shoulders. "Not sure I'd be able to let it go either."

A muscle in his jaw ticked. "Richardson! Get over here." Cameron stalked off to rip the QB a new one over some screwup that Brandon had missed because he'd been too busy prying into his friend's life. Blake wandered over, shoving his Bobcats baseball cap up his forehead. "What'd you say to piss him off?"

"No idea." Normally Brandon would confide in his cousin over his suspicions regarding Cameron. But something held him back. After all, he should respect Cam's privacy. Something Brandon understood.

"I see Mac's here with his jumbotron patrol," Brandon commented.

Blake shook his head. "Man's so far up my ass I feel like I'm walking around bowlegged."

Brandon chuckled. "I take it he's gone full steam ahead with his plan?"

"Mac does everything full steam ahead. He wanted the jumbotron; we're getting the jumbotron."

"Even though it's not what you want," Brandon guessed.

Blake nodded and returned his attention to the team.

They stood in silence for a few minutes, watching the players move through their drills. Blake blew his whistle, then took a quick word with one of the players, Scott Porter. Brandon searched out Matt and saw the kid tossing quick glances to the sidelines, at the Texas recruiter.

Shit.

"So what'd you hear?" Brandon asked Blake when he returned from his chat with Scott.

Blake crossed his arms over his chest. "About what?"

"The recruiters." Duh.

"You mean who are they looking at?"

Why the hell else would he be asking? "Come on, Blake," Brandon growled.

"Obviously they're looking at Cody," Blake answered

Yeah, obviously.

"Who else?"

"Scott," Blake replied while making a note on his clipboard.

Brandon heaved a sigh and looked up at the clear blue sky. "Gonna kill you, Blake."

Blake dropped his clipboard and placed a hand over his chest. "Oh, I'm sorry. Were you asking about Matt?"

"No shit."

Blake grinned. Actually mother-effing grinned. "As a matter of fact, I have had one of the recruiters approach me about your son."

"Yeah?" Brandon glanced back at all the men as though that was supposed to answer the question.

"Would you like to know whom?"

He slid his attention back to Blake. "*Whom*?"

Blake tapped Brandon on the shoulder with his clipboard. "Proper English."

He narrowed his eyes at his cousin. "Annabelle's turned you into a pussy."

Blake turned back to the team. "It's Texas."

"UT?"

"Yep."

Well, shit.

"What's with the clenching?" Blake wanted to know. "I thought that's where Matt wanted to go?"

Brandon's gaze followed Matt's movement across the field. "Only because of Adrienne and football. He can't go to UT."

"Why not?"

"Because it's an out of state school. It's, like, three times the cost."

Blake nodded. "Unless he gets a scholarship," his cousin pointed out.

Yeah, unless that. "He's going to Boulder," Brandon stated.

Blake turned toward him again. "So the two of you have agreed on this? Because the kid practically shit his pants when he saw those giant longhorns on the guy's sweatshirt."

He just bet Matt did.

"Maybe a conversation is in order?" Blake prodded.

"Sorry, are you trying to tell me how to parent my kid?"

Blake held his hands up. "Just saying. It doesn't take a genius to see the two of you aren't on the same page."

"He's a teenager," Brandon pointed out. "We're not on the same page about anything."

"College is a big one, though," Blake reiterated.

"No shit, Blake." Why was he snapping at his cousin? Blake hadn't done anything wrong. "Sorry," he admitted on a sigh. "It's just that his mind is made up and I don't know how to change it."

Blake moved his shoulders beneath his Bobcats sweatshirt. "So why change it? Let him go to school where he wants to go."

So easy for Blake to say that. "Because he's following his girlfriend," Brandon said through gritted teeth. "And we all know how well that always works out."

Blake didn't respond for a moment, but Brandon could feel the guy's focus on him. Studying him.

"You can't protect him from everything," Blake said in a low voice.

Brandon's back teeth gnashed together even harder.

"Look." Blake yanked his sunglasses off his face. "Matt's a good kid. You've raised him right. But if you try to make decisions for him and control his life, you'll only push him away." Brandon opened his mouth to argue, but Blake forged on. "I know that I don't know shit about raising kids, okay? You've got me on that one. But we were both teenagers once and nothing anyone could have said would have changed our minds about anything. And we both know that the cost of the school isn't the real issue here. You could make UT work with scholarships and/or loans."

Fine. Whatever. Blake could just take his opinions and shove them up his know-it-all ass.

Brandon turned and stalked across the field, heading toward the bleachers.

Automatically his gaze zeroed in on Stella, his groin tightening when she tossed her head back and laughed at something Annabelle said. Her neck was long and slender, perfect for dropping kisses and nuzzling his nose across. That thing inside his chest, some place close to his heart, shifted when her soft, throaty laugh floated on the breeze.

And look at him being all sappy, thinking about laughs and breezes and shit. Brandon blew out a breath and leaned his elbows on the top of the fence. He had some time before his first subcontractor meeting of the day and wanted to watch some more of practice before he left. Before he could get into the action on the field, the back of his neck prickled when a clean, flowery scent teased every nerve in his body.

"Did you get your date with Melanie set up?" Stella asked.

"As a matter of fact, I just got off the phone with her," he lied.

Stella snorted and leaned against the fence next to him. "It won't work, you know."

He glanced at her. "What, this master game of seduction we have going on?"

Color flared her cheeks. "You trying to make me jealous."

His gaze dropped to her mouth. What would she do if he kissed her right now? "Don't have to try very hard. Besides, you opened yourself up to that one."

She opened her mouth, then snapped it shut. Yeah, point one for Brandon. "You know, I actually came down here to thank you, not bicker. But for some reason, you bring out the worst in me."

He flicked her nose. "It's called foreplay, sweetheart."

She swatted his hand away, then jabbed him in the chest. "See, right there. Why do you have to do that?"

"Do what?"

"Say things that make me want to smack you."

He leaned forward so their faces were inches apart. The breeze picked up a wayward strand of her hair and blew it into his face. "That's not what you want to do to me."

She groaned and dropped her head back. "You know what? I rescind my thanks. There." She jabbed him in the chest again. "So you can consider my thanks officially rescinded." She took a step back from him. "Gone." Another backward step. "As in not there anymore because you don't deserve a thanks."

He grinned at the pink staining her cheeks. Man, she was something else. A second ago he'd wanted to growl at his cousin to mind his own effing business, and now he couldn't stop thinking about how sexy and adorable Stella Davenport was. "Technically you never offered the thanks, so your counter has no bearing on our conversation."

She tossed her hands up in the air and groaned again. "You're like that brainy guy at school who uses complex sentences to confuse people. That's what you are." She closed the distance between them again and poked that busy little finger of hers right in the middle of his chest. "You're just a big, overbearing smart-ass who wears shirts that are too small for him and gets his shits and giggles by making women all hot and bothered." She turned her finger to herself. "Except me. I'm not hot and bothered. Because I don't even like you." She waved her arm at their surroundings. "I'm talking about other women. Other women are hot and bothered. And on behalf of those poor females, I resent you."

Both sides of his mouth kicked up. "Okay, Stella."

She nodded and took two steps back. "So we understand each other?"

Not even a little. "Perfectly."

"So we're on the same page, then?"

When had they ever been on the same page? "Think we've established that."

She nodded again and gnawed on her lower lip. Uncertain, much? "Great. So my work here is done."

Oh, her work was done all right. She'd successfully made *him* all hot and bothered.

TWELVE

A few hours later, Brandon drove Matt home from a trip to the batting cages, still turned on and frustrated and pissed. Pissed at Stella for digging her crafty little way into a place no woman had been allowed since Trish. And pissed at himself for letting her. Not only letting her, but also enjoying it.

She was his Achilles' heel. Her sass, her brains, her sex appeal. Dangerous combination, all that.

Brandon cleared his throat and glanced at Matt, sure his child would see the turmoil, and borderline hard-on, from the passenger seat. But that would require Matt putting down his cell phone for more than five seconds. Heaven forbid the kid should go one minute without talking to his girlfriend.

"So, you did good at practice," Brandon offered.

Matt lifted a shoulder and didn't take his gaze off his phone. "Yeah."

Brandon blew out a breath as he made his way through town. They drove past Stella's studio, which was filled with kids in black leotards and pink tights. The brief glance inside was enough to see Stella in an off-the-shoulder shirt and another pair of those booty shorts that outlined her perfect, plump ass. One that begged him to cup his hands over so he could yank her against him hard enough for her to see what exactly she did to him.

Focus, asshole.

"Did you happen to notice who was there?" Matt queried.

How could he not notice? Then Brandon realized that Matt couldn't have been talking about Stella, because Matt had no idea what had been going on between them. Or did he?

But yeah, he was probably talking about the recruiters.

"You mean, the recruiter from Boulder?" Brandon tossed out.

"Funny, Dad."

"Colorado Springs?"

Matt sighed and tossed his phone down. "I'm talking about the guy from Texas. The Longhorns, Dad."

Brandon nodded. "Oh him. Right."

Matt narrowed his brown eyes that were so much like Brandon's own. "Like you don't know."

He knew a whole lot more than Matt thought he did. "I'm sensing you want to have a conversation about this."

"Only if you'll listen."

Brandon tossed his son a quick glance. "I always listen."

"When it's what you want to hear."

He didn't do that, did he? He shifted uncomfortably in his seat. "All right. I'm listening." He held up a hand before

Matt started. "But you have to give me a reason other than your girlfriend."

Matt blinked. "Okay. Texas has a better football team."

Brandon turned his truck onto their street. "Life isn't just about football, Matt."

"Okay..." Matt paused, apparently searching for a more acceptable answer. "It's a better school."

Brandon lowered his brow. "In what way?"

Matt shook his head and picked at the hem of his shirt. "Just is."

"You don't even know, do you?"

"I know more than you think," Matt shot back.

Brandon snorted. "Because of all the research you've done?" Had he not done enough? Had he not taken enough time to talk about college and the priorities of a good school? Time had slipped away from him so fast that he hadn't been prepared for the college thing. One minute Matt had been doing eighth-grade science projects, and the next it was time for college submissions.

"I've done enough," Matt answered. "It's a good school, so I don't know what your deal is."

Yeah, he knew UT was a good school. But it was expensive and so damn far away. Brandon knew, as he pulled his truck into the driveway, that the distance thing was just as much of an issue as the cost. It had always been the two of them. Him and his boy. First it had been him and his little man; then Matt had grown up and Brandon couldn't hold on to him any longer.

He threw the truck in park and sighed. "Okay, answer me this. If Adrienne wasn't in the picture, would you even be considering UT?"

Matt didn't answer at first. Then he shook his head and

laughed. "I don't know, Dad. I don't know how to answer that because she is in the picture."

"What if you break up and you realize you hate UT?" Brandon countered.

"Why would I hate UT?" Matt tossed back. "What if I get to Boulder and realize I hate it there?"

Touché. "Okay, what if Adrienne were going away to Rhode Island or Alaska?" Brandon argued. "Would you follow her anywhere?"

Matt unbuckled his seat belt. "I'm pretty sure nobody goes away to school in Alaska." He opened the door and stepped out. "Why are you asking me all these rhetorical questions?"

Brandon followed Matt out of the truck and together they walked toward the front door. "I just want to make sure you've really thought this through. Don't hinge all your future plans on your high school girlfriend."

"We've already had this conversation," Matt pointed out as he opened the front door and dropped his backpack. "I'm not going to make the same mistake you did."

Brandon shut the door and flipped the lights on. Duke came trotting out and followed them into the kitchen. Brandon stroked the dog's ear before pulling a tray of leftover lasagna out of the fridge. "My job as a parent is to do what's best for you."

Matt rummaged around in a cabinet. "You're also supposed to let me make my own mistakes. How am I supposed to learn anything if you're constantly sheltering me? Look, Dad," Matt went on as he set an empty glass on the kitchen counter. "I've given this a lot of thought and UT is where I want to go. And I know the chances of Adrienne and I making it long-term are slim, but it's a chance I'm willing to take." He lifted his shoulders, which were almost as wide as

Brandon's. "And you don't need to worry about the cost, or anything, because I plan to apply for student loans."

Brandon was concerned with more than just the cost. But he knew Matt had made up his mind and nothing Brandon could say would change it. The kid was just as stubborn as he was. A fact that equally frustrated and made him proud.

Brandon heaved a sigh and rubbed a hand along the back of his neck. "It's obvious you've made up your mind. So, if UT is where you want to go, then you've got my support."

Matt's brow wrinkled in confusion. "Really?"

"Yeah. And I'm not saying I hope you and Adrienne break up. She's a good girl who has a promising future. All I'm saying is"—Brandon shifted his feet and glanced at Duke, who'd sprawled across the kitchen floor—"if it doesn't work out, then I'll try and refrain from the whole I-told-you-so."

Matt chuckled. "Gee, thanks."

Before Brandon could yank the kid in for a hug, or any of the other mushy shit that he didn't do well, his cell rang. He retrieved it from his back pocket and answered without checking the caller ID.

"Yeah," he greeted.

"Brandon?"

The female voice on the other end had him pausing in the act of removing the aluminum from the lasagna tray. He blinked, then glanced back at Matt, who'd dropped to the floor to rub Duke's belly.

"Yeah," he answered, deliberately not using Trish's name in front of Matt.

"Have you been getting my messages?" she asked without easing in to any kind of conversation. "Is Matt around? Can I talk to him?"

Brandon stepped around Matt and Duke and let himself

into the backyard through the sliding glass door. "Yeah, he's here. But he doesn't know you've been calling. I haven't said anything to him yet."

There was a long, silent pause on the other end before Trish responded. "Why not? I only want to speak to him for a few minutes. I just... I need to hear his voice."

"I don't know if he'll want to talk to you, Trish."

"How do you know unless you ask him?" she pushed.

"Because I know him." Meaning Trish didn't. Yeah, she'd get what Brandon meant without him having to say it. Not like he was trying to be cruel. But Trish still didn't understand. Matt had let her go a long time ago. To him there was no mother. Only a woman who hadn't wanted him. The grieving process had been long and painful for Matt, but afterward there hadn't been anything. No anger, no hurt. Just nothing.

"He's graduating this year, Brandon," Trish pointed out, as though he didn't know. "I just want to talk to him before that. I need to know that he's okay."

Brandon pinched the bridge of his nose and leaned against the deck railing. "He's fine, Trish. He's—"

"Brandon...," she interrupted. "Okay, look. I was prepared to have a fight on my hands and I'm willing to do this any way you want." She was silent a moment, giving Brandon an opportunity to swallow past the lump in his throat. "I just want to hear his voice, Brandon," she whispered. "Please."

Damn her. Damn her for making him love her, then leaving. Damn her for tugging him along for all those years with empty promises. Damn her for what she'd put Matt through, for making him blame himself for his mother leaving, as though he'd done something wrong. And damn her again for making Brandon feel for her when he didn't want to give her a passing thought. She meant nothing to them, and yet the frisson of guilt that unfurled inside him came without warning.

He wasn't a heartless bastard, as much as he wanted to be toward Trish. She'd reached right back in and fisted his heart in her hands. And as much as he tried, he couldn't bring himself to tell her to piss off.

With a heavy sigh, he pushed away from the railing. "Give me sec," he gave in. "I'll ask him."

"Thanks," she whispered.

Brandon opened the sliding glass door and heard Matt crooning to Duke, telling the dog what a good boy he was. Matt had the animal sprawled on the kitchen floor, rubbing Duke's belly. The lump in Brandon's throat threatened to choke him when Matt looked up with an ear-to-ear grin on his face. The innocence in his son's eyes almost had him telling Trish to forget it. That he wouldn't allow her to drag Matt back to the hell he'd gone through after she'd left. But her broken *please* kept reminding him that she was only human and she was still Matt's mother.

Matt must have sensed Brandon's turmoil, because the smile on his face faded. "What's wrong?"

Duke rolled back over and thumped his tail on the floor when he spotted Brandon. He held his cell phone out to Matt. "Your mother's on the phone. She'd like to talk to you."

The light in the kid's eyes faded, darkening to the familiar confusion laced with anguish Brandon had seen too many times in the past. "Why would I want to talk to her?"

Brandon placed the heel of his palm over the phone so Trish wouldn't hear them. "Just give her a chance, Matt."

Matt's jaw hardened, mirroring the same tug-of-war

Brandon always felt when it came to Trish. "Do you want me to talk to her?"

Matt had never asked him that before, so Brandon had to think about it for a second. "The decision is yours," he answered. "I know you don't have warm feelings for her, but she's still your mom. She sounds sincere this time."

"What do you mean?"

Brandon held out the phone again. "Just talk to her."

Matt's throat worked up and down as he stared at the device. Then he took it, slowly sliding it out of Brandon's hand and placing it up to his ear. "Yeah," Matt greeted.

Brandon stood back while Matt walked out of the kitchen, then settled on the couch in the living room. Would Matt be receptive to the mother he didn't know, after all these years? Would Trish try and backpedal by offering all kinds of excuses and justifications for her long absence?

The situation was so complicated and delicate that Brandon didn't have the first clue how to handle it.

Matt's deep voice floated from the living room. Brandon couldn't hear what was being said and didn't want to eavesdrop. As much as he wanted to know what Trish was saying to him, Brandon also knew it was between Matt and his mother. So he busied himself with dinner, preheating the oven and taking a bag of frozen garlic bread out of the freezer. When that only killed about ten seconds, he moved on to Duke and poured a scoop of food in the dog's bowl. Duke slowly pushed to his feet and ambled to his bowl, his dog collar tags clinking together when he walked. Brandon ruffled Duke's ears, then went back to the fridge for a soda. What he wouldn't do for a beer, but with having a kid, Brandon hadn't wanted to keep alcohol in the house. So he settled for a Coke, twisting the cap off and tossing the thing on the counter.

From the living room, Matt chuckled, followed by a short response. Then he stood from the couch, cell phone in hand.

Brandon eyed the phone but didn't say anything. Didn't press for details. "Quick conversation," Brandon observed.

Matt shrugged and placed the phone on the kitchen counter, without making eye contact. Not good. "She had to go. She said she'd call me next week."

Brandon pulled a sip of his soda. "You gave her your number?"

"Sure."

Brandon nodded and ran his gaze over Matt's too long hair and firmly set mouth. "Everything okay?"

Matt crossed his arms over his chest. "Sure."

Brandon nodded again, because he was an idiot who couldn't seem to do anything else. "Want a soda?"

"Sure."

Brandon lifted a brow as he snagged another Coke from the fridge. "Can we try for something other than *sure*?"

Matt accepted the soda and twisted the cap and offered a half-smile. "Absolutely?"

Brandon returned the grin. "Smart-ass." They drank in silence for a moment, while Duke munched away on his dinner, scattering kibble all over the floor. "Seriously, Matt. No BS. You know you can talk to me."

Matt shrugged again and picked at the soda label. "I don't know. She sounded kind of weird."

"Probably because you haven't talked to her in a while."

"I guess."

More silence.

"She said the first time she called you wouldn't let her talk to me," Matt said.

Why would Trish say that to him? Was she trying to

make him out to be the bad guy? "I'm just trying to protect you, Matt. She's hurt you too many times in the past."

Red flushed into Matt's cheeks. "No, I know. I mean, I understand why you told her no. But she's still my mom. I don't want to be a dick to her or anything."

That was his boy. Always considerate of other people's feelings. "Yeah," Brandon agreed. Then he pointed the tip of his bottle toward Matt. "Except don't say dick." The oven dinged, so Brandon grabbed the bread and stuck it in to cook for fifteen minutes.

"I'm going to do some homework before dinner," Matt announced before he left the kitchen.

Brandon watched him leave with mixed feelings churning in his gut. How far would Trish allow this to go before Matt got too attached again? And what would happen when she eventually stopped calling, like all the other times? Brandon would be left to pick up the pieces.

"You're a sadistic bitch," Stella bit out as a bead of sweat rolled toward her temple.

Annabelle only grinned. "Keep it up with the compliments. You're so good at them."

"Bite me," Stella replied as she pushed through her last set of reps on the weight machine Annabelle had her on.

"And then do ten more," she instructed when Stella finished.

She lifted her head off the machine and pinned her best friend with a glare. "Seriously? Are you trying to kill me?"

Annabelle rolled her eyes. "Oh come on. You're barely breaking a sweat." She smacked Stella's sweaty shoulder.

Stella's leg quivered as she rolled through another ten reps. "When did you get so mean?"

Annabelle tilted her head and offered a sugary smile. "When I met you."

Stella huffed out a breath and stared at the ceiling. "One would think with all the amazing sex you're having with the hot football coach that you'd be nicer. You know, to those of us back on planet Earth who aren't getting any?"

"Well then go get yourself some." Annabelle busied herself with some strap on the machine. "With Brandon, for example."

Stella's foot slipped off the weight. "What? Have you lost your mind?"

Annabelle laughed, then slapped a hand over her mouth.

Stella stood from the machine and grabbed a water bottle. "Okay, next time you come to my studio, I'm going to make you wear my old pointe shoes and you'll have to dance around on your toes until I say stop." Stella paused when Annabelle only laughed harder. "Without the toe pads. I guarantee you won't be laughing when your feet are all bloody and your toenails fall off."

That last sentence put a halt to Annabelle's laughter. She scrunched her face. "Ew, do your toenails actually fall off?"

Stella shrugged, remembering the blinding pain in her feet from hours upon hours of dancing on her toes. "Yeah, you know. It happens."

Annabelle shook her head. "I'm fascinated and grossed out all at the same time."

Stella waved a hand in the air. "What can I say? I'm a slave to my art." At one point in time, those words had rung true. She'd been willing to endure any amount of pain to be the best, to get to the top. She'd hid the pain and her suspicions, until her ACL had given out on her during a grand pax de deux performance. That had been the beginning of the end.

"So, why not Brandon?" Annabelle pushed.

Stella groaned as she retrieved her bag from the floor. "Are we back to this?"

"Well—"

"Something's holding him back," Stella blurted out.

"Maybe Brandon just has a lot on his mind," Annabelle offered. "No, I'm serious," she went on, as though Stella was curious. Which she wasn't. Not even a little. "Trish has been calling—"

"Wait, what?" Stella straightened after pulling a pair of cotton pants out of her bag. "Trish? As in his ex-wife, Trisha?"

Annabelle blinked as though realizing when she'd said. "Did I say Trish?" Annabelle hedged. "Because I meant Carol." Her head bobbed up and down. "She's their third cousin on their mother's side. She lives in New York. You don't know her," Annabelle added in a rush.

Stella narrowed her eyes as she yanked on her pants. "Really? That's the best you can come up with?"

Annabelle's shoulders slumped. "I know. Blake says I can't lie worth a damn." She took a step forward as Stella pulled on her hooded sweatshirt. "I'm sorry, I overheard Blake and Cameron talking. I didn't think it would be right to say anything."

She shrugged and zipped her bag. "Why should I care who he talks to?"

"Right." Annabelle nodded. "You shouldn't."

"I don't." Except she did. Like, a lot.

"Yes, you do," Annabelle persisted. She gripped Stella's shoulders. "You love him."

Stella shook her head. "How could I love him? I don't even know what we have with each other."

"I didn't know with Blake, either. But that didn't stop me from falling for him," Annabelle admitted.

Stella blew out a breath. How could she love him? He drove her nuts. He picked on her and played pool with women named after poodles. He made her hot and drove her home when she'd had too much to drink. He loved his son more than he loved himself. He was also the only man who'd been able to touch her without sending her into a panic. He didn't make her feel like there was something wrong with her because she didn't like to be touched. He wanted to take apart the man who taken advantage of her.

Yeah. She loved him.

"What do I do?" she asked Annabelle.

Annabelle walked her to the door. "You could talk to Brandon."

Or she could eat herself into a sugar coma and then pass out in her own vomit. Yeah, sounded better. Less painful.

Stella opened the studio door, then paused. "Why do you think he didn't tell me?"

"Probably the same reason you haven't told him about Terry. Or Rick."

A shudder ran through her at the mention of two men. One she'd given up everything for. And the other had stolen something much more sacred.

THIRTEEN

Thumping salsa music greeted Stella as she opened the front door. Steeling herself for whatever horrors awaited her, she shut the door and walked toward the ruckus.

Gloria Davenport was dressed in black spandex pants and an off-the-shoulder magenta top with a yellow spaghetti strap tank top underneath. The coffee table had been pushed to the sliding glass door, allowing her mother to have plenty of room to . . . what the hell was she doing?

"Hey, honey," her mom greeted as she swung her arms over her head, then spun around in time with the music. On the television was . . . was it a video game? Or a music video? Stella couldn't tell. Gloria executed a little two-step thing, then dropped down to a lunge. . . . thingy. Whatever the hell.

"Mom . . ." Stella shook her head and dropped her gym bag on the floor. "What?"

"Zumba," Gloria answered. The song ended and the television cheered for what an awesome job her mom had done. Then the program moved into another song and Gloria readied herself.

"God have mercy," Stella whispered to herself.

"Want to join me?" Gloria asked as she swiveled her hips to a slower number. "This stuff kicks your butt. I've already burned, like, four hundred calories."

Stella tapped her leg with the palm of her hand. "Bum knee, Mom."

Gloria laughed as she kept her attention on the screen. "Sorry, honey. I forgot."

"That's all right. I've only told you about five hundred times," she muttered to herself. She flopped down on the recliner and blew out a breath.

"Okay." Gloria put a halt to her dancing, thank goodness, and shut the TV off. "What's wrong?"

"Nothing," she replied automatically.

Gloria jabbed her hands on her hips, which were looking abnormally smooth thanks to the spandex. "You have the look on your face."

"What look?"

"Like you've been chewing glass."

"You know, I've never understood that saying," Stella argued. "If I had actually been chewing glass, I wouldn't be sitting here all calm. I'd probably be bent over the toilet throwing up blood."

Gloria held her hands up. "It's just a saying."

"Well, it's stupid."

"Point taken," Gloria soothed. "I won't use it again." They sat in silence with Gloria fiddling with the hem of her shirt and Stella wishing the floor would swallow her whole. "I know what'll cheer you up." She grabbed for some papers off the coffee table and held them up for Stella to see.

"What're those?"

"These"—Gloria rattled them with a big grin on her face—"are the papers for the lease agreement I signed this morning."

The words Stella had been waiting to hear. "Lease?" she asked, trying not to sound too excited.

"Yep," her mom responded. "For a three-bedroom ranch house about two blocks from here."

Stella shook her head. "You're renting a house?"

Gloria nodded. The idea should have elated her. But for some reason she felt like shit. Like the worst daughter who'd been counting the minutes until her mother left. Some people didn't have mothers. And she'd been wishing for hers to leave.

Gloria glanced at the papers in her hand, then at Stella. "Well, yeah. You've been wanting me to find my own place since I got here."

Stella nodded. "Yeah."

Gloria blinked, then set the papers on the coffee table. "Okay." She came and hunkered down in front of Stella. "What's really wrong?" When Stella didn't answer right away, Gloria took her hands. "Tell Mommy about it."

Stella looked down at their clasped hands. "It's nothing."

Gloria shook her head. "It's not nothing if it makes my baby upset."

But it had to be nothing. If she made her love for Brandon into something, it would fudge all her plans up. Not only did he not love her back, but she'd also start second-guessing her decision to leave. It was the most sacred vow she'd made to herself and she had to follow through with it. Otherwise the regret would be too much for her to live with.

What about the regret over Brandon?

What if they could really have something? What if her

decision to fulfill a lifelong dream dashed away a chance at something real?

She dropped her head back to the chair. "I love a man," she admitted.

Gloria was silent a moment. "Maybe I'm confused. But shouldn't that make you happy?"

Not if the man didn't love her back. And leave it to her mom to make it sound so simple. Everything was simple to Gloria.

"Explain to me why this is a problem," her mother prompted.

"You wouldn't understand," Stella argued.

"Why, because I've never been in a real relationship?" Gloria countered.

Stella lifted her head and looked at her mom. "I didn't mean—"

"It's okay." She sat back on her heels and rubbed a hand over Stella's bad knee. "I know you don't take me seriously. I've never given you any reason to. I wasn't even going to try and give you advice or anything. I was just"—she lifted one shoulder—"going to listen. Because sometimes we need someone who'll just listen."

Going to her mother with her problems wasn't something Stella was experienced with. And how sad was that? Gloria had been too consumed with her own life to notice anything wrong with Stella's. So she'd learned from a young age how to keep everything bottled up. Not to burden anyone else. Handle it herself. Which she had. So much that she'd become good at it. She'd learned the art of humor as a defense mechanism. When someone got too close, throw them off with humor.

Was that what she'd done with Brandon? Was that why their relationship had never progressed? Because she'd been unknowingly pushing him away? Keeping him away from the darkness that lurked underneath the sunshine. Not allowing him to help, because helping herself had become so second nature that she automatically pulled away from someone who had nothing more than good intentions.

"I can't love him," she told her mom.

Gloria tilted her head to one side. "Why the heck not?"

"Well for one thing, he doesn't love me back. He's...cautious." *Like me.* "He's been burned before. So he won't get into a relationship with anyone unless he's sure it's the real deal."

"And why can't it be the real deal with you?"

Stella lifted her shoulders "Because I'm leaving."

"But not forever," Gloria pointed out.

"Yeah, but..." What had been her argument again? She couldn't even remember now. "What if he's moved on when I come back? Or what if they offer me a full-time teaching position?"

Gloria folded her hands on Stella's knees. "Does he know how you feel about him?"

Knowing Brandon, he probably had a good idea. "I don't think so."

Gloria laughed, as though her daughter's logic was hopelessly flawed. "Well, how can he know not to move on if he has no idea how you feel? How do you know he won't wait for you?"

Because Brandon wasn't the waiting type. He'd want to jump in, headfirst, and then Stella wouldn't be able to extract herself. Physically or emotionally.

"Honey." Gloria leaned forward and rested her hands on Stella's thighs. "I may not have any clue what to do in a relationship, but I know what not to do. And it's this."

Stella's brow pinched. "What?"

"Sulking," her mom answered. "Hiding. Not taking a chance."

"I'm not sulking," Stella muttered.

"But you're hiding," her mom pressed.

She'd been hiding for so long that Stella hadn't even realized she'd been doing it anymore. First, hiding behind her dancing. The stage and the movements had taken the place of loneliness and insecurity, instead showing the world a strong, confident young woman who could tackle anything. Then humor had been her vice, masking the loss of her passion and pushing people away before they could scratch too deep.

"I've never really told you about your dad," Gloria went on, surprising Stella with the subject matter. Her mom never talked about Stella's dad. She'd always brushed it off as a casual thing that had resulted in pregnancy and her father hadn't been interested in a baby.

"Yeah, you have," she reminded her mom.

Gloria shook her head. "Not the whole story." She fiddled with a piece of lint on Stella's leg and blew out a breath. "Your dad never knew about you."

She stared at the top of her mom's head, taking in the stray strands of gray hair growing amongst the darker ones. "What do you mean? You told me he took off after you got pregnant."

"I lied," her mom whispered. "He . . . We had one summer together, and I fell in love with him." Gloria swallowed. "He had already made plans to go back to college in the fall. And I honestly didn't think I meant anything to him. He never told me he loved me, never talked about calling me or writing. We were just having some fun. Fooling around like kids do. So I let him leave without telling him how I felt."

"Or about me," Stella concluded, trying to make sense of

her mother's story, which was completely different from the one she'd grown up believing. Why hadn't her mom told her the real story?

"I didn't find out I was pregnant until three weeks after he left. And this was before cell phones and I didn't know his family."

Stella inhaled and tried to squash down the ache in her chest. "Why didn't you tell him how you felt before he left?"

Gloria sat back on her heels and stared at Stella out of tear-rimmed eyes. Was that guilt Stella saw? Or regret? She could never be too sure with her mom.

"Because I knew he didn't feel the same way about me," she answered. "He was already at Notre Dame, and I didn't want to hold him back for some small-town girl who had nothing to offer him."

"So..." Stella glanced around the room, unable to look at her mom. "My father has no idea I exist?"

"Oh, honey, I..." Gloria pushed her hair back out of her face. "I'm sorry."

Stella stood and paced the room. "And so the moral of the story is I should tell Brandon how I feel so I don't live with the same regret, right? Is that why you told me this...this little fable so I don't make the same mistake you did?"

Gloria stood and wrung her hands. "Honey, I...at the time I thought I was making the right decision." She paced the floor, alternating between sniffing and running her hands through her hair. "I was so young, and I didn't really have anyone. Your grandparents had kicked me out of the house, so I went to live with my grandma three hours away. And then after you were born, I was exhausted and over-whelmed." She pinned Stella with watery, sorrowful eyes.

Stella bit back a lump of remorse for lashing out at her mom. "Honestly I never meant for it to be this way. I did the best I could with you, Stella. You have to know that."

Stella's head jerked up. "The best you could, Mom? Really? Dragging me all over the country every few months so I never made any friends was the best you could do? Slipping into a three-week depression after another man walked out on you was the best you could do?"

Gloria's red-rimmed eyes widened, showcasing disbelief at Stella's accusations. But how could she not know? How could she have been so oblivious all those years? "Stella, what're you talking about? That's not how it was."

"Wasn't it, though? That may not be how you remember it, but that was my reality," Stella continued. "You being emotionally unavailable for me when yet another loser took off. And then dragging me to another city with more empty promises that everything would be different. 'You'll see this time, baby,'" Stella repeated the same speech Gloria had given her over and over again. "'It'll all be different now.' That's what you used to say to me. But it never was, Mom. It was never different. It was always the same story no matter where we were. We'd be good for about a month, and then you'd shut yourself in your room for two days when another jerk-off left after getting what he wanted from you. And I was left to make my own dinners and walk to the bus stop so I could make it to my dance classes on time. Then I'd have to bum a ride home from a friend and have to lie to their mom about where you were." Stella plugged on, ignoring the devastation on her mom's face. "I knew, when I got to our apartment, I'd find you in the exact same position you'd been in when I left. Tucked under your covers with a half-drunk bottle of Scotch on the nightstand."

Out of breath and drained from dredging up memories she swore she'd never unearth again, Stella jabbed her hands on her hips and slowly inhaled. Her heart was hammering in her throat, heating her cheeks and bringing forth the familiar bout of panic.

"Stella—" her mom whispered.

"And then," Stella interrupted, "having to watch you parade around with Terry as I tried to hide my disgust when the creep had copped a feel in the kitchen the night before. Knowing I had to hide my feelings about him, because once he took off, you'd slip back into your shell like nothing else in your life mattered." Stella swallowed when her voice broke. "Including me."

Gloria reached for her with a trembling hand. Stella ignored her mother's distress and stepped around her, snagging her purse off the floor. "I can't talk about this anymore." She opened the front door and tossed her mom one final look. "I want you gone when I get back."

The door slammed behind her, shutting off her mom's cry of despair.

Brandon drew his arms back over his head, gripping the golf club with two hands, and took one last look at the empty net on the other side of the yard. He brought his arms down in a wide arc and tagged the golf ball with a satisfying *whack*. And it went flying over the lawn. The little white ball landed in the net, creating a nice dent with a satisfying *whoosh* along with it.

"Not so bad," he muttered to himself. He picked his bottle of beer off the deck railing and took a deep pull, then eyed Duke, who was stretched out on his side on the lawn. "What d'you think, bud? Pretty good for a non-golfer, huh?"

Duke thumped his tail on the grass in show of his support. Yeah, Duke was faithful like that.

Brandon replaced the bottle on the railing and picked up his golf club. Snagging another ball, he dragged the thing over and lined up another shot. This time he missed and the ball sailed into Virginia McAllister's yard. He winced when he heard the ball land in the shrubs.

He hooked his club around another golf ball and braced his feet apart for another shot. He was just about to bring his arms back when Duke let out a deep bark.

Brandon kept the club over his head, not wanting to break stride for what was sure to be a money shot. "Hush," was all he told the dog.

But Duke jumped up off the grass and barked again, this time with more enthusiasm. With a heavy sigh, Brandon dropped his arms. "Dude, do ya mind?" he asked the dog, and turned to see what had disturbed his otherwise introverted animal.

And froze when he laid eyes on Stella, standing just outside his sliding glass door, looking so damn lost and beautiful that the breath left his lungs.

"Sorry," she blurted out. "I, uh"—she gestured behind her—"I rang the bell and no one answered, so I let myself in." She replaced her two-handed grip on a gift bag with tissue paper sticking out of the top. "I saw your truck was here, so I took a chance." She stroked Duke behind his ears after he'd finally made it up the deck stairs to greet her.

"It's fine," he told her.

Seriously? That's all you can say?

She held up the bag. "I have a birthday gift for Matt. I was out and thought I'd drop it off."

Brandon leaned the golf club against the railing. "But his birthday isn't until next week."

"I know," she answered, still petting Duke's head, whose eyes were probably rolling shut. "But I know how busy he is and I had a free moment, so I wanted to give it to him now."

Brandon took the steps to the deck two at a time until he stood in front of her. "He's not home. He's at a friend's house studying for a test."

Stella nodded and dropped her gaze to Duke, who was staring up at her with half-closed eyes while she rubbed one ear and then the other.

"Everything okay?" Brandon asked her after noticing her bloodshot eyes, swollen lips, and tear-streaked cheeks. Brandon wanted to pummel the person who'd sucked the life out of her clear blue eyes and replaced it with misery.

Her gaze flickered to his long enough to know she was about to lie. "Sure." She held the bag up. "I'll come back next week and give it to Matt."

Brandon took the bag from her fingers. "You can just leave it here and I'll give it to him."

She blinked at him, sweeping her dark lashes down long enough to display exhaustion along with whatever else had happened to her. "All right," she answered.

So then...Was she going to leave now? A moment of panic shot through his system at the thought of her turning around and walking out the front door. Of course, it would be crazy for her to stay. In his house. Alone. For the rest of the evening. Where his bedroom was. Definitely dangerous territory.

At the same time, he could use the opportunity to show her he wasn't the ass she thought he was. That they could be capable of having a conversation that didn't either end in them bickering or shoving their tongues down each other's throats.

He gestured toward the golf net on the other side of the yard. "Want to hit a few balls?"

She glanced over his shoulder. "I don't really golf."

"Neither do I." He set the gift bag on the patio table and wrapped his palm around the back of her neck. "But you look like you need to hit something."

She slid him a look as he led her down the deck stairs. "Gee, thanks."

Her neck was slender and cool, just the right size for his palm to fit and tease the loose hairs at the base of her ponytail. He allowed his hand to linger, even though she was perfectly capable of walking on her own. But he liked touching her. Even more than that, he liked how her breath shuddered when his thumb stroked behind her ear.

So maybe their conversations would end with more tongue dancing. Seemed as though they didn't have much of a choice around each other. Fight or make out? No brainer, if you asked him.

He reluctantly dropped his hand, missing her softness, and handed her the golf club. She accepted it, then just stood there with it dangling in her hand.

"You know how to hit a golf ball, right?"

She ran her attention down the club, as though she didn't have the faintest idea how to operate the thing. "I spent every spare minute of my time in a dance studio. What do you think?"

Her question had him grinning and he took a step toward her in order to help her. But she held up a hand to stop him.

"But I'm sure I can figure it out," she told him.

In other words, no touching. Message received loud and clear. He held his hands up. "Have at it, then. Just don't hit it into Mrs. McAllister's yard. I've been on her shit list for about ten years."

She grinned and dangled the club from her index finger and thumb and looked the thing over. Then she gripped it between both hands, but her grip was way too low on the club, and her feet were too close together.

"Spread your legs a little," he told her.

She eyed him over her shoulder.

"Get your mind out of the gutter," he instructed. Although he wouldn't mind joining her there. "Your feet were just too close together."

With a long sigh, she adjusted her footing and lined up her shot. She'd just drawn the club back when he made a noise to stop her. "Now what?" she demanded.

"Don't twist the club when you swing back. Otherwise the ball won't go straight."

She blinked at him and scratched her cheek.

"You don't know what I mean, do you?" he questioned.

She scrunched her nose, which was damn cuter than it should have been. "Not really."

"But you were so sure you could figure it out," he reminded her.

Her foot tapped a rapid rhythm on the grass. "You're going to make me ask, aren't you?"

He grinned. "Yep."

"Fine." She thrust the club at him. "Show me how, O Lord of the Golf Course."

He accepted the club from her. "You're cute when you're cranky."

She narrowed her eyes at him. "I'm not cranky. I'm annoyed."

Brandon aligned himself with the net, noting how Stella had taken a step back when he'd gotten too close to her. Interesting. "A mood that I've become well acquainted with." He braced his feet apart and placed his hands together on the rubber grip. "First of all, your hands should be together like this and higher on the club. Next, when you draw the club back." He demonstrated so she could see. "You want to keep the head of the club level with the ball. Don't twist it like this." He turned the head to the side as she had done. When he shot her a look, her attention wasn't on his demonstration. She yanked her eyes off his ass and pinned them on his. "Care for a more one-on-one instruction?"

She offered him a sweet smile. "Over my dead body."

He shrugged and handed the club over. "Bummer."

She accepted it from him, careful not to touch his hands even though he'd let them linger before letting go of the club. He took a step back and allowed his attention to drop to her plump rear end. Such a nice ass. A perfect handful. All he had to do was take one step closer and he could nuzzle her right in the crook of his hips. He bet she'd fit perfectly there. Maybe even give him a little wiggle and—

"Over there," she told him, pointing to a spot on the grass next to her.

He decided to play innocent. "I'm just standing here," he said with a lift of his shoulders.

She narrowed her eyes. "No, you weren't." She waved her index finger in his direction. "I know what you're doing back there, and I don't want you standing behind me." She snapped her fingers and pointed to the same spot next to her. "Now move your ass."

How's about you move your *ass?*

He snickered and did as instructed, keeping his eyes on hers to prove that he could be around her and not ogle her spankable derriere. And someone ought to give him a medal for that fine piece of playacting. After they established their respectable, or, in his case not-so-respectable, corners, Stella returned to the task at hand. Only she miscalculated her swing, and the club bit into the ground and didn't hit the ball with enough force. It shot about a foot in the air and bounced a few times before settling.

She shoved the club against his chest. "Well, that was fun. But I'm due for some Chinese water torture now."

"Not so fast." He hooked his index finger in the collar of her shirt and put a halt to her hasty exit. He let out a breath and dropped both hands to her shoulders. "Stella, Stella, Stella." He steered her back to where she'd been standing. "We both know the perfectionist in you wants to get this right," he chided, lowering his head to speak in her ear. And yeah, he was right about her ass aligning perfectly against his hips. Sweet Mercy she did things to his libido.

"I'm not a perfectionist," she murmured. Was she breathing heavy? Or was that him unable to control his reaction around her? "I actually pride myself on being an epic screwup. You can ask anyone," she continued. "I hate doing things right. In fact, you could even call me an imperfectionist." Now she was babbling, which meant she was just as flustered and turned on as he was.

"Hush," he told her. Then he brought the club around to her front and placed it in her hands. Because she'd all but gone limp on him, he had to physically wrap her palms around the club. Not that he was complaining. No, he'd use any excuse to touch her. Her chest expanded, nudging her plush breasts against his biceps. The contact created a jolt of awareness straight to his groin, where he instantly hardened. He eased his hips away from her so she wouldn't feel his reaction to her. Stella was already on edge and the last thing he wanted to do was send her running in the opposite direction.

Instead, he wanted to send her running straight to his bedroom.

"Now," he said against her ear. And yeah, he may have

nuzzled her a little with his nose. "Pay attention because I'm only going to demonstrate this one more time. We both know you're not going to be able to fake your indifference much longer."

"You're pushing it," she warned him.

He chuckled against her neck, enjoying the hell out of how her whole body went rigid. Yeah, definitely not indifferent. Then, just because he'd always been one to test his boundaries, he pressed a soft kiss beneath her ear, allowing his lips to linger and savor how incredibly soft she was. How good she smelled and tasted even better.

Her breath huffed out. "Brandon," she whispered. "Stop."

His eyes dropped closed as he inhaled her intoxicating scent. Sort of like a warm summer breeze blowing off the ocean. It was enough to make a man drop to his knees and howl at the moon. Or maybe drop his pants and piss a circle around her. Not exactly romantic, but his primal side wanted to do exactly that so that all the other guys in this town knew to stay the hell away.

"Do I bother you, Stella?" he asked against her ear.

The golf club dropped from her limp hands. "Yes, you bother me."

"Good. Because it's probably not half as much as you bother me."

With the golf club gone, Brandon's hands were free to explore. They went to Stella's thighs first, spreading and spanning her lean muscles, prompting images of them wrapped around his hips. She expelled another long breath when his palms slid up her legs to grip her hips. His fingers ran along the hem of her shirt, skimming her sensitive, creamy soft skin. Damn, how he wanted to drop his mouth there and trail kisses across her stomach. He bet she'd be responsive. Because Stella didn't do anything half-heartedly. No, she threw herself into everything she did with a single-minded determination that was one hell of a turn-on.

"How about some dinner?" he questioned.

"Huh?" she squeaked when this thumb pushed under her shirt and found her belly button.

"Dinner. It's the meal that follows lunch," he explained. "I have some steaks marinating in the fridge."

A flush of red stained her cheeks. "Don't be an ass," she scolded. "I just don't know how you can go from"—she gestured between the two of them—"whatever that was, to offering dinner."

"We could always go back to golf," he suggested.

"I think my golfing days are over."

He closed the distance between them and cupped her face with his hands, tilting her head up so he could speak against her lips. "Stella," he whispered against her mouth. "I'm going to lose my shit if I don't find something to do with my hands, other than shove them up your shirt." He looked into her sky-blue eyes. "Or you can make your way to the front door. The choice is yours."

She licked her lips and toyed with the collar of his shirt. "Do you have any more of that beer?"

FOURTEEN

Stella wandered around in Brandon's spacious kitchen, bypassing the large island for the fridge. Pinned to the stainless steel doors with magnets was a grocery list and a note to remind someone to grab another prescription for Duke's heartworm medication. There were also several photos that caught her attention.

Stella pointed to one with Matt in a navy blue cap and gown, holding a black diploma with Brandon's arm slung around his son's shoulders. Both had ear-to-ear grins. "What's this from?"

Brandon abandoned his chopping at the counter and glanced at the photo. "Matt's eighth-grade graduation."

She scrutinized the photo while sipping on her wine, noting how much Matt had grown since then. "He looks so much younger here."

"You're telling me." Brandon's voice so close behind Stella almost made her spill her wine.

She took another sip to calm her nerves. "I would say it's crazy how fast they grow up, but I wouldn't really know." She turned to face him and almost succumbed to her desire to brush her mouth across his. To hide the heat scorching her cheeks, Stella ducked around him and eyed the dinner Brandon was in the process of preparing. "Need any help with all this?"

He gazed at her for a moment, his clever eyes missing nothing and scanning her face before answering. "No, I've got it." He returned to the counter and resumed his work. "Cooking is one of the many things you learn how to do as a single parent."

Annabelle's revelation about Trish came back, but Stella pushed the curiosity aside. Hell yeah, she wanted to know the story behind that one. She also wanted to know how it was affecting Brandon. If he needed anyone to talk to. If he was worried or confused or hurt. Unfortunately, it wasn't any of Stella's business to pry, nor was she the person to comfort him. Even though she wanted to.

She feigned a casualness she didn't feel and leaned against the counter. "I never pegged you for someone who could cook." When he slanted her a doubting look, she held her hands up. "No offense or anything. I just thought you wouldn't have the patience for all this. Personally I'd rather throw a pizza in the oven and be done with it."

Brandon snorted. "Bite your tongue. Food is a delicacy that deserves time and effort. Can't just be throwing shit together willy-nilly." He snagged a sliced piece of the already grilled steak and held it out to her. "Try some of that."

When she moved to take the meat from his hand, Brandon held it back and shook his head. "Nope. I get to do it and you have to close your eyes."

"Are you kidding me?"

One of his dark brows arched. "Do you trust me, Stella?"

She narrowed her eyes at him. "I'm not sure."

He blew out a breath. "When we sit down to eat, I want you to have an appreciation for the steak. You can't just jump in and attack it. It needs to be finessed and appreciated."

"You do realize it's a piece of meat and not the *Mona Lisa*?"

"Just close your eyes or I'm sticking you with dish duty."

"Not if we use paper plates."

He didn't reply. Just stood there waiting patiently like he had all the time in the world.

She lifted her eyes to the ceiling and decided to appease him. "Fine." She held up her index finger. "But the steak is the only thing that goes in here," she warned with a gesture toward her mouth.

"You were that kid in class who reminded the teacher about the test, weren't you?"

"You say that like it's a bad thing," she protested.

"Just open your mouth and close your eyes before you give your portion to Duke." Then he lowered his mouth to her ear. "Because I don't give my meat to just any woman."

When she opened her mouth to tell him where he could shove his meat, he tossed the piece he'd been holding on her tongue. And, holy shit, it was good. Smoky and spicy and rich. And the stuff damn near melted like butter on her tongue.

"Mmm," she agreed while chewing, swallowing the whole thing at once. "I can't even," she said with a shake of her head. It was the kind of deliciousness found in a five-star restaurant. One that would come with funky garnishes and cost about forty bucks.

Brandon grinned, fully aware of how good he was.

"Right?" he said. "No more blasphemous talk about frozen pizzas."

Stella shook her head. "That was amazing."

He picked up a pair of tongs and shooed her away from the counter. "Now go sit down. I just have to finish with the spinach."

Stella retrieved her glass of wine from the counter. "I can dish my own plate."

"Yeah right. You'll have us eating off paper towels."

"And you've never eaten off a paper towel."

He tossed the spinach around in the skillet and then drizzled more oil on top. "Maybe when I was six." Then he set the tongs down, turned her from the counter, and smacked her ass. "Go. Sit."

Of all the...rude things to do! Smacking her on the ass as though his wandering, yet delightfully playful, hand had every right to make contact with her derriere. Who did he think he was? As though it was supposed to turn her on? As though he knew it turned her on? She sat at the table and eyed his wide shoulders and back, admiring how his T-shirt stretched with just enough tightness to elicit little tingles in her belly. Yeah, the man filled out a shirt like nobody's business.

Before her thoughts went any further, Brandon finished dinner and approached the table with two plates. He set hers down first, because he was a gentleman like that, then took his own seat.

He'd poured some kind of buttery cream sauce on the steak and gave her a healthy dose of spinach and roasted red potatoes.

"Do you cook like this every night?" Stella asked as she placed her napkin in her lap.

"Nah," Brandon replied as he dug into his own food.

"Matt's gone a lot, either with football or his girlfriend." He eyed her as he chewed his steak.

"My mom was gone a lot too," she replied with a shrug. Just shrug it off because it's always okay.

Brandon's silverware clinked against the plate as he cut his food. "Your dad was never around?"

Stella's food sank to the pit of her stomach like a brick at the mention of her father. She'd managed to block out her earlier fight with her mom, even though it had only happened about two hours ago. But she'd pushed it down along with the emotional toll it had taken on her. Anger and hurt over being lied to. Guilt at the look of grief on her mom's face and the way Stella had spoken to her. Driving through town with tears streaming down her face, wondering if there would ever be a time in her life when she'd be at peace. A time when she wouldn't be kicking herself for giving up on her dream for a man. Or taking care of her sick grandmother. Or constantly trying to keep her anxiety in check or pretend she didn't want to throw up when someone got too close to her. How did people live normal lives? How did they go from day to day without waiting for the other shoe to drop?

Tears burned the back of her eyes as she tried to ready an appropriate response to Brandon's question. She drew from her years of practice and pulled herself together. "I never knew my dad," she finally answered, keeping her attention on her plate. If she didn't look at Brandon, he wouldn't see the lies swirling in her eyes. Or the paper-thin control that would snap if she let her guard down.

When Brandon remained silent, Stella risked a glance. His fork was loosely gripped in his left hand, but his gaze was sharp, as though patiently waiting for her to figure her shit out. Waiting for her to sort through the mess of her life so she could confide in him.

Wasn't going to happen. She hadn't even told Annabelle about her fight with her mom, and she certainly wasn't going to tell Brandon.

"I'm sorry," was all he said.

She shrugged again because she was so good at it. "It is what it is. He took off before I was born and my mom did her best with me." Except she hadn't, but Stella left that part out.

"Did she?" Brandon asked.

Stella paused in the act of stabbing her fork into a potato. "Did she what?"

"Do her best with you?"

She snagged the potato and dropped it in her mouth. "Under the circumstances, I guess." Perhaps Gloria had thought she was doing her best.

Thankfully, Brandon let the subject drop. Darkness had fallen while they polished off their meals and talked about other things. Safe things, like the football season and Blake and Annabelle's upcoming spring wedding.

But he knew she was hiding something. She could see it in his eyes when they searched hers, as though looking for the secret she refused to share. While she appreciated that he didn't pry, Stella knew it was only a matter of time before she'd have to come clean. Their relationship could never go beyond casual flirting and heated kisses if she couldn't be honest with him. Being her own worst enemy would put a stop to things with him before they'd have a chance to start.

After dinner, Stella had moved to the living room. Brandon was in the kitchen washing dishes, despite her offering to do them. He'd shooed her out, much the same way he had before, minus the ass pat. Much to her disappointment. Against her better judgment, she'd refilled her glass of wine. Considering what had happened the last time she'd drunk too much, getting an eyeful of Brandon's bare ass in the men's room, Stella should have held off. But the wine was sweet and warm in her system, relaxing her when she otherwise would have been wound tight with nerves. Nerves from her afternoon with her mom and wanting Brandon so damn bad she could hardly stand it.

She sipped from her glass and scanned photos on the fireplace mantel. The framed pictures varied from Matt's football pictures to ones of him in diapers. A five-by-seven in the middle caught her eye. It was a picture-perfect summertime photo at the beach of Brandon on his stomach in the sand, with Matt on his stomach also, perched on his dad's back. Both had wet sandy hair and big smiles and were squinting in the sun. Matt looked no more than seven or eight and Brandon...well, he looked like he always did. Larger than life, bare shoulders, twice as wide as his son's. Strong. Solid. And like he could tackle anything thrown his way. Slay dragons and all that. Because men were supposed to do that kind of thing, weren't they? Stella wouldn't know because she'd never had a man willing to put himself out there like that. Or anyone, really. Including her own mother.

As she studied the picture, absorbing the bond between Brandon and Matt, for the first time she realized what she'd been missing out on. Matt, even though he didn't have a mother, still had everything Stella had lacked. Stability. Comfort. Confidence. But more than that, he had someone who put his needs first.

A tear leaked out, which Stella hastily dashed away. Did Matt realize how lucky he was? Did he know what a prince of a dad he had? A man who would kill himself before allowing Matt to be hurt in any way?

She jolted, sloshing her wine, when Brandon's hands came down on her shoulders.

"Stella," he said in a low voice. "I've ignored this all night. Plus you're breaking my rules. Anyone who cries in my house has to tell me why."

"I'm not crying," she answered automatically.

He chuckled, warm and low next to her ear. Then he turned her to face him and took the wineglass from her sweaty hand. He sighed and cupped her face with his hands. "Stella," he soothed. "Don't you ever get exhausted?"

All the time. She dropped her gaze to his firm mouth because seeing the knowledge in his eyes was too much. "I don't know what you mean."

His thumbs stroked the sensitive skin beneath her ear. "I mean holding up those walls of yours. Don't you ever get tired?"

He had no idea how tiresome it was, making everyone think she was just another face in the crowd. That she wasn't certifiably messed up in the head.

She toyed with the collar of his shirt. "You don't know what you're asking. There are things I've never told anyone." As though on cue, her cell buzzed and Stella knew who it was. With a heavy sigh, she drew her phone out of her back pocket.

PLEASE call me. Let's talk about this, Stella.

Stella shook her head and turned her phone off, still not in the mood to talk to Gloria. Their earlier confrontation was still too fresh in her mind, and she'd yet to work through her own issues. She'd been too busy processing the information.

"Does that have something to do with why you're upset?" Brandon's voice startled her out of her thoughts.

"That was my mom," she found herself answering.

"And you have a complicated relationship with her," he guessed.

Stella snorted as she sat on the couch. "That's putting it mildly." She leaned back, absorbing the soft, cool leather, wishing everything in life could be as soft and giving. "I told you earlier that I never knew my dad," she said while staring at the ceiling.

"Yeah," came Brandon's quiet reply.

"I just found out that I never knew him because my mom never told him about me."

"Ouch," Brandon said.

A humorless laugh popped out of her. "Yeah, ouch. I'd grown up thinking he left my mom after she told him she was pregnant. My mom's been lying to me my whole life."

"At least he didn't choose to leave," Brandon countered.

Stella lifted her head and looked at him. Strong and silent, as though he could chase away her anger and frustration with one swipe of his strong hand. "What?" she questioned.

Brandon shrugged. "Can't blame him for something he didn't know about."

Stella stood. "I'm not angry with him. I'm angry with my mom." She took two steps toward him. "I'm angry because she's been lying to me. I'm angry that she never came to a back-to-school night because whatever guy she was with had promised her the world, or how she wasn't there to celebrate with me with I earned a spot on the Chicago Ballet Company or when I was promoted to principal dancer." Stella couldn't stop the words if she wanted to. Brandon remained in his spot, waiting her out with his usual patience. "She wasn't there when I tore my ACL or when I was taking care of my grandmother while she threw up from the chemo treatments." She took a breath. "She was never there, Brandon."

"I know," he agreed quietly.

She jabbed him in the chest with a finger. "No, you don't know. No one knows what it's been like. No one knows what it's like to have a mom who brings a monster into your house. A man who puts his arm around your mother and then when she's not looking feels you up in the kitchen and tells you to just go with it because he knows you want it just as much as he does." A hefty amount of bile rose in Stella's throat as soon as the words left her. For some people the admission might have been cathartic. To her it was horrifying. To just spew all that ugliness out, with no amount of sugarcoating for Brandon to see, was all her worst fears come to fruition.

She squeezed her eyes shut and spun from him, managing to stay on two feet when the floor tilted beneath her. Perhaps it was the wine. Or perhaps it was the familiar, yet unwanted, anxiety washing over her. Either way, she couldn't stay one minute more and get another glimpse of the pity in Brandon's eyes.

"I have to go," she blurted out.

"Stella," Brandon said from behind her.

"No." She shook her head, snatching her purse from the couch and bypassing Duke. He gazed up at her with those soulful brown eyes as though he understood her sorrow. Stella would have loved to bury her face in his soft fur, but that would have made her pathetic. Sobbing into a dog's neck? Who did that? "I'm sorry, but I can't talk about this."

"Really?" Brandon questioned as he followed her down the hall toward the front door. "Because I'm kind of thinking you need to."

She spun around just as she reached the door, barely able to make out his form when her vision blurred from built up tears. "You don't know what I need." And then she was gone. Throwing open the front door just in time for the tears to flood her cheeks. She thought she heard Brandon plead with her one more time, begging her not to leave. What did he know? He had a perfect life with a perfect son and a perfect aunt and uncle who'd doted on him and given him everything a child needed.

A sob broke free as she fumbled for her keys, only to drop them because her hands wouldn't stop trembling and she couldn't freakin' see because of the tears she was unable to control. They flowed too freely, symbolizing years of repressing anger and pretending to be stronger than she really was. Weren't tears supposed to be liberating? Weren't they supposed to be freeing or some shit like that? Instead all they did was reveal what a fraud she was, exposing her own weaknesses and mocking her.

Stella leaned against her car and buried her face in her hands while she sobbed out years of fear and frustration and anger she'd so expertly held back. She barely budged when a pair of strong hands wrapped around her shoulders and steered her away from her car. Didn't look up when Brandon walked her back inside the house and closed the door behind them. Barely noticed Duke nudging her leg with his wet nose or Brandon pushing him away. Not only was she too embarrassed for the object of all her fantasies to see her like a sniveling three-year-old, but she was also too busy with her face in her hands.

She was lowered to the couch, and Brandon disappeared somewhere. Without a word, he returned with a box of tissues, which she accepted. Without looking at him, because how pathetic was she? She went through about five tissues before coming up for air, then reached for another because she still wasn't ready to look at him yet.

How had she allowed herself to act this way? How did

years of practice and stone-cold emotions erode in one evening?

"Need something to drink?" Brandon asked in a low voice. Quiet and comforting. Cautious.

Stella shook her head and yanked another tissue out of the box. "I'm sorry," she told him.

Brandon tucked a piece of hair behind her ear, allowing his hand to linger on her face. "For what? Being human?"

Stella snorted and toyed with her wadded tissue. "This isn't human," she argued. "This is the funeral scene from *Steel Magnolias*."

Brandon was silent for a moment. "I won't pretend to know what that means."

She laughed, despite the uncontrollable garden hose spewing from her eyes. "Most men don't." She pulled in a shuddering breath. "I hate her," she whispered.

Brandon put an arm around her shoulders and ran his fingers through her hair. "No, you don't."

"You have a really annoying habit of trying to tell me how I feel," she shot back.

"Not trying to overstep bounds or anything," he reassured. "But you wouldn't be this upset if you hated her. You're this upset because you love her."

She blew out a breath, thankful the waterworks had finally subsided. Her eyes were dry, but the rest of her felt carved out and hollow. "I guess you're right." Brandon's arm along the back of the couch, cradling her head, felt good. Comforting and strong and solid. The perfect juxtaposition to her life. And how ironic was that? A man who was all wrong for her in every way represented everything she'd spent her life looking for. She sounded like a living synopsis for a Nicholas Sparks movie.

"Does she know?" Brandon asked, voice low and deep.

"Does she know my love/hate relationship with her?"

He chuckled, which rumbled deep in his chest. "Smart-ass. Does she know she brought a man into your life who took advantage of you?"

Stella continued to shred the tissue in her hands. "She does now," she answered, remembering their earlier confrontation. The confusion and hurt in her mother's eyes. Stella's regret over her outburst and finding it so easy to talk to her own mother that way. What kind of daughter did that? Moisture welled in her eyes again, reminding Stella she was a long way from self-awareness.

Brandon's arms tightened around her shoulders. "Don't do that again."

"Do crying women make you uncomfortable?" she queried. Even though she doubted much of anything made Brandon West uncomfortable.

"Depends on what they're crying about," he answered. "But you?" He gave her hair a playful tug. "Makes me uncomfortable as hell."

Instinctively, Stella pulled away but Brandon's arm tightened on her shoulder, preventing her escape. His nose nuzzled her hair. "Don't think you need to hide from me, Stella. Seeing you cry makes me want to comfort you. All my chivalrous instincts come out, but if I put my hands on you, we both know where it'll lead."

"But you're putting your hands on me now," she pointed out.

He grunted some noncommittal answer and pulled her tighter. His heartbeat sure and even beneath his chest contradicting the up and down of her own heart.

"He never raped me," she blurted. Because, for some reason, she needed him to know.

"You don't have to tell me about it, Stella," Brandon said.

But she needed to. Didn't he realize she'd never be able to move forward until she forced herself to confront it?

"It's okay," she pressed. "But I need you to know that he never forced himself on me like that."

Brandon turned to look at her. "Any kind of force on a woman is too far," he told her. "I don't care what kind of contact it is. Force is force."

She nodded, understanding his logic and feeling her insides melt at the fierceness in his eyes. "The first time it happened, I was shocked. So shocked that I thought someone was playing a practical joke on me. Because something like that couldn't be real, right?" she asked Brandon as though he had the answer. The muscle in his jaw ticked. "At first I tried to play along with him when he'd 'accidentally' touch me. But then his advances became bolder, cornering me in the kitchen and slipping his hand under my shirt, telling me that my mom wouldn't care."

More tears leaked out, as Stella remembered the paralyzing fear of a man twice her size, knowing he could overpower her with little effort. Not having a clue how to fend him off or protect herself. So she'd stood there while he'd breathed heavily in her ear, touching her breast with one hand and stroking himself with the other. A shudder trickled through her body. "After a few times I started staying the night at a friend's house. I don't think my mom even noticed I was gone."

Brandon cursed under his breath. "How old were you?"

Stella swallowed to quench her dry throat. "Fifteen."

He abruptly stood from the couch, leaving her cold and missing his solid weight next to her. "And you never told anyone?"

"What was I supposed to say? That my mom's boyfriend

cops feels on me in the kitchen and I stand there and let him?"

Brandon loomed over her and gripped her shoulders. "You tell someone that you're being molested by a sick bastard who deserves to have his dick sawed off."

She gazed into his eyes, seeing the fury and retribution she'd always longed to see from her mother. "Why are you so angry?"

"Because I want to kill him, Stella." He gave her a gentle shake. "I want to slowly take him apart for destroying you like that. It's because of him you don't like to be touched, isn't it?"

After that, any time a man got close she'd automatically think about Terry and his sour breath on her neck while he got off on touching her. Eventually the memories had prevented her from being able to get close to anyone. The thought of any person invading her personal space or putting a hand on her made her want to throw up.

"Yes," she whispered.

"Then, yeah, I want to fucking kill him."

"That's"—she shook her head, trying to find the right words—"just about the sweetest thing I've ever heard."

He drew back at her response and gave her a puzzled look. "Sweet?" he echoed.

Her mouth turned up, despite the heaviness of the conversation. "Yeah. No one's ever stuck up for me like that before." She lifted her shoulders. "It's kind of nice."

Brandon plowed his hands through his hair, then pinned her with a look. "You have to talk to her."

Stella shook her head, knowing who he was talking about. "I can't." When he looked unconvinced, she went on. "You don't know her. She won't understand."

Brandon stalked forward, then squatted in front of her.

"It doesn't matter if she understands. You have to tell her for *you*. You'll never be able to put it behind you if you don't open up about it."

She toyed with the soft hair on his forearms, wishing they'd just wrap around her and offer some comfort. "But I just did open up about it."

He shook his head. "Not the same thing. She needs to know what's going on in here," he added with a palm over her heart. She knew he meant the gesture in a totally nonsexual way, only using his hand to get his point across. But her traitorous body couldn't stop responding to his touch. How big his hand was compared to her, how the warmth bled through the material of her shirt and bloomed across her chest.

And she knew he recognized the arc of sexual tension between them because his nostrils flared and his pupils blackened his eyes. It wouldn't take a lot to lean forward and press her lips to his. But tonight wasn't the night for that and Stella liked to think she was levelheaded enough for that.

Something behind them vibrated, but neither moved to check on the sound. Brandon's gaze dropped to her mouth and the air between them froze for a split second. Just an instant, but long enough for them to realize the moment had shifted to something deeper.

Brandon dropped his head, then pushed to his feet. Her eyes roamed over his broad back as he snatched his cell phone off the coffee table. He stared at the screen for a moment.

"I need to get this," he told her.

She nodded and didn't get up from the couch, too exhausted to move even if she wanted to. "Sure."

He stepped away, leaving her bereft in the wake of his

departure, already missing his strength and quiet reassurance. Somehow he'd slipped past all her barriers and made himself right at home.

With a deep sigh, Stella sank farther back into the couch and closed her eyes. Her body felt heavy and weighed down, drained from the evening. Going from wanting to jump Brandon's sexy bones to crying like a maniac had left her feeling empty. The weightlessness of sleep crept into her bones, despite her mind's warning not to succumb. She didn't want to fall asleep on Brandon's couch, but she slipped anyway and the last thing she remembered hearing was Brandon muttering his ex-wife's name.

FIFTEEN

The first thing Stella noticed when she woke up was how different her bed smelled. Musky and spicy like... Irish Spring.

Irish Spring? What the...?

What happened last night? Talking to Brandon... yes, she remembered that. That weird seductive game of golf... definitely remembered that. Breaking down in his driveway, which had led to her pouring out all her dirty stuff... unfortunately remembered that.

With a groan, Stella fell back on the pillow, then inhaled deeply when Brandon's scent floated around her. Damn, his bed smelled even better than he did. She rolled over and buried her face in the pillow, drawing in his essence and conjuring an image of him lying in the bed. The sheet low on his hips, barely concealing the goods underneath. Yeah, he probably slept naked. Brandon threw off heat like nobody's business and probably couldn't be bothered with a trivial thing like boxers.

As mouthwatering as those images were, because *damn*, it still didn't answer how she'd gotten here. Why hadn't she just gone home?

The phone had rung, which he'd answered, and then...what?

Had she fallen asleep?

But if she had, why wasn't she on the couch, where she'd been last night? Or, better yet, why hadn't he woken her up and sent her packing?

As she sat up again, she heard a noise. Voices. Two male voices. Brandon and Matt. Then the smells hit. Something frying. Fatty and greasy, like maybe bacon.

On cue, her stomach growled. She slid from the bed and groaned when the room spun. She grabbed the night-stand for support and knocked something over. She picked up the overturned picture frame and replaced it by the lamp. When she righted the photo, something in her chest turned over. The shot was of Brandon sitting in a chair, holding a newborn Matt probably just hours after he'd been born, given the hospital bracelet fastened to this tiny wrist. Stella picked the photo up for closer in-spection, memorizing every detail of Brandon looking exhausted and way too young in his backward baseball cap and Blanco Valley High School T-shirt. But it wasn't his youth that struck her. It was the pure, unadulterated adoration and love on his face as he gazed down at the baby. A little boy who'd been unplanned but who had been loved and wanted from the moment he'd entered the world.

The scents from the kitchen prompted another growl from her stomach. Stella found a mirror, ran her hands through her hair, and tried to dispel the image of Brandon carrying her to his room. Tucking her in.

The voices from the kitchen grew louder as she walked on bare feet down the hall. Brandon said something, his voice deep and gravelly from sleep, to which Matt laughed. The crackle and sizzle of cooking bacon accompanied the wafting smells, along with freshly brewed coffee. Brandon was leaning against the counter and, Holy Lord, had his shirt unbuttoned, sipping from a mug. His casual, barefooted, ruffled bed head had her stomach turning over and overwhelming the hunger she'd woken up with.

Matt turned from his place at the stove as he tossed another piece of bacon on the pan. His brows pinched in confusion at her appearance. "Hey, Stella," he greeted as he tossed a look back and forth between her and Brandon.

Brandon just smirked at her from behind his mug, which said *World's Okayest Dad.*

She managed a smile, which probably came across as more of a grimace. Oh Lord, she hoped Matt didn't think she'd done the nasty with his dad. How horrifying was that?

"Morning," she muttered, then stood in the middle of the room while Matt cooked breakfast and Brandon sipped his coffee. Why didn't he button his shirt already?

He must have caught her ogling the cut of muscles because his smirk bloomed into a full-grown grin. "Hungry?" he asked.

She eyed the plateful of pancakes and inhaled the sweet scent of bacon grease. "Actually, yeah."

His grin remained when he set his mug down. "Have a seat at the table."

Why was he so damn happy? Who was this cheerful at...she eyed the clock. Six forty-five? Who even got up this early?

She did as instructed and waited while he grabbed a plate from the cabinet. He and Matt exchanged conversation while Brandon plopped some pancakes on the plate, then added bacon.

"You eat like this every morning?" she asked as the food was set in front of her.

Brandon eyed her like she'd lost her mind. "Growing men need their protein."

"I wouldn't really call bacon and pancakes protein," she argued.

"It's not," Matt called from the stove. "Dad just likes the fat."

Brandon ambled back to the counter and smacked Matt upside the head. "Don't be a douche."

Stella couldn't help but grin at the easy banter between the two.

"Sleep okay?" Brandon asked when he took a seat with his own plate of food. Only he'd piled three times as many pancakes and half a package of bacon.

"Geez, save some for the starving people," she commented while eyeing his plate.

Brandon paused with his fork halfway to his mouth. "Why do you have to hate?"

She grinned and cut into her pancakes. Matt was still at the stove, pouring the last of the pancake batter into the pan. She glanced at him, then at Brandon. Stella leaned closer to Brandon and lowered her voice. "Um"—she shifted in her seat when one of his dark brows lifted—"what exactly happened last night?"

"You mean after you fell asleep and I carried you to bed?"

Heat flooded her cheeks at the image of him carrying her, then laying her beneath his covers. Had his touch lingered? Did he sneak any peeks while she'd been out of it?

No, Brandon would never do that. He was too honorable to take advantage of a woman in that way. On the other hand, if something had happened between them, wouldn't she have remembered?

"Relax, Stella," Brandon soothed. "I tucked you in nice and tight and that's all."

She nodded. "Okay." More nodding, because the disappointment she felt was ridiculous. Wasn't it? "Good." They ate in silence while Matt shut the stove off and filled his own plate. "Except, why didn't you just wake me up and send me home?"

Brandon eyed her over the rim of his coffee cup. "Didn't think you were up to driving home. Figured you were better off staying here."

"Oh," was all she said. "Thanks."

His brow arched again. "Don't mention it."

Matt joined them at the table, crowding the space with his plate and glass of juice. He nudged Brandon's plate to make room. Brandon nudged back, which Matt answered with a shove to Brandon's shoulder.

"Hey," Brandon replied, and pushed Matt back.

"Dude, move over," Matt said.

The play was like watching two brothers rather than father and son. Stella coughed into her drink to hide her grin.

"Stella, you should come shooting with us this weekend," Matt announced.

Stella glanced at the kid while Brandon choked on his coffee. "Shooting?" she questioned.

Matt cut into his pancakes. "Yeah, Dad and I go into the mountains with our rifles."

She glanced at Brandon, who was still recovering from shooting coffee out his nose. "If you go up there to shoot Bambi, I want no part of it."

"Bambi?" Matt repeated with a wrinkled brow.

Brandon smacked Matt on the shoulder. "She means deer. And I doubt Stella would be into that."

Did he not want her to go? Was it some sacred father-son thing that he didn't want her impeding on? Was she not worthy to partake of their time together?

"Actually," she said to Matt, "that sounds like fun."

"Fun?" Brandon repeated. "Shooting a rifle sounds like fun?"

She shrugged her shoulders. "Why, is it not fun?"

"Hell yeah it's fun," Matt confirmed.

Brandon whacked him again. "Watch your language." He directed his attention back to Stella. "I only meant that it doesn't seem like something you'd be into."

Stella leaned back in her chair and eyed him from across the table, meeting the challenge in his eyes. "Why? Because I teach little girls how to point their toes? Or because I used to spend just as much time in a tutu as I did in regular street clothes?"

Brandon shot a look at Matt, as though pleading for help. Apparently Matt wasn't on board because he only chewed his food in silence. "Uh . . . yeah?"

Matt shook his head. "Dude, wrong answer."

Stella leaned forward and glared at Brandon; then she placed her hand on Matt's shoulder. "I would love to come shooting with you."

So, yeah. Showed him, didn't she?

Later that night, the Bobcats were playing like shit during their game against the Alamosa Maroons. Cody had thrown for two interceptions before Blake had yanked him at half-time. Things had turned around slightly in the third quarter when the Bobcats had narrowed the point gap to one touch-down. Matt hadn't had much play time, only seeing the field for about half the second quarter before Blake had pulled him. Brandon had kept his protests to himself, trusting that his cousin knew what he was doing, even if his kid getting benched made every parental bone in Brandon's body want to protest.

"What's wrong with you?" Stella asked for the fourth time since halftime.

Knowing he'd been unusually quiet, Brandon dug for another cheese-drenched chip and searched his mind for an excuse. "Just trying to enjoy these Michelin-star-worthy nachos."

She snorted and scanned the action on the field. "Nice try. When you go quiet, something's wrong."

Did she know him that well? "Actually I'm pondering whether or not to go easy on you or school you in the art of shooting."

She smirked at him. Her long hair was down, with a chunk of it draped over her shoulder and pooling around her breast. "By all means, don't feel the need to go easy on me. I can give as good as I get."

Yeah, he didn't doubt that for a second. "You know, you don't have to go if you don't want to," he blurted out.

"Why would I not want to?" she countered. "It sounds like fun." She looked at him again, hypnotizing him with those clear blue eyes. Honestly, they were like looking into the waters of a warm Caribbean sea. Not that he knew what that looked like exactly, but it seemed like a good comparison.

"I'm just concerned for someone who's never used a gun before," he hedged.

Her brow pinched in disbelief. "How do you know I've never used a gun before?"

Stella, the petite, lithe ballerina who floated around with all the regal air of an aristocrat handling a twelve-gauge? Call him crazy, but he couldn't picture it.

"Have you?" he questioned.

An adorable pink stained her cheeks, one he wanted to kiss away. "Well, if you must know, I haven't. Not that it'll make a difference. I'm sure I can handle a gun as well as you can."

Poor little Stella Davenport. She hated admitting there was something on the planet she'd yet to master.

"I mean, how hard could it be to aim and pull the trigger?" she went on.

He slanted her a look. "It's a little more complicated than that, but sure."

"If I can do a triple pirouette on my toes without any toe pads, I'm sure I can handle a gun."

He nudged her shoulder with his. "I don't know what that is, but it sounds dirty." *Seriously? Could you be a bigger jackass?*

She grinned and wiggled her eyebrows. "If you think that's hot, you should see me lift my leg up over my head."

The chip he'd just taken a bite of went down the wrong way. "Can you really do that?" he asked through bitter coughs to clear the food from his pipe.

But she only shrugged and watched the action on the field. "You'll just have to use your imagination for that one."

Oh, he was using his imagination all right. Only her leg was over his head instead of hers. Setting the borderline dirty banter aside, Brandon had no doubt she'd been the best dancer on the stage. Because Stella threw her heart and soul into whatever she did. She was too competitive to allow anyone to show her up. Being forced to give up her passion had to have been crushing for her. Brandon had never given it much thought, beyond his good fortune that her retirement ultimately led her to Blanco Valley. But after everything she'd been through, and then having to walk away from the only thing that had given her sanctuary? She was a thousand times stronger than he'd ever given her credit for.

"Do you miss it?" he asked her.

Stella's gaze followed the Bobcats as they intercepted the ball from Alamosa. The crowd around them surged to their feet and the band fired up. "All the time," she answered after they retook their seats.

Brandon placed his empty nacho tray at his feet. "You were the best, weren't you?"

She looked at him, the melancholy darkening her usually bright eyes punching a hole in his chest. "You know I was."

Without thinking, and disregarding the game and fans around them, because Stella had a way of making everything else melt away, Brandon cupped her chin. She didn't protest when he tilted her head up. Didn't pull away when he stroked his thumb over her lower lip. Perhaps her willpower was as weak as his. Perhaps she was as tired of fighting the pull between them that seemed to grow stronger every time they were around each other. Whatever it was, Brandon wasn't about to question the silent permission her eyes were giving him. Because they dropped closed in anticipation, waiting and inviting him to kiss her. And who was he to deny a beautiful woman? They both wanted it, both craved it, both needed it more than their next heartbeat.

Their lips pressed together, fusing with a sweet, yet burning desire. Stella moaned and dug her fingers into his forearms when he teased her slick lips with his tongue. A shiver ran through his body, surprising him because a woman had never made him shiver before. Weren't the ladies the ones who were supposed to shiver? Stella had a way of forcing his body into a strange territory of the unknown. It turned him on and scared the shit out of him at the same time.

Just as he was about to release her, because they were surrounded by cheering football fans, Stella's mouth parted and her tongue sought his. Not one to disappoint, Brandon kept the kiss going, meeting the stroke of her tongue with one of his own. He chased her, exploring the heat of her mouth and swallowing her surprised gasp.

Then she jumped back and yelped.

What the hell?

"Oh, I am so sorry," Rhonda Powell exclaimed as she brushed her hand over Stella's back. "The kid behind me bumped into me. I swear I didn't mean to dump my ice all over your back."

Biggest line of shit if Brandon ever heard one. Rhonda was as devious as they came and had been trying to shove her number in Brandon's back pocket for months.

Stella turned and eyed the pile of ice on the concrete behind her. The withering look she tossed Rhonda could have melted said ice into a puddle. "It's all right," she told the woman with a sweet smile. "Some of us just aren't blessed with grace and balance."

Brandon managed to hide his chuckle as Rhonda's fake-as-shit smile faded and was replaced with a ripe reddening of her cheeks. He eyed the patches of moisture on Stella's back and was surprised Rhonda hadn't dumped the stuff inside Stella's shirt.

Then Rhonda turned her attention to Brandon, dismissing Stella with a flick of her gaze. She placed her hand on his shoulder, which quickly turned into a slow caress. "I didn't get you, did I?"

He wrapped his hand around her wrist and removed it. "No, Rhonda, your aim was spot on." Then he faced forward, shrugging her off the same way she'd done to Stella. "You all right?" he asked Stella.

Stella lowered her head and chewed her lip. Did she have any idea how damn cute she was?

"The steam coming out of Rhonda's ears was worth that entire thing."

And what about the kiss? Had that been worth it too? Before he could question that further, the crowd ceased cheering, then groaned in unison. His attention whipped toward the field just as Beverly Rowley whacked him on the knee with her orange and black pom-pom. "Hey, that's Matty down there."

Brandon yanked his attention to the field to see the play action had stopped, and the team was gathered in a cluster near the end zone. His son was on his back, both hands gripping his right shin as blood poured down his leg.

Beside him Stella gasped. "So much blood," she whispered.

Brandon was just about to haul ass to the field when his cell vibrated from his back pocket. With his attention still riveted on his kid speaking to Blake and clutching his leg, Brandon retrieved his phone and saw a text from Cameron.

Don't rush the field just yet.

Yeah, Cam knew him. Knew Brandon would get a look at his child's bloody leg and need to be right there next to him.

As though sensing the panic quickly building and tensing his body, Stella placed her hand on his leg, squeezing with silent reassurance. She loved Matt; he knew that. She'd do anything for his son and he loved her for that. Her devotion to him was more than Trish had ever given Matt and Matt deserved that devotion. The kid deserved more than Brandon could give him on his own.

"He'll be okay," Stella muttered.

He leaned forward and gripped Beverly's shoulder. "What happened?" He hated that he even had to ask. Damn it, he should have been paying closer attention. That was his kid out there, playing the game he loved, trying to land a scholarship, and he'd been too busy falling more in love with Stella. Drowning himself in her crystal-clear blue eyes, trying to imagine a future with them together.

"Couldn't tell," Beverly answered. "It looked like he collided with another player. I saw the other kid's leg fly up; then Matt went down."

The only thing Brandon could think of was that Matt had taken a cleat to the leg.

On cue, his cell buzzed and Brandon pulled Cam's text up.

Took a cleat to the shin. Pretty deep gash, looks like he'll need stitches. Blake's releasing him from the game if you want to come grab him.

Stella must have read the text message over his shoulder, because she stood at the same time as he did and followed him down the bleachers. Brandon reached the bottom as Matt limped off the field with the help of two other players.

His stomach twisted at the sight of blood oozing down Matt's leg. The crowd applauded, showing their support for their player as he exited the game.

"You don't have to come with me," Brandon told Stella, but secretly absorbed her strength next to him.

She followed him through the gate that led to the field. "I want to."

He stopped with a heavy sigh. Why did she insist on constantly inserting herself deeper in his life? Why did she have to make it so difficult for him to keep her at arm's length?

"Stella—"

"Please let me," she said in a rush. "Look, I…" She licked her lips and eyed Matt being carried toward them. One of the coaches had given Matt a towel to ease the flow of blood. "I know this is kind of shitty timing, but I never really thanked you for last night. You've done a lot more for me than you realize." Her voice trembled. "I need to do this for you."

He gazed down at her, knowing he wouldn't have told her no anyway. Even if she weren't standing on the sidelines of a paused football game, pleading with those damn wounded eyes of hers. Because he wanted her there, knowing she was leaving and would eventually break his heart. He wanted her there.

With a quiet nod, he turned as Matt approached. Brandon's stomach turned over again at the lines of stress and pain etched across his son's face. Sweat beaded his forehead and ran down his temples. Someone had tied the towel around Matt's leg, which was already soaked in blood.

Brandon wrapped his arm around Matt's shoulder to help him limp off the field. Stella did the same, and Brandon wanted to order her to back off. She had a bad knee and had no business taking on Matt's weight. But he knew she wouldn't listen. She was stubborn like that. And, as she'd said, it was something she needed to do for him. So he let her.

SIXTEEN

If Brandon didn't stop pacing, Stella was going to handcuff him to a chair. Of course, she'd need to find a pair of handcuffs first.

But still, he was driving her nuts.

After sitting in the waiting room for half an hour, while blood continued to ooze from Matt's leg, they'd finally admitted him. They hadn't allowed Brandon in the X-ray room and Stella had had to physically drag him into a chair, so he could bounce in and out of said chair every ten seconds. He'd consumed about three cups of coffee, offering her one with every sip. When she'd asked if they had a skinny white chocolate mocha, only to make the guy smile, he'd snarled at her.

Because of the situation, she'd forgive the snarl.

"Please sit down," Stella said to the ceiling after Brandon had scared an eighty-year-old woman when he'd crumpled his third coffee cup a little too hard.

With a heavy sigh, Brandon plopped into the chair. "What's taking so long?" he muttered.

"Maybe there's a line," she joked.

Brandon glared at her, then checked his watch again. They'd been there for almost an hour and it was just edging past eleven p.m. "How long does it take to do one X-ray?"

"I'm sure he's fine. They'll probably just stitch him up."

Brandon grunted and crossed his arms over his chest. "You didn't have to come, you know. If you're tired, I can drive you home."

If they hadn't been sitting in an emergency room, waiting for news on his son, she would have smacked the man. "You keep saying that, and I keep telling you I want to be here. Besides, if you leave to drive me home, you might not be here when they finish with him."

Brandon scratched the scruff on his face. "Yeah, that's true."

She placed a hand to stop the bouncing of his leg. "He'll be fine," she reassured him. "Matt's a strong kid."

He blew out a breath and scrubbed a hand through his messy hair. "Yeah."

"I meant what I said earlier," Stella said.

Brandon leaned his head back in the chair and closed his eyes. "You mean about not wanting any of my nachos? I told you you'd be hungry."

She grinned, despite the situation. "No. And for your information, I'm not hungry."

"Okay. Then you must be talking about the comment you made about me looking like an Adonis in this sweat-shirt."

Stella smacked him on the shoulder, barely resisting the urge to run her palm over the tense muscle. Kind of like the way Rhonda had. Stella snatched her hand away at the memory. "Your kid has a hole in his leg and you still manage to be a smart-ass. Impressive."

"What can I say? It's a special talent."

No doubt. "I'm talking about my hastily thrown out gratitude on the football field, surrounded by huffing, sweaty high school kids."

Brandon nodded as though she'd jogged his memory. "Oh, that." He flicked her on the nose. "Yeah, it was a special moment, wasn't it? The only thing lacking was some violins and conveniently placed mood lighting."

"Still with the jokes," she commented. "Do you keep them on index cards so you can memorize them for moments such as this?"

He gazed at her, then narrowed his eyes, which were heavy with exhaustion. "Obviously I won't be anymore."

Before she could respond with something along the lines of, *Can I sit on your lap and maybe wiggle around a little?* the double doors swung open and a frazzled-looking nurse strode through. "Mr. West?" she called.

Brandon immediately stood. "How's Matt?"

She smiled, clearly sensing a distressed parent when she saw one. "He's fine. The doctor gave him some pain pills and is just going to stitch him up real quick."

Relief sagged his bulky shoulders. "So no damage was done to his leg?"

The nurse nodded. "Yes, his X-ray came out clean. It's nothing more than a nasty gash." She offered Stella a smile, probably thinking she was Matt's mom. "As soon as he's stitched, the doctor will have some paperwork for you to sign, and then he'll be discharged."

Brandon nodded. "Thank you."

"Of course," she replied; then she disappeared back through the doors.

Brandon retook his seat with a long sigh.

Stella elbowed him in the ribs. "Told you he'd be fine. Kid's probably as hardheaded as you are."

"I resent that," he countered without looking at her. Then he was silent for a moment. "I should call Trish," he said quietly.

The name had Stella's back going rigid as she remembered what Annabelle had said about Matt's mother calling to rekindle a relationship. Brandon still hadn't confided in her, which had sent silent alarms in her head. She'd wracked her brain for days trying to come up with a reason for his reluctance. A lack of trust was the only thing that made sense. Because she was leaving, Brandon still held a part of himself back.

"She's been calling," Brandon said, pulling Stella from her thoughts and confusing her. Brandon looked up from his phone and pinned her with a gaze full of conflict. "Matt doesn't know."

Stella shook her head, trying to make sense of his words. "Brandon, what're you talking about? Matt doesn't know what? That she wants to talk to him?"

"No, they've spoken." he informed her. "He doesn't know that she left the circus and bought a house in Oklahoma." The muscle in his jaw ticked.

"How do you know she hasn't told him that?"

"Because he hasn't mentioned it," Brandon answered.

Stella turned in her seat and placed a hand on Brandon's arm, as much for comfort as to plead with him. "Don't you think you should tell him?"

"I told Trish I wanted to talk to Matt first."

How long had Brandon been keeping that from Matt? "And have you talked to him?"

Brandon turned his pained expression to her.

Stella swallowed and removed her hand from his arm, missing his warmth. "So that's a no."

He stared at her for a moment as though he wanted to say something. But what?

Brandon snorted. "Matt will hate me when he finds out I knew and didn't tell him." He shook his head. "How can he go through this again?"

And she'd been obsessing over why Brandon hadn't chosen to include her? What a selfish ass she was.

"Matt hating you isn't possible," she urged him. "He worships you, Brandon."

Brandon laughed without humor. "You don't get it, Stella. I'm all he's got. I'm the one person in his life he's supposed to trust. The only one who hasn't ripped the rug out from under his feet. How do you think he'll take it when he finds out I've been keeping this from him?"

"She's the one who left," she told Brandon, hoping to get through to him. "She's the one who stayed away." She gripped his scruffy jaw with both hands and urged him to look at her. "You're not responsible for her actions."

His jaw tensed. "But I'm responsible for my son's happiness."

"He's seventeen, Brandon. He's not a kid anymore and you can't protect him forever."

He blew out a breath. "What if I let her talk to him, then the calls stop like they did before?"

Stella released his face before she did something really stupid like kiss him. One kiss a night was enough. "Then it's her loss."

Stella's heart ached when Brandon rubbed a hand over the back of his neck. "Yeah, but I'll be left to clean up the mess, just like when Matt was little."

"And you'll do the best you can, because that's what you

do," she reassured him. "That's what good parents do. And you're a good parent, Brandon. Don't let her make you feel inadequate. You never stop trying to be better for Matt, and that's what makes you different."

He slid her a look with a raised brow. "You mean like how your mom did for you?"

"Yeah, well." Stella attempted a laugh but failed. "Just consider Gloria Davenport an example of what not to do."

He was quiet a moment; then she almost jumped out of her chair when he touched her chin and turned her face toward him. "I'm sorry you went through all that, Stella. Your mother doesn't deserve you."

The last little piece protecting her heart fell away. Just tumbled into an abyss before she had a chance to snatch it and put it back where it damn well belonged. Brandon had no business saying things like that to her, and he certainly had no business making her feel like a happy ending was possible for her. Messed up people like her didn't get happy endings. They didn't have smokin' hot, heroic men like Brandon looking at her like she was the answer to all his problems. She'd only create more problems for him.

Didn't he know to stay away from her?

"Brandon," she whispered, fighting tears and knowing she'd lose. "Why do you have to make it so hard?" She attempted another laugh, only this one came out as half a sob. "I mean, you wear shirts that are too small, you drive me home when I'm drunk, you let me cry on your shoulder, and then you say things like that. And you expect me to be able to walk away from you?"

His grip on her chin tightened. "So don't."

She blinked, trying to force back tears that kept threatening. "Don't what?"

"Don't walk away," he said again, his voice nearing a rough whisper. "Don't go to Chicago."

A heavy breath whooshed out of her. His request was her happy ending and worst nightmare all wrapped into one desperate plea. Her whole life she'd dreamed of a man like him, despite the fears that had prevented her from ever getting close to anyone. One who'd look at her like no one else existed. One who'd take her for who she was, flaws and dirty secrets and all. But also one who understood the final dream she'd yet to fulfill, that was her pièce de résistance.

But fate had to be just that cruel, didn't it? Just like everything else in her life, she'd been presented with something she couldn't have. Given a snippet of the future she'd secretly wanted for herself, only the timing was all wrong.

Why was it always wrong?

She opened her mouth, ready to jump at his words, but the declaration died in her throat. Why couldn't she do it? "Brandon, I..."

He cleared his throat and released her chin. "I'm sorry. That was wrong of me."

No, wait!

"I told you I would never ask you to give up your dream, and I meant it," he went on. "I just thought..." His words trailed off as his eyes searched hers.

He just thought what? That they could have a real shot together? That whatever was between them was strong enough to go the distance?

She opened her mouth to say something, anything, when Matt pushed through the double doors. And the second Matt stepped into the room, Stella knew the moment had been lost. Like a hot air balloon slowly sinking to the ground, so had her chance with Brandon. He'd given her a window, and

all she'd been able to do was sit there and question everything like she always did.

The moment was lost, and she feared she'd never get another chance.

Stella had decided it was time to talk to her mother,
just to round out what had shaped up to be a miserable
weekend. Today was the day she was supposed to go
shooting with Matt and Brandon. But after last night in
the ER, when she'd behaved like a royal jackass and
basically thrown Brandon's invitation back in his face,
she hadn't been in the mood. Although she'd suffered
from a heavy dose of guilt for letting Matt down, Stella
simply hadn't been able to face Brandon. She shot him a
quick text, telling him she wasn't feeling well. He didn't
respond. She told herself it was for the best, because she
needed some time away from him. Space to clear her
head and decided what her problem was and why she always screwed everything up.

So, yeah. Perfect time to have it out with her mother.

Besides, it was past time. Gloria's calls and text messages had eventually stopped and the silence had only
served as a reminder to Stella. Sometimes Gloria's silences
could be louder than her tantrums.

She turned her car into the driveway of her mother's
new house, taking in the clean and well-manicured lawn.
Gloria had never been much of a housekeeper. No, Stella
had been the one to wash the dishes, vacuum, and clean
the bathrooms. She'd even made sure there were fresh
flowers on the breakfast table. So the quaint '50s ranch
with potted mums and a garden gnome at the base of a tree
threw Stella off.

She turned off the car and walked toward the front door.

Gloria had even decorated the heavy wood with a fall wreath, full of orange and yellow flowers and a burlap ribbon.

Maybe the homeowner had decorated before Gloria had moved in. Yeah, that explained it.

A second after Stella rang the bell, the door was flung open and Gloria was there, throwing her arms around Stella's shoulders before she had a chance to brace herself.

"Oh, honey," her mother gushed.

Stella managed to stay upright with taking the brunt of her mom's weight. Gloria clung tight, as though expecting Stella to run away before they had a chance to talk. To be honest, Stella's initial instinct had been to do just that. A fleeting moment of panic had snapped into her spine, whispering at her to shove her mom away. That she didn't like displays of affection or anyone touching her.

But Brandon touches you.

Yeah. Funny how he'd become the one person who didn't send her into a panic.

Gently, Stella removed her mother's arms and stepped back. She offered a smile at the flash of hurt in Gloria's eyes.

"I'm sorry, come in," Gloria invited.

Stella stepped through the door and noticed how good the place smelled. Like sunshine and freshly baked bread. Her mom had baked?

When Stella was growing up, Gloria had been incapable of microwaving a simple bowl of mac and cheese.

No, not incapable. Unwilling.

"What's that I'm smelling?" Stella queried as she followed her mom into the house.

"Oh, that's apple cinnamon bread." A nervous laugh

popped out of her mom. "Just something new I'm trying. Would you like some? I just took it out of the oven."

Again, her instinct was to say no. To turn around and try this again another day, that she didn't have the strength or the energy to deal with this. But something in Gloria's gaze, and unabashed amount of hope, gave Stella pause.

Maybe her mother was turning over a new leaf. And if she could, why couldn't Stella?

"Sure, I'll try a slice," she told her mom.

Gloria's mouth turned into a grin, like a kid who'd been given permission to eat a cookie before dinner. She disappeared into the kitchen and Stella took a seat on the couch to wait. Where had all this furniture come from? It was inviting and comfortable, just begging Stella to pull her feet up and curl under a blanket.

"Is all this yours?" she asked her mom when she reappeared with the food.

Gloria glanced around the room. "It came furnished. I just added some photographs and fresh flowers." She handed Stella a slice of bread with dark brown stuff spread on top. Gloria gestured to it. "That's apple butter. I made that too."

Stella picked up the bread and studied it. Smelled good. And still warm. "When did you start baking like this?"

"Just over the last couple of days..." Gloria's gaze bounced around the room as her words trailed off.

Great. She was eating guilt food.

Nevertheless, it was good. Spicy and soft and...homemade. That word threw Stella for a loop because, as a kid, homemade had been a novelty. A luxury that other kids enjoyed. Not poor Stella Davenport who had to walk to school and dance in secondhand toe shoes.

Shit, she really needed to stop living in the past. Were

her demons her own fault for always comparing her present to her past? For measuring everyone around her with what she'd known growing up? Was that what she'd been doing with Brandon?

Expecting things with him to implode because that had always been her standard.

"Mom—"

"Honey—"

They spoke at the same time and quieted at the same time, waiting for the other to continue.

"Go ahead," Stella said as she polished off the last of the apple bread.

Her mom waved a hand at her. "No, you go."

"I'm sorry for the way I spoke to you," she started, not knowing what else to say.

Gloria shook her head. "I deserved that—"

"No, you didn't," she interrupted. "There are a dozen different ways I could have handled that, and I shouldn't have spoken to you the way I did. I'm sorry." She wadded up the paper towel. "And I'm sorry for ignoring all your calls. I know I upset you, but there were some things I needed to sort out before we could talk."

"Honey, about Terry—"

"I don't want to talk about him," Stella barked. Really, she didn't want to talk about any of it. But, at the very least, she needed her mom to know she wasn't angry anymore. That she was making an attempt, however poor that attempt was, to put it all behind her.

Her statement must have thrown Gloria for a loop, because she opened her mouth, then snapped it shut.

"But, honey—"

"Mom, please," Stella urged.

Gloria took a seat next to Stella on the couch. "You

have to know that I..." She rocked forward on the couch and wrung her hands. "If I'd had any idea what he'd been doing..." She shook her head and blew out a shuddering breath. "God, I can't believe I brought that monster in the house with you," she muttered in a harsh whisper. Had she meant for Stella to hear that? "You were my little girl and I was supposed to protect you and I've failed in so many ways." The tears muddling Gloria's voice threatened Stella's own tears. Gloria swiped at her eyes but refused to look at Stella.

Stella wrung her own hands at the impulse to comfort her mom. But touching and affection had never come easy for her, so the desire to put her arm around her own mother contradicted her comfort zone. Finally, she laid a hand on Gloria's shoulder. "You haven't failed, Mom. He was a creep who should have known better."

Gloria whipped her head up and pinned Stella with tear-filled eyes. "*I* should have known better, Stella." She jabbed her index finger in the middle of her chest. "Don't you get it? I was the mom. It was my job to take care of you and keep you safe and I brought that prick into our home and he violated you." She dropped her head into her hands and cried. "The thought of what he did to you...How could you ever forgive me?"

Stella's own tears flowed, a feeling she wasn't used to. She'd never been a crier. Didn't get emotional or sappy over stuff other women did. But the sight of her mom, old and broken and crying over the little girl she'd wronged, hit a deeply buried place inside. A place she'd kept hidden for a reason, for *this* very reason, and her mother's tears exposed it. Just shined a big ol' fat light on the damn thing so that Stella was powerless to force it down.

"Of course I forgive you," Stella whispered. "I just

wanted you to see me." She chased away her own tears, hating herself for allowing them to fall. "You never saw me, Mom."

"Oh, honey." Gloria thumbed one of Stella's tears away. "You came barreling into my life before I was ready, always looking up at me with those big blue eyes full of undying trust and love and I didn't know the first thing to do with you." She shook her head. "You scared me to death. You were the best thing I ever did," Gloria whispered. "What I was always the most proud of."

The words Stella had spent her entire childhood desperate to hear had finally been said.

Gloria wiped her eyes. "Goodness I haven't cried this much since my hamster escaped and got eaten by the neighbor's cat."

Stella chuckled, despite the heaviness hanging around the room. Leave it to her mom to crack a joke in the middle of sniffling into a tissue.

"Did you bury it?" Stella asked.

Gloria laughed and dabbed her eyes. "There wasn't anything to bury. My mom made the cat's owner buy me a new hamster. Sadly, that one, Richard the Third, died two weeks after I got him." She blew out a wistful sigh. "He was the last hamster I ever owned. Actually, he was the last pet I ever owned."

They sat in silence for a moment, nothing but the ticking of a wall clock making noise. "I'm sorry," Stella said again.

Gloria placed a hand on Stella's knee and squeezed. "Honey, you have nothing to be sorry for. I'm the one who's screwed up."

Stella knew those words would be the last of their heartfelt talk or any kind of journey down memory lane. As painful as it had been, Stella couldn't help but feel a moment of relief that the two of them had aired their feelings.

"Hey, what'd you say we go buy a hamster and name him Richard the Fourth?"

Gloria gave Stella's leg another squeeze. "Oh, sweetie," she said with more tears in her eyes. "There was no Richard the Fourth."

Typical smart-ass comment from her mom. And yeah, Stella kind of liked it.

SEVENTEEN

Brandon eyed the pink satin shoes dangling from Stella's slim fingers, unsuccessfully trying to hold back the distrust that was mingling the horror in his gaze. "Not just no," he told her, "but *hell* no."

She offered a smile that didn't quite reach her eyes. Was it just him, or was something up with her this morning? "Relax, they're not for you." She held the shoes out for Matt.

Matt blinked but didn't take them. "Uh..."

Brandon yanked the shoes from Stella's grasp.

Stella's bright blue eyes narrowed at him. "Will you calm down?" She jerked the odd-looking shoes back. "They're not for him to wear."

With a hesitant reach, Matt accepted the shoes and turned them this way and that. "Not that I don't appreciate your... gift," his son said, "but what am I supposed to do with them?"

Stella clasped her hands behind her back. "Just think of them as a token of our time together. Most dancers take years and years to get into a pair of toe shoes. I'd say you've earned them."

"Toe shoes?" Matt repeated while still scrutinizing them. "They're so odd-looking. And they look like they'd kill."

Stella shrugged. "They're not so bad if you have enough padding shoved around your toes. You eventually get used to the pain."

Brandon eyed Stella as she spoke with Matt, thinking she was different this morning. The feistiness that lit up her eyes whenever she was around him wasn't there. What had changed since they'd seen each other last? Her guard was thrown back up and he didn't know why.

"Matt, give us a minute." Brandon wrapped his palm around Stella's bicep, loving how cool and soft her skin was. He ushered her outside so Matt wouldn't overhear.

Stella's eyes hardened as she pulled her arm out of his grasp. He thought about holding on, because he loved touching her, but he didn't want to piss her off further. "What're you doing?"

"What's up?" he prodded.

Her cool eyes blinked. "What'd you mean?"

Brandon crossed his arms over his chest and braced his feet apart, fully prepared for a battle. Nothing was ever easy with this woman. "I mean the attitude. The blank stares. The fake smiles. What's up with you, Stella?"

Something flashed across her eyes for a brief second. If Brandon hadn't been looking, he might have missed the fear that darkened her gaze. But he was too good, knew her too well to dismiss whatever walls she was trying her hardest to throw up. "Nothing," she said.

"Nothing," he repeated.

She nodded. "Yep, nothing."

It was a bullshit answer if he ever heard one, but he didn't call her out on it because he didn't want to scare her off. Because he knew she'd run scared if she had any idea what was going through his mind or what he wanted to do to her.

Except...yeah, screw it.

He got all up in her personal space, practically wanting to pound his chest in triumph when her narrowed eyes widened. Yeah, he had her right where he wanted her. She pretended she was such a good actress, but her gasp gave her away when he snaked one arm around her waist and tunneled the other in her thick hair.

She opened her mouth, probably to tell him to go to hell, but Brandon cut her off with a fierce kiss. The sort of kiss that stole her breath and cemented the reality that he could never let her go. Hell yeah, this was what he'd been fantasizing about since being at the hospital with her. Actually in the entire time he'd known her, he'd wanted this. To mess up her hair with his fingers and make her lips swell with kisses so deep that neither of them could think straight.

And as her tongue tangled with his, that was exactly what happened. Brandon lost all train of thought, forgot why he'd dragged her out to the sidewalk and left his confused kid behind. Forgot why he'd demanded to know what had killed the light in her eyes. Because all that mattered was the heat of Stella's mouth and the bite of her sharp nails in his shoulders. The way she wedged a leg in between his and sucked the breath right out of his lungs.

Damn it was good; she was good; the whole thing was—

"Hey, buddy, this is a family town."

Stella immediately jerked away from him as though

they'd been caught red-handed. He supposed they had and Brandon scanned the faces passing by them for whoever had destroyed a perfectly sexy moment.

Stella stepped back and shook her head. Panic slammed through him as she reached for the studio door. "Nope," she said. "Not doing this with you."

Damn if he was going to let her walk away after she'd just kissed the shit out of him. He grabbed her arm to stop her hasty retreat. "Do what, Stella?"

"Whatever it is you're doing," she shot back.

Brandon spared a glance inside the studio to check on Matt. The kid was leaning against the wall, playing on his phone. "And what is it you think I'm doing?"

She spun around and tugged her arm free. "I don't know what you're doing, Brandon. And that's what pisses me off. Because whatever game you're playing with me—"

"Whoa, what the hell?" he demanded. She thought he was playing with her? She was the one who blew hot and cold so often that he didn't know which way was up.

"You've made it clear from the very beginning that you don't want a relationship with me," Stella told him. "Then you go around kissing me and making me feel like..." She shook her head as her chest heaved. "Like..."

He crowded her again, needing to hear her say exactly how she felt. "Like what, Stella?"

Her gaze snapped to his and she shoved him away. "I don't know, all right? I don't know how you make me feel. But I know that I don't like it."

She didn't like it? Yeah, now she had a small dose of what he'd been going through. He hated the way she made him feel because it was new and different. She made him itch and come alive at the same time. Scared shitless and safe. Whatever the hell that meant. How can someone be terrified and feel good at the same time? The woman was a walking contradiction who drove him crazy as often as she turned him on.

And then he laughed, because he was the jackass who'd allowed it to happen. "Yeah, welcome to my world, sweetheart."

Stella shook her head. "What's that supposed to mean?"

What did that mean? It meant that she rocked his world. It meant that he didn't know what to do with her because she was leaving and would only break his heart when she didn't come back.

He shook his head, more at his own stupidity than frustration with her. It wasn't her fault. She was just being Stella. It was his own damn fault for chasing after her like some panting teenager who couldn't get his hormones under control.

"Nothing," he finally said. And he left her standing there like the asshole he was.

Some days Brandon wished he smoked. He heard the stuff took the edge off and calmed nerves. Because that was what he needed. Something to cool the death grip he had on his steering wheel before he tore the thing in half.

Or just get laid.

Yeah, that was good at taking the edge off.

Except the only woman he wanted for that was ignoring him. Because he'd seriously blown it with her. What kind of asshole asked a woman to give up her one and only dream for him?

Yeah, this asshole.

What had he been thinking, asking Stella not to go to Chicago? He'd allowed his fears of her not returning to run his mouth off. To blurt out what he'd been thinking for months. And why should she stay? What did she have to stay for?

He was no better than all the other assholes who'd taken advantage of her.

He sighed and rubbed a hand over his face. He picked up his cell, dialed her number, and stared at the screen without connecting the call. He didn't deserve her. She'd been through too much, been abused one too many times, for him to only continue the same pattern. With a grunt of disgust with himself, Brandon tossed the phone down and gripped the steering wheel with both hands.

As he'd been sitting in the waiting room at the hospital, hearing her tell him Matt was going to be fine, soaking up her strength, Brandon had realized he hadn't done enough. Hadn't done enough to show her he wanted more. How could she know he wanted something deeper than touching and kissing and flirting if he didn't put himself out there? So he'd blurted out the words and then been hurt when she hadn't jumped at the opportunity to give up everything for him. He knew he needed to put himself out there in order to show her, and he thought simply asking her had been enough.

The truth was, he'd been selfish to ask her to stay, and if he was going to gain her trust, he needed to give it in return.

So what did he do now?

Brandon turned off the highway to pick Matt up from practice. Technically he wasn't supposed to be participating, at least until his leg healed enough. To be honest, Matt had been damn lucky his muscle hadn't been torn.

There were only a few games left in the season until the playoffs and Matt needed to be in top shape. Brandon knew that impressing the recruiters was more important to Matt than anything. Right now, his sole focus was gaining a scholarship to UT. The idea of Matt going to school in Texas still didn't sit well with Brandon. But the kid had dug his heels in and there was little chance of changing his mind.

He pulled into the high school parking lot as the team was finishing practice.

The day had turned cooler, with a crisp breeze bending the bare branches of the aspens and bringing with it gray clouds. Brandon snagged his coat and shrugged it over his shoulders to ward off the chill.

He walked onto the field and caught sight of Matt just before he disappeared into the tunnel leading to the locker room. Blake and Cameron had hung back to speak to one another.

"Please tell him he's not allowed to miss Monday night football for a woman," Cameron ordered Brandon.

"Were we doing something for Monday night football tonight?" Brandon asked.

Cameron crossed his arms over his chest. "You two were supposed to come over to watch the Broncos."

Shit, he'd forgotten. He'd been too busy kicking his own ass for blowing it with Stella.

Cameron snorted and shook his head. "You're both assholes."

"At least I have a good excuse," Blake commented.

Cam glared at Blake. "Celebrating your ten-month anniversary isn't a good excuse. Hell, that's not even a real anniversary."

"It is to Annabelle," Blake argued. "And you're jealous because I go home to a woman every night and you go home to your fist."

Brandon chuckled and Cameron slugged him on the arm. "What the hell are you laughing at? You go home to a teenager and your dog."

"That's not what I hear," Blake muttered.

Cameron lifted a brow and Brandon tossed his cousin a quizzical look. "What're you talking about?"

"That you've been spending a lot of time with Little Miss Dance Teacher," Blake said with a grin.

"And who do you hear this from?" Brandon asked.

"Notice he's not denying it," Cam commented.

"Annabelle," Blake said with a shrug, while ignoring Cameron's comment.

"How the hell does Annabelle know?" Brandon questioned.

Blake looked at his cousin like he'd lost his mind. "Don't you know women tell each other everything?"

"And still not denying," Cameron threw in.

"Will you shut up?" Brandon ordered his friend.

Cam held his hands up in surrender. "Just saying."

"What's going on there?" Blake asked.

"Nothing," he answered.

Blake and Cam exchanged a look.

"Really?" Cameron queried. "Because didn't she go with you to the hospital when Matt had to get stitched up?"

Brandon shook his head. "That doesn't mean anything." Even as the words were leaving his mouth, Brandon knew they didn't hold water. That he was lying to himself as much as lying to his two closest friends.

"Yeah, it does," Blake commented after studying Brandon in silence. "It means more than you want it to."

"It can't though," Brandon said quietly. "She's leaving."

"Yeah, but not forever," Cameron pointed out.

"That's not true," Blake corrected. "She's looking for a permanent teaching position." He eyed Brandon. "You don't trust her to come back," Blake concluded. When Brandon didn't respond, Blake sighed. "Stella's not Trish."

Logically, Brandon knew that. But his heart, which had been hurt too many times, hadn't gotten the memo. It kept whispering to stay back, that she had heartbreak written all over her.

Blake rested a hand on Brandon's shoulder. "Just think about this. The two of you kept pushing me into something with Annabelle. You could see what I couldn't and knew that she'd make me happy. Where would she and I be if I had allowed my fears to take over?"

Brandon knew his cousin was right. The problem was, Brandon had been living with his fears for so long, he wasn't sure he knew what to do without them.

But didn't she at least deserve for him to make an effort?

EIGHTEEN

Brandon pulled up to Stella's studio just as his phone rang and Trish's number flashed across the screen. With a groan he picked up the device and seriously thought about ignoring it. But given her situation and the fact that she'd been having weekly conversations with Matt, Brandon reconsidered.

"Yeah," he answered on the third ring.

"I want Matt to come see me," Trish said by way of a greeting.

Brandon glanced out the driver's side window and caught a glimpse of Stella twirling across the dance floor, then executing some sort of jump. She was the most incredible thing he'd ever seen.

"What?" he asked Trish.

"I want him to know that I'm here to stay," she informed Brandon in a shaky voice. "I want to see him."

"I don't think he's ready for that, Trish."

A sob came from the other end of the phone. "I think he is." Trish was quiet for a moment; then her soft cries filled the line. The sound was like a fist around Brandon's heart, then tightened when he imagined Matt's reaction when Trish bailed on him again. He'd be devastated all over again, heartbroken, and Brandon wasn't sure he'd survive another round of watching his only child pick up the pieces after another loss.

"Is there at least a picture of him you can send me?"

Brandon sighed and dropped his head to the steering wheel. Just when he thought he had things figured out, knew exactly what he needed to do with Stella, life threw him another curve ball. And the harder he swung, the more he missed.

"I understand your hesitation," Trish continued. "I've let you down in the past, so I don't blame you at all for being wary. But don't you think the decision should be his?"

"I'm used to making the decisions for him," Brandon muttered. But even as the words left his mouth, they sounded...wrong. Making decisions for his grown son?

"But you can't keep doing that." She paused a moment. "And I'm not trying to tell you how to parent him. But he's old enough to decide for himself. Don't you think?"

"I need to understand what your intentions are."

Trish blew out a breath. "I want to rekindle a relationship with him," she explained.

"Yeah, I get that. But I've heard all this before and so has Matt. What happens after that?"

"I want..." Her words trailed off, as though she hadn't thought that far ahead, which created a sick feeling in the pit of his stomach. "I want to know all about him. I want to know what his future goals are, what he wants to study in college. I want to know what kind of food he likes to eat and what he does in his spare time."

See, those were the things she should already know about him.

"I know I should know all of these things," Trish said, as though she'd read his mind. "I can't go back and undo all the mistakes I've made. But I'm here now and I'm asking for one more chance."

"Trish—"

"I'm sorry for everything," she blurted out. "For not being strong enough when you needed me, for leaving." She blew out a breath. "I never meant to hurt you, Brandon. But when I left, I knew I was leaving Matt in good hands. You were always better at it than me."

Brandon's eyes dropped closed. What did she expect him to say? That it hadn't been about leaving Matt in capable hands? That Matt had needed a mother, no matter how inadequate she'd felt?

"Trish—"

"You've done a great job with him," she interrupted. "Matt's a fine young man and I couldn't be more proud."

"Trish," he pleaded again, but what he'd planned to say dissolved. His first instinct was always to brush her off. But something in the back of his mind told him to wait. The voice sounded suspiciously like Stella's, urging him to take a step back, to stop hovering over Matt and let the kid experience something without Brandon acting as his safety net.

"I need your word," he told her. "I need to know you won't hurt him again."

"Of course," she answered immediately. "And you'll always be number one in his life, Brandon. I get that. I'm not trying to take over or take him away from you. And the last thing I want is to hurt Matt again. I'm just asking for this one last chance."

As Brandon sat in his truck, staring into Stella's studio, he knew what he needed to do. He knew letting go of Matt was better for the kid than constantly trying to shelter him.

"All right, Trish. Maybe we can take a road trip to Oklahoma after he graduates. But that's my condition," Brandon warned. "I want to be there the first time. After that, if Matt decides he wants to see you again, then that's his decision to make."

Brandon practically felt Trish's sigh of relief. "You have no idea how much that means to me," she gushed.

He wanted to tell her not to get her hopes up, but he bit his tongue. Because maybe he would be better served as well by being a little more open-minded.

"Yeah, well…" Brandon broke off when his voice had grown thick. "I can't make any promises about visiting this summer. But we'll try."

"Understandable," Trish responded; then the line went dead. Brandon had the feeling she hadn't wanted to give him a chance to change his mind. He ought to. True, he hadn't felt anything for her in a long time, but she'd been his first love. His first everything and Matt's mother. A part of him had always been grateful to her for giving him the most precious gift, even when he'd been hating her for leaving them.

He blew out a breath and dropped the phone on the passenger seat. As he exited the car, he thought about Matt and the conversation he'd had with Trish just last week. Brandon replayed the laughter coming from Matt's bedroom, how he'd been telling Trish about Adrienne and their late-night trip to the emergency room. The conversation had been like any other normal exchange. Easy, lighthearted. Mundane.

Brandon had had the urge to warn Matt that it was a fantasy. That his mother had always had her own agenda. How would Matt react once Trish skipped out again? And would Brandon be able to hold him together this time?

But maybe this time Matt needed to experience it for himself. Maybe what he needed was for Brandon to step back and allow him to have whatever relationship with his mother that he wanted.

He yanked open the door to Stella's studio and was greeted by the soft strings of a violin. The gentle crescendo of the music matched the fluid motions of Stella as she glided across the floor. She moved like her bones were made of liquid, as though she were born to be in motion.

Brandon leaned against the door frame and watched her. There was something innocent and carefree about her dancing, knowing she was in her own world, not thinking or worrying about anything else. Watching her uninhibited, with all those guards lowered and defenses turned off, made the ache inside his chest grow. How could he have ever thought he couldn't wait for her? Stella was worth all the time in the world and he'd wait forever if he had to.

Stella came down out of a jump, one where her legs had done the splits in the air and her head thrown back. When she landed, her gaze landed on his. He expected to see surprise. A demand that he get out because he was invading her privacy and personal time. Instead she stood there in the middle of the floor, breath coming fast and short, skin glowing from perspiration.

In a word, she was the most beautiful thing he'd ever seen.

"I didn't mean to interrupt," he told her.

"Yes, you did," she replied.

Her cheeks were flushed, matching the rash of heat

across her chest that was covered in a fine sheen of sweat. Damn if he didn't want to give her a good tug until she stumbled against him. Maybe she'd gasp in surprise. But she'd come willingly and let him touch his mouth to hers.

He took a step closer. "Actually, I didn't." He scanned her features, committing her beauty to memory and how her blue eyes always darkened when she was around him. "I like watching you. It gives me peace."

She jabbed her hands on her hips and tilted her head. "What's wrong?"

Nothing. Everything. "What do you mean?"

She took a step closer, giving him the opportunity to inhale her scent. It was fresh, despite the fact that she'd been dancing. She lifted her arm and touched the spot between his eyes. "Something's happened."

Her touch melted his insides and reminded him how much softer she was than him. How much more innocent and sweet. She calmed the turbulence he'd been carrying around since their last encounter. He'd been confused and pissed at himself for screwing up with her. But after laying eyes on her and feeling her gentle touch, his mind cleared.

"I wanted to apologize about yesterday," he said.

She gnawed on her lower lip, tempting him to back her against the wall. "I was cranky too."

"Trish wants Matt to come visit her," he blurted out.

Her lips parted, which only furthered his need to kiss her, if only to force everything else to melt away. "And you should let him," she replied. Funny how she knew what he was talking about.

"I know, it's just..." He sighed. "I can't watch him go through that again." Brandon shook his head. "I don't know what I'll do if he ends up hurt again."

"You can be there for him," she said.

"It isn't enough," he said more to himself than to her. "I wish I could take it from him."

She cupped his cheek. "Because you're a good dad. Matt's lucky to have you." Her silky palm felt like a puff of fresh air over his heated skin. "And he's a strong kid. He'll survive because you've taught him well."

Brandon's brow pinched and he took a moment to absorb her petite fingers sliding into his hair. "You have an awful lot of faith in me."

"Why wouldn't I?"

"Because you should know better," he warned her.

She crossed her arms over her chest. "Maybe *you* should know better."

"Better than what?"

"Than to be that dumb."

"Come again?"

She sighed as though exasperated. "You don't give Matt enough credit."

"How do you figure that?"

"You try to protect him too much," she pointed out.

"See, I figured that was kind of part of my job description as the parent," he argued.

She sighed and spun away from him. "Can't we ever just have a normal conversation?"

"Apparently not," he agreed. "Maybe we should get the kissing thing out of the way now so we can go back to taking shots at each other."

She spun back around to face him as her cheeks flamed red. "Will you stop joking around?"

He rubbed a hand along his rough jaw. "Actually, I was being serious."

She groaned. "You're impossible to talk to."

Brandon gestured toward her. "Yeah, and you're so Dr. Phil."

Her brow pinched. "What?"

He turned to leave, more frustrated with himself than her. "Nothing. Forget it." He should have known better than to try and be around Stella when his head was full of other junk. She clouded his thinking and within two seconds of laying eyes on her refreshing beauty he'd resorted to his old habits. Pushing her away. Making her feel like they weren't compatible enough to have a simple conversation. She'd tried to comfort him, and he'd lashed out at her.

Just as he reached the door, her hand landed on his forearm. "Don't leave mad." He stopped but didn't face her. "Besides, you forgot the obligatory kissing. An encounter between us can't end unless we mingle with some heavy breathing and ass grabbing."

He chuckled, despite the tumult flowing through his veins, courtesy of his ex-wife and a woman he wanted more than anything but didn't deserve. "Maybe I'm trying to change things up a little. Predictability is boring."

"Predictability isn't boring," she countered. "I thrive on being predictable."

Well, that was a load of shit. He glanced at her over his shoulder. "Are you saying you want me to breathe heavily on you and grab your ass?"

She attempted a smile that didn't quite reach her eyes. Yeah, she was as conflicted and confused as him. "Yes, but maybe in a less Ron-and-Hermione kind of way."

"Who?"

One side of her mouth kicked up. "From *Harry Potter*?" she queried, obviously trying to jog his memory. "Completely awkward kissing scene between two people who have no chemistry?"

He turned fully to face her and tilted her face up to his. "You think we have no chemistry, Stella?"

She shook her head as the blush in her cheeks deepened. "No, that's not what I meant—"

"So you think I breathe heavily and ass grab like an awkward, redheaded teenage wizard?" he questioned as he used one arm to tug her closer and the other slid back into her hair.

Her breath hitched. "So you do know what *Harry Potter* is."

He nuzzled her nose and grinned in satisfaction when her breath shuddered. "Anyone who's raised a kid knows who Harry Potter is."

Her fingers dug into his forearms. "Matt doesn't really strike me as a *Harry Potter* fan. I figured he would have spent all his free time throwing a football around and rolling in mud or something."

"He went through an awkward phase," Brandon answered. Then he leaned back slightly and lifted a brow at her. "And rolling in mud? That's what you think boys spend their time doing?"

She lifted her shoulders and toyed with the buttons on his shirt. "I don't know. I don't exactly have a lot of experience with teenage boys."

Her hands flattened on his chest. "I think we should stop talking and commence with the ass grabbing now."

One of his hands slid lower but stopped just short of the prize. "You sure? Because it sounds like your confidence in my abilities to squeeze your rump to your satisfaction have faltered."

She pulled back a little. "You realize the whole *Harry Potter* thing wasn't a real comparison, right?"

"Sounded real."

She wiggled her hips to encourage him. "Maybe you should give it one more go to prove your ass-grabbing skills are superior to Ron Weasley's."

To prove her wrong, he slid one palm lower, smoothing it over the gentle curve of her backside to where it rounded out to a perfect handful. He grinned when her pupils dilated and her lips parted with a gentle breath.

"Aren't there two hands back there?" she urged.

"Pushy, aren't you?" His other hand joined the first one and glided over her spandex-covered rump. He applied gentle pressure and nudged her even closer, until she could feel the evidence of what she did to him beneath his jeans. She gasped, fanning her breath across his neck and accelerating his heart rate. He bent his knees and dipped his hands lower so the tips of his fingers could feel the groove at the tops of her thighs.

She sighed against him again and fisted her hands in the material of his shirt. He took advantage of her open mouth and stole a kiss, fully intending on the contact being nothing more than a brief spark. His way of reminding her how easily she always melted against him. But she surprised him when her tongue swept out and prodded his lips open.

Her tongue swirled around his, sucking the breath from his lungs with her softness and determination. His hands palmed her ass tighter as he turned them and backed her toward the closest wall. He had no idea where they were or if the wall was there. He remembered seeing a wall close by when he'd walked in the door. Yeah, he was pretty sure it was there. If not, then he'd just toss her to the floor.

She grunted when her back hit the plaster and rattled a picture by her head. Had he pushed her with too much force? His blood was pumping through his veins too hard, seizing all thought and handicapping his ability to notice anything beyond Stella and her hot body wiggling against his. He shoved his knees in between her legs and spread them to accommodate his hips. She took the position a step further and wrapped one of her long, leanly muscled legs around his thigh. One of his hands abandoned her ass and hooked over her leg, tugging it higher.

Damn, she was hot, matching his burning desire with her own. One of them moaned; he wasn't sure which because the sound pumped through his system.

Then she doused the flame when she tore her mouth from his. "Brandon," she said with a rough whisper.

He wasn't finished with her yet, so he dropped kisses along her neck. Satisfaction hummed through him when she tilted her head and gave him optimal access to the sensitive spot beneath her ear.

"Brandon," she said again in a louder voice.

He only grunted because he didn't want to take his mouth off her long enough to answer.

"We have to stop," she told him.

He chuckled against her ear. "That's funny."

But instead of getting back to business, she gave his shoulders a shove. "We're in public."

"So?" He bent his head to get another taste of her skin, because who the hell cared if everyone could see them? But Stella obviously had other ideas, because she shoved him again.

"We can't continue with something we won't be able to finish."

His mind cleared of hazy lust and was able to focus on her words. Finish. Yeah, he got what she meant. If they weren't in the middle of her studio, she'd be taking his clothes off instead of pushing him away. While the kiss had been hot as hell, like get-thee-naked-ASAP scorching, he was grateful one of them had their head on straight. Because his sure as hell was never screwed on right when he was around her.

"Brandon." Her tongue darted out to lick her still-swollen lips. "About what you said at the hospital..."

"You have to go, Stella," he blurted out. Because nothing like ripping off the Band-Aid.

She tilted her head as though she didn't understand. "I have to go?" she repeated.

He backed away and removed her hands from his shoulders. "I know what I said about you staying, and I want you to forget that." His thumbs scraped along her knuckles. "You need to do this. Get that teaching job that you want so badly."

She shifted against him and his eyes almost rolled back in his head when her hips nudged his. "Brandon, I don't understand what you mean. You asked me not to go to Chicago, and now you're telling me to leave?"

The thought of her walking out of his life and never returning made him want to chew glass. But she'd repeatedly told him she'd come back and it was past time he showed her some trust. "I was being selfish. I mean, yeah, I don't want you to go. But I can't ask you to do that, because this job means something to you." He tilted her chin up. "And you mean something to me. So you need to go and do this." She opened her mouth and he thumbed her lower lip. "You'll hate yourself if you don't. And then you'll hate me and I can't live in a world that you're not a part of."

She averted her gaze, probably her way of hiding the tears she didn't want him to see. "I could never hate you," she whispered.

"Well, I don't feel like testing that theory out."

"But I thought this was a deal breaker for you," she reminded him. "I thought you had all kinds of trust issues."

"I'm working on those," he told her. "And you're worth waiting for."

A single tear rolled down her cheek, which he swiped away with his thumb. "No one's ever put my wants first before."

He buried his nose in her hair and inhaled deeply. "I'm not trying to break any records."

She pursed her lips. "They may not even offer me anything."

"Stella. They'd be crazy not to."

She shrugged. "I'm just saying. There's a chance I'll be back."

He flicked his thumb over her cheek. "And I'm just saying. Go for what you've always wanted. Get that job and be happy."

Even if her achieving her dreams meant breaking his heart.

NINETEEN

The following Friday the Bobcats lost their game, sending premature whispers among the town as to whether or not they'd actually make the playoffs. Blake hadn't seemed worried, at least when Brandon had seen him after the game. Yeah, he'd been pissed at the three fumbles by various players. But he still had faith that his players could pull themselves together for the rest of the season. There were only two games left, so Brandon hoped they could too.

On Saturday, after the loss, Brandon had to get up early and take care of some business. Considering one of their projects was about to close, which they desperately needed the payout from, Brandon hadn't balked at giving up his Saturday morning. By the time he'd finished punch lists and walk-throughs with clients, he was on his second travel mug of coffee. When he'd left the house at seven that morning, Matt had still been asleep but Brandon needed some time to talk to him. Trish hadn't called back since her last phone call about clueing Matt in. And Brandon hadn't had time to speak with him.

Correction: Brandon had been putting it off.

The subject matter was a slippery one, and he'd been spending the past week pondering how to broach the topic. There was no telling how Matt would react and Brandon needed to be prepared for anything. And he needed to get a move on before Trish took matters into her own hands and broadsided Matt with the announcement.

Brandon pulled into his driveway and downed the last of his coffee. The stuff had gone cold, but the caffeine was too precious to waste. He was just getting out of the truck when his phone rang. He glanced at the caller ID and tried to settle his heart when Stella's name flashed on the screen.

"Hi," he greeted as he stepped out of the truck and shut the door.

"Hi," she answered back with a soft voice.

Brandon's steps faltered when Stella didn't say anything else. He shoved his car keys in his pocket. "Stella?"

"Yeah, sorry. I just..." He heard her expel a breath. "I forgot to tell you before that I worked things out with my mom."

Brandon grinned as he opened the front door and was greeted by Duke. He gave the dog's ears a brief scratch before heading to the kitchen. "I'm glad to hear that." Was that all he could say? "Are you two all right now?"

"Yeah," Stella said with a sigh. "We talked over a loaf of homemade bread. She even made apple butter to go with it."

Brandon opened the fridge and took out leftover roasted chicken. "Thought your mom wasn't much of a cook?"

Stella laughed, which set his teeth on edge because he wanted to be near her. He wanted to see the laughter light up her eyes. "She's not. I guess she was feeling adventurous." She paused a moment. "Anyway, I just wanted to thank you."

"For what?"

"Just for being there and listening. I didn't take the time to tell you before and I felt bad."

"You don't need to feel bad, Stella. I was just doing what anyone else would have done," Brandon answered. He tucked his cell phone between his shoulder and ear as he unwrapped aluminum from the chicken.

"Did you?" she questioned. "Are you saying you could have been anyone sitting with me and holding my hand while I cried about my shitty childhood?"

Well, when she put it that way...Yeah, Brandon supposed she was right.

No, he *knew* she was right. What he didn't know was why he was trying to downplay the whole thing. He'd be an idiot not to know the moment they'd had and how the intimacy had brought them to another level.

He blew out a breath and closed his eyes. "Stella." He pictured her lying on her bed, hair spread out beneath her, bare legs tangled in cotton sheets. "You're welcome," he said instead of asking her what she was wearing. Because how wrong would that have been? Here she was thanking him for a profound moment, and all he could do was think about her in bed.

"I have a class in a few minutes, so I have to go," she told him.

"Okay."

So why wasn't he hanging up? Or why hadn't she?

"Bye, Brandon." The soft click in his ear was like a gunshot to the chest.

Brandon resumed his lunch preparation as Duke ambled up behind him, trying to put Stella's soft voice from his mind. And his need for her. He turned and tossed a piece of chicken in the dog's direction. But Duke wasn't the quickest bullet in the gun and the chicken landed on the floor.

"Gotta be faster than that, boy," Brandon commented.

Duke eventually found the meat and lapped it up. Then he sat and wagged his tail back and forth across the floor.

"No more," Brandon told him. Duke's ears perked up and his head tilted. "You're already spoiled." He gave the dog another ear rub. "Where's Matt?" Brandon asked as though Duke could answer. "He was supposed to feed you this morning."

When Duke didn't answer because, yeah, he was a dog, Brandon left the kitchen in search of his son. Matt had never been a real late sleeper and rarely ever spent his Saturdays in bed or even holed up in his room. He was either out with friends or with Adrienne.

The fact that Matt hadn't appeared yet left Brandon wondering if he was feeling all right.

The hallway leading to the bedrooms was quiet. Almost too quiet?

Had he left?

No, Matt wouldn't have gone anywhere without texting Brandon where he was going. He'd taught his son to be more responsible than that.

Matt's bedroom door was closed, so Brandon knocked. "Matt?" he called when no answer came.

Was that a muffled response? Brandon pushed the door open and stepped inside. The blinds were still closed, preventing sunlight from penetrating the dark interior. The bed was an unmade mess with the comforter hanging halfway off the bed and one pillow on the floor by the nightstand.

Matt was seated on the floor, leaning against the footboard and cradling his cell phone. His hair was still untamed from sleep and he'd yet to change from the basketball shorts he usually wore to bed.

"Hey," Brandon greeted from the doorway. "You want some leftover chicken for lunch?"

Matt stared at his cell phone while turning it over in his hands. "Sure," was his muttered response.

Brandon eyed his slumped posture and the fact that he'd yet to look Brandon's way. "Everything all right?" he asked his son.

Matt only shrugged.

Okay, then. "Did you get into a fight with Adrienne?"

"No."

Great. One-word answers. Matt had never really been the typical sullen teenager. But he was sure as shit putting new definition to that term now.

Brandon leaned against the door frame and crossed his arms over his chest. "What's going on, Matt? Whatever it is, you can tell me."

Matt still didn't look up from his phone. "I think you already know."

Brandon narrowed his eyes. "What're you . . ." His words trailed off as it hit him like a kick to the midsection. "Your mom called you, didn't she?"

Matt sniffed and nodded.

Brandon uncrossed his arms and scrubbed a hand over his head. Shit. Trish was supposed to have waited for him to talk to Matt. As much as he'd like to blame his ex-wife for jumping the gun, Brandon knew it was his own fault. He'd been putting it off because he hadn't known how to broach the subject with Matt. His job as the parent was to protect his child, to shield him from hurt. The truth was, he hadn't wanted to have the discussion in the first place. He'd sort of been hoping Trish would have changed her mind.

Brandon stepped into the room, searching for something to say. An apology seemed inadequate but, damn, his kid was confused just like he feared would happen.

"She said you and her talked about seeing her next summer," Matt announced.

"Well..." Brandon started to explain, then stopped himself. "Yeah. But you and I were supposed to talk about it first."

"Why?" Matt turned his pleading gaze to Brandon. "Why would we talk about it first?"

Brandon blew out a breath and scrubbed a hand down his face. "Matt...it's a delicate situation."

"Are you going to try and keep me from her?" Matt asked, point-blank.

The question came out more as an accusation, which Brandon wasn't sure if Matt intended. His gaze was hard and unyielding, and this certainly wasn't the reaction he'd anticipated. He sat on the floor next to Matt and leaned against the footboard. "Of course not," Brandon immediately answered. But when Matt stared back, unblinking, Brandon explained further. "Matt, I don't want you to be hurt again."

"Because I get it," Matt went on.

They sat in silence for a moment, each trying to process the sticky situation and sort through their feelings. Trish had been absent from their lives for so long, and yet she was still causing turmoil.

"Do you want to go see her?" Brandon asked.

Matt played with his phone, turning it over in his hand and running his finger across the screen. "I don't know," he answered with a shrug. "I haven't felt anything for her in so long that I…" He blew out a breath. "It's just weird, you know? Talking to her after all this time."

Yeah, Brandon knew. He knew better than anyone.

"I used to hate her," Matt said in a low voice.

Brandon gazed at his son, staring at his strong profile and the dark stubble that darkened his jaw. He saw so much of himself at that age, and yet Brandon had done his damnedest to make sure Matt grew up better than him. To teach him not to make the same mistakes Brandon had.

"You never hated her, Matt," Brandon answered. "You loved her. That's why her absence always hurt so bad."

Matt didn't answer, only shrugged his bare shoulders, which Brandon took as agreement. He knew because he identified with Matt's pain, with his conflicting feelings. He'd hated Trish for a long time, too, until he recognized his hate as pain for the woman he'd loved leaving them.

"I get why you didn't want me talking to her," Matt said.

"I thought you'd be mad," Brandon admitted.

Matt shrugged again. "Nah. I mean, it's weird, talking to her and stuff. She sounds…happy, though."

Trish had always sounded happy when she'd call in the past, but he didn't tell Matt that. Matt sounded optimistic. More optimistic than Brandon expected, and he didn't want to burst the kid's bubble, even though his need to protect was still overpowering his need to let go.

"I'm sorry, Matt,"

"What for?"

Brandon stared ahead, at their feet resting next to each other. "I don't know. I guess I always blamed myself for her leaving. You deserved better and I couldn't give it to you."

"Dad," Matt said, and Brandon finally looked at him. "You did your best. And we were always good, right?"

Brandon nodded, not trusting his voice to come out right.

"You were enough," Matt went on. "You always gave me enough."

Those were words that he'd needed to hear for so long. He'd even tried telling himself that he didn't need the affirmation from Matt. He shouldn't have needed it. But damn he had. After Trish had taken off, his confidence as a parent had been shaken. Cracked. Handicapped, if you will, or whatever the hell one wanted to call it. He'd blamed himself for Trish leaving, for not giving her whatever she'd needed to make her stay. A part of him thought Matt had blamed him too. It had been a shitty thing to consider, especially since Matt had been so young and a three-year-old's mind didn't work that way.

Brandon cleared his throat and searched for something to say. Something other than, *Guuuuuuh.*

"So should we, like, hug now?" Matt asked.

Brandon nudged Matt's shoulder with his. "I don't know, do you want to?"

They were both silent for a moment.

"Hugging's cool," Matt finally said.

"As long as we don't do it in front of your friends, right?" Brandon joked. He couldn't be sure, but he wore Matt actually blushed. And damn if that didn't make Brandon feel warm and fuzzy inside.

"Dad," Matt responded with a half chuckle, half choke.

Yeah, my thoughts exactly.

"Do you think she means it?" Matt asked.

Brandon pulled in a breath and slowly blew it out. "I don't know," he answered honestly. "But I think she's trying."

"Yeah," Matt agreed. "Do you think she feels bad? I mean, I know she always says she does, but do you think she's for real?"

Brandon turned the words over in his mind, knowing what Matt needed to hear. He didn't want to lie to the kid, but he also always had a hard time knowing what went on in Trish's head. "I think she has a lot of regrets," he told Matt.

"You think I should give her another chance," Matt guessed.

At first, no. He hadn't wanted Matt to give Trish another chance. Because she didn't deserve it. She'd had an opportunity to be a wife and mother, and she'd chosen to leave. To have another life. But now? Now he wanted Matt to be better. To rise above the bitter man Brandon had once been. The one who'd hated Trish and blamed himself for everything.

"I think the decision is up to you." He slung an arm around Matt's shoulders. "Look, your mom's made a lot of mistakes. Some I'm sure she wishes she could take back. But she's still your mom. And without her, I wouldn't have you." He nudged Matt's shoulders and Matt finally looked at him. "Yeah, the years after she left were hell. But I got you out of it and you're worth all that."

Matt looked away, triggering a frisson of relief in Brandon's system. Neither of them had been good at the huggy, kissy, mushy thing.

Despite that, sitting next to his kid, having a talk they should have had years ago was...nice.

Matt's phone rang. Brandon withdrew his arm from around Matt's shoulder and glanced at the phone when Matt picked it up. The display screen said *Mom.*

Matt stared at it for a second.

"Make peace with her," Brandon told his son. "She's trying."

Matt nodded, and Brandon stood to give him some privacy.

"Dad," Matt called, stopping Brandon at the bedroom door. He turned and eyed the kid who'd turned his world upside down eighteen years ago but had been worth every stressful second. "Thanks," Matt said.

Brandon only nodded, because his heart was in his throat. He turned to leave just as he heard Matt say, "Hey, Mom."

Now, *that* had him smiling. Go figure.

"Are you sure you've packed enough sweaters? Because you know Chicago gets really cold this time of year." Gloria was perched on the edge of Stella's bed, inspecting every item she was throwing in her suitcase. As though she were some invalid who didn't know how to pack for herself.

"For the tenth time, I've got enough cold weather clothing," Stella answered back with practiced patience. She shot her mom a look as she dug through her underwear drawer. "I did live there, you know."

Gloria offered a smile that didn't reach her eyes. "Yes, I know."

All her old ballet paraphernalia, including her toe shoes, toe pads, flats, and a few leotards, was stuffed in a box at the top of her closet. When she'd missed out on her last choreography job and had returned to Blanco Valley—feeling horrendously sorry for herself—Stella had shoved all the stuff away and hadn't looked at it since.

She grabbed the box and opened it. The familiar smell of rosin still brought back memories of every ballet class she took. That was when she'd known true peace, doing something for herself and letting go of all the ugliness that had followed her childhood around.

Stella picked up one of the toe shoes and ran her fingers over the frayed satin where she'd cut around the boxed end of the toe. Cutting the satin, then burning the material made for better grip on the floor. She'd also ripped the inner leather lining out so the shoes would bend easier with her foot. She lifted the shoe to her nose and inhaled deeply. The nostalgic feeling flooding her system fought with the nagging in the back of her brain. The one she'd had since her encounter with Brandon in her studio.

He'd told her to go because he knew how much this opportunity meant to her. Because he was selfless and would never ask her to compromise herself for his benefit. Her heart had swelled with love for him, turning her resolve into a giant question mark.

Was she making a mistake by leaving? By making Brandon wait for her? And would he really wait?

She knew his trust issues wouldn't go away overnight, even though he was working on them. What if he decided she was gone too long? Or wasn't worth waiting for?

For the first time in years, she'd started to second-guess her decision to leave Blanco Valley. Even though it was temporary, Stella had never been totally sure if she'd want to come back.

She wanted to resent Brandon for upsetting her plans. For being so damn sexy and wonderful that now she didn't want to leave him. But it wasn't his fault. It was her own fault for thinking she could get attached to him and still be able to walk away. To pretend this choreography job was more important.

She turned her pointe shoe over in her hand one more time before replacing it in the box.

"I still think you'll regret not going to the game tomorrow," her mother said from the closet doorway.

Tomorrow night was the Bobcats' final regular season game. If they won, they clinched their division and earned a place in the playoffs. Last season they'd barely missed out on the playoffs, but the town was hoping for a more victorious outcome this time. Annabelle had tried her hardest to urge Stella to come tonight. But she just couldn't. She couldn't sit there next to Brandon, because they always managed to find each other at the games, hear his deep voice, feel his wide shoulders brushing hers. She needed distance if she was going to keep her resolve and follow through with the plans she'd already made.

"I'll be fine," she told her mom, even though that wasn't what her mom had asked.

"Are you sure?" she pushed. "You don't even need to be there until Monday."

Stella glanced at her mom and attempted a carefree grin. "I have a lot to do still before I leave."

"Okay—" Gloria said, then stopped and tilted her head. "I think someone just knocked on your door."

Stella sighed and left her box of ballet stuff on the closet floor. "It's probably Annabelle so she can make me feel guilty again."

She reached the front door and swung the thing open. Her heart double-timed, then fluttered, literally fluttered, when she saw Brandon on her doorstep. He was tall and wide and gorgeous with dark sunglasses shading his eyes and a backward baseball cap covering his thick brown hair. His jeans were faded and worn, with a tear near the pocket.

And his Bobcats hooded sweatshirt only emphasized his thick shoulders.

She bet the sweatshirt smelled good. She bet it was soft and warm and smelled like his skin and soap all mixed together into one toe-curling scent.

He grinned at her when she only stood there staring at him. "Stella?"

She blinked herself out of her trance so she could stop fantasizing about slipping her hands under the sweatshirt. "Sorry," she said, then stood back for him to enter. "Come on in."

He brushed past her and, yeah, he smelled like something that ought to be labeled "Insta-orgasm." A gift bag with tissue paper spurting from the top dangled from one of his hands. He yanked his sunglasses off and hooked them in the pocket of his jeans. Her eyes followed the movement, exploring how the soft denim cupped his package like he was about to rock a 501 Blues commercial.

Or maybe an underwear commercial. Something for Joe Boxer, or anything that would keep his impressiveness the center of attention. Because, *damn*.

"Stella." His voice was low and rumbly. She'd spent enough time with him to recognize the need lacing the words.

He tipped her chin up with his index finger and lowered his mouth. She didn't have time to prepare herself for his touch. And maybe he'd done that on purpose so she wouldn't have the opportunity to push him away. Not that it mattered, because she wouldn't have pushed him away. He ought to know that by now.

He jumped right into the kiss by encouraging her lips open with his tongue. And she allowed him, because every time he kissed her, she forgot how to think. How to react. The only thing she was capable of doing was standing there, because the man fried her brain. She kissed him back because it was too good not to throw her whole body and soul into it. The gift bag dropped from his fingers, allowing his arm to wrap securely around her back. His large palm splayed across her hip, then moved to cup her rear end. Images assaulted her of the other night in her studio, when he'd so skillfully maneuvered her against the wall, creating a delicious tingle in her midsection.

He groaned and took the kiss up another notch by angling his head and delving his tongue deeper. His other hand, the one holding her chin, slid back into her hair.

They needed to stop. Not only was her mom loitering somewhere in the back of the house, but also things could easily escalate to a place they had no business going.

So she pulled away, forcing back the reluctance threatening to take control.

"You don't play fair," she accused.

Brandon smiled and swiped his thumb across her lower lip. "I never claimed to."

She gripped the front of his sweatshirt with two fists. "But see, I really need you to."

He snickered and gripped both her hips, holding her to him. "What's the matter, Stella? Do I make you weak in the knees?"

And then some. But giving him the upper hand was out of the question. She needed to keep it for herself or else she was done for.

Hell, you're already done for. And since when did you ever have the upper hand with this guy?

So what was a little lie? They made her feel better and gave her the illusion of having her shit together.

She pushed away from him and wiped her mouth with the back of her hand. "What's in the bag?" she questioned, because avoidance was sometimes a good thing.

His gaze zeroed in on her as though he knew she damn well *didn't* have her shit together. In fact, if she wasn't mistaken, it looked as though he wanted to say something. And not some smart-ass comment, just to keep up their tradition of taking swipes at each other. No, there was something else on his mind. Something deep he needed to say, but she'd derailed him.

Normally she'd give herself a pat on the back. But the usual victory that followed one-upping Brandon wasn't there.

He snagged the bag off the floor, just as her mother made an appearance.

She offered Brandon a smile, as though she knew exactly what they'd just been up to. Knowing her mother, and probably the way Stella was toeing the line of hyperventilation, Gloria probably did. "Hello, Brandon."

He nodded. "Ms. Davenport."

Gloria's gaze volleyed back and forth between him and Stella. "Well, I need to get going." She gave Stella a peck on the cheek. "I'll be back in a few hours," she said, then was gone.

The silence between her and Brandon was too thick for Stella's comfort. Was he upset that she'd stopped the kiss? Had he changed his mind about wanting her to leave?

"What time is your flight?" he asked.

She shoved her own internal battle away. "Nine-fifteen."

"What're you doing with your house?"

"I'm only going to be gone for six weeks," she answered. Stella had put a hold on her mail and Gloria had agreed to stop by just to check on things.

Brandon nodded, then handed her the bag. "Matt and I put something together for you."

Her hand was damp and trembling when she took the bag from him. His bigger hand closed over hers, as though sensing her building anxiety. "It's okay," he told her.

What was okay? They were okay?

"I don't have to go," she blurted out.

Brandon's hand froze over hers. Then his grip tightened. "Don't be stupid."

"Um...thanks?" Yeah, not what she'd expected him to say.

"I'm serious," he reiterated. "Don't throw away what you've been working for."

What about what they were throwing away? "I'm just saying," she went on. "If you asked me to stay, I would."

Brandon dragged his thumb across her knuckles as they both still gripped the bag. "I already told you, I won't ask you to do that. You'd need to make that decision on your own."

What did that mean? How was she supposed to respond to that?

"Are you saying you want me to stay, but you don't want to ask me?"

"Of course I don't want you to go," he told her. "Especially since you may not come back. You think I like the idea of never being able to drag you off to bed?"

She leaned away from him. "Oh, and that's all you're waiting for?"

He chuckled and tucked a piece of her hair behind her ear. "I'd be crazy not to."

"So you really don't want me to go?" she asked him again.

Brandon blew out a heavy sigh. "Stella," he said. His hand left hers and he threaded his fingers through her hair. "I'm saying if you really don't want to go back to Chicago, it needs to be what you want, not because I asked you not to go. You've lived your life for other people for too long. It's time you started living for yourself." His deep brown gaze searched hers. "Do you understand what I'm saying?"

"I don't know what to say." She swallowed. "I'm not used to people...caring about me this much." She wanted to lean in to him. Just bury her face in his neck and slide her hands beneath his sweatshirt so she could feel the dips and ridges of his back.

He tapped her chin with his index finger. "See, that's where you're wrong. It's not just caring, Stella. It's love."

Her breath huffed out the same time a tear leaked over her lashes. She whipped her head up right as Brandon departed and closed the front door behind him. The soft *snick* matched the hitching of her breath as he shut the door on whatever she'd been planning to say.

Stella swiped a tear away and dumped tissue paper out of the gift bag. Inside was a five-by-seven framed photo of Matt and Brandon, Matt in his football uniform and Brandon with his arm slung around Matt's shoulders. Both were grinning, both handsome and full of life.

On the bottom of the frame were the words *I left my heart in Colorado.*

Mine.

The word whispered in her mind, teasing her with what she could have if only she had the guts to come out and claim it.

Stella ran her index finger over the carved words, replaying Brandon's brief visit and wishing she'd taken the chance to come out of her shell.

She placed the photo on the hall table and snagged her cell phone from her purse. Her fingers trembled as she dialed Annabelle's number.

"Hey," her friend answered on the second ring.

"Do you think I'm making the right decision?" Stella came out and asked.

"Yep," Annabelle answered immediately.

Stella sighed, leaned against the front door, and slid down to the floor. "Annabelle."

Her friend giggled. "Well, you've got to give me something to go on, Stella. I don't know what you're talking about."

She thunked her head back on the door. "Do you think I'm making the right decision by leaving?"

"It's what you want, isn't it?"

"Yeah, but what if fate is handing me my one and only opportunity at happiness. With something real. I mean, what if this is a test and by getting on that plane tonight I'll end up failing miserably." Stella pushed to her feet and paced around the entryway. "And then while he's waiting, Brandon bumps into some gorgeous supermodel who says something witty and they end up getting married. And then they have three children who, of course, will be just as gorgeous and star in dozens of Ralph Lauren ads. And I in my grief take up a hobby of collecting something really stupid like porcelain dolls, which becomes an obsession and I name them absurd things like Prissy and Muffin." Stella took a deep breath and forged on. "And Brandon lives happily ever after with his Ralph Lauren family, occasionally thinking about that ballerina he used to know, and I'm just the loony old woman who talks to her dolls."

Annabelle was silent a moment. "You've given this a lot of thought, haven't you?"

"I'm serious, Annabelle. I don't want to talk to dolls."

"So don't talk to your dolls."

A hysterical laugh bubbled out. "See, you're not helping."

Annabelle chuckled. "I'm sorry, but that was a humorous and surprisingly well-thought-out monologue. Not to mention ridiculous."

"It's not ridiculous to me," she argued. "It could happen."

"It'll never happen," Annabelle countered.

Stella leaned against the wall. "But how can you be so sure? That's what I'm struggling with. How can I be sure I'm making the right decision?"

Annabelle sighed. "I don't know, Stella. I don't think anyone is ever really sure about anything. But the fact that you're questioning yourself this much ought to tell you something."

Stella was silent as she pondered Annabelle's words. "Yeah," she finally answered.

"Look, Brandon said he'd wait for you, right?"

"But what if he doesn't?" Stella threw out.

"When have you ever known Brandon to go back on his word?"

"Yes, but what if he doesn't?" she pressed again.

"Stella," Annabelle said on a groan. "You have got to stop being your own worst enemy."

Stella closed her eyes and lowered her head. "You're right, sorry." She scraped her toe along the floor. "I think he told me he loves me."

"You think?" Annabelle repeated.

"Pretty sure," Stella admitted.

"Of course he does," Annabelle said with a smile in her

voice. "You know he'll wait for you, Stella. But can you wait for him?"

She'd waited her whole life for a man like Brandon West and would wait another lifetime if she had to. "Of course I can. I'm just not sure I want to."

"I think you've got your answer, then."

TWENTY

The marching band launched into an escalated fight song as the Bobcats' final game of the season ticked its way through the fourth quarter. The Lewis-Palmer Rangers were the favorite to win, especially since they were reigning state champions. So far, they'd forced the Bobcats to earn every bead of sweat and grass stain decorating the exhausted but motivated players. Brandon knew the team wouldn't go down without a fight, and the Rangers were definitely sporting for one. Seeing as though the lead kept volleying back and forth between the two teams, it was obvious they weren't going to just hand over the division title.

But the Bobcats knew what they were up against. No way were they going to have a repeat of last season, making it all the way to the end only to slouch away under the heavy cloak of disappointment.

The score was currently 27–21 with the Rangers in the lead. The Bobcats fans, who'd packed every last square inch of the bleachers, should have calmed in light of their team slowly fading. But they'd yet to lose faith.

The fourth quarter wound to its final minutes with Cody receiving the snap. The two girls in front of Brandon surged to their feet and waved the orange and black pom-poms in the air. Wyatt Thompson, the Bobcats' running back, easily received the ball. But the victory was short-lived when he was tackled and flipped over onto this back.

The crowd sent out a groan, and the two girls in front of Brandon sat down again. He turned for a second, ready to make a comment about the game, then remembered he was alone. Because Stella wasn't there.

Her plane had left last night, taking his heart along with it. Logically, he knew leaving was the best thing for her. Stella needed to fulfill her dreams; otherwise she'd never truly be happy. Yeah, he wanted to be with her and yeah he'd wait for however long it took. Even if it meant never seeing her again. However, deep down he'd held out a small sliver of hope she'd change her mind. That she wouldn't be offered the teaching position she so wanted. That had been his pesky trust problem trying to poke its rabid head up. He'd shoved it down as they'd stood in her foyer yesterday. The words had been there, dying to be released.

Just stay.

Unfortunately, he knew only thinking about himself wouldn't do either of them any good. If they had a shot at something real, whenever that would be, then he needed to show her some trust.

The gesture made him feel like he was literally out on a limb. Walking a thin wire two hundred feet above the ground with no safety net underneath. Though his gut told him he wouldn't fall, Brandon couldn't help the fear that lingered.

But, damn, he missed her. Missed her snarky sense of humor that made him laugh every time. He missed the fire that shot in her clear blue eyes whenever he pissed her off. Missed the feel of her lithe body against his, her lips, her soft hair. But most of all he missed how she made him feel. Whole. Worthy. Like he could get through anything as long as she was with him.

The play on the field resumed, snapping Brandon's attention back to reality. Matt was currently on the sidelines and possession of the ball had been turned over to the Rangers. It was third and one, but the running back fumbled his hand-off. Blake called his last time-out. The clock had twenty seconds left in the game.

Brandon's gaze tracked Matt, then skittered over the UT recruiter who'd been carefully making notes on his clipboard. As a compromise, Brandon had decided to take a driving trip to Austin so he and Matt could tour the UT campus. Winter break was coming up and he figured that would be a perfect time to visit the college his son wanted to attend. Plus it would give him a distraction from missing Stella.

The Bobcats' time-out ended and the players dispersed. The clock resumed with the Rangers still having possession of the ball. The Cats needed an interception something fierce; otherwise they could kiss this game good-bye.

Sweat built up on Brandon's hands as the announcer made some vague comment about the risk the other coach was taking. He wasn't really paying attention to the white noise of the band; the cheerleaders, who'd been back-flipping all over the place; or the crowd, including the Beehive Mafia seated behind him and alternating between screaming at the field and making off-color comments to one another.

The Rangers moved into position to kick a field goal, and both of the stands came to a hush as the action amped up. Brandon's gaze skittered to Blake, who had his ball cap pulled low over his face and arms crossed tightly over his chest. He assumed the strategy of the Rangers was to kick a field goal, putting them up by three and then running the clock down. Things didn't look good for the Bobcats, but the fans weren't giving up hope. They were on their feet, cheering for their team, encouraging them, even though the game was slowly slipping through their fingers. The clock ticked down, like the countdown to an execution as the kicker readied himself, then sprinted forward. His foot made contact with the ball, and their fans' noise level escalated as they assumed the ball would sail through the goalposts and bring them the win. But out of nowhere a Bobcat defensive lineman jumped up and successfully blocked the ball.

The stands around him roared to a deafening level when the ball went flying and spiraled out of control. Both teams made a mad dash for the thing, creating a chaos of confused but determined players.

Brandon's heart hammered up to his throat as the Bobcats on the sidelines jumped up and down. Blake and Cameron ran down the length of the field as the ball rolled and was attacked by about six different players, Matt included. Only two of those players bore the orange and black uniform. An air of desperation and anticipation clung to both sides of the stands. Then someone was up clutching the ball tightly to his side. Brandon blinked at the orange and black of the Bobcat uniform, belatedly realizing it was *his* kid as Matt screamed down the field toward the end zone. The announcer screeched some frantic message of unbelievable playmaking and, "Holy Jesus, folks, look at that kid fly!"

The crowd went ballistic, on their feet, screaming and waving their hands and pom-poms as Matt raced against the time clock.

Four seconds.

Three seconds.

Brandon's heart slammed harder in his chest as he watched a full season of hard work and determination come down to one play that could save the game. Part of him couldn't believe he was watching the same player who used to struggle with agility and balance. And, son of a bitch, the realization hit Brandon as he followed Matt's movement down the field. How instrumental Stella had been in Matt's playmaking. Brandon would never have believed that ballet training could have had that much of an impact on Matt's football game. But it had, and Brandon reluctantly admitted how much he'd underestimated Stella. How little credit he'd given Matt's time in her studio.

He snagged his cell phone to send her a text, saying...well, he wasn't sure. But he felt he needed to talk to her. But before he could compose a message, Matt's feet flew past the five-yard line, then crossed the end zone just as the clock hit zero.

The players held the celebrations for one more minute while they got in formation for their field goal. The noise of the bleachers was a loud hum of kids hollering and stomping their feet as the kicker lined up. He easily made it, and the hum turned into a roar. The players and coaches immediately rushed the field, headsets and helmets flying in the air as they rushed the players. Brandon's ears rang as the band fired up another song and the fans roared and stomped the bleachers. The stunned faces of the opponents and their coaches matched the shock reverberating through the Bobcats fans. The game should have ended with the Rangers' field goal. Instead their team had pulled a stunner out of their asses and scored a touchdown with twenty seconds left on the clock.

The former state champions, the ones who'd been favored to take home the win, filed off the field, heads hung in defeat and shock. The Bobcats continued to maul and pile on top of each other on the field.

Soon the fans followed, rushing the field as parents looked for kids and girlfriends looked for boyfriends. The field quickly turned into a mass of celebrating people, plain-clothes mixing with jerseys and sweat and exuberated players.

Brandon knew he'd never find Matt in this mess, so he stayed in his spot as people moved all around him. Some hugging and celebrating with others and some trying their best to get to the field. Behind him Beverly Rowley told some kid to "Move your ass, pronto." Virginia chastised her friend for the language and reiterated to the kid that he needed to speed himself up. Brandon only shook his head as one of them bumped into him from behind.

"Aren't you going to get down there and find Matty?" Virginia asked.

Brandon turned to face her. "I'll find him after the game," he told her. "He's probably with his friends anyway."

Virginia gestured to a spot next to him. "Where's your game friend? The one you're always making googly eyes at."

For a second, he almost feigned ignorance. After all, denial had been easier than admitting that he made "googly eyes" at Stella. Or that he even missed her. But what was the point? Virginia, as well as the rest of the Mafia, knew there was something special between him and Stella. He'd been an idiot for not seeing it sooner and an even bigger idiot for letting her leave.

However much he knew she loved what she was doing, and needed this opportunity, her departure hurt like a son of a bitch. Cut him deeper than Trish leaving.

"She's in Chicago," he told Virginia.

Virginia squinted at him, then was jostled from behind. Brandon placed a hand on her shoulder to steady her. "Chicago?" she repeated. "What the devil is she doing there? Don't you love the girl?"

Brandon blinked at her, thrown off by her blunt question. Which was stupid because Virginia had never been subtle about anything in her life, including her continued threats to have Duke thrown in a shelter for eating her roses. Then he grinned because, yeah, he loved Stella. "Yes, ma'am, I do."

"Well, why'd you let her leave?" Virginia demanded. "Doesn't she know how you feel?"

"Uh…" He'd sort of told her, in a roundabout way he assumed she'd figure out. Maybe not the best tactic.

Virginia rolled her eyes. "Men," she muttered to herself. Then she smacked him on the arm. "And don't call me ma'am. Makes me feel old."

She finally made her way down the bleachers, but Brandon remained in his spot. The field was still a mess of people and players, as were the bleachers. People were either trying desperately to exit or were hanging around talking about the win. Excitement and euphoria hummed through the crowd and should have dragged Brandon along with him. After all, he'd just watched his son rush the field with the rest of his team and celebrate what they'd been working toward all season.

Unfortunately, none of it meant anything without Stella.

Stella stood at the window of her Chicago apartment and watched the powdery snowflakes slowly drift to the ground. They landed in the narrow alley below, barely clinging to the ground because the temperature wasn't quite cold enough for them to stick. She lifted a mug of hot cocoa to her lips as a mother cat and her kittens darted from one side of the alley to the other. They barely dodged the garbage truck that stopped by every Tuesday to empty the Dumpster. Normally Stella enjoyed watching the antics of the cat family, the way the kittens bounded all over the deserted alley and played with the trash that occasionally blew down the street. But tonight, Stella wasn't into it. Her gaze tracked the movements without really seeing anything. Even her hot cocoa was lukewarm and bland.

Maybe her lackluster mood was because she was so exhausted. Yeah, that had to be it. The six back-to-back classes she'd taught that day, not to mention the extra hour she'd spent with a student who'd been struggling with her triple pirouettes, had taken it out of her. Thus had been her schedule for the month since she'd left Colorado.

Her feet hurt, her knee throbbed. And she was lonely.

Which was strange, because she was surrounded by people all day. Students, other teachers, her roommate. So how could she be lonely? Where had this ache in her chest come from? She'd finally achieved what she'd wanted. *Rapunzel* was scheduled to premiere next week, and her artistic director had already offered her a permanent teaching position. All she had to do was sign the contract. The offer hadn't been a surprise. She'd known they'd come at her with something. But what had been a surprise were the second thoughts clouding what should have been elation. Her mother and Annabelle had flown out and taken her to a congratulatory dinner. They'd laughed, drunk champagne, and went to a show.

But in the back of Stella's mind had been those pesky second thoughts. As though accepting the offer would be a mistake. But how could fulfilling her dreams be a mistake? Stella knew she had some time to think about the offer. Her artistic director said he needed an answer by the time *Rapunzel* wrapped. Two weeks. But Stella had the feeling she wouldn't need two weeks. Why take that much time to decide on something she wasn't sure she wanted anymore?

Stella had yet to figure that one out and she supposed that was the reason for her melancholy mood tonight. Beyond just being tired.

Behind her, Jessica, the roommate the company had set her up with, came out of the back bedroom. Stella turned and pasted a smile on her face and lifted the mug to her lips.

"Are you sure you don't want to come?" Jessica asked as she wound her scarf around her neck.

Stella eyed the woman's red hair, which was styled in loose, perfect curls. "No, I'm good."

"You want me to bring you some pizza back?"

The thought of some Chicago-style pizza should have made Stella's mouth water. Instead, her stomach continued to turn over. "No, I'll just heat up some leftovers."

Jessica strung her handbag over her shoulder and

turned to leave, but she stopped at the last minute. "Oh, I almost forgot to tell you—you've got some mail on the counter."

"Anything exciting?"

Jessica shrugged. "Looks like mostly junk. But one of them looks like a handwritten letter."

A letter?

Her roommate smiled and opened the door. "You've got a secret admirer I don't know about?"

Stella snorted. "Yeah right."

"Don't wait up," she responded, then shut the door behind her.

The apartment was silent once again, leaving Stella alone with her thoughts. Sometimes she'd go back to the dance studio and use the alone time to practice. She always loved an empty studio where she could crank up the music and dance however she wanted. But lately she hadn't been interested. And what was even more disturbing was that she didn't know why.

Maybe she should have gone out with Jessica and her friends. Perhaps an evening out with other women would do her some good. Just some old-fashioned fun to take her mind off...

Brandon.

That's what was bothering her. And Stella knew that walking down to the corner pizza place wouldn't erase her mind of the man who'd let her leave.

Funny how she'd sworn she'd never give up her dreams for a man again, and here she was considering walking away from it all for one.

How messed up was that?

Stella set her mug down and groaned. When Brandon had initially asked her to stay, she'd been over the moon.

To the point where she'd been ready to throw her arms around his neck and scream yes! But then he'd rescinded it by saying it was a decision she needed to make on her own. As much as her brain understood, her heart had a harder time catching up. He'd told her she'd hate herself if she let the opportunity go by. And she knew he'd been right. This was something she'd needed to do. But after being faced with an offer of a full-time teaching position, all she'd wanted to do was call him just so she could hear his voice. Instead she'd called Annabelle, who'd squealed and booked a plane ticket so they could celebrate. And then she'd gone back to feeling lonely. Like something was still missing. Still unfulfilled.

At first she'd been unwilling to identify what the missing piece was. The thing that kept her up at night watching stray cats out the window. She wanted Brandon.

Not only that. She also wanted him to want her back.

Okay, yeah, she knew he wanted her. But she wanted him to want her enough to come after her. To be that guy who booked a red eye, then showed up on the doorstep all disheveled because he'd been up all night and hadn't really thought his plan through because all he could think about was getting to *her*.

Except real life isn't the movies.

And Brandon had done the noble thing by letting her leave. He'd been selfless by sacrificing his wants for her happiness.

Stella got that. Really, she did.

And she loved him for his chivalry. Men like Brandon West were one in a million.

Yeah, and you're seriously thinking about choosing a teaching job over him.

God, she was an idiot.

Was she really going to give up a once-in-a-lifetime guy
for a teaching job? Her entire adult life, she thought this was
what she'd wanted. Ever since losing out on that other job,
her sole focus had been getting back here. To recapture what
she'd lost. For a man.

What had she been trying to prove by coming back here?

She'd left her house. Left her mom, her best friend.
Brandon. At least she still had her studio. She hadn't
been able to bring herself to give that up completely.
Even though she wasn't there to run the thing, she
still missed her students. Their smiles, their enthusiasm.
Misty, the woman Stella had hired to run the place,
called regularly and kept her up to date. But it wasn't
the same.

She missed it all. Missed home.

Stella pushed away from the window, grabbed her mug,
and dumped the contents down the sink. So now she was
good and depressed...or even more depressed. Normally,
she'd call Annabelle, but those conversations always turned
to Brandon.

Maybe she should just call him. They hadn't talked
much. She supposed he thought he was giving her the time
he thought she needed. At first she had. But now? Now she
just wanted to hear his voice.

She snagged her cell phone from the counter and was
about to dial his number when her gaze fell on her mail.

More specifically the letter Jessica said she had.

Ms. Stella Davenport, along with her address, was written in a handwriting she didn't recognize.

So that ruled out Brandon.

Bummer.

But still...who would write her a letter? Who even wrote
letters anymore? Most people just texted or e-mailed.

The thought that someone took the time to handwrite something to her was sweet. No one had done that in years and now her interest was piqued.

She set her phone down and picked up the plain white envelope.

There was no return address, no other markings that would indicate who'd written it.

Without thinking further, Stella tore open the envelope and unfolded the paper inside. It was a simple lined piece of paper filled with neat handwriting. Handwriting that she recognized and caused her heart to squeeze painfully in her chest.

Brandon had actually written her a letter?

For a second, Stella contemplated throwing the paper in the trash. Because she didn't want to see. She didn't know if she could bear to see Brandon's heart poured out for her. Didn't want his true feelings revealed and further remind her of the mistake she'd made by leaving him.

But she read anyway, because she couldn't help herself.

Stella,

When Matt was six, he fell off his bike and hit his head on the concrete, knocking two teeth out of his head and sending us to the emergency room. He cried and shook while the nurse gave him five stitches on his chin. I was shaking just as badly, though I did my best to hide it. Because, you know, big tough dad and all that. I was only twenty-four and still didn't know what the hell I was doing with a kid. But Matt would look up at me with those scared, teary eyes and I would at least try to fake my way through everything. It scared the shit out of me when I saw the blood pouring from his chin and the tears stream-ing down his face. The fear that goes through you when you see your child sitting on a hospital bed is unimagin-able.

But...I've got to be honest with you, Stella. Walking away from you that day at your house? Knowing you were on a plane and flying hundreds of miles away, possibly for good? All that brought the same fear back. The same help-lessness of seeing Matt being stitched up, the same fear gripping my heart came rushing back the moment you left. Because for the first time in my life I've finally found some-one. That one special person I never really realized I'd been waiting for. She was finally here and I let her walk away, like a righteous idiot.

Despite that, it's a decision I would make again because that's where you belong. I wouldn't have been able to live with myself if I had kept you from something that meant so much to you. You light up when you're teaching and the thought of students being deprived of your smile and warmth would have been a greater crime.

I don't want you to think that letting you leave was easy for me. And it wasn't because you don't mean anything to me. Or that we don't mean anything. Being with you has brought more smiles to my face than anything in recent years. Even if you did frustrate the shit out of me some-times.

I don't think I'm even going to mail this to you. But I just kind of needed to get everything out, you know? Cathartic, I guess you could say.

Matt misses you and so does Duke, the big dummy.

And okay, I miss you too. Like, a lot.

It actually kind of hurts sometimes. More than when Trish left.

I'm not really sure what else to say. Except that I love you. But I'm pretty sure you already know that.

Stella's fingers trembled as she crumpled the letter and tossed it to the counter.

Her loved her?

The big oaf loved her.

For weeks she'd been floating around in a fog. In a limbo, not knowing whether she should be coming or going. Now she knew what she needed to do.

TWENTY-ONE

Brandon rested the butt of the Winchester against his shoulder and took aim. With a slow exhale, he squeezed the trigger and held back a smile of satisfaction as the old whiskey bottle shattered in the quiet air. A flock of birds that were brave enough to endure a Colorado winter scattered out of a nearby tree and disappeared into the overcast sky. He dropped another round into the pipe, cocked the hammer, and moved down the line of bottles he'd set up in the distance. Normally Brandon didn't go shooting alone. Matt almost always jumped at the opportunity, but he'd opted to spend the afternoon with Adrienne. Brandon hadn't pushed the issue, nor had he called Cameron. His friend would probably shit a brick if he found out Brandon had gone shooting without him. But he hadn't been in the mood for company.

To be honest, he hadn't been in the mood for much of anything for almost two months now. The other day Matt had called him a "grumpy shit who needed to remove the stick from his ass." And because he knew his kid was right, Brandon had opted not to smack him upside the head for his language. He had been a surly SOB and he couldn't fault Matt for calling him out. And he was pretty sure Matt, and everyone else, knew the reason for the dark cloud following Brandon around like an incurable disease. But just because he was aware of the reason for his dark mood didn't mean he wanted to talk about it. Or think about.

Even though he was thinking about it right now. Or all the time.

Damn it, he'd come up here to get away from his thoughts. To escape the memory of a woman who'd left her imprint on him. On his soul. So deeply that he couldn't even close his eyes without seeing her. Feeling her lips on his. Hearing the last words she'd spoken to him. It had been during a phone call he'd impulsively made a few weeks ago. Just to hear her voice. Because he was masochistic like that. He'd told himself he was going to stop calling her, to stop obsessing over a woman he couldn't have. So he'd called her one more time. At least he'd told himself it was the last time.

So far he'd stuck to his guns and hadn't called her again. And she hadn't called him. Probably just as well too. Cut the cord and all that. But, damn, he missed her. Like, a lot.

Way more than he should.

And he shouldn't be surprised. He'd known being away from Stella would be torture, even as he'd told her to go. Doing the right thing sometimes sucked.

At least Stella was happy now. Knowing she was where she belonged, doing what she'd wanted for so long, was the only thing that kept him going.

From his pocket his cell buzzed, but Brandon ignored it.

He wasn't in the mood to talk to anyone. So he shouldered his rifle again and blew up some more bottles. It felt good, blowing shit up. Since he couldn't go around picking fights with people, blowing bottles up was the next best thing.

He supposed.

His cell buzzed again. With an irritated groan, he set the gun down and grabbed his cell. Matt's number showed on the caller ID. Brandon hit the ignore button, then grimaced as a text came through.

Need to talk to you. Stop sulking and call me.

Brandon grit his teeth and sent a reply.

Is it an emergency?

Not exactly, but... Matt replied.

But what? Are you bleeding? Being held at gunpoint?

Matt's reply was slower to come this time.

Um...No??

Have you been abducted? Is Adrienne unconscious?

Dad, seriously...

Brandon felt his mouth twitch. Was he actually trying to smile?

If it's none of the above, stop calling me. I'll be home later.

His phone buzzed one last time.

Fine. But don't come bitching to me about not trying to warn you.

Warn him? About what? Being a miserable son of a bitch?

Oh, wait. He was already there.

Brandon pocketed the phone again, deciding to leave it on instead of turning it off. Then, as he grabbed the gun again, along with more rounds, something behind him caught his attention. A slight noise.

A tingle danced its way down his spine as Brandon

shouldered the rifle and turned to greet his unexpected guest.

Brandon had always thought if he ever laid eyes on Stella Davenport again, he'd know exactly what to say to her. That he'd grab her in his arms and kiss the hell out of her, then carry her off someplace where they could start their lives together. But the reality was nothing like how he'd played it in his head. It was confusing and wonderful and scary as shit.

He opened his mouth to say something. Anything intelligent or romantic and earth-shattering. But nothing came out. He cleared his throat, but that didn't help either.

"Hi," Stella greeted.

Brandon's gaze roamed over her loose hair, which kept blowing across her face in the cool breeze, her long legs wrapped in a pair of tight jeans, and a cream sweater that looked as soft as her skin.

"Hi," he finally managed.

She tucked her hair behind one ear. "Matt told me where to find you," she informed him.

Don't come bitching to me about not trying to warn you.

She took a step forward and cut him off before he could start firing questions at her.

"I'm sure you're wondering what I'm doing here..." she started.

Brandon rubbed a hand along the back of his neck. "You could say that."

Stella opened her mouth, then shut it. She shook her head, then dropped her gaze to the ground. "You didn't give me much of a choice."

Say what?

"I wanted to call you every day," she went on. "Each morning I woke up, I wanted to just drive to the airport and board the first plane back to Colorado. I kept telling myself that I'd made the right decision. That being in Chicago was where I belonged. That I was happy, even though I wasn't." She chuckled. "I actually thought that telling myself that I was happy would make it so."

Brandon turned her words over in his mind and tried to make sense of them. But he didn't understand what she was getting at or how they explained what she was doing here.

"I didn't want to come back here," Stella explained. "I needed to make a clean break from everything if I was going to move on."

Brandon took a step forward. "Move on from what, Stella?"

But she ignored his question. "But you've never played fair, have you?"

Brandon's stomach turned over. "What're you talking about?"

Stella didn't respond to his next question either. She reached into her back pocket and withdrew a piece of paper. Brandon's mind tried filling in the blanks as she unfolded the thing and held it up for him to see.

And his mind was still playing catch-up as everything clicked into place. His own handwriting, which hadn't been meant for anyone's eyes but his, was on display for him to see. To remember the flood of emotions he'd been dealing with in the weeks following Stella's departure. They were a cruel mocking of his own weaknesses. The torment that was Stella's absence and the longing he hadn't been able to escape.

Demanding to know who she'd gotten the letter from was on the forefront of his thoughts. But seeing her standing in front of him, more than a mirage that he couldn't touch, trumped why's and how's.

"Stella, I—"

"I read it three times," she interjected. "After I read it the first time, I crumpled it up and tossed it in the trash. I couldn't stand it." Stella turned the letter over in her hands and smoothed out the rumples. "I was already miserable there, constantly second-guessing my decision to leave, and then..." She shook her head. "Well, after about a day, I dug the thing out of the garbage and reread it. I was going to call you," she announced. "But the idea of hearing your voice and not seeing you made me feel a little sick to my stomach."

Brandon swallowed, hard. The lump in his throat had doubled in size since he'd laid eyes on her. "So you just hopped on a plane out here?"

"Basically. Well"—she lifted her shoulders—"first I had to pack up all my stuff, then tell my artistic director that I needed to turn down his offer. Nothing like walking away from a dream offer to tell the man you love that you can't live without him."

There were so many unexpected shocks in those sentences that Brandon didn't know which to address first. But Stella beat him to the punch by taking a step forward and holding up a hand.

"Just give me a minute before you say anything," she said. She inhaled deeply and slowly let it out. "It wasn't supposed to be like this. I was supposed to go back to Chicago and live out the rest of my days as an instructor. Maybe indulge on the occasional slice of Chicago-style pizza. But then... but then I got there and it just felt all wrong. Like I had fallen into a bad dream. At first I thought I needed some more time to adjust to a new living situation and a new schedule. But it only got worse and I slipped into this sort of daze that I couldn't wake up from."

The lump in Brandon's throat continued to grow. He

wanted to tell her to stop. To start cutting his heart into pieces. Because he knew he couldn't have her. There was no way she was back to stay, because that would be too good to be true. With the exception of Matt, nothing had ever worked out that perfectly for Brandon. He'd accepted his fate without Stella, as much as it killed him. He was prepared to move on with his life, and here she was throwing everything out of whack.

"Stella, I need you to explain to me what you're doing here," he demanded.

"I'm trying," she told him.

He came closer to her. Close enough to see the flecks of gray in her eyes. Close enough to wrap his hands around her slim shoulders and dig his fingers into her soft flesh. "Try harder. Because I can't handle watching you walk away again."

"Weren't you listening to anything I said?" she shot back. "I left a teaching contract for you. An opportunity I'd been waiting for for years. For you, Brandon."

He squeezed her harder. "I didn't ask you to do that. I told you it needed to be your decision. To be what *you* want."

"It was my decision," she argued back. "And this is what I want. Do you really think I'd walk away from all that for just anyone?"

He gave her a gentle shake, because he needed her to understand. He couldn't stand the thought of him being the reason for any regrets. "Damn it, Stella. I need you to be sure. If you come back here, it needs to be for good. You can't just pop back in, then leave again."

She dropped the letter and gripped the front of his sweatshirt with both hands. "This is for good. This is it for me, Brandon. Do or die time. Do you get it?" Her breath huffed in and out and matched the heavy thumping of his own heart. "And why are we yelling?"

A laugh popped out of him because, if he didn't laugh, he might drop to his knees and bury his face in her stomach. He lowered his forehead to hers. "Damn, Stella."

She looped her arms around his neck. "I loved it, you know," she whispered.

"Loved what?"

"The letter you wrote me. It was the greatest and worst thing I'd ever read," she said.

Brandon's brow pinched as he leaned away from her. "Worst?"

She played with the string from his hood. "Because it only solidified that I'd made the most awful decision of my life. And it was something I needed to fix right away."

"Stella—"

"I never would have been happy there," she butted in. "I need you to understand that I've done this for me."

Brandon grinned despite the turmoil churning his stomach. "So this was a completely selfish move?"

"Totally," she agreed. "I'm only thinking about my own happiness."

His hands moved from her shoulders, down the sleek indentation of her spine so his palms could squeeze the perfect globes of her ass. "As long as we're being selfish...I don't want you going back."

"I have no plans to go anywhere," she assured him. Then she pressed her lips to his and grinned against him.

As much as it killed him, Brandon pulled away from her softness. "I'm serious, Stella. You know what I've been through. If there's even a doubt in your mind, then this can't go any further."

"I know what you've been through," she agreed. "I know

you've been disappointed and hurt by people you were supposed to trust. And you also know what I've been through. I walked away from my dream before for a man, and I swore I wouldn't compromise myself like that ever again. But this time I know it's right. This time I know the guy's worth it."

A breath Brandon hadn't realized he'd been holding slowly released. He held her tighter, pulled her closer as though still afraid she'd run away.

Stella leaned away from him. "You know this is for real, right? That you're stuck with me?"

Brandon gave her another kiss and grinned against her mouth. "As long as you can handle my stinky dog and two men dirtying up the kitchen."

"Just keep the bathroom clean." She leaned farther away when he tried to kiss her again. "And I'm going to need you to buy some paper plates."

He quickly stole a kiss. "Hell no. You keep your blasphemous paper plates out of my house."

"What if it's our house?" she questioned.

He pinched her rear end. "You know it'll be your house too."

She swatted his arm. "No, I mean we buy a place of our own."

A place that was just his and Stella's? Where they could start fresh and make new memories...sounded like heaven to him. "Okay, I'll agree to that on one condition."

One of her brows lifted. "Really? You're going to start throwing conditions at me?"

"Just hear me out."

She blew out a breath. "All right."

"You let me put a big-screen TV with surround sound in the living room, and you can bring your damn paper plates."

"A big-screen TV?" she asked as she ran her hands up and down his arms. "You mean like a place where we can snuggle up and watch old movies?"

Brandon blinked. "Actually, I was thinking of a place Matt and I can watch ball games."

He waited for her to smack him, to tell him in his dreams. Instead she just grinned and wrapped her arms around his neck again. "You realize that I don't actually need paper plates, right?"

"Yeah, I kind of figured that."

"That you and your smelly dog and pretentious cooking skills are enough?"

"You think my cooking skills are pretentious?" he questioned.

Her mouth twitched. "I think you could mix in a TV dinner every once in a while."

"Okay, I'll tell you what. We'll buy a new place together, with a sports room, and I'll let you eat a microwave dinner on the couch every once in a while."

"Gee, you'll let me?" she said around a grin. "Aren't you the sweetest?"

"Aren't I, though?"

She gave him a hot, openmouthed kiss. One with tongue and teeth and two months of separation and longing finally coming together. When they broke apart, they were both breathing hard and touching everywhere their hands could reach.

"I don't need the damn TV dinners, Brandon," she said as her hands found the flesh beneath his sweatshirt. "I just want you."

He sucked in a breath and held himself back from yanking her sweater over her head. Instead, he picked her up and her legs found their way around his hips. "Now that we've got that straight." He started walking with her hanging on to him. "Let's go find a tree I can back you up against."

Stella buried her face in his neck and giggled. Brandon tightened his arms around her and felt the cool breeze dancing around them. And for the first time in his life, he allowed himself to hope.

Two weeks later

"Hey, listen up," Blake called from the front of his spacious living room that boasted vaulted ceilings and giant windows.

The murmur of the crowd died as the coach commanded the attention of his players and their families.

"I just have a few things I'd like to say before we eat," Blake went on.

In late February, Blake had organized a team dinner at his house. Everyone and their sister was there because it had been a hell of a season of ups and downs, capped by a game no one ever thought they'd make it to.

Brandon scanned the crowd and spotted Cameron talking to a parent. He kept looking until his eyes landed on Stella. His heart turned over in his chest every time he looked at her, as though realizing for the first time that she was all his. He still couldn't get used to the idea that she only had eyes for him. She laughed at something Annabelle said, then gave him a little finger wave. He answered with a wink, then grinned when her cheeks stained pink.

She was so into him.

Just as much as he was into her.

And of course it was his own son who brought her back. Matt had found that letter on his dresser and taken matters into his own hands by mailing it. His own son had seen what Brandon had failed to see. He'd been brave enough to take a leap of faith for both of them, and Brandon owed him for that.

Matt came up next to him while cramming a puff pastry thing in his mouth. "Have you tried one of these yet?" Matt asked with a mouthful of food. "So good."

Brandon elbowed him, then jerked his head toward Blake. "You're supposed to be listening."

Matt shrugged. "I can listen and eat at the same time."

"First I want to thank everyone for coming today," Blake continued. "Especially to my gorgeous fiancée for providing all the food." All heads turned toward Annabelle, who blew Blake a kiss, totally oblivious to everyone staring at her. "If it hadn't been for her, you all would be eating Ritz crackers and slices of cheese."

A low chuckle danced over the crowd.

"But most of all I want to thank the parents for allowing me to coach your kids," Blake went on in a more serious note. "These are the hardest-working, most determined bunch of boys I've ever had the pleasure to work with. Coaching them for the past two seasons has been the most fulfilling thing I've done in a long time." He cleared his throat. "A lot of people had written us off. They thought the Bobcats were finished, thought we'd never do anything but lose. But your boys have shown them down isn't always out." He glanced around the room. "Now, we may not have taken the state title this year, but the fact that we even made it that far was beyond anyone's expectations for us. I don't know about you, but I plan on seeing our name at the end of that bracket next year as the state champs."

The players hooted and pumped their fists in the air.

Blake grinned. "I'm getting the finger wave from my fiancée, so dig in to the food she's made for us."

The crowd dispersed, with the parents approaching Blake and the players going straight for the food.

Beside him, Matt shifted. "I've gotta get some more of those puff things." Then he was gone.

Brandon immediately went in search of Stella because he'd been away from her too long. But he stopped short and spun around when someone pinched his ass.

Stella grinned. "So feisty."

"You'll pay for that," he growled, then swooped down for a wet, deep kiss.

When she came up for air, she swatted him on the shoulder. "There are kids here."

Brandon snorted and looked around. "And most of them have done a lot worse than that."

Stella hooked her arm around his waist and led them toward the already lengthy buffet line. "Blake gave a nice speech."

"Yeah," he agreed.

They stopped at the end of the line and Stella turned toward him. "Are you sure you don't want me to go with you tomorrow?"

He and Matt were leaving in the morning to visit Trish in Oklahoma. At first Matt had insisted on going by himself, then he'd relented and asked Brandon to go with him. Brandon had pointed it out, but he sensed that Matt was scared. That he wasn't yet too old to need his father by his side. And Brandon had been happy to agree, because it had always been the two of them and he wasn't going to leave Matt high and dry just yet.

Brandon sighed and tucked a strand of hair behind Stella's ear. "This is something Matt and I have to do."

"Will you guys be okay?" Stella queried.

Brandon glanced at his son, who was standing with a group of other players. "He's handling it in his own way. But yeah, he'll be fine."

Stella slid her hands up his chest. "And what about you? Are you nervous?"

"Me?" He'd been so busy worrying about Matt that he hadn't really taken the time to process much. "I thought I would be, but no. And as long as I have you to come home to, I'll be perfect."

"Aw." She slid her arms around his neck. "What fortune cookie did you get that out of?"

He chuckled and kissed her. "Smart-ass."

"Hey." Cameron bumped him from behind. "Get a room already."

Stella grinned at him. "You wouldn't be feeling lonely, would you?"

Cam narrowed his eyes at both of them.

"Anyway," he went on. "I heard the recruiter from UT gave Matt a letter indicating their interest in him."

Brandon couldn't help his smile, even though UT hadn't been his first choice. But Matt had been bursting with excitement when the letter had come in the mail three weeks ago. "Yeah, the three of us are going to Austin during the school's spring break to tour the campus."

Adrienne had already been accepted, so Matt had hurried and applied. Brandon had urged him to wait, just to see if some kind of scholarship was going to come through. Matt's response had been a huge grin and, "If I don't get a scholarship, I'll just apply for loans and other scholarships." But the kid was bound and determined to stay with his girlfriend. Yeah, that had freaked Brandon out at first, but Adrienne was a good girl and he'd taught

Matt well enough to hammer some common sense into the kid.

Bottom line, he was happy, had good grades and a goal. Brandon couldn't ask for much more than that.

"We're making a whole trip out of it," Stella expanded. She grinned up at Brandon. "While we're in Austin visiting UT, I'm making Brandon take me to see Cirque du Soleil."

Cameron furrowed his brow. "Seriously?" he asked Brandon. "Acrobats?"

He gestured toward Stella. "Do you forget who you're talking to?"

Stella poked Cameron in the chest. "You'll be doing the same thing for a woman someday."

Cameron vehemently shook his head. "Not a chance. The only thing I do for women is get them off."

Brandon smacked him on the shoulder. "Dude."

Cam shrugged. "Just keeping it real."

"Yeah, real dumb," Brandon shot back.

Stella just laughed because she knew, at the heart of it, Cam was a good man. "You'll eat those words one day, Cam. Just wait and see."

Cameron shook his head. "Not happening."

Brandon chuckled as his friend ambled away.

Stella poked him in the ribs. "What're you laughing at?"

"Nothing," he immediately answered. But when she lifted a brow, he cleared his throat. "Just that I used to say the same thing."

"No, not you," Stella teased. "You would never have been that pessimistic."

"I was happy in my pessimism."

"No, you weren't."

He blew out a breath and lowered his head. Yeah, she'd caught him red-handed. He'd never truly been happy before, despite what he'd told himself. He'd been miserable in his mistrust and lonely as hell. Until Stella had come along and thrown his world off its axis with her colorful outlook on life, guarded eyes, and her inability to take his bullshit.

He tightened his arms around her. "Yeah, you're right." He dropped a kiss on her nose. "How do you always know these things?"

"Because I'm a genius. You ought to know that by now."

What he knew was that he'd just really started living, and it all began on the day she'd thrown up on his shoes.

Love Always Wins in Champion Valley!

Cameron Shaw has one love
in his life: football.

And then Audrey Bennett
walked into his life.

Let the games begin...

A preview of
Changing the Rules follows.

ONE

Audrey Bennet had been on the road for almost six hours. The two extra double shots she'd hastily tossed back with a chocolate scone at daybreak had long since worn off, leaving her with the jittery aftereffects of a caffeine crash. As a rule, she usually avoided caffeine altogether, simply because her nerves were almost always edging on this side of shot. Not that Audrey had issues with anxiety. Usually. But thanks to both her parents being type A personalities with a bit of OCD thrown in, Audrey rarely understood the meaning of calm, cool, and collected.

So yeah. Coffee had been a bad choice.

However, today she'd made an exception, given the fact that she hadn't been sleeping lately and needed to make the drive from Boulder to Blanco Valley. Wherever the hell that was.

She'd never heard of it and had almost had a stroke when she'd pulled the route up on Google Maps a few days ago.

She'd opted for the long way down I-25 instead of adding to her nerves by winding her way through the mountainous Colorado interior.

Audrey glanced in the rearview mirror at her passenger, who'd been alternating between sleeping and talking to her stuffed cat. The thing was named Jellybean and had long since turned from its original pink to a questionable brown. Audrey had meant to wash it, but Piper had yanked the cat from Audrey's hand with a trembling lip that had cut straight to Audrey's already broken heart. Because Piper had been through so much lately, with the loss of her mother to cancer and being forced to move away from her home to live with an uncle she'd never met, Audrey had let the subject of washing the putrid stuffed animal rest.

Spending so much time with a six-year-old had taught Audrey how to pick her battles. That, and stuffed animals were not to be messed with. Whatever. If Piper could live with a stuffed cat that smelled like apple juice, and possibly chicken nuggets, then so could Audrey.

A sign for the Blanco Valley city limits came into view, and Audrey practically cried tears of relief. Or maybe pain, because her legs had gone numb about an hour ago.

Then a sign welcoming her to Champion's Valley flew past.

What was Champion's Valley?

Was that the same as Blanco Valley?

Whatever. Audrey didn't care. She just wanted this drive over already. Long car trips had never been her cup of tea, or coffee in this instance. She'd much rather hop on a plane and be there faster. But she'd needed her SUV to haul a small trailer full of Piper's things and suitcases for Audrey's extended stay.

"Are we almost there?" Piper quipped from the backseat.

Audrey glanced in the rearview mirror again and offered a comforting smile. Jellybean was wrapped in one small arm and the other was playing with the hem of her shorts.

"Almost, sweetie."

"I'm bored," Piper announced.

Audrey ground her teeth together and reminded herself that the poor girl had been in the car as long as Audrey had. And the crash from the caffeine was making her extra cranky.

She made a left turn and followed the directions toward the high school football stadium. "Why don't you watch your movie again?"

"I don't want to," Piper answered.

Well, why would she? She'd only watched the thing about four times.

"Okay," Audrey said, searching her brain for something for Piper to do. "What about the pile of books on the seat?"

"I already looked at them all," Piper offered.

Well, shit.

"Audrey?" Piper asked.

Audrey's heart cracked open again at the child's soft tone. She'd been through a whirlwind of emotions the past few weeks, alternating between crying and asking when her mommy was coming back. Audrey had cried with her and tried answering her question as best she could, knowing Piper's little six-year-old mind wasn't capable of understanding fully. What did six-year-olds know about death? Did they understand it was permanent? Did Piper know she'd never see her mother again? Never hear her voice or hug her or hear Dianna tell her little girl everything was going to be okay?

Audrey gripped the steering wheel harder at the unfairness of the situation. Piper was a sweet, loving, outgoing girl who'd lost her only parent and would be forced to live the rest of her life wondering why. Why she didn't have a family. Why she didn't have a mom to tuck her in at night or teach her how to wear makeup. Piper deserved the very best. She deserved to feel safe and loved and whole.

"Is my uncle Cameron nice?" Piper asked when Audrey didn't respond to her.

Audrey swatted away the fresh tears that almost fell. "I don't know, sweetie. I've never met him."

"Why can't I stay with you?"

Audrey's eyes dropped closed at the question Piper had asked a dozen times already. As much as she'd love, and give anything, to keep Piper with her, it just wasn't possible.

She spared the child another glance in the rearview mirror. "Honey, we talked about this, remember? Your mom wanted you to stay with family."

"But you're my family," Piper argued.

The statement pulled a smile from Audrey. "Not in the way your mom meant."

The poor girl didn't understand any of it. She didn't understand why her mom had died, and she didn't understand why she had to live with an uncle she'd never met. But Dianna had been explicit in her wishes. She'd awarded custody to her half brother, Cameron Shaw, and she wanted Audrey to deliver Piper. To help make the transition easier, she'd said. Audrey didn't understand it either, but Dianna hadn't had any other family and Piper's dad had never been in the picture. Her job simply was to deliver Piper to her uncle and stay until Piper was comfortable with the man.

But what kind of man was he? Audrey's brow furrowed as she came to a red light. From what she knew, Dianna and Cameron hadn't had much of a relationship. Dianna had been tight-lipped about it, only saying Cameron's father had left his mother and remarried, and Dianna had been born several years later. She said she'd met him a few times when she was little, but as she'd gotten older, Cameron had stopped coming around. Audrey suspected that maybe the mysterious Cameron Shaw had resented his much younger half sister, even though Dianna had never said as much. Audrey hoped that wasn't true, because what kind of asshole would resent his little sister for a situation that wasn't her fault?

In any event, if Dianna had entrusted the life of her little girl to Cameron, then he couldn't be that bad.

Right?

All Audrey knew about the guy was that he was in his midthirties and coached high school football. She didn't even know if he had a family of his own. Oh God, what if he already had kids and didn't want another? Especially one he didn't even know?

No, Dianna knew what she'd been doing when awarding custody of Piper to her brother. If Dianna trusted him, then Audrey would too.

But if Audrey even sensed a flicker of something not right with the guy, she'd whisk Piper away so fast his head would spin. She'd fight for custody of the little girl herself.

"Why don't you read one of your books to Jellybean?" Audrey suggested. "We'll be there in a minute."

Silence filled the car, followed by a muffled, "'Kay."

The light turned green at the same time that her phone vibrated from the cup holder. Probably Evan, Audrey's boyfriend of three months who hadn't been comfortable with her driving. She blindly reached for the phone just as she heard a loud *pop* and the car jerked wildly to the left, almost veering her into oncoming traffic.

From the backseat, Piper yelped and Audrey barely

stuffed back a curse as she gripped both hands around the steering wheel. She knew a popped tire when she heard one and cursed her shitty luck after already having been on the road for six hours.

"Audrey?" Piper called out with fear lacing her voice.

"It's okay, honey," Audrey soothed, while trying to keep herself calm. She jerked the car into the next lane, ignoring honks and other drivers whipping around her. The shredded tire, which sounded like it was in the back, thudded around the rim and bobbled the car all over the place. She managed to pull the SUV over, while narrowly missing a handful of cyclists. The thing jerked to a stop, then rested crookedly, hanging halfway in the bike lane and half into traffic where impatient drivers were forced to maneuver around her.

With a sigh she tossed the gear in park and leaned her head back on the headrest.

"What happened to the car?" Piper asked from her car seat. "Is it broken?"

Audrey blew out a breath and opened her eyes. "Audrey really wishes she could curse right now," she whispered to herself. Then she pasted a smile on her face, for Piper's benefit, and turned to face the girl. "The car's not broken. I just need to take a look at the tire."

Piper blinked and hugged Jellybean closer. Her chubby cheeks were red and her once-neat ponytails were loose, allowing the girl's blond curls to stick to her cheeks.

"It sounds like the car broke," Piper said again.

"It's not broken." She reached back and rested a comforting hand on the child's knee. "But I need you to stay in your seat while I get out and look at the tire. Okay?" When Piper nodded, Audrey grabbed a book from the seat and dropped it in Piper's lap. "Here, read this to Jellybean. I think she's bored too."

Piper picked Jellybean up and bounced it on her knee. "Jellybean was asleep, but the broken car woke her up. She was dreaming about jelly beans."

Of course she was. Jelly beans were Piper's favorite thing in the whole world. Aside from her stuffed cat.

Audrey got out of the car and ignored the glares from other drivers. Like it was her fault her damn tire blew and forced her off the road. But she ignored them anyway and gave the rear driver's side tire the middle finger as she tried to figure out what the hell to do. She had a spare, but it was buried in the back end of the SUV, underneath suitcases and bags of food. Her father, who was a dentist, had shown her countless times how to change a flat tire. He said he'd never wanted his little girl to be unprepared should she ever find herself in a situation such as this. She almost grabbed her cell from the car and called him with a tear-filled thanks. Instead she shot the blown tire another glare and yanked open the back hatch to start removing suitcases. She needed to get to the spare and her other tools.

Once the suitcases and bags of food were unloaded, which she'd done while mentally alphabetizing curse words, she retrieved the spare, along with a wrench and the jack.

Someone honked as she set the spare next to the car, and Audrey barely resisted the urge to flip them the bird.

Piper stuck her head over the backseat. "Are you gonna fix the car?"

Audrey grinned and ignored the bead of sweat rolling down the middle of her back, even though the temperature was in the sixties. "You bet, sweetie."

Piper bounced in the seat. "I'm hungry."

Of course she was. Next thing, she'd have to go to the bathroom.

Audrey set the jack on the ground and dug around for a snack. She handed the girl a baggie of goldfish and a Fruit Roll-Up.

"Stay in your seat, please," she reminded the six-year-old. Because Piper, God love her, had the attention span of a puppy.

Piper bounced back in her seat and fired up a conversation with Jellybean. Audrey smiled, despite the inconvenience of the situation and the fact that she was essentially leaving her best friend's daughter with a stranger and Audrey would have to say good-bye. She forced the lump out of her throat and tried not to think about having to leave Piper. She loved that little girl as she would her own and the idea of being away from her tore her guts up. There would be no more makeovers, no more whimsical stories, and no more sticky kisses. A tear escaped, but Audrey managed to pull herself together.

She'd just set the jack and wrench on the ground in front of the flat when a deep rumbling behind the trailer caught her attention. A shiny yellow Camaro slowed to a stop; then the rumbling quieted and the driver exited the car.

Great. Probably some guy who thought she didn't know shit about changing tires. Just because she was shy of one-twenty and average height didn't mean she didn't know how to handle things herself. Men always underestimated her.

"Need a hand with that?"

The voice was deep and low and tickled long-forgotten places. Places Evan had yet to discover. Strange. This guy pulls over to offer help, mutters six words, and all of a sudden sparks were igniting all over the place. Like she was some nun who'd never heard a sexy voice before.

Audrey jabbed the wrench on the first lug nut and twisted. The thing didn't budge. "I've got it," she responded with a glance at his brand-new AND1s.

The stance of his feet widened. "Looks like you're struggling."

She spared him a glance... way the hell up because, *damn*, he was tall. But she couldn't get a good look at his face because the bright afternoon sun shone just over his shoulder and blinded her. Her only impression was long legs and wide shoulders. Oh, and don't forget that voice. "I know how to change a tire," she told him.

"Never said you didn't," he responded, and squatted next to her.

She continued to work on the lug nut and loosened the first one. She kept at it until the nut came all the way off and fell to the pavement.

The dude next to her tensed. Audrey wasn't sure how she could feel the tension in him, but somehow she just knew. Sort of like how the air shifts when someone enters a room. He wanted to correct her. He probably thought she was doing it wrong. He had another think coming if he thought he was going to tell her how to change a tire.

Audrey was a bit of a perfectionist who liked to do things herself. She was independent like that.

"You should loosen all the nuts before you take them all the way off," he told her.

Audrey's mouth quirked as she loosened the next lug nut. "I appreciate your help but—" Holy hell, were all the men in Blanco Valley walking Calvin Klein ads? Audrey had just meant to toss him a dismissive glance, long enough to convey her message that she didn't need help. But the overwhelming hulk of a man who'd hunkered down next to her had captured her attention. No, not just captured. Commanded. Deep blue eyes, sort of like staring down into the deepest part of the ocean, held her gaze from beneath the bill of a Blanco Valley High baseball cap. The shadow from the hat slashed across his straight nose, which was perched above a mouth so firm and full that Audrey actually felt a flutter somewhere in her belly.

Shit, what had she been saying?

Oh, yeah. She'd been about to tell the guy to take a hike when she'd been rendered speechless by a pair of dreamy blue eyes and a mouth that probably delivered toe-curling grins.

One of his dark brows arched. "But...?" he prompted.

She blinked and tried to regain the composure she had before he'd shown up and tied her tongue in knots.

"But I know how to change a tire." And hadn't she already told him that? To prove her point, Audrey went back to loosening the lug nuts. The second one was proving to be trickier, which was just her luck. She turned the wrench, with no progress.

The guy, who'd yet to give a name so Audrey had decided to dub him Gorgeous Baseball Cap Guy, reached out to take the wrench from her.

She shot him a look and he held his hands up.

"May I?" he asked.

Audrey shot a glance at the car and spotted Piper bobbing her head up and down in the window. She probably had to go to the bathroom, in which case, she needed the tire fixed STAT.

Reluctantly, she passed the wrench over and moved aside for him. Mr. Gorgeous Baseball Cap Guy took her place in front of the tire and worked the lug nuts with ease.

"I take it you're one of those independent types," he commented while loosening one nut after the next.

"It's faster if you take each one off first," she pointed out instead of confirming his way too astute observation about her.

One side of the full mouth kicked up. "It really isn't." He loosened the final nut and slanted her a look. "You have control issues as well?"

Audrey opened her mouth to argue, because that was always her first reaction to everything. Correct. Control. It was sort of a vice for her and one she'd been trying for way too long to fix. And also probably why she hadn't had a relationship that lasted longer than three months. She'd come to learn that men didn't take well to their girlfriend constantly correcting everything they did. She had a coping mechanism for when she felt her anxiety skyrocketing and the urge to nitpick came clawing to the surface. Unfortunately, reciting designer labels alphabetically tended to annoy people just as much as her control issues. But Evan didn't seem to mind. Evan was a sweet guy.

"I'm not controlling," she found herself saying, and ignored the look of disbelief that flashed across Mr. Gorgeous's blue eyes. "It's just that when I see something that I feel could be done better, I say something."

"But you weren't doing it better," he pointed out.

"In your opinion," she argued.

He nodded as though he understood. "Controlling," he said again, and any forgiveness she had been about to offer him was obliterated.

She reached for the wrench. "I think I can take it from here."

"Just give me a sec." He placed the jack under the car

and raised the thing as though it were nothing more than a child's toy.

"Okay, then." Audrey attempted to shoulder him out of the way, but it was like trying to move a cement statue. She had a brief impression of a solid shoulder underneath his hooded sweatshirt before backing away. Her first thought was, why would a man like him hide all that goodness beneath a bulky sweatshirt? But her second thought of, *Hello boyfriend* immediately smacked away any improper thoughts.

"Impatient little thing, aren't you?" he asked with a smirk as he removed the lug nuts.

She narrowed her eyes at him. "Maybe I'm not the only one with control issues."

His smirk turned into a full-blown grin, and holy Alexander McQueen, the man had some serious wattage. "So you admit you have control issues."

Was he for real? In the time he'd been distracting her with his pearly whites, he'd removed the tire and replaced it with the spare. And in probably half the time that she could have done it. But, still. There had been nothing wrong with the way she'd been removing the lug nuts.

"I could have done that," she told him.

"Yeah," he agreed as he replaced the lug nuts and tightened them with little effort. "Except you were doing it wrong."

His grin widened at the same time that his gaze dropped to her chest. It took a second of heat flaming Audrey's cheeks for her to realize that he was checking her out. But because it had been so long since a man of his…caliber…had shown any interest in her, Audrey could do nothing more than stare and blink. Yeah, real sexy. No wonder she went a year in between boyfriends.

Gorgeous Baseball Cap Guy handed over the wrench

with that maddening smirk still causing all sorts of flutters in her belly.

Focus. You're here for Piper. Not to get noticed by hot Good Samaritans.

She took the wrench from him and they stood at the same time.

He braced a hand on the roof of her car and leaned forward. Was he meaning to crowd her? Intimidate her with those wide shoulders and eyes so blue it was like staring at a crystal-clear lake? Except Audrey didn't feel intimidated. The spark that flamed to life took her off guard because... well, had she ever felt anything like that before? She couldn't remember.

"You know, it's customary to say thanks," he pointed out.

"Thanks," she offered.

His grin turned to a chuckle as his gaze dropped to her chest once more. He dropped his hand from the car and gave her a mock solute. "Have a good one. Try not to shred any more tires."

Then he strolled away, moving with a grace that kept Audrey riveted in her spot for longer than it should have. Did Evan walk like that? Like he owned the ground beneath his feet? Better yet, why did she keep comparing the two men? Evan and Gorgeous Baseball Cap Guy were nothing alike. Evan was shorter and not as... overwhelming? Yes, that was a good word for the man. Overwhelming. Evan wasn't anything like that and Audrey liked him just fine. He made her laugh and held doors open for her. Gorgeous Baseball Cap Guy was bossy and too big.

Too big?

Women drooled over men like him, and all Audrey could

think about was how he'd taken over and kept looking at her boobs.

He helped you out when no one else would stop.

Yes, but why couldn't she get over the fact that he made her skin itchy? Evan didn't make her skin itchy. Thing was, Audrey wasn't sure if that was a good thing or a bad thing.

She blinked and realized she was still standing by the car, and Piper had once again pressed her face to the window. Audrey cleaned her tools up and replaced everything in the rear of the SUV. Back inside the car, Audrey's phone kept beeping. Then she remembered she'd received a notification when her tire had blown.

"Put your seat belt back on," she instructed Piper as she started the car and pulled out into traffic.

"Did the car get fixed?" Piper questioned.

Audrey glanced over her shoulder and changed lanes. "Yep, good as new."

"I have to go potty."

"We'll find a place to go at the high school."

Piper was silent a moment. "What's a high school?"

Audrey picked up her phone as it beeped again. She thumbed the screen while navigating traffic. "It's where bigger kids go to school. We're meeting your uncle there."

Piper fell silent again as she pulled up a text from Evan. Audrey grinned as she thought about his deep brown eyes and silly sense of humor. He probably would have called a tow truck for her and then made sure Piper was taken care of. Evan was a gem of a guy who—

This relationship isn't really working out for me.

Audrey scowled and scrolled through the messages, looking for the, *It's not you, it's me,* pushing past the hurt knifing through her chest.

A second later, her phone buzzed again and another text came through.

It's not you, it's me. You're a really sweet girl, Evan wrote. *But I can't be in a relationship right now. I need to focus on me.*

Audrey stopped at another red light and resisted the urge to toss her phone out the window. Dumped via text message. Story of her life. Despite that, she'd expected better from Evan. She'd expected a relationship with a guy who took her to see *Wicked* to last longer than three months. Evan was supposed to be the real deal. Guys like him didn't come along very often, and now she was filing yet another relationship into the Said and Done part of her life.

She huffed out a breath and leaned her head against the headrest. Of course she was hurt. She'd liked Evan. Could have even grown to love him if he'd given the relationship a chance. Maybe it was her. Maybe she had *damaged goods* stamped across her forehead. Why else couldn't she pin a guy down longer than it took for the leaves to change color in the fall?

Audrey's eyes jerked open when someone honked. The light had turned green, so she pressed forward and turned right toward the high school. It didn't matter. He was just another guy in a long string of men who hadn't been able to stick. All that mattered now was Piper and easing her transition into her new life with her uncle.

Except she was reasonably attractive, right? Yeah, Audrey was pretty sure she could hold her own. Guys liked blondes, and five-six was a decent height. And she stayed in shape by jogging every morning. Audrey gave herself a once-over, glancing from her jeans to her button-down and giving herself a nod of approval. Then she did a double take to the missed button on her shirt as she pulled into the high school parking lot.

"Shit," she whispered to herself.

Maybe dressing in the dark hadn't been such a good idea after all. The gaping hole her missed button had created had afforded Gorgeous Baseball Cap Guy a straight shot to her hot-pink bra.

She only hoped Cameron Shaw wasn't anything like him.

ABOUT THE AUTHOR

Erin Kern lives in north Texas with her husband, two kids, and their dog. She loves barbecue, Texas sunsets, antiquing, and high school football games. The first book in the Champion Valley series, *Winner Takes All*, was published in August 2016 and was inspired by Erin's love of Texas football, small towns, and happy endings.

When she's not at the computer working on her next tale, she can be found spending time with her kids or curled up with a good book.

You can learn more at:

ErinKern.com
Twitter @erinkern04
Facebook.com/ErinKernAuthor

Fall in Love with Forever Romance

SUGARPLUM WAY
By Debbie Mason

The *USA Today* bestselling Harmony Harbor series continues! As a romance author, Julia Landon's job is to create happy-ever-afters. But she can't seem to create one for herself—even after a steamy kiss under the mistletoe with Aiden Gallagher. After a bitter divorce, Aiden has no interest in making another commitment; he just wants to spend quality time with his daughter. But with Christmas right around the corner, both Aiden and Julia may find that Santa is about to grant a little girl's special wish.

Fall in Love with Forever Romance

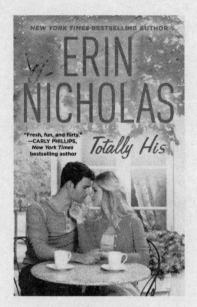

TOTALLY HIS
By Erin Nicholas

In the newest of *New York Times* bestselling author Erin Nicholas's Opposites Attract series, actress Sophie Birch is used to looking out for herself. When her theater catches fire and a cop scoops her up to save her, she fights him every step of the way...even though his arms feel oh-so-good. Finn Kelly can't help but appreciate how sexy the woman in his arms looks...even if she's currently resisting arrest. But when Sophie finds herself in trouble again, can Finn convince her to lean on him?

Fall in Love with Forever Romance

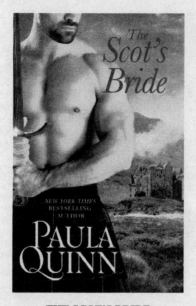

THE SCOT'S BRIDE
By Paula Quinn

For readers of Karen Hawkins, Monica McCarty, and Hannah Howell.
Charlotte Lindsay refuses to abide by Patrick MacGregor, the barbaric
highlander assigned to keep her out of trouble. But what's Charlie to
do when her biggest temptation is the man charged with keeping her a
proper young lass?

Fall in Love with Forever Romance

BACK IN THE GAME
By Erin Kern

Fans of *Friday Night Lights* will love the heartwarming Champion Valley series by best-selling author Erin Kern. Stella Davenport swore she'd never let anything get in the way of her dream—until sexy, broad-shouldered Brandon West walks back into her life. Brandon knows that love only leads to heartbreak, but Stella is a breath of fresh air he didn't even know he'd been missing. When she's offered her dream job in Chicago, will he be willing to put his heart on the line?

LETHAL LIES
By Rebecca Zanetti

Long-buried secrets and deadly forces threaten Anya Best and Heath Jones as they hunt down the infamous Copper Killer. Will they find love only to lose their lives? Fans of Maya Banks and Shannon McKenna will love Rebecca Zanetti's latest sexy suspense!

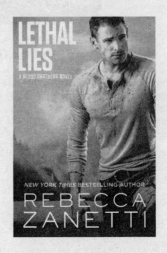